Imogene's Eloise

Inspired by a true-love story

MARGUERITE QUANTAINE

CK PUBLICATIONS
Published in the United States by
Cantïne-Kilpatrick
Post Office Box 925, Silver Springs, Florida 34489-0925
ISBN 978-0-940548-01-5
First Edition

Cover art adapted by M. J. Cantïne from an unsigned artist postcard published in 1904 by M.M.Vienne.

Imogene's Eloise is a work of fiction inspired by a true story. Names, places, characters and events are either used fictitiously or the product of the author's imagination. Any resemblance to actual people, living or dead is unintentional and entirely coincidental.

This book contains several passages that were previously published in the *Antiquarian*, *Long Island Times*, *Venus Ezine*, *St. Petersburg Times* and margueritequantaine.wordpress.com by Marguerite Quantaine © 2000-2014

For the woman who became my life

ACKNOWLEDGMENTS

I would still be obsessing over minutiae and unable to let this book be if it wasn't for a mutual dedication to detail executed by my punctuation editor, Jennifer Daniele-Calafiore.

I'm forever indebted to my sister, Susan, for her confidence in me, and my sister Kate, who provided me with the tools needed to complete this long writing process.

I especially appreciate the extra attention and generosity of time given by those who have shared my beeps and blogs and those who regularly comment on my Facebook posts including Adrianne Miller, Kieran York, Sunita Kripalani, Mary Anne Frett, Ann Breckenridge, Alice Cantine, Caroline Filler, Bree Toms Couch, Di Delanoy, Charlyn Heard, Doug Humphrey, Sunny Alexander, Rogena Mitchell-Jones, Ana Delgado, Linda Bale, Mary Margaret Perry, Julie Molthop, Amy Nabinger-Bieger, Carrie & Jan Carr, Susan Cicero, Kate Dana, Cathy Rowlands, Kathy Brodrick, Mercedes Lewis, Kaysi Peister, Deb Rondeau, Maite de Tapia Escribano, Barb Martin, Leighann Parker, Amber Stewart, Jennifer Rogal, Jenny Lee, Gena Ratcliff, Bren Nelson, Steve Cantrell, Tom Schoenbeck, Diane Hollifield, Deanna Siano, Donna Wells, Dawn Habschied, Helen B. Fremin and Suzanne Harding

Ultimately, a writer is only as good as her muse. Mine has been the same for forty-five years. No words were ever imagined or created to accurately express the eternal gratitude I feel for the inspiration Elizabeth provides.

Thank you.

ONE
Saturday Morning, March 14, 1970
Blink!

Imogene awoke wondering if she was awake, disquieted by eyes stuck open before complete consciousness settled in. She contemplated how long such had been so, and if she should move — or, if she even could move, sensing something besides the weight of her body holding her down.

She spotted an inky spider up there where her stare met the 15 foot alabaster ceiling directly overhead and followed it as it scurried across the embossed floral ornamentation bordering the upper wall, then down to the long, high, black lacquered fireplace mantel where it instantly blended in.

It occurred to her she was home.

Her chin doubled as she arched her head up to look downwards over her torso, through the thick tickles of the silver fox faux fur collar on her Kelly green worsted wool coat, past the tiny rhinestone studded stockings covering her knees, and onto the salt encrusted buckle of a solitary saturated leather boot.

That explains the stiffness and profuse sweating, she thought.

Still, it took the sudden sputter and clank of the antiquated radiator to startle her, yanking her sideways enough to propel her off the couch and onto the floor, face first.

"Again," she groaned. "Same as last night."

She blinked. Last night? She squeezed her eyes shut and held them there for a bit before blinking again. And again.

It might have been the sharp pain resulting from the slight smashing of her head against the polished parquet floor that caused a delayed awakening of her voice.

"Oh no," she coughed, dislodging bits of inhaled cat hair caught at

1

the back of her throat. "Oh no," she repeated, wiping the molt from her tongue with her wrist before pushing herself perpendicular.

If someone had been there with her as she staggered up, insisting that the night before was all a dream, she might have believed it so. But for the remnants of a yellow rose scrunched under the red kid glove on her left hand, its thorn embedded near her wrist. But for the anxiety rising in her flat (though viable) chest, the vision of the woman's face glossing over her eyes, the faint scent of Shalimar left lingering on her clothes from when they danced, slowly, to something by the Beatles. Or was it *Something* by the Beatles? The uncertainty puzzled her.

And, oh, by the way — why did she dance with a woman? She never had before, not even with her sisters.

"Think!" she ordered aloud. "Why was I on the...? And where is my other...? How could I still be dres...? This *headache*. From falling off the couch?" She squinted. "Or, possibly? Could it be, say, the result of...what? Falling off my barstool?" She cocked her head. "I fell off my barstool?"

Gasp, wham! Imogene's right hand hit her forehead hard, followed by a silent "ow-w" as she lowered herself back onto the couch, cradling what she hoped wasn't a brain tumor.

"You fell off your barstool?" she whined, mortified by the oozing image. "You looked at that woman and you *fell* off your barstool?"

Her head dropped back to the top cushion as her arms reached upwards, pleading to no one and nothing in particular for mercy before surrendering, letting her face roll sideways in direct line with the mirror mounted on the open closet door.

She expected to see the reflection of a demure girl with chestnut eyes and auburn hair aesthetically cropped to shoulder length. A *Mademoiselle* magazine mademoiselle who dresses fashionably by color coordinating her shoes with her belts and scarves, and matches the finish on the buttons of each outfit with a complementing shade of jewelry. A young lady of presumed propriety; one who never leaves home without her hair lacquered, her makeup spritzed, her head covered, her hands gloved, her embroidered handkerchief hidden in her cuff and her wits about her.

Instead, she saw where the embroidery of a throw pillow left creased impressions on her cheek, her hair horizontally tangled wherever it wasn't vertically flat and matted, her nylons sagging at the knees, her coat wrinkled and askew.

And, too, she knew there wasn't a part of her body that didn't ache from the vague memory of the night before, or hunger from the yearning the morning-after had imposed.

"Hells-bells, Imogene," she said to her tarnished reflection, recalling the woman's lips brushing the very cheek where a wide, dried riverbed of mascara now flaked from a bit below her eye to shy of her chin. It prompted a peculiar spasm.

She sat up, elbows stiff, arms braced with hands clutching the couch cushions as her thoughts retraced the woman's fingertips gliding off Imogene's shoulder and downwards to where her pink silk shirt was tucked snugly into her matching skirt-and-vest ensemble. Easing her hand up under the vest, the woman rested it on the small of Imogene's back where it lingered until shortly after the music stopped and an intense quiet alerted them to their being the last couple left swaying on the dance floor.

It all began careening back. Imogene could almost feel the softness of those lips near the rim of her ear and hear the gentle whisper of the woman's voice suggesting they go back to her hotel.

"I just want to hold you," she coaxed.

"Not until we're married," Imogene simpered.

That's when a bloodcurdling scream occurred.

Oh no, not on the dance floor while in the arms of the credible cover girl. No. The bloodcurdling *scream* sending Imogene into the air and spinning with her hands gripping at her opposite shoulders and squeezing in humiliation came with the recollection of those wedding words, spoken to the woman after meeting her only minutes earlier.

"Not until we're *married?*" She cupped her hands over her mouth and wailed in censure of herself, "Oh-h my. Oh no-no-no. I didn't say that to her. Did I? I did not say that. I did not. I didn't. *I didn't!*"

Imogene stopped on the verge of tears, her fists clenched so tight in front of her mouth that the knuckles went from pink to white and back again. Painfully aware of her furrowed brow and unable to relax it, she began shaking her head instead.

"I did, I did, I did. I said that. That's exactly what I said," she lamented, stripping off her clothes and stomping her way through the conclave kitchen to her compact bathroom, stepping into its clawfoot tub where streams from a wide-mouth showerhead began to pummel her before she thought to let the water warm, or remove her boot.

It didn't initially faze her.

As she lathered up, frames of the preceding evening began flashing back to the moment she was snatched from the woman's arms, followed by the woman's failed effort to hold on as Imogene uttered (what she'd later learn was) a gin-tinged "ba-bye."

Imogene froze, focusing on the bizarre sequence of herself being carried through a rowdy crowd, passing Juni, the come-hither Italian Amazon bartender whom she'd never seen smile at any of her other wannabe suitors during the entire time Andy Wink urged her to frequent Johnny's. Juni, who tossed a yellow rose to the woman being blocked upon Wink's directive, but not before the woman caught Juni's rose and hurled it over the heads of Wink's broad brigade as Imogene stretched to catch it.

"Wink!" Imogene heaved, her lips pursed with rebuke, at the precise moment the shower water registered too hot for rinsing her hair with one hand while trying to dislodge the soused leather boot with the other.

Her screech bulleted out from the bathroom, ricocheted off the kitchen, flew through the studio, sailed under the door, burst into the hallway, and resonated down the stairwell to the foyer at the very moment Charles Frank ambled in.

TWO
Sunday, May 8, 1966
Charles In Charge

If you stretched Yosemite Sam to roughly six foot three, trimmed his thickset, tangerine mustache back to lip width, removed the bent brim hat hiding a bramble of matching hair, conceded the wild eyes, and exchanged the cartoon Calvary blues for a brindle brown suit that looked like it once was a cannon wad, you'd find the mirror image of Charles Frank.

But unlike the six-shooter Sam, Charles had a weighted way of walking, and slurred-spit way of talking, making him a target of hooligans, hookers, and those seeking handouts on street corners. As such, he avoided people whenever possible and suffered them when not.

Love hadn't been kind to Charles, nor he to it, due mostly to his inability to consummate his first marriage and finding no other woman interested in marrying him once they learned such to have been so. It wasn't that he didn't like women. He did. He simply didn't desire them (or anyone) in 'that' way. As he saw it, marriage required getting creepy-crawly close. Charles wasn't willing to do that.

Fortunately, his principal employment had been that of a factotum (a word he used to discourage prying). It complemented his cracker-barrel ambition to live out his days placidly and die detached — with some exceptions. And, lately, that exception had been for the girl living directly above him in apartment #3.

• • •

When Mr. Singer (who looked so much like the author Isaac Bashevis Singer that most believed it *was* him) first bought the Victorian

5

whitestone near the corner of Central Park West and 85th Street in the Spring of 1946, it had been for himself and his wife, Anna, along with Charles, who served as their driver, gardener, maintenance man, and *faux-naïf* friend.

"Good day," Charles would say to Mr. Singer every morning. Singer would nod. "Yanks look good," Charles would say whenever the team won a game. Singer would nod. "Better bundle up," he'd say at various times come autumn. Singer would nod. "Happy holidays," he'd offer, regardless of whose holiday it was. Often, Singer would nod. The two had been conversing like that for years, ever since meeting outside Katz's Delicatessen on Manhattan's lower East Side.

It happened one night when Mr. Singer was hurrying home with a brown paper bag smelling of hot corned beef, rye seeds, brown mustard, and garlic pickles when he saw Charles crouched low on the Ludlow Street curb and sat down beside him.

"*Nu?*" nudged Singer, gently. "Trouble?"

"Scared," mumbled Charles, feeling both vulnerable and vanquished.

Singer nodded before adding, "Of?"

"Everything. Scared of it all."

Mr. Singer looked around at the tires of cars speeding east on Houston Street towards the river, and the shoes of shoppers stopping or stumbling, trying to avoid them. "But not of this curb," Singer clarified.

Charles turned toward the man sitting in his neat navy suit with his thin dark tie hanging from his starched white shirt. He wore a teardrop tweaked fedora trimmed in a blue grosgrain ribbon clamped tightly down on his head. A swollen-tipped nose separated his two slightly bulging, roasted umber eyes set back under mountain-peaked, wooly black brows, all contrasting a face that seemed never to have seen sunshine.

"No," conceded Charles. "Not of the curb."

"And, not of food?"

"No."

"And, not of a job?"

"No."

"Well then," Singer said, patting Charles on the shoulder, "not such a *dybbuk* after all."

He rose slowly and motioned Charles to follow him to a nearby apartment building he owned where the two men shared Singer's sandwich, washed down with a Dr. Brown's Celery Soda. Then Charles slept soundly on a borrowed bed in a back room, the prelude to an affinity with Singer that would bond them for forty-some more years.

• • •

Originally, the West 85th Street whitestone was a four-story home. It had a nursery, nanny, and maids quarters on the top floor, the Singer residence on the center two, and Charles' lodgings occupying half of the of ground floor, with one door opening to the black and white tiled front foyer, a back door opening to a courtyard, and a third door leading down to a massive boiler in the basement that Charles was paid extra to maintain.

Distinct from the rented redstones on the balance of the block, visitors entered the Singer home by walking down three marble steps to an old-world terrace stretching the width of the building. It provided an air of privacy with a high-walled ledge where stoop sitting was discouraged by the presence of wrought iron spike tips sticking upwards every six inches.

At the time, the Singers were in their late thirties, expecting their first child in October. The whitestone had been a gift to themselves for finally succeeding in starting the family they'd desperately tried to conceive after marrying more than a decade earlier.

But shortly after they'd all moved into the grand old residence, Anna miscarried in such a way as to take both the life of their unborn baby and all hopes of ever bearing another.

"I'm so very sorry," Charles choked.

Singer turned his head and looked into Charles' eyes, pleading for it not to be so. Charles put his arm around Singer's shoulder and they sat down on the cold stone steps leading to the street together. They wept aloud.

Afterwards, the three became a family united by loss, resigned to grow old together on a fusion of routine, duty, and deep devotion.

At least, that was their strategy until the day Anna became winded climbing stairs and Mr. Singer moved the two of them into the Belnord, a nearby building with elevators and a doorman.

It left Charles as the custodian of the whitestone, now divided into six large studio apartments with kitchens and baths on the two center floors, and eight single rooms sharing one hallway bath on the top. The upkeep created by male tenants scratching the dark oak floors, filling fireplaces with refuse, clogging plumbing with food scraps, and putting cracks in plaster walls to display posters, hang sports jerseys, and girlie calendars was endless.

"Couldn't you find someone more responsible next time?" Charles invariably asked of Mr. Singer as they repainted yet another wall, or repaired an interior shutter on a front bay window, or reupholstered a couch, or replaced a chair.

"Yes, yes," said Singer. But he never did, not even when the studio for rent was directly above that of Charles, subjecting him to noises from bouncing balls, roughhousing, hard heels, or frolicking on furniture late at night.

"I want you to seal that door to the hall locker," Mr. Singer instructed, "and open the one sealed off inside this studio so I can rent it as a one bedroom."

"But, but," Charles protested, "Where will I keep the mops and pails for washing down the upper halls and stairs?"

"Nu? You don't have space for these things?"

Charles did. His place was as sparse as servants' quarters without the furniture Mr. Singer provided for his other renters: convertible couches, chairs with ottomans, tables with reading lamps, mirrored dressers, and a wall of bookcases for displaying keepsakes — sometimes even books. It wasn't that Singer hadn't offered Charles furnishings, because he had. Singer was a *mentsh* among men about such things, as kind as he was generous. But Charles politely declined, having always been a make-do man. Anyhow, it wasn't about the space. It was the thought of having to drag equipment up and down the stairs.

"It's a fine apartment," Charles conceded, secretly wishing it could be his, if he had someone to share it with now that he was well past sixty and his cat was old.

"We'll get double what we did without the bedroom," Mr. Singer calculated. "Three hundred fifty a month. Maybe four."

"That cubbyhole is barely wide enough for a double bed," Charles worried aloud. Not that it mattered. Mr. Singer had up his mind.

The morning they finished the conversion and began removing the sheets protecting the apartment's furniture, Mr. Singer turned to see a petite, red-haired girl dressed in a salad-green coat with contrasting hat and gloves standing in the apartment's doorway, mesmerized. He followed her eyes as they tip-toed the length and width of the room, alighting upon each detail like sunbeams filtering through the windows. She spoke with reverence.

"This is the most beautiful room I've ever seen in my entire life."

Singer tried to hide the pride he felt by pooh-poohing her words. "You must not have been in very many rooms."

"None like this," she marveled. "Not ever."

She twinkles, Singer told himself. *Like my Anna.*

"What's that you have?" He pointed to the red inked classifieds the girl clutched.

"Oh, I'm sorry." She extended her hand. "My name is Imogene LaPin. I was hoping to be shown this single room advertised for twenty a week." She showed Singer the ad he'd placed in *The New York Times*. "I heard you talking from the lobby, so I came up. I didn't mean to intrude."

She's polite, Mr. Singer thought, *and the same age my girl might be if she'd lived.*

• • •

Mr. Singer sensed he and his Anna would have a girl. They gave thanks for her each evening of the one hundred and forty-nine days from the calculated date of conception to the dusk of the day his daughter died. The loss still stabbed at him like a short, sharp dagger to the heart, twisting and twisting. It swamped him with self-reproach, as if he could have prevented it.

The doctors claimed otherwise. The police said it wasn't unusual. All those even remotely familiar with the tragedy insisted he'd done nothing wrong.

And yet, he was tormented. He felt punished.

They'd been waltzing around the bedroom, rich with a fragrance of honeysuckle and the hi-fi sound of Nat King Cole crooning *I Love You, For Sentimental Reasons* when Anna broke from his arms and doubled downward into a gushing pool of blood.

Singer was stunned at first, unaware of why Anna fell or what needed doing. It was when he dropped down to his knees for her that he saw the translucent sac in a sea of gelatinous red. Stretching to scoop it up while balancing Anna in his arms, he lunged them onto the bed, hastily wrapping mother and daughter in the pulled-free percale before lifting them up and charging out the door.

"Let my Anna live," Singer beseeched. "Let my child see me, once. Let me hear her voice, once. Please, oh *please!*"

Struggling to see through the spate of tears swelling his eyes, he leapt up from the terrace onto the sidewalk and sprinted into the traffic of Central Park West where the piercing cries of his ancestral Yiddish prayers were easily understood.

What followed was a blur. He knew it was a Checker Marathon cab that stopped, whose occupant, a dapper chap named Harold, dressed in his night-at-the-opera best, vaulted out with the driver in tow. Together they lifted the stricken Singers into the back seat of the cab that then zigzagged through cross-town traffic to Mount Sinai Hospital, delivering them soaked in a senseless sorrow.

Now, twenty years later, he stood staring at a guileless young girl while consumed by thoughts of his dead daughter, thinking *if she'd survived I'd be watching over her now.*

"One hundred dollars a month, furnished" Singer proffered. "Including utilities, except for a phone. But you must get a phone. Could you pay that?" He was prepared to go lower.

"Could I?" She was astonished. "Oh, yes, yes!" she danced, throwing her arms around him. "You don't know what this means to me, truly you don't. Thank you. *Thank* you!"

Charles dropped his mop. He couldn't believe what he'd seen and heard Mr. Singer do for a girl he'd never met. "Mr. Singer!" he started to say. But before he could, the shadow of a street corner wrapped in a whiff of rye surprised his senses.

"Charles here will be changing the locks this afternoon, but you can move in later today if you'd like. Knock on his door behind the stairwell in the lobby if you need anything."

The two looked at each other, water welling in both sets of eyes, wondering why the other was near tears. Mr. Singer patted Imogene on the shoulder saying "There, there," before abruptly turning to go.

He never looked back.

THREE
Saturday Morning, March 14, 1970
Imogene & Charles

Imogene answered the knock on her door wrapped in a white, Egyptian-cotton terrycloth robe. The Vaseline she'd slapdashed on to remove her mascara (but neglected to remove before showering) now flowed from both eyes, creating a murdered mime effect.

"Good morning Charles, how are you, I'm sorry, I'm late, need to run, hope it can wait, thanks for stopping by..." she jabbered, intending to close the door in his face.

"You screamed, Missy," Charles inserted. He pointed to her feet. "Your boot's leaking."

Imogene never questioned why he addressed her as Missy, right from their introduction years earlier when *she* was the one standing in the doorway and he was inside that very room, holding a mop she now needed. Since people had been calling her by names other than Imogene all her life, she accepted each as a term of endearment because, frankly, she liked the thought of endearing herself to others. But that was before, this was now, and all she wanted was for him to go so she could leave.

"The shower water," she relented. "It hit me too hot."

"But are you okay? You look like you might not be."

Imogene leaned back to peer into the pocket mirror on the inside door used to spot makeup errors before venturing out. She winced at the evidence of having jumped from the tub into a fogged filled room without wiping the medicine chest glass to check her reflection. Instead she quickly towel dried her hair and combed it straight back, planning to tie it with a silk scarf, like that of a Vogue model in Chanel suit.

"I'm fine. Trying something new. Something different. You know how that is."

"No." He stared a while. She waited a bit. Finally he offered, "I'd hate to think you were in some kind of trouble that I didn't see until too late. I'd feel responsible, somehow."

It wasn't that Imogene didn't appreciate Charles. She did. He'd never intruded into her life, while always watching out for her. If he heard a strange knocking on her door late at night, he took the time to climb the stairs and redirect visitors to the right apartment, because she didn't entertain later than eight. And, separate from the other tenants, she never had to wait to get something repaired or replaced. She never had to pay for it, either. There seemed to be an unwritten, unspoken agreement that her apartment came complete with Charles.

So, under any other circumstances, she'd chat and be gracious. But this day, time was of the essence, because she knew she'd lose her mind if she didn't hasten to chase her heart.

"I met someone last night."

"Well, Missy, say no more." Charles turned, talking while walking away. "Sorry to have held you up. Glad you're okay. I am that."

"Thanks, Charles." She watched him shuffle down the hall using his garden glove to dust the oak banister and begin descending the steps before calling out, "Charles!"

"Yes?"

"Can I borrow your mop?"

"I'll leave it for you in the lobby, Missy."

Imogene leaned back against the door and closed her eyes. "See?" she quietly said to herself. "You're riled up without cause. If you'll calm down, everything will be fine."

She bent and unzipped the squishy boot, kicking it off, so hard, it went flying across the room and landed on the Hepplewhite sideboard where her tomcat, Pansy, was lounging. This perceived assault caused the cat to soar up, catching his claws on the cover of the book that was under him, sending both through the air and crashing to the floor. Scaring her cat acted as the catalyst for Imogene's tears to flow.

"Oh, Pansy," she blubbered. "I'm so beside myself I forgot I had a pussy. How could that be?" She picked up Pansy and hugged him as he squirmed and growled. "My poor little, dear little, innocent little, perfect little Pansy. It's just that I met someone last night, Pansy. And, I'm positive she's the person I've been looking for all my life, even though it never occurred to me I was looking for her. But, really Pansy, I must have suspected it. Mustn't have I?" She snorted and scowled. "Is that right? Mustn't have I?"

She distractedly removed a starched and ironed white linen handkerchief from her robe pocket and smeared the mascara from her bloodshot eyes with it, rubbing the mixture of tears and makeup residue over her cheeks and her nose, leaving a sheen of blackened Vaseline behind. Then she put Pansy down to walk over and retrieve the book from the floor and a photograph that had fallen from it.

It gave her pause.

• • •

Imogene's mother nicknamed her Dolly. She said it was because Imogene was petite, still only three feet through fifth grade, not reaching a full five-foot height until turning thirteen.

"You were like a big, brown-eyed doll that I could ribbon and bow to my heart's content," she'd repeat forever after. "You'll always be my little Dolly."

Her mom liked to recount how, when Imogene was five, she was given a blonde haired blue-eyed doll for Christmas that she quickly christened, Eloise.

"When I grow up, I will marry Eloise," Imogene vowed.

Her mother listened dotingly, ever amused by the resolve shown by this runt of her litter of six. "How can you be sure she'll say yes?"

Imogene returned the doll to its box and tenderly blanketed it with white tissue before crawling up on her mothers lap, placing her dainty little hands on her mother's cheeks, and looking determinedly into her mother's ice blue eyes. "Don't worry, mom. Eloise will."

Three years later, when her father moved the family from the former right side of the tracks to the new-and-improved right side of the tracks, all the children's toys were mysteriously lost. But Imogene still had the 1951 serrated edge monochrome Christmas photo of herself and that doll, preserved as her Beatrix Potter bookmark.

Thenceforth, the photo was automatically transferred from one cherished book to another throughout her childhood. It moved gingerly between all of the *Anne of Green Gables* and *Nancy Drew* series. It graced pages of *The Bobbsy Twins, Aesop's Fables, A Dog of Flanders, Little Women, Rebecca of Sunnybrook Farm,* and *A Child's Garden of Verse.* It proved as suitable a separator for the pages of *Hamlet* and *Macbeth* as it did for the poems of *Edna St. Vincent Millay* and *Emily Dickinson,* the desperation of *Mrs. Dalloway,* the lessons of *To Kill A Mockingbird,* the caliber of *The King Must Die* and the versifying of *You Can't Go Home Again.* Ultimately, it accompanied Imogene as she boarded a bus bound for college with *The Group* stuffed in her purse, and remained her primary page-keeper when moving to Manhattan the following year.

Now, Imogene stood, fondly studying the photo, feeling the consequence of serendipity. To think, she'd actually met and promptly fallen in love with a real-life blonde haired, blue-eyed doll of a woman, whose name was...?

Frankly, there's no word to describe the sound Imogene emitted when sucking in the revelation, gagging on it, gurgling, and then coughing it out like a Pansy hairball.

"I didn't say my name. She didn't tell me hers. Oh-h no." Imogene felt faint. She began to shake. "Pansy," she whimpered. "Come help your poor momma."

The cat moseyed over and she picked it up, hugging it high enough on her shoulder and close enough to her face for the cat to sample some Vaseline residue. Imogene interpreted it as cat caring and found it cathartic.

She sat with the cat on the couch where her coat had been left in a heap, searching its pockets for clues, finding another handkerchief, this one embroidered with shamrocks to match the coat's color. Pansy started to caterwaul at being held too tight. Imogene mistook it as her cue to share.

"We didn't tell each other our names. There wasn't time." Pansy squirmed. "No, Pansy, it wasn't like that. It was late. The place was packed. The music was loud. I'd had enough. I wanted to come home to you and make the whole night go away." Pansy swatted Imogene's nose hard enough to gain release from her grip. A trickle of blood appeared and clotted before crusting, not that Imogene noticed. Instead, she kept right on whimpering. "Frankie Vali was playing on the jukebox next to my stool where, you know, Wink pays extra so I can sit there and set my ice water on it." Pansy clearly did *not* know, but remained attentive. "He and Juni have the whole thing worked out. Girls wanting to meet me send over a drink. I look her way and mouth, thanks. Wink switches glasses with me and drinks it. Then he gestures to Juni to tell the girl I'm not interested."

She quietly visualized the scenario that had played out on every Friday night for a year once she and Wink escaped the after-service Oneg Shabbat at The Village Temple on 12th Street and walked the seven blocks up and half block over to Johnny's where Wink acted as Queen to his ladies-in-waiting.

"Week after week. You'd think they'd all have caught on."

Imogene closed her eyes and began to run her fingers through her hair, stopping now and then to hold onto her scalp, carefully walking herself through it all again.

"It was precisely 11:58. I'm certain because I'd looked up at that big old pink neon clock near the cash register when the door swung open. Juni flipped the overhead spotlight on to nail the person coming through. All eyes shifted towards the blonde there. Her head turned in my direction. I took one look at her and fell off my barstool, flat on my face."

Imogene lowered herself nose-first onto the floor in an effort to recapture the moment.

"All of a sudden the woman was there turning me over." Imogene rolled over onto her back and lifted her arms in the air. "She took my hands and pulled me up." Imogene rose. "Then, while scooting me back onto the stool, she looked me straight in the eyes and said, 'I bet you do that for all the girls.'"

Imogene issued a euphoric squeak, remaining stuck in the schmaltz of the remark for a full five seconds before darker thoughts opened her weepy eyes wide to a possibility that petrified her.

"She was with someone." Imogene shook her head "No. No one. No." And yet, "Yes." Using her hands to frame the chain of events, she began again. "The woman came through the door. Our eyes met. I fell on my face. She helped me up, set me back, and scored the come-on quip. Then what? Oh, yes. Dory intervened. She took me by the shoulders, told me to stay put, and left me a glass of water that tasted funny. Piney. Then Dory, what? Disappeared?" Imogene slowly swiveled her head as if she was back in the moment, surveying the scene, putting all the players in place. "No. No, she went to tell Wink. That's it. She turned away, leaving the woman, where? Across from me, standing at the bar, before sitting down next to...oh-h shit."

Imogene instantly placed her hand over her mouth, surprised by the vulgarity she'd let slip, since she was never, ever vulgar. True, she could be annoying when conveying the detailed history of basic information. And she was often loud, due to years of elocution training for being a stage actress before accepting she wasn't a team player and deplored waiting around while other cast members missed their marks or forgot their lines.

But the more she dwelled on being a person of propriety, the more she weighed the naturalness of the unfortunate 's' utterance with the circumstances. At last she decided it was an accurate use of the word, spoken intuitively and in earnest, ergo, allowed with reservation, as long as never expressed in mixed company.

Once she'd absolved herself of any etiquette error and returned her attention to the events of the night before, she felt a surge of anger take hold.

"She was with that tramp." This time there was no dictum debate.

Imogene saw the display 'Miss Tramp' made of herself when she arrived at Johnny's dressed more for monkey business at The Plaza or The Drake than slumming at an all-babe bar. They'd taken an instant dislike to each other, expressed in glares; Imogene, because she knew a sleaze when she saw one — the tramp, because she knew Imogene wouldn't touch her with a ten foot pole. She wouldn't even touch the pole.

"No," Imogene concluded. "No-no-no. She *met* Miss Tramp there."

That started Imogene pacing and plotting and wandering in and out of her closet, not knowing what to wear, starting with a training bra, fresh socks and a pair of white cotton panties with the word 'Saturday' embroidered in pink near the lower left leg opening.

"I need to find Miss Tramp's name. Would Wink know? No-no. Wink wouldn't know. Regardless, I can't grill Wink or Miss Tramp about the woman." Imogene stepped into her panties and pulled them up before swirling about, flopping a sock in the air with her left hand. "Juni, maybe? Would Juni know her? No." Imogene whipped around and twirled a second sock with her right hand. "Juni couldn't know her because the woman told me, what? She was just in town for the weekend. That's it. She was visiting here from..."

Pansy came running when Imogene yelped, expecting to be scooped up.

"I don't know! I don't know where she's from, how she got here, where she's going back to, whom she's going back to, or even *if* she's going back to someone." She looked down at Pansy and implored, "Is she here alone? Is she taken? And, why oh why didn't I get her name?"

Pansy circled in and out between Imogene's legs, pushing up against her as he lead her to the kitchen before jumping onto the countertop where he was accustomed to being served.

Imogene removed the vintage Bunker from its dainty hook over her white porcelain two burner stove to open a fierce smelling can of Figaro tuna. Squeezing the pincer handles on an angle, she absentmindedly slopped all the juices onto the floor, splashing her legs, ankles and feet.

"Meow," said Pansy. Imogene stroked "you're welcome" before shuffling back through the living room, opening the top shutter on one of the four bay windows and peering out.

"Do you think it's warm enough for Keds?" she asked the cat (as if Pansy ever left the apartment after being born in a Long Island basement two years earlier). "No matter. Let's review," she began, pulling a pair of knee high socks over her fishy feet, lopping her head to and fro with each remark. "I didn't tell her my name. She didn't tell me hers. We didn't swap numbers. She's here for the weekend. I don't know where she's from. She doesn't know where I am. I was so nervous I chugged Dory's piney water. We danced. Did she approach me? No. I played charades. Yes, that's it. I pantomimed a request to dance." Imogene bowed her head in shame. "I am such a moron."

Looking back up, it came to mind, "And we did dance a bit, to *Something* by the Beatles. That's when she said she was staying at the Manhattan Hotel on 8th Street."

Imogene stopped to listen to herself. "What did I just say?" She closed her eyes and silently mouthed Manhattan Hotel on 8th Street, finishing with a "Bingo!"

That's it, she thought. *That's all I need to know.* She leapt in the air, ecstatic, before grabbing her clothes from where she'd dropped them on the floor — rationalizing, she'd be more easily recognized if she wore the same outfit as the previous night. Forget that it now looked like it had been up a pig's ass, she was dressed and off on a cloud of confidence, without taking time to examine her face in the handy-dandy door mirror, or suspecting the outside temperature had plummeted, or checking the directory to see if there even was a Manhattan Hotel on 8th Street.

There was not.

FOUR
Friday The 13th Into Saturday March 14, 1970
Night & Day

Andy Wink was pissed.

Dory Fenton knew that once he descended the back stairs into the barroom's cavernous quarters he wasn't to be disturbed. Yet there she was, blasting out his name over the cover of red-bulb nightlights as if the upstairs was on fire and they were all doomed to die. He dropped his pants and bared his chest to calm his buyer and prove he wasn't wired before buttoning up his 501's and excusing himself.

"What the hell, Dory?"

"It's Imogene, it's Imogene! Come quick."

"Imogene?"

"She got a stranger to dance. I saw her do it the second I was coming to get you. I sat her on her stool and told her to stay put. And then, on my way down here I looked back, and that's what she was doing. Making moves on that woman."

"Can't be," Wink shushed. "Mo's never looked sideways at a woman except to check out what she's wearing. There's no way she made a pass. Now get it together and go stand in a corner until I finish up."

Wink returned to confer behind rafter-high cases of unopened liquor bottles while Dory fidgeted. Minutes later a butch sailed by, stuffing a plastic bag inside the pocket flap of her Big Yank flannel shirt and taking the stairs up, three steps at a clip.

"You can come out now, Dory," Wink called, counting a roll of sweat stained bills, "and tell me everything I don't already know."

This is what Wink knew: It wasn't quite midnight when he began worrying about his buyer being late. It concerned him because he was counting on that dependable score as funding needed for his wedding

20

day, now hours away. When he finally caught sight of his hemp-head crossing the dance floor to his downstairs lair, the music changed to a Frankie Vali hit, so he took a split second to glance over his shoulder to see the front door pop open and trouble walk in.

As a stark contrast to most sapphics entering Johnny's with little fanfare, this outsider earned the attention of everyone in the place. He pegged her as subtlety stunning at taller than average and elegantly thin, her flaxen hair (as light and lustrous as his own) styled in a costly cut. It made him wonder if her eyes were also as bright, feeling an impetuous flow of jealousy engulf him. He couldn't see what color they were from that distance, but somehow he knew they were blue.

Too, he was enough of a fashion aficionado to detect she favored designer labels; a navy wool turtleneck with reverse-pleat slacks complemented by a matching, three-quarter length car coat, its upturned collar wrapped with a cashmere scarf, executed with panache.

Wink sensed the lady was heartbreak for anyone looking twice at her. Whom she wanted, or who called dibs on her was irrelevant. This was the variety of lesbian Wink avoided, knowing she'd see through him — unlike his Imogene who dressed with a flair devoid of worldliness.

He whipped his head around to where Imogene should have been sitting on her stool next to the jukebox, waiting for him to finish with business, not that she knew what he was up to. Mo (his pet name for her) was someone who trusted more than she should, the kind of character flaw he sought and encouraged in others. But he couldn't spot Imogene through the gathering crowd, near to where the imposing woman was now standing.

"Are we doing this or what?" his buyer called out.

Wink's reply was a wicked look, following her down the stairs without a second thought.

That ended the minute Dory invaded his turf, hysterical.

"Where's my drink?" snarled Wink.

"I set it down on the jukebox when Imogene fell off her stool."

"How many times have I told you, don't do that? Anyone could pick it up and drink it."

"So what? It's water."

"No, it's not. I tell you to order water from Juni. That's our Dory-code for gin."

"Then why not tell me to get you gin?"

"Because everyone with half a brain knows the rotgut bar blend is toxic. You can't leave a glass of Bombay sitting free without knocking a booze looter for a loop."

"Uh-oh."

"What, uh-oh?"

"After Imogene fell off her stool..."

"Why do you keep saying that?"

"Because she did! Some blonde number came through the door and Imogene saw her and she was up and then, kaboom, down on the floor."

"What? Was she hurt?"

"No, Wink, she was too loopy to be hurt."

"Loopy?"

"Yes, loopy. Happy-dippy. Moonstruck."

"Imogene was moonstruck?"

"That's what I'm trying to tell you, Houston. We have a problem!"

"Maybe she caught her boot on the stool rail — that's why she fell."

"Fell, yes, Wink, but head-over-heels, flat on her face. She fell, and the woman sailed over and picked her up and says..." Dory stopped to catch her breath before heaving it out. "I bet you do that for all the girls."

"Oh-h," Wink had to admit, "that's good."

"No!" fumed Dory. "It's not good. It's not right. It's not fair. I've been waiting to make my move on Imogene for months, but you said, no way. *No way*, you said. And now, in comes this lipsticker to steal my thunder before I even have a chance to...to...to..."

"Spit it out, Dory."

"To score, dammit!"

But Wink was only half-listening, letting her steam while he schemed. He knew he'd need Dory to break whatever bond the blonde might now hold over Imogene and he didn't want Dory (whom he privately referred to as Dorydumbdyke) going ballistic on him.

"Is that all?"

"No, that's not all. I told her to stay put and have a drink of water."

"You gave Imogene my Bombay Gin?"

"I thought it was water!"

"Did she drink it?"

"Yes, of course. She chugged it."

"She *chugged* it?"

"She did. And when I left to get you, I turned around and saw her invite that woman to dance." Dory was pacing, panicky and roast red.

"Calm down. Tell me what she said."

"I can't calm down, Wink. I had the person I've been hot on for months chug gin. Gin I gave her because I thought it was water. And now you tell me it wasn't even watered-down gin. Which means she'll blame me once she sobers up. As in, not *your* fault, but mine! I was the one who left her stalking a dangerous woman that she hit on to dance." Dory had become frantic. Frantic and seething. Frantic and seething and flailing her arms.

"Tell me what she said!" Wink yelled.

"Who?"

"Imogene, you twit! What did she say to get the woman to dance?"

"Nothing!" Dory demonstrated. "What she did was hold her left hand out, palm up, with the fingers pointing hell-bent towards that woman. Then she took her right hand and held it directly above her left palm with her first two first fingers pointing down. Then she *twirled* her fingers around in circles like she was drilling a friggin' hole!"

Wink jerked backward. "My God! She might as well have laid down and spread eagle."

"I know that! You think I don't know that? You think every woman in the whole damn place doesn't know that? You think the woman she hit on doesn't know that? Huh? *Do* you?"

Now Wink was pacing. "Look, Dory, all's not lost if you'll do as I say and help me get her out of here."

"Why? What's in it for me?"

"Help me get into a cab and I'll tell her you're interested in her. I'll open that door." Wink was lying through his thirty-two capped teeth, but knew he did so to a desperate woman he didn't care about beyond that moment and what she could do to aid and abet him.

"You'd do that for me?"

"I will."

"Then why the hell haven't you done it before now?"

"Because she never showed any interest in women! Dammit Dory, I'm as upset about this as you. I mean, if what you say is so, I had *no* idea."

Wink was being honest. Imogene attracted and rejected women. She flunked the fag-hag tag altogether. And in her display of general indifference to most men, she made it clear she'd rather die in the gutter by her own hand than marry one.

True, she said she'd marry him, but under contracted conditions. Theirs was to be a toy union, without intimacies, for the exclusive benefit of his career and perceptional place in society. And, since it was now past midnight, this was their wedding day.

Not that Dory knew. Not that he'd tell her because (to him) Dory was less than nothing; one of those posers who professed a love for other women, but didn't love herself *as* one. Instead, she went to extremes to make herself look, sound, and act like a man whose aim was to seduce lesbians with machismo.

"It behooves me to understand why any woman desiring women would ever choose a man-mimicker like you," he'd often said to her. "No offense."

"No offense taken," she slapped back. "Because it behooves me to understand why any man desiring men would choose someone as nelly as you. Admit it. I'm more of a man than you, and *twice* the woman."

"Perhaps. But I'm more of a lady than you could ever be."

They'd drunk to that, many times.

Now Dory sat on a crud-encrusted step, surveying him, trying to determine if he was telling her the truth; weighing her options and realizing she had none.

"What'd'ya want me to do?"

"Collect our coats, then go flag a cab."

"What'll you do?"

"Get Imogene. I'll carry her out of here if need be and take her home. We'll deal with the rest of this in the morning after she's slept it off and we've had time to make things up while sorting this out."

"What if there's no cab?"

Dory's incessant what-ifing to even the simplest plan always managed to perturb Wink. It was why he tolerated, but didn't like her, and knew there wasn't a way in a mental institution imagination that Dory and Imogene could ever click as a couple.

"You can find one if you jog the half block to Fifth Avenue, flag it from there, and bring it back to here."

"But we live in opposite directions. How will I get home?"

"Gee, let's see. How about, after we've gone you flag yourself another cab? My treat."

"Fine," she relented, tired of his taunting. "I'll see you out front."

When they reached the top of the stairs Wink and Dory spotted the blonde interloper sitting with Imogene at a table near the edge of the dance floor. Dory reacted first.

"Imogene's sitting on the woman's lap! There's an empty chair beside them and she's..."

"I can see that, Dory. I have eyes in front of my head you know."

"I'm going to..."

"You're going to get our coats and meet us out front. I'll put an end to this right now."

Once Dory had steamed her way through the crowd to the cloakroom, Wink summoned several of his friends from the floor, women who were miffed at the prowler for trespassing on private property. Not that Imogene belonged to them — but they'd played fair for the year Wink had escorted Imogene to Johnny's. They respected her privacy while enjoying the fanfare provided by Wink, who acted the role of Elsa Maxwell with favor and flare.

The fact was, Wink had once been resented as an intruder to their all-girls club, but he'd since earned the honor of belonging there. Rated prettier than most and more generous than all, Wink was the sparkle that went out of the room whenever he left it.

But on that night Wink crossed a line strictly forbidden by Juni, bartender extraordinaire and guardian of Johnny's *Kiss-Met Law*.

FIVE
20 Years Earlier, March 1950
Juniper Barry, Big Mike Bolla & Easy

Juniper Barry treated her name like an ugly birthmark needing to be hidden. As the target of small town sanctimonious residents who knew her parents were illiterate alcoholics, she'd been subjected to dogged ridicule because of it, in and out of the schoolroom.

In fact, on the day she was born the attending midwife showed no discretion in retelling the story of how Juniper's folks foolishly believed they were naming her after the berry used to flavor gin, "too damn stupid to know the difference" in the spelling between their own last name and that kernel of fruit.

Now, thirteen hundred miles and twenty years later, Juni still cringed at the thought of her true name being revealed to anyone in Manhattan where she'd fled as a teenager shortly after the crash that killed her parents and the weeping willow they hit while motorcycling, blotto, through the local graveyard.

She didn't stay for their funeral, having no money to pay for it, no relatives, no friends, and no way to prevent being placed in an orphanage at fifteen, the legal depository for the godforsaken then.

Instead, the minute the coroner released her parents' personal effects, she shoved a mother-of-pearl handled switchblade down the inside of her mom's salvaged knee-high leather boots, donned her dad's black leather jacket (after scouring his blood off the studs), pocketed the gold wedding bands wrested from her parents fractured fingers, and flagged down the first semi coming towards her, seeing it as her get out of Kansas free card.

• • •

It would be Juni's great good fortune that the eighteen-wheeler she hitched was traveling directly from the vineyards of California to a liquor distributor located on the lower east side of Manhattan. The driver, having made a wrong turn trying to circumvent Emporia, saw (what he thought was) a young man on the dark road late at night and took a chance in welcoming him aboard.

"Where you heading?" Big Mike Bolla asked when the tall, wiry wayfarer climbed into his semi.

"New York City," Juni muffled.

For a split second it took Big Mike by surprise. He was accustomed to conversing with young men in his rig and even sharing an occasional bed with one if it was proposed and seemed safe. But this was the first time he'd let a woman into his transport, all six feet of her, plus a lethal three-inch heel on her boot.

"Ever been there before?"

"Nope."

"Someone there you're meeting?"

"Nope."

"Anyone there you know?"

"Nope."

"Well then, you picked a safe ride and authority. Manhattan is my town."

Juni crossed her fingers and held her breath in hopes her luck had finally changed.

"My name is Big Mike Bolla."

"Mine's Juni."

"Happy to meet you, Juni!" he enthused, offering to shake in kinship. "Have you been hitching long?"

"No," she flinched, startled by his grizzly-size hand, and a rounder version of his elastic face that mimicked Stan Laurel's of Hardy fame, crowned with a monkish haircut encircling a balding head. If he grabbed hold and wouldn't let go, she hoped she had the wherewithal to stab him. Determining *where* might prove problematic. There was a mountain of him to consider.

"Well, you're wise to refuse my hand. Hitching isn't always safe. But go ahead and relax. You got nothin' to fear in me." Big Mike pulled the chain releasing a blast from his horn that every kid waving out a window wants to hear, easing the tractor-trailer back onto the road. "You can adjust the radio if you want. There ain't much on this time of night. Foley, Williams, and Ernie Ford mostly. I favor the Ford fellow myself."

"No, I'd rather just sit for a bit if you don't mind." Which she did, quietly, for a full five miles before drifting off to sleep.

• • •

Forty-nine miles outside of Kansas City, Missouri heading east on Highway 40 was a truck stop renting white one-room cabins with navy blue doors and red rocking chairs out front. A neon *Goodlookin' Homecookin'* logo flashed over the glass ball Cities Gas pumps 24 hours a day, year round. Acclaimed for having the best food, cleanest sheets, and fastest take-out of any fill-up between there and St. Louis, long haul truckers treated its proprietors like family, paying homage to Ma Fitz, who personally served hundreds of them daily, and Pappy Fitz, who never met a colicky engine he couldn't fix overnight.

But the crown jewel of the tireless duo was their daughter, an eleven year old hellion who pumped the truckers' gas and cleaned their windshields while smooth-talking anyone within earshot into buying her latest knickknackery and not-altogether-legal fireworks from stashes she kept hidden in the trunk of a 1938 Buick Roadmaster that was smashed in, jacked up, rusted out, and left for feral cats to inhabit behind the restaurant's chicken coop.

"Stayin' over, are ya, Mister Mike?" hoped the girl as she gingerly hoisted herself up on top of the diesel's hood to check its windshield wipers for wear.

"Not this trip. Hardly have time to grab some of your mom's meat loaf sandwiches and pecan pie before gettin' us back on the road. Would she have any of that peppermint tea brewed to calm the queasy in my stomach?"

"Absolutely-positutely! And some fresh made lemonade to churn it right back up again. You might want to jelly jar some of it."

"Don't say."

"Do say!"

Big Mike chuckled his way into the restaurant while the girl finished up. Then she casually swung herself through the driver side window like a towheaded capuchin monkey expecting a treat and plopped down on the tattered leather seat behind the steering wheel.

"You and Big Mike married?" she needled Juni.

"Nope."

"Didn't think so."

"Then why...?"

"To show I'm right."

"Well, you are."

"Thought so."

"You married?"

"Me? Jeepers no. I'm only eleven. But I'm never getting married. No siree. No man's ever gonna to tell *me* what to do!"

"Not even the guy you work for someday?"

"I won't work for a guy."

"Oh no? Then what'll you do?'

"I'll do whatever I darn well please. Same as now."

"Pretty sure of yourself for a pip-squeak aren't you?"

"Pretty sure and pretty apt to stay that way!"

Juni laughed. Big Mike had spoken fondly of the girl before they got to the stop, and now she could understand why the kid was so well liked. Her self-confidence alone was contagious.

And who could resist her sweet pink lips framing teeth with a cute little space between the front two. "I'm told a girl with a space between her front teeth grows up to be a beauty," Juni teased.

"Then how's come you don't have one?"

"Because I'm no beauty."

"You are if I say you are, and I say you are, so don't be lettin' anyone say different."

It was the first time in Juni's life anyone suggested she might be worth a second glance. "What's your name, kid?"

"Easy."

"Easy? That's an odd one. What's it short for?"

"Come easy, go easy!" she grinned on her way up and out the window as Big Mike was about to open the door. "Don't be a stranger, Mister Mike. And take good care of the little lady."

"I'm no lady," Juni shouted out after her.

"I knew that!" Easy shouted back.

The balance of their trip to New York was less engaging than the ten minutes spent with Easy Fitz. It was a glint of time Juni revisited often over the next twenty years, occasionally as a spirits raiser, but most often when a woman with charm waltzed into one of the places where she tended bar.

All tolled, she'd worked at clubs much worse than Johnny's, but none much better, most of them opening up on a shoestring and closing down on a raid. Having always been hired by a middleman and paid in cash, she wasn't privy to the bar's ownership. That was for the best and certainly safer. Big Mike hinted the dives were mob controlled payoff places. Not that she cared.

Before they reached Manhattan's Little Italy, Big Mike knew the sordid details of Juni's lamentable life, and she knew he was a low man on the Sicilian totem pole, driving his last rig of bootleg liquor across country. Diabetes flare-ups had made it impossible for him to ride the roads any longer, so he'd been reassigned to a bartender gig at a rough-and-tumble saloon in the center of the garment district with the front half utilized as a refuge for rummies and roustabouts, with the back serving as a clearinghouse for stolen goods.

"You ever tended bar, Juni?"

"Firsthand. I could make gimlet out of a Limey and a pine cone."

"Hah! That's a good one. By golly, I'm gonna use that the first time some Brit wanders in wanting a Pimm's."

If she feared Big Mike might turn her over to the authorities once he discovered she was fifteen and alone in the world, she needn't have.

"Sad fact? You look twenty-five."

She checked her reflection in the mirror taped to the rider side visor and saw he was right. Dark circles looped her bleak brown eyes and light lines creased her forehead.

"Not much I can do about that now." It wasn't like Juni to cry, but she was on the verge.

"Aw-w-w, buck up girl. Once you get some sound sleep and a little beef on those bones you'll look a full nickel younger."

"Well, I guess that's preferable to looking like jailbait. And to think that kid labeled me a beauty."

"You mean Easy? That's because she sees it all as it should be, not as it is. But you'll get there." He whipped out a roll of twenties and peeled off ten. "Tell you what. This'll get you started. You can pay me back whenever, if you want. It makes no matter-mind to me. I was glad to have you along making this last trip my best ever." He scribbled a map to a Village address on the inside of a Hershey's wrapper, told her who to talk to, and pointed her in the right direction. "I'll call later with details. You can start working tomorrow."

"As what?"

"A bartender. What else? You'll get an afternoon shift 'til you prove yourself. But if you keep your hands outta the till and off the swill, you'll do fine."

That's all Juni hoped for from the get-go: a place to stay and a way to make it on her own. Big Mike had vouched for her, no strings attached.

Their paths seldom crossed after that, but Juni knew in her heart she could depend on Big Mike Bolla to be there for her if need be.

SIX
Early Saturday Morning, March 14, 1970
Juni & Nadine & Izzy

Juni fancied being bartender extraordinaire and Patron Saint of Johnny's. She trivialized the Saint misnomer (being neither Catholic nor pious), but accepted it as so. Watching over lovelorn lesbians by nurturing them in their hours of need had provided her with a purpose.

Every afternoon at four she'd unlock the street and vestibule doors before flipping on the rose tinged wall lamps and low watt bar spots, making it as bright as it would get inside for ten hours until closing at two. The blacked-out front window preventing sunlight was a privacy standard for all gay bars in the city once the New York State Liquor Authority established a rule that barred the serving of alcohol to homosexuals. Some restaurants even went so far as to post notices on their doors that read: *Gay? Go away!*

That archetype of blatant bias had eased up a bit after the uprising at the Stonewall Inn the year before, but Juni knew it remained dangerous to be a homo in New York. The Charles Street Police House was proof of that. Days earlier an illegally detained kid in fear of being jailed for being gay jumped out the station house window and impaled himself on the fence below. A full page photo of the skewered boy headlined the *Daily News* with officers mocking him. It engendered public outrage.

The faceoff began years earlier with the organization of sip-ins by the Mattachine Society to test the Liquor Authority rule. Their polite protest grew into a lawsuit dominating the dialogue at Julius', a renown west Village tavern where nothing obstructed the picture window view of young men with imposing good looks lining the bar and crowding the staging area near a revered fry cook turning out the best burgers in Manhattan.

For more than a century, Julius' had been a legendary actors and artists haunt for poseurs, popinjays, poof, rakes, coxcombs, Molly, flamboyant fop and dandies, all past aspersions to the modern day slurs of sissy, queen, Mary, faggot, fairy, nellie, Nancypants, pansy and queer. The Mattachine confrontation exacted a compromise: the Liquor Authority regulation would not alter Julius' history as long as cruising was kept to the back room tables.

Once, when a priest was arrested at Julius' for soliciting a young man for sex, a flyer was taped to the front window alerting patrons of the raid. The posting wasn't meant to hide the truth of what went on behind closed doors. It simply served as a heads-up.

At least, that's what Juni heard through the grapevine of barhopping regulars to lesbian haunts, all more secluded, highly secretive, and completely disassociated from men's.

The gist of it was, such stark differences existed between male and female homosexuals, often their sole link was the partisan preference proviso. Whereas men frequented buggery bars, bath houses, public toilets, rest stops, movie theatres, parking lots, parks, the docks, backcombs, sand dunes, meatpacking coolers, quickie rate motels, and the Rambles in reckless pursuit of anonymous sex, women either met at private parties or the few lesbian bars scattered throughout the boroughs, seeking the kind of Cinderella romance that begins and ends with the same someone to wake up to each morning.

"Say what you will about women's liberation," Juni warned all lesbians broaching the topic with her, "after generations of being treated as recreational sex objects by men, the worst thing we could do is adopt that random slam-bam attitude towards each other." Nevertheless, she saw her way of thinking start to fade. It made her feel old and obsolete at thirty-five.

Liquor Authority aside, when it came to opening a gay bar in New York City, there were always those eager to ignore the law. Even if it required paying mob henchman, bribing beat cops, or contributing large sums to fund political candidates, opportunists lined up to provide gays with places to be fleeced.

In that respect, the rebellion at Stonewall sold newspapers, produced sound bites, set benchmarks, and altered the perception of being openly gay in New York for some — but such would not be the reality for the majority.

"Equality?" Juni would say. "Not in my lifetime, sister."

To prevent the possibility of arrest, Johnny's put a policy in place. Whenever anyone was about to enter the premises, a buzzer rigged to the outer front door would warn Juni to flip a switch that simultaneously changed the music and aimed a bright, white spotlight directly at the vestibule, temporarily blinding the person coming through, law-enforcement included. It gave the ladies enough time to either break apart and stay put, or escape through side and back doors into alleyways. In three years time, Juni had briefly blinded thousands of the unsuspecting, but Johnny's had never been successfully raided.

• • •

When the femme fatale floated in two minutes before midnight on that Friday the 13th, Juni was as agog as most of the regulars watching her gallantly help Johnny's mascot, Imogene, up off the floor before squeezing onto a seat at the bar next to a prima-donna known as Knockers Nadine.

"Can I get you something?" Juni tried not to stare into the femme's eyes.

"Two Canadian Clubs with a bottle of 7up on the side," ordered Nadine. "And not that Mist stuff either, Juni. I'll pay the premium."

It surprised Juni that the two knew each other. True, Nadine was flush with cash, but whatever she flaunted by way of fortune she lacked in sophistication. "I'd rather the lady speak for herself, Nadine."

"C.C. and seven," thanked the woman, revealing a space between her two front teeth.

Nadine snapped. "Back off, Juni. You're spoken for and she's mine. So go. Hug your bud vase. We have some unfinished business."

It wasn't true that Juni was taken, but she did place a fresh yellow rose in a crystal vase on the bar each day, alluding to a lover. Occasionally, she'd have the rose delivered to herself by messenger with a mushy card enclosed, causing the girls to whistle and cheer. But more often, she bought one from a sidewalk vendor on the way into work. It saved hurt feelings and fended off flirtations. She knew if she couldn't go home with all of them, she shouldn't go home with any.

The truth was, in the twenty years since shedding Kansas and adopting New York as born and bred, she'd grown into her skin and could have her pick of the lezzy-litter. Her Irish heritage of sable locks, emerald eyes, and ivory skin had blossomed once she'd shed poverty and welcomed womanhood. She still wore boots with three-inch heels, but had added frilly blouses to her black leather wardrobe, her mom's gold band to her left hand, and her dad's on a chain around her neck. It served to create a dual persona that warded off ruffians and kept the peace without requiring a bouncer to be present.

All the same, she wasn't about to mince words with Nadine over old inamorata rights, but neither was she going to stray far from someone that might be her long ago little well-wisher.

Nadine ogled the woman. "Thanks for remembering my birthday."

"I didn't. Somehow you knew I'd be in town for the night and the limo left me here. If the driver hadn't said the boys were inside I wouldn't have come in."

"Well, forget that. As long as I have you now."

The lady laughed. "You don't! I'll stay for a drink, but that's it. Call it a birthday present if you want, or reward for finally admitting to getting older — in public no less."

Nadine ignored the stab by changing the subject. "What's with the salivating kid over there?" She'd motioned towards Imogene who was back on her stool next to the jukebox, staring while chugging who-knew-what.

Juni couldn't tell if Nadine's inquiry irked the lady, or she just felt frisky. Whichever, she immediately stood and sauntered over to the Seeburg where, while avoiding eye contact with Imogene, she dropped in a few quarters and made some selections. Then she pivoted and sauntered back to the bar.

"Down dyke," Nadine warned. "People are arrested for less lechery in this town. Besides, that kid is definitely jail bait."

By then Juni had delivered their drinks. "The girl's of age," she corrected. "But a newbie. At least, I've never seen her swoon over anyone. Before now."

"Does she come here often?" the lady ventured.

"Every Friday night for about a year. She sits and watches. Doesn't even shake hands."

Before Nadine could warn Juni about shutting up or losing her tip, Imogene had won the lady's attention via a zany charade and the two were gliding off to join the crowd on the dance floor swaying to *Something* by the Fab Four.

"Damn you, Juni!"

"Oh come now, Nadine. Those two were sure-fire on sight."

"Keep rubbing it in, Juni. See how rich it gets you."

"What's her name anyhow?"

Nadine lit a Gitanes, inhaled, then picked a piece of tobacco off the tip of her tongue before spitting out, "Izzy."

"Unusual. Short for Isabelle, maybe?"

"Eloise Fitz, although she's incognito here. So, there's a freebie on tap for anyone who spreads her real name around."

Juni felt her heart jerk. "Known her long?"

"Met in a moment of weakness on the Boardwalk in Ft. Lauderdale. Summer of '67."

"She doesn't strike me as being weak."

"Well I don't strike myself as being stupid, either. But I was when I didn't nail her down when I could."

"Spare me, Nadine. You might have gotten lucky once, but you never had a chance with that one. She must have been rebounding."

"Something like that."

They both glanced over toward the dance floor in time to see Eloise's lips nestled near the edge of Imogene's ear as they slowly came-to on the dance floor, thirty long seconds after the music stopped.

"I'm now, officially, road kill," Nadine conceded.

It pleased Juni to no end. "Refill?"

"Yeah. Make it a double, dammit."

Juni intended to reintroduce herself to Eloise the minute Nadine scored elsewhere out of spite, but Andy Wink ruined her plans by breaking Johnny's Kiss-Met Rule, plainly posted on the vestibule wall for all those entering the bar to see:

"Any two who kiss after meeting within these hopeful walls, let no one put asunder for so long as they remain on these premises. Failure to comply will result in your immediate removal, subject to banishment."

Yet there Wink was, lifting Imogene from her perch on the intruder's knee and carrying her through the barroom while a few of his paid lackeys ran ramrod.

Juni reacted unpredictably. She plucked her yellow rose from its vase and pitched it to Eloise who lobbed it to Imogene who effortlessly caught the rose within an instant of being whisked out the door.

The part-cheering-part-scuffle eruption that followed, with Wink's women muscling-up to Eloise and accusing her of theft, required Juni to jump up on the bar and whistle for quiet. "Belly up to the bar, babes! One free round on the house."

It gave Eloise the distraction she needed to barge out of Johnny's.

SEVEN
Early Saturday Morning, March 14, 1970
Nadine & Eloise

By the time Eloise got outside, the taxi had pulled away from the curb and was heading towards the intersection at the far end of the block. She stood in the middle of the street, focusing on the tail lights, her arm poised in the air overhead, hoping to be reflected in the rear view mirror, wishing the girl would somehow see her, tell the driver to stop, and she'd get out.

When the cab slowed, Eloise dropped her arm, held her breath, and waited. But as soon as the traffic light switched from red to green the taxi sped up again, quickly disappearing into the dark, dank March morning.

"Hey Miss Silly, lost your filly?" Nadine mocked. She'd exited Johnny's garbed in a white lynx coat the length of her 5'5" frame, its front open to expose the electricity of her taupe sweater dress clinging to every dip and peak of her body, purposely providing a walking peep show for public view. Flicking a lit butt into the air like a torpedo she added, "Well, don't be so dismayed darlin'. God knows you had better taste three years ago."

Eloise took a last look up and down the street in case the taxi circled the block to return for her. Otherwise, except for Nadine's red Jaguar parked illegally near Johnny's front door, the street was predictably empty. Those who didn't frequent Johnny's by foot or cab parked their cars in a nearby gated garage to thwart being bullied or beaten. Nadine preferred to tempt fate. It made her dangerous in oh-so many ways.

"Better taste in what?"

"In women, of course. When did you start chasing chicken anyway? Don't you find us big girls tits-illating anymore?" She straightened her shoulders and shimmied, laughing when Eloise looked away.

Eloise shivered over to where Nadine posed. "What makes you think I ever did?"

"Come now, love. You might have jumped ship, but that doesn't mean we weren't hotter than hell once under a Miami moon. Besides, this is New York. You're in *my* town now."

Eloise knew that last part was probably true. Nadine had married enough rich men and bedded enough wealthy women in her forty-five years to extort a Park Avenue penthouse, a Pines seaside cottage, a Boca condo, and money to survive in style for as long as necessary.

"I'm meeting someone."

"Don't tell me you're here with James." Nadine knew otherwise. She'd collected on a debt owed by an old hedonist of hers who'd been eager to solicit the young hustler Eloise befriended in Portsmouth where Nadine learned Eloise had retreated. The plot was desperate and pathetic, even for Nadine, but she was lonely and bored and could afford it.

At 31, Eloise was often mistaken for a fag-hag accompanying closeted benefactors and their belladonna boys to charitable events. The only other time she and Nadine met, Eloise was the plus one for a 35 year old closeted gay guy at his sister's Coconut Grove wedding. Later that night, swayed by the allure of browned bodies, umbrella drinks, Motown music and the curiosity to see a palatial suite at The Fontainebleau, Eloise caved in to Nadine's advances. But by morning she regretted what she'd never done before and committed to never letting it happen again.

It's not that Nadine wasn't attractive in a 'Mrs. Robinson' way. She was. The Sassoon pageboy, Revlon nails, Mary Quant eyelashes, Lancôme lotions, Millot Crêpe de Chine perfume, Claire Haddad peignoirs, and Birks Crown jewels were all proof of that.

Rather, Eloise discerned Nadine was a Mrs. Robinson for real, as if cloned from the character in *The Graduate* who briefly married a same-name plastic surgeon in the calculated gain of a hefty divorce settlement. It made Nadine the shade of sly not to engage for any reason on any level.

"No. Not James. He's in Portsmouth. I'm here with friends of his."

"In that case, you can catch up with them after I take you home and do unto you as I would have you do unto me."

Eloise stood staring at Nadine while mulling things over. Like how there was something strange about Johnny's, and how the women made leaving it difficult, and why the limousine driver dropped her there after he'd been paid to be at her disposal. One thing was for certain: she couldn't go back into the bar, not even to phone for a cab.

"Come back Little Sheba," Nadine parodied.

Eloise looked down at her feet in an effort to hide her dismay. "Don't you think you're a little out of my league?"

"Okay, what's going on here, Iz? You're not still thinking about having a romp with that chicory, are you?"

"Romp? Is that what you're calling it these days?"

"Forget it, Izzy. That kid isn't interested in you."

"You think not, huh?"

"Absolutely not!"

"The bartender said..."

"Juni said what you wanted to hear. That's what bartenders are paid to do."

"Then why did she try to help me?"

"Help you? What makes you think she was trying to help you?"

"What makes you think not?"

"Wake-up, woman! The word is that brat's getting married today. If anything, she was looking for a fast, free ride before breeder season."

"Married?"

"Yeah, the tiny tart. Setting you up like that."

It made no sense to Eloise, from the second she was blinded by the bar light to that teeth chattering meet on the street with Nadine.

"The trouble with you, Nadine, is that you always think the worst of people."

"Hell, lady, I *am* the worst of people!" She slinked over to her car and flung open the driver's door. "That's what makes me so D-cup desirable."

It was true. Nadine took pride in herself for being the person she peddled. Eloise wished her no harm for that. Nonetheless, she rued the day they crossed paths while admitting, if they hadn't, they wouldn't be where they were, sparring over the girl who got away.

"Where's your other half, Nadine?" Eloise hoped she was slouched asleep in the car.

"Simone? I left her home for you."

"You didn't."

"And it's a good thing, because the minute you made that rather spectacular entrance tonight, I tagged you as all mine. We both want it. Why squabble?"

"You're brazen, Nadine."

"And you're still here, Izzy. Whoever the kid is, she's not coming back. It's cold. It's late. You're lonely. I'm hungry for your loneliness. It doesn't take a genius to formulate the finale."

With that, Nadine eased into the Jag, revved the engine to get the heat going, and leaned over to roll down the passenger side window while inching the car forward to where Eloise teetered on the curb.

Eloise bent to look in, impervious to Nadine's shamelessly overexposed cleavage.

"Izzy, Izzy, Izzy," she cooed, patting the tawny leather seat with her helpful hand. "Dare I say...coming?"

EIGHT
Early Saturday Morning, March 14, 1970
Dory & Izzy

Dory was half way home to her Chelsea apartment when she told the cab driver to do a one-eighty back to Johnny's and "step on it." She hoped to get there in time to find the person who'd caused her angst an hour earlier, but couldn't believe her luck when spotting the woman stranded outside the entrance of the bar as a red Jaguar peeled off leaving a trail of tire tracks.

"There's an extra tip in it for you if you slow down long enough for me to offer this lady a lift," she bargained, "and if she accepts, circle downtown towards the West Village while we chat some."

"You got it!" The driver loved being dispatched to Dykedom, one of many callous labels for haunts that catered to butches like the one in his back seat. They didn't pay as well as his faggot-freight, drag queen cargo, sea-fairies, or convention-queers, but he knew all homos flashed more cash than straights on the graveyard shift, so he took as many calls from pervert places as possible.

Dory rolled down the window. "You wanna share a cab?"

"Absolutely, yes. Gee, thanks! That would be great." Eloise jumped into the back seat of the taxi, eager to thaw from the steadily declining temperature. "It can't be more that 20° out."

"Cold enough to kill a feral cat."

"That's an awful thought, but yes. Poor things. I hope we don't see any. I'd want to stop and help somehow."

A sucker for strays, Dory concluded. Like shooting ducks in a bucket.

"I'm Dory. Didn't I see you inside Johnny's earlier?"

"Izzy." Eloise gave Dory a quick quizzical once-over before offering her hand. "Yes, I saw you, too. That's odd. You weren't...?"

IMOGENE'S ELOISE

"Following you? No, no. Not that you aren't followable. Ha-ha. That's not even a word is it? Followable?"

Dory began stammering, uncomfortably aware that she was close enough to her adversary to see her eyes were as blue as the bubble gum cigars dispensed at the birth of baby boys. The same cigars sweet tooth butches like to bite into at times. Two of which were tucked inside her jacket, ready to offer as an after-chew in case she got lucky. Which meant, they were stale.

"I...I thought I left my...my gloves inside so I circled back...but, oh, looky here." She held up her gloves wondering if 'looky here' wasn't the kind of femme phrase she ought to think about giving up. Still, a save is a save. "I'm heading uptown. Where can I drop you?"

Eloise hesitated, thinking, *could this woman who is working so hard at perfecting the mannerisms of a man be wacko, or just a walking-talking contradiction of a croaky voice Elvis impersonator using way too much pomade? And, the English Leather aftershave is overkill. There's no other cab to flag. But this butch appearing out of nowhere feels dicey.*

"The Manhattan Hotel on 8th Street."

"Did you catch that, driver?" Dory punched the back of the seat. "Take the lady to her place, first."

"I heard it," he said. "But there's no hotel on 8th Street."

"There is," Eloise assured. "That's where I left my bags."

"Nope. No hotels on 8th Street. Not in Manhattan. In Brooklyn maybe. That could be."

"No sir, it's here. It's having a grand opening. It's a big, beautiful place with teal interior, a brass and glass entrance, red carpet and matching doorman. Very snazzy."

The cab driver clicked on his radio. "Tony here, 285, come back."

A crackle and pause preceded the reply. "Where you be, Baloney? Over."

"Broadway heading south. Over."

"Where's the fare? Over."

"Any new hotels opening named Manhattan? Over."

"We had a call from a (static)...on Eighth Av..."

"Come back."

"...Royal...thea..distr...opened...week...no...Over."

"That's it," Eloise confirmed. "The Royal Manhattan. On 8th, like

I said."

"Eighth Avenue ain't 8th Street, lady." The cab driver hung a right at NYU and passed by Washington Square Park, set to head up Sixth Avenue before turning west on 14th. "Hey base, you got a cross on that? Over."

"...forty-four...forty-five. Over."

"Roger that."

Dory pressed her back to the door so she could distance herself while scrutinizing her captive. Her bravado resurfaced. "Don't sweat it, we'll get you there."

"Oh, I wasn't worried," Eloise tapered off, "about that."

"What then? Can I help?"

"It's nothing. Except, the girl sitting near the jukebox. Were you with her?"

"Um," Dory stalled. "Which one?"

"The redhead on the stool."

"Oh, her. I was helping her out, that's all. A lipsticker who can't hold her liquor."

"I didn't get that impression. It seemed more like she was slipped a mickey. Does it happen there much? Because the bartender didn't strike me as the type who'd allow it."

"I can't help you. I mean, if that's why you were at Johnny's. To spy."

"No, no. Not that. We first met tonight. And, I must have told her wrong about where I'm staying. If there's no listing, I can't imagine how she'll find me."

"Gee. That's tough. You'll have to call her."

"I didn't get her number."

Dory quickly faced forwards. "No? Well, she's probably listed."

"I didn't get her name, either."

"That's not good. I would have taken you for being better at pickups."

Eloise let it go. "Is there anyone you can think of who...?"

"No-o. Can't help ya. I mean I might have seen her around a time or two before, but she's always alone. Not that I'm a regular or anything."

The cab had caught all the green lights going uptown and was slowing to a stop. "Well, this is me." Eloise reached into her pocket for the fare.

"Let me get it," offered Dory. "My treat."

"That's very nice of you." Eloise felt foolish for misjudging the strange little woman. As she slid out of the cab she bent back in to say, "Thanks again for helping me. If you believe in Karma, you can count on someone returning the favor someday. I hope it's soon. You deserve it."

"I'm not a believer," Dory lied.

"I knew that. But it's okay. Karma will find you."

Dory continued watching Eloise as she closed the car door and disappeared up the steps and through the lobby doors. Sinking back into the seat, she caught the cab driver eyeing her in his rear view mirror. By the way he lowered his look, she knew he knew she'd lied; probably even why.

"London Terrace, same as before, Miss?"

"Yes, 23rd Street, Ninth Avenue side."

After riding the twenty blocks in silence, Dory followed through and doubled the tip. She felt it was well worth the satisfaction it gave, knowing there was no chance of Imogene ever seeing Eloise again, not in a city of eight million strangers. Wink was compelled to plead her case now. Imogene might even seek her for comfort. She'd emerge as the hero.

"Thank you," she spoke to the mirrored reflection of the driver's eyes.

His admonition came after she'd exited the cab and he rolled down his window as she turned away. "I wouldn't want to be you if either of them finds out."

But Dory kept on walking, undaunted, convinced they couldn't find out, or find each other. The very thought of either happening was, at best, ludicrous.

NINE
June 1943 ~ June 1968
Andrew Winklehoffen

There's a wrong side of the tracks in every town and Andrew Winklehoffen grew up on his, having been ripped from the arms of a woman condemned to Dachau, only to become the illicit son of a Gestapo couple fleeing Germany with forged papers and passports. The rage that his new Nazi parents harbored over Hitler's defeat was replaced with an unmitigated loathing for the boy, resulting in a misguided unification that their marriage, alone, had failed to achieve.

Because by all accounts, Andrew was born an abomination — an effeminate boy whose face was far prettier, skin was softer, and hands were more delicate than anyone else subsisting in the coal tar community near the foothills of Cheat Mountain, West Virginia.

"Don't you dare cry," his mother warned after beating him with a belt for saying he was hungry. She felt no remorse when slamming the smooth brass buckle into his back, ever careful never to mar his face (as if it was sacred ground and she was securing her seat in the hereafter by sparing it). "No kid of mine cries without good reason, and hunger's no good reason. If it were, I'd be sobbing all day. Do you see me blubbering? Well? Do you?"

"N-n-no."

"No, what?" she threatened by raising the leather strap overhead to let loose again.

"No, Mrs. Winklehoffen," Andrew cowered. He'd never been allowed to call her mother, momma, or mom, which was fine with him. He always felt suspicious of the woman, wondering, *who was she? Who was she, really?*

His uncertainty was understandable judging by their physical disparities. She claimed an eighteen year age difference between them, but it looked more like thirty. The jowls on her sallow face sagged. Her milky grey eyes had wide, red under-lids. Her lips turned inward covering teeth angled backwards. Her ears were twice the size of his, on a head half as big, and her dry, sandy hair was always wrapped in a wiry wad, bobby-pinned atop her head like a pile of poo.

"I bet you think you're better than me, don't you, mister?"

"No, Mrs. Winklehoffen."

"Because you aren't, you wretched little bastard. And don't you ever forget it either!" Then she hit him again for the hell of it.

• • •

Andrew endured fourteen years of his parents' contempt before his reinvention of 1956. After coercing money from a pasty-skin family man he'd accommodated near the Marlinton C&O railroad station, he buried himself below a burlap bag on a potato truck heading east, arriving bruised and near broke at the Fulton Fish Market in lower Manhattan, willing to do whatever (and whomever) it required to survive.

First, he modified his name to Andy Wink, then engaged the metamorphosing aid of a coterie of priests who held court every Saturday on the sands of Riis Park, sunbathing, imbibing, and trading Andy off among themselves with a faith in secrecy, a hope of discretion, and a pretense of charity in the guise of their bartered house boy.

"They were good to me in innumerable ways," Wink later recounted. "Each of them grew genuinely fond of me. Of course, I serviced them. That was a large part of it. If payment hadn't come at the expense of parish poor boxes I might still be employed."

Once he shot from short and thin to tall and strapping, the priests pooled their resources to provide Wink with a flat on West 86th Street, a modest bank account, and introductions to well-heeled communicants seeking a hireling who demonstrated judiciousness. Wink's skills were compensated in cash, gifts and impeccable references. For nearly a decade, it proved the ideal set-up for the insatiable young stud. That is, until a curate confessed to fits of jealousy while watching Wink evolve from an engaging young boy into an enchanting young man.

The priests who began as his clients and became his friends were all identified, chastised, and dispersed to faraway lands, creating repercussions among parishioners who weren't told why their fathers had been banished. It left Wink on his own once again.

But this time he wasn't a despised little boy fleeing a despicable home. Instead, he was two weeks past his twenty-fourth birthday, out for a stroll on the streets of New York, and confident of finding new benefactors that would be delighted to support him in the style to which he'd become so comfortably accustomed.

"You're walking a rabbit," Andy laughed at the attractive redhead bouncing along on the sidewalk towards him as he exited Central Park.

"You're walking a cat!" she returned with gusto.

He would forever think it funny, how they met like that, as if he'd been given an unearned gift from out of the blue. Or, maybe it could be proclaimed as a miracle, for those who believed in such phenomena.

Andy Wink did not.

TEN
Saturday Morning, June 8, 1968
Andy Wink & Imogene LaPin

Wink was vivacious. He didn't walk so much as prance, turn so much as swirl, stand so much as pose, nor speak so much as sing in a blithe timbre, all of which Imogene interpreted as neutered. Because that's what Imogene's mind did with anything that caught her fancy. She rendered people, animals, inanimate objects, and French adjectives alike as female; a propensity she'd shown from childhood.

It took Wink awhile to catch onto her idiosyncrasy of modifying genders, mistaking Imogene as daft — but in a distinctively charming-chirpy way.

"What's your pretty kitty's name?" she gushed while stooping to kiss his cat.

"Walt Whitman."

"She's so sweet."

"He."

"Oh yes she *is*. She *is*. She *is* a pretty kitty! How old is she?"

"Can't say. I'm cat-sitting *him* for the day while his owner is on the Island." He was more amused than rankled, but equally explicit.

"Long?"

"Fire."

"No. Will he be away long?"

"Oh, sorry. I thought you meant Long Island. And, I was answering, Fire Island."

"I'm funning you. I was going to say 'Pines' before predicting you'd say 'Fire' if I said 'Long,' so I switched in mid-josh."

"Ah-ha!" he tried trumping her. "A chest player!"

"Strictly in banter these days. It used to be, rather than give up my queen, I'd joyfully kill off the bishops and the knights and the king."

"I said, *chest* player, as a double entendre."

"And yet, you ignore my expertise in disregarding that." She stood and saluted him. "I'm Imogene LaPin."

"I'm Andy Wink." He flashed her his platinum grade golden boy smile. "Is that French?"

"Imogene?"

"LaPin."

"*Oui.*"

"Well," he ventured, looking her over, "that explains the eyes, skin, thin limbs, and delicately organized attire. But not the auburn hair, nor the pleasantries."

"*Sacré bleu et parbleu! La tournesol géant m'a trouvée!*"

"Translate."

"Sacred blue and egad! The giant sunflower has found me out!"

"That's what *sacré bleu* means in French?"

"*Pourquoi?*"

"I always thought they were curse words."

"Yes, if said as one word. *Sacrébleu!* But, I said it as two. *Sacré bleu.* That earns me a pass from the powers that be." She swatted the air.

"God?"

"A nickname for Goddess. But I speak in the vernacular."

"Which is?"

"Betty. The 'be' in 'powers that be' is short for Betty," Imogene clarified, as if it was common knowledge rather than singularly inspired.

"That explains it then. All but the hair."

"I'm an American with ancestors in bloody revolutions on both sides of the Atlantic."

"How very henna-esque."

"*Très bien! Très bien!*" She threw her hands in the air. "*Je l'avoue! Arrête de me battre!*"

"What?"

"Okay! Okay! I confess! Stop beating me! I'm French in last name, mostly."

"Whereas, Imogene is...?"

"Poorly printed Shakespeare, silly. At least," she struck a stance, "so it be thought." She curtsied. "You see, milady, when the first manuscript for his play, Cymbeline, was published, the character,

Innogen, with two n's, was printed Imogen. They'd set the n's so close together it looked like an 'm', giving birth to the name for that notable redheaded beauty."

"Of course. I can see it now. A half French, half English, all-American girl."

"Well," she disclosed, "between us pretties? If you ask the *boulanger* at La Pâtisserie in the West Village, he'll swear I'm three-quarters croissant."

Right then is when Wink would come to say it hit; the propriety portion of Andrew Winklehoffen officially fell in love. At least, he fell as in love as he'd ever been, or would ever be, with a woman who viewed him as a sunflower girl.

"Let's pledge to tell each other everything, shall we?" he enthused.

"Agreed, if some of it can be true."

They shook hands in earnest.

"I feel as if we've always been friends, Imogene."

"I feel you feel so, too."

They'd returned to the park, acting as any other upper west side family on an ordinary outing: he with his cat hissing and she with her rabbit hopping. At 79th Street they crossed a half-moon bridge and climbed the old stone steps to wander amongst the Shakespeare Garden flower beds until they located a rustic, twig slatted, cement bench to dub as their own.

By then he'd lied about his name. Not the Andrew portion, but the surname which, after escaping Cheat Mountain, a priest had ascertained was Kohen, and that he was two years older than he'd been told. Instead, he offered 'orphanage' as the explanation for his past.

"How long have you had the hare?"

Imogene checked her wrist. "About three hours now."

"No watch?"

"Don't own one."

"Interesting. A woman who tells time by freckle."

"It's an art."

"Does bunny have a name?"

"Martini."

"Gin, or vodka?"

"No doubt, Vodka."

"Because...?"

"Her owner's name is Olive."

They laughed together. It became the immutable glue that bound them as fated friends for another nineteen months.

ELEVEN
Wednesday Afternoon, August 7, 1968
Wink & Imogene

For the first year Wink and Imogene saw each other daily, always on weekdays, mostly after work, and sometimes late into the night. Twice a month they'd spring for lunch at Katz's Delicatessen, where they'd feast on brisket sandwiches, garlic pickles, and Radeberger Pilsner. On Friday nights they'd attend services and the Oneg Shabbat before heading to Johnny's, and some Saturday mornings they'd breakfast at The Parlor in the Village where Wink maintained a booth for himself and guests.

She told him she was the purchasing manager for an advertising agency with corporate offices in the Tishman building on Fifth Avenue. He told her he supervised the programming and punch cards operations for entering data into the ceiling-high block-long computers at a Wall Street investment house.

At first, he wasn't sure whether her job was more fiction than reality. Until then, he'd known of no other women in positions at that level of authority. But one day she invited him to attend a Purchasing Managers Association of New York luncheon where she'd be introduced as the first ever female member.

"Talk about breaking the glass ceiling," he offered by way of congratulations.

"Hardly."

"Well, cracking it then?"

"More like washing it while hanging upside down on a hook. I mean, it's not like I had to vie for membership. I got in by default through our corporate standing. But you're right. A first is a first and it's required I attend this once."

"If it was me I'd be strutting my stuff."

"Oh I will be. You're my stuff."

Wink was accustomed to Imogene being a make-the-most-of-now person rather than one who assumed things lasted indefinitely. She thought him fanciful for mapping his future beyond breakfast. He resisted at first, having always catered to whatever his calendar dictated, but soon he began forgoing his habits in favor of her spontaneity.

There were other things he found compelling about her as well, like the way she rejected the notion of obligatory respect given to people in positions of authority.

"Alleged authority," she'd stress. "That person did nothing to earn my respect and I'm not in the charity-respect business." She didn't fear speaking her mind, or altering it soon after weighing the next person's input. If someone required she justify her reversal, she'd say, with certitude, "I am woman!"

Then there was the ease with which she'd ask clarification to whatever was proposed, regardless of how ignorant she appeared by doing so. She said it guaranteed the respondent felt smarter and more valued as a result. Wink eventually realized the tricky tactic was a big part of Imogene's simulated personality.

"So we're clear, kiddo," he warned as they entered the event, "I'm on to you and your disingenuous elicitation."

"No you aren't."

"How not?"

"You view questions as a blah-blah conversation stimulant. I view them as bait." She stood in the doorway pretending to search for their seats while timing their entrance. "It's like, one person goes fishing on a sunny day and returns nine hours later with nothing but a bad burn. Another goes fishing on a rainy day and comes back in nine minutes with dinner. The difference, my big man?"

"The bait?"

"The bait!"

Wink blanked. "I don't get it."

"Any question I pose has primarily one purpose. To gain insight into the emotional intelligence and cultural literacy level of another person by letting him assume it's superior to those of mine."

"Which gets you, what? Other than them thinking you're foolish."

"It gives me control of the conversation. And once I get it, the last thing I mistaken for is a fool."

Wink knew it was true. Whenever men were present and she finally entered the fray, the spotlight switched to her and remained there. "You think it would work?"

"What's that?"

"Instead of acting dense, what if you're assertive by saying something that riles rather than soothes the male ego."

"*Every*thing riles the male ego," she scoffed.

"Maybe. But you sit there and get them to salivate for sport, even when there are plenty of women to go around. Hell, I've seen you make fags fawn once you get your devil on."

"At least gay guys are a challenge. These fellows in here?" She fluttered her eyes at two men stumbling past them. "I could tell them I hate them and some would still want my number, or be set on giving me theirs."

"A Hamilton says you can't."

"A Jackson says I can."

"Oh you are so *on*, princess!"

They were the last to be seated, near the dais, at a large, round table in the company of eight other managers, all male. Six were wearing generic blue suits from sale lots, their drip-dry shirts fastened with polyester, pointed-tip, skinny-width ties. Two wore blue, one red, two stripes, one geometric pattern — all clip-ons. The other two were budding Wall Street men: one in a black suit with a powder blue shirt and flat-bottom tie fixed in a Windsor knot with a dimple; the other in a dark chocolate suit and pale flaxen button-down collar shirt with a leather bolo fashioning eighteen karat gold aglets and a flattened nugget slider.

Yet none were as impressive as Wink (towering three inches over the next tallest at the table) in a custom made Adam of London mohair suit, white silk shirt, paisley tie with matching festoon hanky, and Bruno Magli Italian loafers, all gifts from satisfied clientele.

They stood when Wink pulled Imogene's chair out, sitting after she gestured via a slight flitter of her hand. Then they returned to their conversation in a huddled manner with subdued tones, plainly put out by her presence.

Their conduct made Imogene keen as a fox stalking prey. It

reminded Wink of something she'd told him — of how she'd been terribly alone in New York, but not terribly lonely, and somewhat mystified by her inability to care deeply about others, yet not bothered by it.

"It's like I'm emotionally bankrupt," she'd said.

• • •

Imogene LaPin possessed the kind of approachable good looks that people pursued: not beautiful, but pretty, with shoulder length locks framing pronounced cheekbones planted in a light whipping cream complexion.

Admirers were regarded as a free meal ticket to her, as long as they suggested a restaurant with cloth napkins and a menu of fresh foods served by waiters who were immaculate, reticent, and polite. Otherwise, she showed no interest in men, finding the City reserve so embarrassingly abundant, it didn't demand she date any of them more that once.

"Committing names and numbers to memory is pointless," she told Wink, "since I'm seldom honest about giving out my own."

Unfortunately, women annoyed Imogene mercilessly by what she perceived as their perpetual pursuit of male attention, acting shamefully coy whenever one entered their arena, and all too willing to accept second-class status once eye contact was made. It left her in an odd kind of limbo as neither a misanthropist nor a preferentialist. Wink saw her as someone who was passionate about life and living, but dispassionate about people, and asexually adrift.

• • •

"Pardon me," the black-suited man finally addressed Wink at the behest of the rest, "but we aren't allowed to bring our wives to these functions. It cramps our style and requires censoring ourselves. No offense to her."

"No offense taken," Imogene interjected. "But we aren't married."

Black-suit responded with disdain, peeved that she had the audacity to interrupt. "I'm not interested in what your relationship is, all

I..."

"As amused as I'd be by watching you put your other foot in it," she began again, "allow me to save you from yourself. My name is Imogene LaPin."

He spat back. "Is that supposed to mean something to me?"

"Holy-moly," mumbled bolo tie. "You're the new member on the agenda, I. LaPin."

"I am," she verified graciously, "and I apologize for any need you feel to tidy up the conversation while I'm here. But if you do, I'll assure you, I won't be back, regardless of how patronizingly endearing you're no doubt capable of being."

"That's impossible," black-suit disputed.

"What?""

"Ad Age reported your firm snagged the Nixon bid."

"True."

"You're saying they hired *you* to manage purchasing?"

"Hired, no. Promoted, yes. Purchasing, forms design, in-house production, invoice approval, phone installations, equipment acquisitions, expense records, mailroom management, and interior decorating to be accurate."

Bolo tie shot forth. "So, Tricky-Dick. Have you met him?"

"I have. Once."

That's all it took.

"My name is John MacDonald," black-suit conceded, followed by fast introductions from the rest, each one standing and leaning forward to offer his hand as an act of instant cordiality while Wink sat back, watching his twenty disappear.

Once the minutes were read, announcements made, and Imogene was given a tepid applause, the food was served without further interruption in the chatter. Her new cohorts proved eager to learn what happened to the fellow Imogene replaced (quit), if anyone famous ever wandered the agency halls (off and on), if Nixon would win (yes), and if shenanigans went on behind closed doors (confidentiality clause).

At times the topic reverted to business — like who knew the cheapest, fastest and best supplier of engraved business cards versus thermograph, while those saddled with mimeograph machines cranking out hundreds of purple-ink copies were eager to discuss new duplicators using paper plates to produce thousands of high quality in-house impressions. Wink suffered through an hour or so of "what do you use, Imogene?" and "what do you think, Imogene?" and "where do you go, Imogene?" before the talk got down to the predictable nitty-gritty.

"So, you're not married?" John asked Wink.

"Not yet."

"Intentions then?"

"More like terms to get hitched as long as neither of us fall in love before St. Patrick's Day, 1970."

"I am shocked!" John turned to Imogene. "I would have taken you for a romantic."

"That I am, through and through."

"Then why the fail-safe date? What's the problem?"

And here it comes, thought Wink.

"Oh, there's no problem," Imogene toyed. "I simply don't like men."

Spoons dropped. Coffee slopped.

"I'm sorry?" John assumed he'd heard wrong.

"I don't like men," she reiterated.

"You mean, some men? Or, all men?"

"Pretty much, all. The few I favor I treat as women. It makes this more of a girls club than a boys club for me."

"Are you saying you're a...lesbian?"

Imogene knew she held their hearts in her hand, perfectly primed for gentle squeezing. "I don't have an answer to that yet."

Bolo tie joined in. "Then what is it you don't like about us?"

"The physique. The features."

"For instance?"

"I don't like all that body hair."

"Me, neither," confirmed a striped tie. The others turned toward him. "Well, I *don't*. That ape look creeps me out. Creeped my wife out, too, before she met me."

"You're hairless?" red-tie guy wondered.

"Pretty much. It's very light, what's there. So, is that all Imogene?"

"My, no." She parted her lips for a moment, casually blotting the corners of her mouth with her napkin. "I don't like the way men spit, scratch, or extol the emitting of foul odors and sounds as proof of their manhood."

Geometric-tie sympathized. "I can see how a lady would find that public adjusting of stuff revolting. And the snot stuff, too. If a woman did that in public...yetch!"

The men mumbled their agreement, as if innocent on all charges.

"I don't like the way men spread their legs when they sit," Imogene continued.

"I always try to rest my right ankle on my left knee when I sit," said John. The pointed ties raised their hands with affinity to him.

"I'm profoundly put off by the way sweaty men treat furniture as a welcome mat for their stains."

"That makes my lady go all Squirrel Girl," said one.

"If I come in from hoops and even think about sitting down before showering, mine howls bloody murder," said another. All others grimaced.

"I recoil at coarseness," she continued, "including explicit vulgarisms and the locker room banalities men use to debase the women in their lives."

Silence.

"And, one more thing. I abhor the way you're enthralled by violence."

"True," John concurred. "There's too much violence these days."

"Of course, there *are* male anomalies," Imogene added. "As Mz. Wink here can attest to."

Bolo-tie raised his hand. "Me, too! I can attest to that."

"And, sex with men?" John dared, feeling entitled.

Imogene shrugged. "It's unnatural. I've never even entertained the thought."

Later, after agreeing to meet at the same table the following month and saying the last of their adieus, Wink walked Imogene back up Fifth Avenue to her workplace.

"Mogy, I must say, your objections detailed everything I like about men."

"Isn't that the point, Wink?" Imogene slipped her arm through his as they leaned closer to talk. "Aren't you attracted to men in the identical way a straight woman would be?"

"I suppose."

"You'd think science and society could grasp that. Instead, people concentrate so much on the cozying-up part of couples, they miss that homosexuals view heterosexual intimacies as aberrant behavior. Plus the cringe factor to other mannerisms, tendencies, features, and interests. I think, someday, scientists will admit that pure homosexuals are incapable of voluntary inbreeding with pure heterosexuals, qualifying the two as being different species."

"Say, when did you get to be a whiz at this? We've never discussed it at all."

Wink suspected it might have something to do with her disappearing to Long Island every weekend in the company of an agency colleague and her cousin. He wagered their 'cousinship' was a cover for being lesbians — a code Imogene hadn't yet deciphered. Because as savvy as Imogene proved in business, she remained wide-eyed in Wink-world.

"I'm being objective is all. Right now it's way too simplistic for scientists to admit it as so, and too contentious for religionists to dare accept."

"Maybe. But I still don't understand how you got away with saying all you said today."

"Oh, that. It's honesty. People love being told the truth, even when they don't like what they're hearing."

"You might be right."

When they got to her building, Imogene handed Wink three business cards with numbers scribbled on the back. He handed her a twenty.

"So, you'll be calling bolo boy?" she suggested.

"You're such a brat! You picked up on him, too?"

She was walking away, backwards, while answering. "Not entirely. The cream colored card is his. He *begged* me to give it to you."

TWELVE
Early Saturday Morning, March 14, 1970
Under The Wire

Emboldened with the remnants of a dead yellow rose and the singular intent to find the woman who wanted to 'just hold' her, Imogene abandoned the safety, warmth, and security of the home where she led a simple, serene, sometimes superficial, but essentially satisfying life. The blasts of cold air whipping at her bare head didn't deter her. The discovery of a paltry two tokens and pocket change in a coat created more for fashion than for warmth didn't discourage her. Not having the woman's name, phone number, or address of where she was weekending in a city of millions didn't faze her. Because when it came to love, Imogene LaPin was an idiot.

Already shivering as she quickened down the cement steps of the IND subway station, Imogene entered a cavern even colder than the out-of-doors. Desolate during that early Saturday morning hour, it seemed eerie and unsafe until she heard and felt a familiar screech and rumble arriving a full thirty seconds before the train appeared.

Although it moved like a powder burn that couldn't possibly stop in a flash, the train did exactly that, popping open its doors, then chugging them shut, offering her a choice of the mostly vacant vinyl covered, cotton-padded seats. She settled on hugging a steel pole instead, the lurch and roll of the train swaying her back and forth, causing her to swirl at intervals as she stood the distance, making stops at Columbus Circle (where a mobster would soon be murdered), 42nd Street (where dreams of names in bright, white lights linger), 34th Street (made famous by retail rivals), 14th Street (where those who couldn't afford the bargain basement of Gimbles shopped at Klein's on the Square) and on to the 4th Street exit in the West Village. All the while she was focused on the flimsy facts of an unnamed female in an unnumbered room being registered at an unknown address on 8th Street, that two mile vein of mischief-making through the hub of Greenwich Village.

Imogene began her hunt by walking the South side of 8th Street from Fifth Avenue to Avenue D near the East River, searching the facades of hundreds of buildings and expressions on as many bystanders to no avail. Upon reaching Skid Row, where the impoverished huddled in cardboard boxes insulated with layers of salvaged newspapers, and Bowery bums accosted anyone foolish enough to venture by — even she was surprised no one approached her.

Only a scraggly red kitten stalked her for the stench of dried tuna juice on her ankles and legs, encouraging Imogene to lift it up and stick it inside her coat. Together they walked the north side of 8th Street back west again, past Second Avenue and onto Third; past the BMT line on the corner of Broadway and the many mom-and-pop storefronts; past the high-rises of the rich on Fifth Avenue with southern views of Washington Square, and across the mega intersection of Sixth Avenue where the Women's House of Detention commanded its own concrete island; then onward towards the Henry Hudson.

There was no hotel.

Disquieted but not discouraged, Imogene crossed over to the south side of 8th Street and trudged back towards Fifth Avenue, retracing her steps. Along the way she'd foolishly discarded all the wads of tissues used to stuff her bra, refilling the hollows with a stretched out sleeping kitten. She hoped it was sleeping anyhow. She felt reluctant to check as she walked the length of 8th a second time.

By eleven the damp, piercing cold that gripped the city had burrowed into her bones. Her toes felt like sticks of stone. The skin on the back of her hands had crusted, cracked, and was oozing blood clots. Her hair was drooping and dripping. Her face was a mass of wind burned splotches, and her bottom lip stung from where she'd nervously nibbled away the skin.

Desperate for refuge from the polestar that had proved to be her Waterloo, she chose the one public telephone booth on the street: a grimy, garbage strewn, urine soaked, metal and glass enclosed shelter near the trendy Orange Julius take-out window where all the pretty people were lining up to buy their morning raw egg juice jolt. Once inside, she carefully closed the folding doors against their clearly visible world and began to cry. Not the little leaks-from-eye-corners kind of tears, or stoic crest of water wrestling the lips of stringent lids. No, no. Imogene's were those hard, cruel, inconsolable, coughing, choking, desperate sobs; the kind that build and fester over years of neglect, scarring an isolated heart.

Suddenly, something so remarkable transpired, it made Imogene want to live long enough to tell someone else's grandkids. As she shook and sobbed through an overdue metamorphosing from naive child to full-fledged blubbering fool — the phone rang.

Imogene stopped dead. She stared at the handset for the time it took her auxiliary self to summon up her finest phone voice. But before her automaton self could activate, the ringing ceased. She waited, fixated for another minute before cautiously lifting the receiver up between pinched fingertips. First, she spit on the earpiece, using a circular motion to wipe it off on her coat at the pointed bend of her elbow. Then she spit on the mouthpiece and did the same. Finally, after repeated hesitations and pained facial expressions, she conjured up enough courage to dial by using the pinky knuckle on her left hand.

"Operator," said the voice on the line. "How may I help you?"

"I need to find a woman." Imogene was astonished by the hoarseness of her own voice.

"Honey, you're going to have to speak up. I can barely hear you."

"I can't speak up. I'm...I'm...crying," she choked. "And I'm alone." She choked a second time. "And I have no tissues because the kitten was cold." She coughed. "And the handkerchief that I carry because my mom says a lady is never without her handkerchief...my hanky is a wet gob inside my pocket. And I don't," she moaned, "I don't know what to do."

"It's all right, honey."

"Help me?"

There was a brief silence, just long enough for the operator to scope the situation. "Well, honey," she encouraged in a warm, smooth tone, "you tell me what I can do and I'll try my best. Now go ahead and speak as low as you want. I'll pay closer attention. Okay?"

"Yes," Imogene gulped. "Thank you."

"Can you tell me where you are?"

"I'm in the filthiest, most disgusting phone booth in the whole wide world."

"Uh-huh. Could you be a little more specific, honey?"

"On 8th Street."

"In what borough, sweetheart?"

"Manhattan."

"The Village?"

"Yes. Greenwich Village on the west side. Why?"

"I wondered if I was close by."

"Are you?"

"I'm close enough if need be."

"Okay."

"Now, take a deep breath before telling me what's wrong."

"It's that, I met this girl. This woman. Last night. I met her at a bar where my sort of prenuptial party was kind of being given because I'm supposed to maybe marry Wink today. We said we would by St. Patrick's Day if we were both still single."

"I see."

"But last night I met someone. And, now I can't find her. The woman."

"To invite to your wedding?"

"No-o-o," Imogene whined. "No, I'm not getting married now."

"Even if you don't find her?"

"I have to find her. I must. I just, just, just must."

"Of course you do, dear. I understand."

"You do? Because I don't."

"You will."

"I will?"

"You will. Is this the first time you've cared deeply about someone?"

"Yes,"

"Well then, you'll see. You'll be fine."

"Okay."

"Are you feeling a little better now?"

"Yes," Imogene lied as her despair resurfaced. "No."

"Then you go ahead. Let it out. It's all right. But...maybe...first...can you tell me the woman's last name?"

"No." Imogene sniffled, blotting her eyes on the cuff of her coat before wiping her nose on the sleeve. "Not her first name either. I was so, so..."

"Confused?"

"No."

"Distracted?"

"No."

"Smitten?"

"Yes! Smitten. That's it. That's the word. I was so smitten. It was like I *knew* her. Like she'd always been inside me trying to find me. And when she did, it never occurred to me to ask her name."

"It happens," the operator heartened. "Did she say where she lives?"

"No. She's not from here." Imogene swallowed hard, trying to hold back more tears, feeling like she'd already cried all the brown in the irises out. "She said she was just in town for the weekend."

"Well, honey, you see how that's going to make it more difficult, don't you?"

"Uh-huh."

"Can you tell me anything more about her? Is she here visiting someone? Any idea where she might be staying?"

"That's the thing. She said she was staying at the Manhattan Hotel on 8th Street. And I've walked the length of 8th Street from way over in the East Village to almost the Hudson. Both sides of the street. Part of it twice." Imogene laid her arm on the metal shelf intended to hold a directory that had long since been stolen, and leaned over to rest her forehead on the back of her hand, feeling anxiety rise in her throat all over again. "I couldn't find the hotel."

"Hold on a sec," said her operator (for the woman was now Imogene's operator, and the desire to triumph had returned to Imogene because of her). "I'm looking at the latest Manhattan yellow pages under lodgings and you're right. There's no Manhattan Hotel listed. Are you sure that's what she said?"

"Yes," Imogene swallowed hard. "I think so. I'm pretty sure so."

"Well, I'll tell you what let's do. Let me start at the top of the list of hotels in Manhattan and I'll read each of them out loud to you. Then you tell me if anything sounds familiar. How would that be?"

"You'd do that for me?"

"We'll do it together. Are you ready?"

Imogene nodded.

"Are you ready, sweetheart?"

Imogene nodded harder.

"Are you?"

"Yes."

And with that the operator began to read each name and location of every hotel in Manhattan while Imogene stood in the stagnant stickiness of coagulated pee, listening to the compassionate voice of one who was trained and paid to provide telephone numbers and street addresses, but not empathy, and not hope.

About thirty minutes into reading all the data of each hotel (in case even a scintilla of it might jar Imogene's memory), the operator reached the listing to The Plaza.

"Not The Plaza," Imogene said, wearily.

Then the worst imaginable thing happened.

The line disconnected.

The operator was — poof — gone, dealing a death-blow to Imogene's ear.

"No, no, no!" Imogene screamed into the mouthpiece, over and over, hitting the receiver on the metal shelf and then on the phone box, again and again as if it was a sledgehammer and the act of banging it would make the cracked hard-plastic talk. "No! No! No!"

"Honey! Honey!" the operator summoned.

Imogene halted mid-hit. "Ohmigod, I'm sorry. I thought we were..."

"Honey, sweetie, I think I've got it. Something told me to check the addendum to the new phone listings, and there is one. Could it be the Royal Manhattan Hotel on Eighth Avenue?"

For a split second Imogene was perplexed, thinking *how could anyone leave out a crucial word like 'Royal' and switch the address of a street to an avenue? Was it intentional? Did she not want to be found?*

"Yes," Imogene said. "It could be. It must be." There was a tacit moment of quiet conquest shared between the two before Imogene asked, "How can I ever thank you?"

"You just go find her, and when you do, hold onto her for dear life."

"I will. Thank you. Thank you."

"You're welcome, dear. Good luck!" Click.

Imogene remained still, staring to the sound of a dial tone, feeling battered and drained. She was hungry and dirty. Her eyes were nearly swollen shut. She knew she needed help and that there was no one in the world she could count on to come to her rescue.

Except?

Imogene LaPin dialed Andy Wink.

THIRTEEN
Early Saturday Morning, March 14, 1970
Imogene's Gentle Men

Wink hadn't slept.

Twelve hours earlier he'd been certain of his future as a married man, primed to enjoy a standing in a community that would envy him for his ideal marriage to the perfect wife. Now? Who knew? He checked the French boudoir clock on a shelf above the stove while frying himself two eggs in a tablespoon of bacon grease. It was 6:30. He'd dumped Imogene onto the Danish modern couch in her apartment five hours earlier, fully clothed except for the one boot he managed to remove that was sodden from her stumbling off the curb into a slush puddle of probably piss outside Johnny's.

By itself, the unfortunate mishap had infuriated him. But to add insult to injured pride, he'd soiled his hands when removing the boot, nelly-freaking and flinging it backwards over his head. The very thought of gutter grime on his hands was enough to make Wink fume and exit in a huff. Now he sat simmering in a stew of if-onlys, adding imaginary salt to his manufactured misery while stirring the proverbial pot.

If only that annoying woman hadn't invaded their turf and upset their marriage plans. If only Dory hadn't gone all faux-balls-ballistic. If only Juni hadn't egged the uproar on by sacrificing her yellow rose. If only he'd have wrested the damn rose from Imogene's clutches and destroyed when he had the chance.

"None of this is my doing," he dismissed, wishing there was someone else to blame. He checked his reflection in the gold leaf mirror riveted to the side of the claret red refrigerator door, intended partly as a deterrent to his eating unwisely, but mostly so he could admire himself. "If this proves to be our demise," he resolved, "then by queendom come, someone will pay! I'll be there when she wakes up. I'll act inflamed!"

Or not, he decided. It depended on how much she remembered and whether or not he knew her better than she knew herself. He'd believed he did, even though they'd met a mere eighteen months earlier. Now, that argument was hard to make, chiefly because Imogene didn't see, hear, or think of herself as others did. Instead, she operated intuitively, sailing along like lyrical poetry, seemingly unaware of the impact she made on those around her.

The first time he witnessed her nescience was when he was aroused from a nap in the boxy bedroom off her studio by a hard knock on her apartment door.

• • •

"Donald, what a pleasant surprise. Come in, " Imogene urged without touching. Not a kiss. Not a hug. Not a handshake. "Why didn't you tell me you were in town?"

"I was afraid you wouldn't want to see me."

"Silly boy. Why wouldn't I?"

Donald Ponde and Imogene LaPin were schoolmates for six years of junior and senior high. He was a tall, studious-looking fellow with dishwater blonde hair, grass green eyes, and a self-effacing style trapped behind black horn-rimmed glasses and plaid short-sleeved shirts, each fitted with a pen protector in the left chest pocket. In Donald's mind, they'd been best friends all that time. But to Imogene, Donald was solely someone she'd known longer and liked better than most. Ideally, he might have made a decent enough sister.

During their senior year, Donald dated Cassie Crone, arguably the most beautiful girl in the school, Cassie was a gullible, dimple-cheeked cheerleader whom Imogene knew to be both genuine and kind. She saw Donald and Cassie as a model twosome sharing similar interests and compatible religions from families of equal financial and social status.

At times, Donald and Cassie would double date with Imogene and her pretend boyfriend, Morgan Newcomb, an astute fellow with enviable looks, a sonorous voice, and advanced intellect. Classmates predicted Morgan and Imogene would marry someday, but privately, the two had never even kissed.

"I suppose we should go to the prom," Morgan mentioned during an accelerated game of nine-hole one crisp May morning before school.

Imogene had been studying the game of golf in the event she became an executive who'd need to play it someday, not that anyone credited women with being capable of holding prized positions requiring links skills. Of course, there were exceptions, and in many ways Imogene was viewed as exceptional—as long as it didn't entail activities involving perspiration, teams, dirt, lifting, carrying, standing, heights, subjugation, exercise, blood, foul odors, loud noises, or typing. Her maternal and nurturing skills were also highly suspect, limited to the protection and care of dogs, cats, birds, butterflies, garter snakes, spiders, and salamanders. But never, *ever* people.

"If you'd like, Morgan. But my mother's husband said, should I attend, I must be home by ten." She checked his stance, hoping to duplicate it.

Morgan drove his ball nearly 100 yards, straight down the greenway. "Her husband isn't your father?"

"You could call him that," she clarified while teeing up, "as long as it's not the traditional use of the word, father. Or, husband." She hit her ball half as far, and sliced it a skosh.

"I get what you mean. Mine, too."

"Oh yes?" she offered, careful not to reveal more of her to him than he to she.

"Pugnacious as well," he confessed, retrieving their tees. "He contends it's the drink."

They walked the green, heartened by a bright-blue, cloudless sky and the dreams of freedom it evoked, quietly summing up their commonalities: bad dads, an elitist manner of conversing, and the tenacity of a caged crow committed to fleeing the coop.

• • •

"I've something to say!" Donald blurted.

"Fine, but gee, what's it been? Three years? I'm putting on coffee. Come in!"

He entered the room, unaware of the bedroom door cracked open to his left, or the man on the bed there, pretending to nap. "I've been waiting to say it for nine years."

"That's a mighty long time to be holding it in."

"It is, Mo. That's why I drove all night to get here."

Except for Wink, she hadn't been called Mo or Mogy much since leaving Michigan. New Yorkers tended not to be nicknamers, unlike Donald and Wink, who'd both given her the moniker of Mo from the minute they met.

"Okay then. Let's have it."

He cleared his throat, lifted his chin, and clasped his hands behind his back in an effort not to falter. "I love you. I've always loved you."

"I suppose, in your own way," she neutralized.

"I love you, Mo. I want you to marry me."

She laughed. "No you don't."

"I do."

"But what about Cassie?"

"We broke up on prom night."

"No."

"Yes."

"Why?"

"I said I was dating her was so I could be near you."

"*What?*"

"It's true. I fell in love with you in seventh grade and told her so."

"Which explains why I never heard from her again."

"You left town the next day."

"That, too."

"Without a forwarding address."

"The point being?"

"Were you running away from me?"

"No-o. I was running away from home."

"That's not funny."

"That's why I was running away from it."

"You're serious?"

"Perfectly. I was leaving it all behind in a general obliteration kind of way."

"What about Morgan?"

MARGUERITE QUANTAINE

"Morgan?" The name had slipped her mind. "Oh, Morgan! Who knows?"

"What about your folks?"

"I'm still glued to my mom. That hasn't changed."

"Not your dad?"

It baffled her. "Did I ever even once mention my father to you?"

"No."

"And, how long have we been chums?"

"Nine years."

"I rest my case."

"What about your siblings?"

"Scattered in different directions. We write." She motioned him toward a brocaded wing chair rescued from a street corner near Sutton Place. "Sit. This all requires coffee."

"No."

"No to sitting, or no coffee?"

"I didn't come for coffee. I came for an answer. Will you marry me?"

Imogene didn't flinch. She wasn't gentle. "Never."

Donald stood, stupefied. He'd prepared a response to yes, no, maybe, and someday. But she'd trumped him.

Turning to go, he noticed a man asleep in her modest bedroom and assumed, wrong. It kept him from saying good-bye.

Wink remained lingering over the espied conversation between Imogene and Donald, the one he would lie about overhearing, but fail to forget. It made him realize how often he beheld Imogene unwittingly sabotage the will of women and mangle the hearts of men. He knew it wasn't her intent to wreak havoc; it arose because whatever went on inside the minds and hearts of others had never transpired inside hers.

• • •

"When she finally does call," Wink fussed, "she'll probably have forgotten it's our wedding day." But by then, even his anger was conflicted. He'd regarded marriage as a despicable form of social climbing, suppressing his own desperate need to fit in. But he accepted he'd have to conform if he was to climb the corporate ladder any higher.

Okay, he mentally pinched himself, *so I'm not exactly on the ladder. But I've been around enough boardrooms to understand the agenda requiring marriage to ensure a promotion.* He mentally pinched himself harder. *Okay, okay! I've been 'on' enough boardroom tables and 'was' the agenda. Still, any excuse of not being a family man won't wash for refusing me a raise once Imogene is my wife and I claim Pansy as my stepkid.*

"How the hell did this happen to you?" he berated his mirrored image. "Everything was going smoothly until that vamp showed up!" Wink always paused to give the devil her due when it came to good-lookers. "Of course, if she'd been a he you can bet I'd be having him bummy side up this morning for breakfast."

He buttered an onion roll and placed the eggs on it, popping the yolks to let them soak in before sitting down to think about his regular tricks who'd asked about his impending retirement.

They were all told the same thing about Imogene: intellectually speaking, she was quick-witted and well read, without any need to fake knowing something she didn't, while sometimes dumbing down about things she did. He felt it contributed to making him a hit at every social event they attended where a savvy woman on his arm was necessitated.

But it was what Imogene didn't know that proved invaluable, specifically those traits distinct to Wink, like the underbelly world of hustling, scoring, skimming, and coercion. He knew the weakest link had always been his reliance on Imogene's chastity and naïveté and the fact that, up until a few hours earlier, no matter whom Wink introduced Imogene to, she displayed no more than surface emotions. She was winsome when she wanted to be and attentive when needed. But, regardless of how rich, attractive, or interested others were in her, Imogene had no need to bond.

"I can't decide if she's asexual, frigid, or clitorisless," he once said in an effort to end Dory's pestering.

"Clitorisless?"

"It isn't Scrabble, Dory. It's Imogene."

That had been Wink's ace in the hole. Imogene knew he was gay. Neither assumed she was. Both agreed there'd never be any degree of intimacy between them and that, if either fell in love, he or she could depart without feeling beholden. Their union would be based on perception, opportunity, tax codes and showmanship.

At least, it might have been. But now that Imogene was in play, Wink knew he needed to stop her in her tracks.

He consulted his boudoir clock again and hissed. Only twenty minutes had elapsed.

FOURTEEN
Saturday Afternoon, March 14, 1970
Imogene & Wink

Wink wandered into the living room of the two-bedroom apartment he occupied with strangers since his priest payouts ceased. So many young men had answered a stream of ads to share the place that he'd stopped keeping track of names as long as the rent was paid on time. The fellows currently crashing there during tricking hours would have been evicted by noon if he'd married Imogene. Not now.

Having finished with breakfast, he stretched out on the living room couch, planning to read the morning papers until eight o'clock, before walking to Imogene's, shaking her awake if need be, and demanding an answer as to what their future held. Instead, he dozed until an incessant ringing aroused him. He grabbed for the phone, assuming it was her.

"So, Imogene, you're finally up!"

"I've been up. And out."

"What? Where are you?"

"In the Village."

"Where there?"

"The phone booth across from The Parlor."

"Gimme the number."

She hadn't anticipated him being angry and was regretting her failure to predict it before taking his return call on the third ring.

"What's with the delayed pickup, Mo?"

"I was trying to think."

"Of?"

"The best way to tell you something."

"Why aren't you here, with me? Have any idea how worried..."

"I've been looking for her." There. It was out. It was over.

"No." Her admission deflated him. He'd hoped she'd lie and tell him what he wanted to hear — because that's what best friends do best. Lie.

Okay, she thought. *So it isn't over. What the hell is wrong with me, not to have considered him as part of this?* "I know where she is," she spoke in spite of herself. "I think I do. I mean I don't, but I'm hoping I do."

"No."

"Wink..."

"No," he repeated, as if she was sitting next to him, reading the *Times*, savoring fresh perked coffee, buttering a bialy and listening to Johnny Mathais, feeling smug and secure. "We're getting married in three hours. We're getting married."

"Wink. Listen to me, hon. Are you listening?"

"I don't want to listen. I want you to get back here. Now!"

"Wink." She paused. "I've been searching since six this morning. You know that's not like me. Risky. Erratic. Stupid, even."

"I love you, Mo," his voice cracked.

She let the three words linger for a moment, giving him the respect he deserved before replacing them with three more.

"I'm sorry Wink." His silence was searing. "You know...when I was a kid my mom said the words 'I'm sorry' were the two most useless words in the English language. They're afterthoughts of aftermaths. Cruel compensation. Believe me, Wink, I never intended to be cruel. But I can't."

"Can't?" He hoped she meant 'can't leave' him.

"I can't marry you, Wink."

He muffled the mouthpiece and turned his face away.

"You can't marry me," she added, but by then he'd slipped down onto the floor, covering his eyes with his hand, pressing the receiver into the carpet in an effort to cloak the transmission of his hurt. All she could do was wait.

"We'll work it out," he tried. "We always do."

"No."

They remained strung together by dead air for the time it took them to steady their voices and accept the separate despair being felt.

"Please, Wink? Help me?"

"Why should I?"

"Because I need you. And, if it were the other way around, I'd help you."

"No you wouldn't."

"I'd try."

"No you would not Imogene! You've no idea how I feel right now. You don't understood how much I care for you. Admire you. Feel lucky to be your friend. You don't."

"Wink! Wink, listen to me. I didn't get her name." Her hand masked her mouth, pressing back the desperation of that reality. "I don't understand what's going on inside me. How I'm being so bold when I'm so scared. Why I'm trembling thinking about her." She struggled to speak. "All I'm sure of is...is that I saw her and...my heart...my heart fluttered. And my lungs, Wink. My lungs *seized*. Because. I don't know. I felt her in there somehow. And now it's been like...like I have this...this euphoric sense of...of spinning."

"That's the Bombay gin wearing off, honey." He resorted to flippant because it's what they both did best. Flippant was how they conveyed their affection. Maybe flippant would bring her back to him? It was worth a shot.

She was grateful for his infusion of levity. Mirth always made everything easier. But, hey! Wait just a darn minute.

"Bombay gin? *What* Bombay gin?"

Oops.

"It was all Dumb Dory's doing," he swore. "She tried to hide her guzzling by carrying it around like a glass of water. She shouldn't have set it on the jukebox and you shouldn't have drunk it. Haven't I told you and told you not to pick up drinks at bars?"

"You told me not to put mine down because a stranger would pick it up."

"Well? See?"

"Dory put it down, not me, and Dory isn't exactly a stranger."

"Believe me, she's stranger than you think."

They both grinned into the mouthpiece before taking a collective breath.

"Other things, too, Wink."

"What other things?"

She scratched her brow with the cuff of her coat and propped herself up against the booth door, weary, but feeling safe again. "Remember when I told you about being a camp counselor in Great Barrington three years ago?"

"Vaguely."

"I told you how one of the teens in my care wanted to know what it meant to have a stirring downstairs."

He recalled he wanted to protect her from the world, believing maybe he could. "Yes."

"I didn't know what she was talking about, Wink. And, you said you didn't, either."

"Christ."

"It was a kosher camp, Wink. It couldn't have been Christ."

"No, Imogene." His voice was tender now. "I mean, Christ, as in, I'm caught, I lied."

"About the stirring?"

"Hell yes about that. I mean, what's the point? I can't explain it. Not to you, anyhow." He sighed. "But, dammit all, Mo, I was prepared to lie about a whole lot more. I was ready to say that woman last night was all a drunken illusion. I was going to deny she existed."

"You were? Why?"

He swallowed hard, took it slow. "The truth is, I knew what was going on with you. I saw how you looked at her. I felt you resist me when I lifted you from her lap. When all your strength drained away the moment you caught that rose. And then, later, while I cradled you as you slept, all the way home in the cab. I knew."

"You couldn't have known-known."

"You were smiling in your sleep, sweetie."

"Was I, Wink? Because as awful as I feel after what I've been through today, I'm all aglow inside."

"It showed."

"And, honestly Wink, I wouldn't want you to stay with me if it was you. I'd probably want you to feel as guilty as I do right now. But I'd let you go."

"Let *her* go."

"I...can't." The words hobbled out with a new awareness of how much she'd hurt him, and of how many others she might have hurt in similar ways. She was ashamed of herself if so.

In spite of it all, she knew how empty their life together would be if she married him, and the agony that would remain as hers, alone, if she failed to find the stranger in the night who seemed to have absconded with her very soul.

"How the hell am I supposed to let you go, Mo?"

"You already did, hon. As I lay sleeping."

• • •

That should have been the end of it and the finish of them. He should have hung up and she should have taken the subway home and neither of them should have ever crossed paths again, despite how close by they lived. That's the nature of life in the city; it's more likely for a visitor from Iowa to recognize a former classmate while strolling through Central Park than for Manhattan neighbors to run into each other anywhere.

But Wink wasn't willing to give up and Imogene wasn't ready to let go.

"I'll make you a deal," he suggested. "We'll have breakfast. I'll call Charlene at The Parlor and tell her to seat you at my window booth."

"Free food? That's the deal? Hmm, what to do, what to do."

"The *deal* is, I talk and you listen."

Imogene moaned, "O-o-ka-ay."

"I'm warning you though, I'll tell you everything. What being with that woman will mean. What the lifestyle entails. No sugarcoating. You'll know what you're getting into before you give me up. Because, even if you find her, she won't stay, Mo."

"You don't know that."

"I know her type. I know it's your first, and the first one never stays. They aren't meant to stay. And she's not even the first *act*, Mo. Not the stage directions, or the credits rolling. Your first is like the notes a writer forgets are in his pants pocket before tossing them into the wash, then curses the loss the rest of his life. He could wind up with a bestseller, but he still thinks it might have been better if he hadn't lost those first notes. That's the way it is. Slow start. Fast finish. Endless regret."

"It doesn't have to be."

"Yes, it does. Whatever you think, or want to believe, you can't change it."

"Wink..."

"No! I'm going to tell you what she'll say to win you over, and how she'll play you, and how it will hurt when she dumps you for the next girl who catches her eye. And you're going to listen to me, Imogene. You're going to acknowledge everything I say until I'm persuaded you understand every word."

"I said, okay."

"No. Not okay. Because you aren't going to like the truth."

"The truth? When has anybody ever told me the truth, Wink? When did you? And how will the so-called truth upset me more than I am right now?"

"You didn't need to know before."

"Yeah, well, maybe I did." She wished that he'd give in and give up.

"Then it's a go?"

"Yes," she relented. After all, she was hungry. What part of her could pancakes hurt?

"One more thing."

"I'm groaning here."

"Once you're seated, Charlene will give you a pen and extra place mats."

"Why?"

"Turn them over and write down everything about last night, this morning, now, and right up until I get there."

"All of it?"

"Every word you spoke. Everything you did. Every thought you had."

"Then what?"

"Then you'll give it to me so I can hold onto it for that someday when she leaves you. And she *will* leave you, Mogy. What you write will be my someday told-you-so."

When Imogene hung up the receiver she turned her attention towards The Parlor's plate glass window. She could see Charlene summoned to the phone at the cashier's counter, listen, look out and wave, return the handset, walk to the front door, open it, and motion her to come.

FIFTEEN
Saturday Afternoon, March 14, 1970
Charlene's Story

On the way into the restaurant where she'd worked 12-hour shifts waiting tables for two years, Charlene noticed Miss Imogene slouched in the phone booth across the street. She thought it odd.

Charlene knew Miss Imogene and Mr. Wink were getting married later that day at The Village Temple four blocks away. The wedding idea seemed like a sham to her, Mr. Wink being gay and all, while Miss Imogene was, well, she never quite knew what to think of Miss Imogene. Talk about weird. Irrespective of how bubbly Mr. Wink was, Miss Imogene remained as predictable as ice crystals on refrozen peas.

The early morning snowfall had turned into a grey muddy slush that Charlene stomped off her tennis shoes before entering the restaurant. It meant her feet would be wet and cold for most of her shift. Charlene daydreamed about buying a pair of red rubber boots like Miss Imogene often wore on such days, wondering if this was the year she could afford it.

She never needed boots before moving to New York and couldn't get used to needing them now. Back home in Georgia her feet were always dry as red road dust, even when bare. It made her ache for the warmth of the southern sun and the living left behind.

Not that it was much of a life, picking pecans with her sister and selling them to testy travelers lost along Route 84 winding west from Dothan, Alabama, past the groves in Brinson, and on to the Atlantic coast. But it was all she'd known for her first seventeen years. It seemed like fifty ago instead of two. And not so much as a souvenir post card from her momma since.

$$\bullet \; \bullet \; \bullet$$

Charlene Deane adored her momma, a big, buxom, burly black woman with hands the size of ping pong paddles capable of lifting Charlene up like the munchkin she once was and hugging her silly if such be the plan. An earnest scripture reader who thought the sun rose on Charlene's head and set in her heart, Momma Deane was as strict as a hickory stick switch and as diligent as an ant clearing mud from a shoe-mashed mound.

One morning when her momma was alone in the groves cracking paper-shells and singing praises to the Lord, a gentleman farmer visited her with his pistol drawn. Beginning nine months after that, her momma's preacher never missed an opportunity to bellow, "Charlene is the ivory outcome spawned by the devil's doing that day!" It made her the target of ridicule at school and a cause for concern among all the Confederate ladies in town, each one fearful that her husband did the deed and that their children were related by damnation.

In contrast, Charlene was the envy of her half-sister, whose blackstrap molasses face matched that of their momma, but whose dolls were as waxen as Charlene alone.

Some said Charlene grew up to be sexually deviant as a result of the shunning she suffered by the man who loved her momma like most men love naughty pictures and nasty talk. But she knew such rumors were rubbish because, even as a fledgling, she recoiled to male voices, resisted male advances, and loathed their insolence when offering to "pack some real black into her."

Fortunately, her momma had been her champion, raising her up to greet each day as if it were a gift to her alone. Charlene believed her momma's love would never end, and still couldn't accept that it had.

By fifteen, Charlene had grown to a razor's edge shy of five-ten, with a flat, firm body and a glow only innocence owns. She lived as a white elephant on the segregated side of town, being bussed to an integrated school where the boys her age were shorter, so kept their distance when tormenting her with vulgarities, and the girls renounced her as a freak, turning their backs whenever she appeared. It left Charlene prey to loneliness.

The one person showing any interest at all in the child was the physical education teacher, Miss Janey, who treated Charlene as her personal prize.

"She has such potential as an athlete with such purity and strength," Miss Janey buzzed in the teachers' lounge on registration day while her colleagues listened, suspecting it was more like the girl was such-such temptation for the beefy old broad, presumed to be canoodling with Miss Evans of Home Economics.

One Friday after the final bell sent students scurrying to everywhere but there, Charlene reported to the shower room at the request of Miss Janey, where she was surprised to find her teacher wrapped in a towel the size and quality reserved for people pictured at beach resorts in magazine advertisements.

Miss Janey greeted her with a soft, damp kiss to the cheek. "Thank you for coming my dear." Charlene liked being kissed by this woman who had once murmured, "I want you to know you can always confide in me," so close to her ear, Charlene discerned the enticing scent of Tabu on Miss Janey's neck. "Think of me as your *best* friend."

Sadly, Charlene had no other friends. Because of it, she thought of Miss Janey all the time, night and day, awake and asleep. She looked to Miss Janey for inspiration and relied on Miss Janey for approval. She tracked Miss Janey's every move. She believed she'd willingly die for Miss Janey and realized she was in love with Miss Janey when she began to swoon while gazing at the moon with thoughts of her. (But after she walked into a tree while out swooning one night, she stopped looking up unless she was sitting down.)

"Why'dya send for me, Miss Janey?" Charlene stood with her chin pressed into her neck and her eyes angled upwards like every Southern-colored addressing whites had been taught. Even though her skin was whiter than the ever-tanned teacher, Charlene cowered because she always did as told.

"You're not in class now, dear. No one's here but us. So, there'll be none of this 'Miss' business. Call me Janey. All my real friends do."

Charlene liked the liberty of saying Miss Janey's name without the prefix.

"Janey," she smiled. It was a wide, unwary, emancipated smile.

"You're blossoming, dear. Why, you're already six inches taller than me!"

"Yessum Miss. I mean, yessum, Janey. Yessum, I am."

"Your momma must have mentioned that it's time you find out

what it means to be..." She paused, cunningly. "I'm sorry, dear. How old are you?"

"Fifteen."

"Fifteen? My-oh-my that's hard to believe. Or, did your momma tell you that to keep you her little girl a bit longer?"

"Oh no, Janey!" Charlene's head bounced up. "My momma don't lie ta me."

"That's good," Miss Janey cajoled. "That's the way a momma should be." She began stroking the girls arm lightly, above the elbow. "But there's a difference between a good lie and a bad lie. You understand that, don't you?"

"I heard talk of them bads, but never did hear of them goods."

"Good lies involve those where someone might get hurt if the truth came out. Like if you were to tell the other students that you're my pet. Now, we know that's the truth, but telling them might hurt their feelings. Make them mad. So, if anyone calls you the teacher's pet, you'll need to say it's not so. That's a good lie. And, I'll tell the same good lie. You understand, don't you Charlene?"

"Yessum," she good lied. Because truth was, Charlene didn't give a rat's ass about the feelings of her tormenters.

"Have you ever lied to your momma, Charlene?"

"Only good ones!"

Perfect, Janey thought. "The school nurse records say that you haven't reached puberty yet. Is that true?"

"Pu-ber-ty?"

"You mean your momma never told you about the birds and the bees?"

"My job's to feed the birds leftover nut bits, if that's what you mean. And I reckon I can make paste for a bee sting as good as any."

Miss Janey moistened and rolled her lips. "It's a term, dear, a polite way to differentiate between men and women. Your momma sent a note forbidding you to attend health class. Did she take you through that talk at home?"

"No. Don't suppose so. Don't need ta know 'bout menfolk though. I hear dirty words spoke, all hushy 'tween those who wanna make me feel poorly. It don't much. But..."

By then Miss Janey had taken Charlene's hand and was leading her through the locker room towards the showers.

"Yes, Charlene? But what?"

"If *you* were to tell me, I'd be mighty thankful, 'specially if it's 'bout my sister. She been bleedin' down low. Heals up some and darned if she don't go get cut again. If that's what's all 'bout, I don't want *nothin'* of that."

"No," Miss Janey soothed, sitting Charlene down on a locker-room bench. "That's not what I had in mind. We can talk about that later, although it might present a problem."

"What, Janey?" Charlene loved saying her name. She could say it and say it. Write it and write it. Think it and think it over and over. Janey. Janey. No Miss, just Janey.

"Your momma might want to be the first one to tell you. And if I do..." she baited.

"You tell me! I swear, I won't tell my momma. If she asks, I'll act all surprised like. Not ta worry none 'bout me, Janey. I love you!"

How had that slipped out? Charlene began to tremble, thinking she'd said something wrong, something forbidden, something she'd never confessed to anyone but God, who likely already knew.

"And I love you Charlene. You know I do."

No, Charlene thought, *I didn't know. I didn't dare hope it. But I know now. Janey loves me. She does, or why else say it?*

How happy the three little words made her. How eager.

The teacher handed Charlene a towel and told her to get undressed, to wrap the towel around her, and to meet her inside.

"We're going to shower together," said Miss Janey. "It's what best friends do."

"They do?"

"Trust me."

It was Miss Evans who filed the anonymous tip informing the police of what was going on between Charlene and her teacher. By then Charlene was turning eighteen and obsessed with the coach who had disguised her megalomania as love for the beguiled child.

To avoid arrest, Miss Janey left with Miss Evans, both quietly quitting without saying their goodbyes. As part of the agreement, Miss

Janey called Charlene from a pay phone on her police escorted way out of town and instructed the girl to answer all questions put forth by law enforcement, truthfully.

Charlene obliged the woman in whom she'd lost herself, unaware of the toll it would take on her heart. Afterwards, Charlene's momma upped the agony ante by telling Charlene she no longer had a home, nor a family who wanted anything more to do with her.

It didn't take much thinking time for Charlene to find her way north to New York City where she quickly landed a job at The Parlor to begin a new life clouded with mixed regrets.

She'd been born the bastard of a mother raped by a white man, rejected by her stepfather, separated from her stepsister, pawed by men-friends and relatives alike, treated with contempt, seduced, betrayed, and discarded by her teacher, deceived by the law, denied justice, and scorned by a religion that professed love and forgiveness.

• • •

"I be twenty come August," she said to herself while waiting for Imogene to cross the street, "and skin me alive if I ain't standin' here frettin' over some rich white bitch who gots the finest red rubber boots I ever did see, but don't got sense 'nuff ta wear 'em on as pissy a cold mornin' as be this."

SIXTEEN
Late Saturday Afternoon, Saturday, March 14, 1970
Imogene & Charlene

Imogene had always been optimistic about her future, certain of her choices, composed, clean and orderly. Pretty orderly. Orderly enough. But now?

She mulled it over while walking to where Charlene held The Parlor door open, replaying Juni's voice in her head giving the two minute warning before all of them went from being night drinkers to morning drunks. A casual look to her right was all it took to disintegrate and feel an entirely new person soar up from her ashes. Well...floundered up anyhow.

"Mornin,' Miss Imogene." Charlene was concerned. "You okay this mornin,' mam? You be lookin' a little rheumy-eyed."

"I'm fine thank you, Charlene," Imogene politely lied. Then added with mild irritation, "But Charlene, how many times must I remind you? It's not Miss Imogene. It's Imogene. Or, Mo. Friends call me Mo."

"Oh, I won't be doin' that, Miss Imogene. I done made that slip once. I won't ever again be callin' white women anything but what be safe."

Imogene glanced over her shoulder at Charlene as they walked to the booth Wink reserved at noon each Saturday and paid for whether they used it or not.

"Whatever are you saying, Charlene? You're white."

"I ain't." Charlene was indignant about it. "The man with the gun who forced my momma be white. And I can't hide my skin bein' white. But my blood is as black as black can be and I not be 'bout ta forget it."

Imogene sat staring up at the girl, thinking what she heard couldn't

87

be so. She'd assumed by her manner of speaking that Charlene was from the rural south, but knew she could as easily be a method actress rehearsing for a role. One never knew if the person serving you today would reappear as a star of stage and screen tomorrow. New York was ripe for it.

As for Charlene, she displayed no interracial stereotypical characteristics. Her hair was a thick, soft, burnt-brown, cut short and combed straight back. Dimpled cheeks accented her oval face complementing thin lips and grey eyes with long, linear lashes. Her hips held one of those flat backsides emblematic to high society inbreeding and her feet were gracefully small. Even so, she wasn't a particularly pretty girl, but certainly a handsome one. And tall! Imogene thought Charlene could easily become a model, or stewardess. But black?

"I don't mean to be disrespectful, but..." Imogene dared, before Charlene flashed her a 'better not say it' look.

This woman, Charlene thought, *has been a bee sting in my butt from the first drizzly day she marched in here wearing those bright red boots and behaving as wily a woman as I ever did see.*

Imogene had intended to ask if Charlene's mother hadn't gotten her by another means, but stopped short, figuring if Charlene wanted to be black, let it be.

"I'm sorry about your momma."

"No reason, Miss Imogene. Wasn't you who forced me into this world. Didn't mean ta make ya think so."

"No, no. You didn't. I meant." She shrugged. "I don't really know what I meant. Sorry."

Miss Imogene was now making Charlene the sorry one; sorry she'd begun a conversation with the starchy little thing and sorry she depended on Wink's generosity that obligated her to help the woman.

It wasn't that Miss Imogene hadn't tried to be friendly. But Charlene knew better than to trust any Easter-lily-white-ass woman. *Pure* Easter-lily-white, that is. And to Charlene, Miss Imogene was as pure as any Easter-lily-white-ass got.

Why, look at the way she had Mr. Wink bobbing and spinning like a tin top. Charlene knew Mr. Wink was as dandy as one of those three-dollar bills she'd heard about. Yet here he was, dilly-dallying after Miss Imogene; about to marry her.

Lordy, lordy, Charlene questioned herself as she helped Miss Imogene pull her coat off and out from under where she sat, *what in the world was that boy thinking? And, why was Miss Imogene acting so wiggly?*

Not that Charlene truly cared one way or the other about either of them. ""Don't you be turnin' a blind eye ta Mr. Wink," Charlene would sometimes remind her window reflection. "He still be a man."

Charlene felt repugnance for men, especially for the one who had raped her momma, and for her momma's husband who should have loved her in spite of her not being his own.

"As if I was my momma's fault," she'd hiss. "As if she chose to have me."

But even repugnance was too mild a word for how she felt about the detective who tricked her into telling him things she never would have. It took her a bit of thinking, but she understood what made all of it wrong now. Still, it didn't justify the lies the detective told in order to unravel her. The memory of it scalded her eyes at times.

Charlene thought, too, about the shame the preacher man spread, making her Momma choose between Messiah and Pariah Land. She bet the baby Jesus would have a thing or two to say about it.

"What that be movin' in there, Miss Imogene?"

"Oh thank goodness!" Imogene opened her blouse enough to free the grimy red tabby from her bra and kissed it. "I was afraid she died."

"It be a mighty dirty kitty ta be kissin' like that, seeing how you always be polishin' the fork afore usin' it and wrappin' a napkin 'round the Heinz bottle afore fixin' your fries."

Imogene kissed the kitty again. "She's my lucky pussy."

"If you say so, gotta be, but gimme-here. I'll dust it up some and set a saucer down back yonder 'til you be gone."

"That would be good of you, Charlene, a blessing on you. I swear it is."

Charlene held the kitten high, inspecting it. "Has kitty gotta name?"

"Petunia."

"But it be a 'he' kitty, Miss Imogene."

"Petunia," she repeated.

Charlene went to nestle the kitten in a corrugated box lined with torn strips of newspaper and set down dishes of warm milk and scavenged sardines before returning to Imogene's table carrying a copper colored plastic, black top pot of freshly brewed coffee.

"You sure you be okay?" she caught herself saying despite everything inside her telling her not to. "What with Mr. Wink and the wedding and all?"

"Yes. The wedding's fine." Imogene had been staring out the window, lost in thought. "That is, it would be fine if I were going to be there." She turned towards Charlene. "Which I'm not. So there's that."

For the first time Imogene was looking up at her, exposing 'racketycoon' eyes: wounded whites with smeared black bandit-style skins where mascara had liquefied and dried under the swollen red and blotchy puffy parts. They were eyes that Charlene recognized as once being like her own.

"You ain't gettin' hitched?"

"No."

"Does Mr. Wink...?"

"Yes."

Suspicion shot through Charlene. Her lip curled as she envisioned Mr. Wink cheating on Miss Imogene and Miss Imogene finding out Mr. Wink was to skedaddle. Maybe he intended all along to say one thing but do another, burdening Miss Imogene to forever dwell on where their love went and why it had cost her a heart. "There be a new man?"

"No."

"Missus then?"

"Yes, Charlene. There is."

"Sonofabitchin' no good bastard men. Every pissin' lyin' cheatin' slimy last one of 'em."

"No-o," quieted Imogene. "No. Not Wink." She touched the girl's arm lightly. "It's *me*, Charlene. I'm the no good, bastard, slimy whatever it was. Not Wink. She's for me."

"Oh!" said Charlene taken aback. "Oh-h," she repeated, surprised by the gentleness of Miss Imogene's fingertips on her arm. "Well, I 'spect that be different, Miss Imogene."

"Why, Charlene? How is it different?"

"Can't say I'm willin' ta say. But somethin' inside tells me, when

90

Mr. Wink gets here I bet he won't be wearing a pair of eyes like you got."

"Hmm. Maybe Wink wears his eyes on the inside."

"That'd be why his mascara don't run. But I never did see a sad hearted fella look as pity-faced as you."

"I look that bad?"

"Yessum. You oughta be tidyin' up some."

"Thanks for your honesty and concern, Charlene, but I'm too beat. All I need right now are some extra place mats, please."

"Yessum, Miss Imogene. You sure that be all right 'bout me sayin' just Imogene, mam?"

"Yes. Or, Mo."

"I right-like Mo," Charlene smiled at her for the first time. "Will seven mats do? Ten?"

"Better make it ten."

Imogene welcomed the fresh amiability and informality. Charlene had a tendency to be gruff with her, especially on cold and rainy days. But now she was being attentive. Even kind.

"I be taking that there dead flower, Mo?"

"No, no!" Imogene blocked her from disturbing the remnants of the yellow rose she'd arranged on the table before her.

Charlene recognized panic in Imogene's voice. "That be from your lady?"

"It is."

"Yessum," Charlene empathized. "I feel the same 'bout shower room floors some days."

Imogene took the blue Bic pen Charlene handed her, flipped over the delivered paper mats and began printing in neat letters on a blank backside.

"What you be writin'?"

"A confession. An explanation. My death sentence, perhaps. Maybe a bit of each."

Charlene left her alone to do what Imogene felt needed doing, but continued checking on her at intervals, watching from an acceptable distance. She felt the two of them were pilgrims on a common road.

Charlene had traveled to its end, while Imogene was starting out, unaware of the forward battles and backwards slides where love-muggers hid, eager to strip all sanctity from a woman's soul.

She grumbled aloud while filling the metal top, tilt-a-spoon sugar canisters and fluted glass shakers, dropping a pinch of salt over her opposite shoulder with each, accepting that she hadn't yet recovered from her first trip down that road. Yes, she'd made it to the dead end and survived, but she couldn't let go and didn't believe herself capable of making it back.

"Humph!"

"What's that humph about, Charlene?" the grease-cook barked. He'd stalked her from the day she'd first walked through the Parlor door.

"A loud thought s'all," she barked back.

"About me? Is that it? About my offer to take you to see Liston's comeback in June?"

"More 'bout how sweet you be on them smack-back games."

"You got me there," he bragged. "Boxing, football, hockey — whatever. Only men lust for the brutal sports."

"You be wrong, rutabaga. Women lust for love. It be the most brutal sport of all."

After the lunch crowd cleared, a young floor washer pestered Charlene to let him start the cleanup early. She didn't hear him at first because she was zoned out, revisiting her conversation with Mr. Willabeez, the janitor whose voice was too high and step too soft to escape Johnny Reb's radar.

Willabeez wisely distanced himself from all school scandals until Charlene told him she'd been banished. First he gave her the contents of the tin can he used for stowing change snaked out of drains and swept up from hallways. Then he revealed Miss Janey and Miss Evans fled to New York City to find jobs in a school system with more closets than all of Georgia had for hiding. Charlene preferred to think Miss Janey was teacher-napped by Miss Evans, or possibly blackmailed into leaving her behind.

"Whitemailed what it was," she scoffed, aloud, as she rolled three stainless steel utensils into each logo stamped paper napkin. "Maybe I should tell Miss Mo 'bout the storm that starts the second she say she be queer."

"Can I Charlene, can I? Let me start washin' the floors now. Will it be okay? It's awful cold out and slow here today."

"I 'spect so." Charlene didn't care. She'd refocused on Imogene who had finished writing and was busily numbering the paper mats.

The morning events made Charlene curious about where Imogene and Mr. Wink had met and what made Imogene think he was some sort of financial whiz. One of The Parlor regulars told her Mr. Wink dealt drugs to stockbrokers, servicing the richest ones with noontime quickies; even admitted to being one of Wink's tricks for a time.

Imogene didn't strike Charlene as someone who was wise to the secreted side of Mr. Wink. Not that Charlene was about to tell her. Nope. No way.

Once The Parlor was deserted of all but a few stragglers on counter stools, the penetrating odor of frying oils and onions was slowly swabbed away with Pine-Sol and Clorox. Imogene hadn't looked up, except to reach out and touch the wilted rose before her. It prevented Charlene from catching her eye, even after dilly-dallying near her booth several times.

Charlene was now longing to learn where Imogene met her lady friend. Had it been at a bar, a club, a party? Or, was it at one of those private places she'd heard about, where old lovers gather to compare notes on past conquests hoping a trade-off might result in a better grade of failure? Could that be where Miss Janey might go? Had Imogene ever met Miss Janey? Was such an encounter even probable?

The squealing of brakes from a taxi out front brought Charlene suddenly back, alerting her to Wink's arrival. She watched through the window as he leapt from the cab carrying a Saks Fifth Avenue shopping bag, a bouquet of daffodils, and the face of victory usually reserved for the roar of the crowd.

"Uh-oh," Charlene said. "Fire in the belly of the nelly."

SEVENTEEN
Early Saturday Afternoon, March 14, 1970
Gender Bending

Wink flagged a cab outside his apartment and rode around the corner to Imogene's place, giving the driver an extra tip up front to wait while he dashed inside to grab things Imogene might need, especially if she'd left to lesbian hunt that morning without changing her clothes.

Everything indicated she had. The place appeared to be the same as when he dumped her unceremoniously onto the Danish modern couch hours earlier, the one misfit piece in the room.

"I can't get rid of it, Wink," she'd argue. "This apartment came furnished, so it's not mine to pitch."

"But everything else in here is period."

"It would hurt Mr. Singer's feelings if I removed it."

"Then have *him* do it. Whoever heard of worrying about a landlord's feelings anyhow?"

"He's my friend."

"Friend-schmend."

"I can't afford to replace it."

"I bet we could find something on Sutton again. Their discards are preferable to this."

"The couch is brand new, Wink."

"Now you're making my case for me."

"It's a trundle bed."

"No kidding?" He crouched down to pull out the frame. "That is too cool for school."

Standing there now, visualizing that conversation caused him to scrutinize the disarray of the room he'd missed at first glance: pillows out of place, her robe in a pile, a book on the floor with a photograph sticking out, an ankle boot on the sideboard. He quickly removed the boot, fearing it was bad luck to leave it there. Not that he was superstitious.

He searched the wastebaskets for that damnable rose she'd clung to, hoping to find it and piss on it before flushing. Alas, no such luck.

In the bathroom, he tested the bristles of her toothbrush on a tissue. They could have dried naturally in the hours since she left, but he packed it, along with a tin of Colgate powder.

Her makeup was put away, which wasn't at all like Imogene. Usually, whatever she applied in haste in the morning she'd put away at night. *How odd*, he thought. *I've never seen her go out without her face in place. Base, blush, lips, and lashes.* He envied her long, naturally curved lashes. His were as long, but so embarrassingly straight, he had to crimp them by using a metal clamp that often jammed, resulting in hysterics.

"Oh Mogy," he mused aloud, "we wear the same brand mascara."

Finding a zippered pouch in the vanity under the sink, he filled it with the cosmetics, adding a wide tooth comb, white cotton washcloth, and fresh bar of Crabtree & Evelyn goats milk soap. Then he returned to the front room.

Her wardrobe consisted of expensive apparel purchased as drastically reduced close-outs from upscale stores. Everything was hung neatly, a clear indication Imogene did nothing but get up and go out. Otherwise, clothes would be strewn from her having changed her mind at least three times before finalizing on what to wear. Sometimes they'd be out the door and half up the block before she'd scamper back for a different purse, catching up to him with the same purse and an entirely altered ensemble.

It agitated him to find her red rubber boots there. He knew she'd have worn them on such a cold, damp day if she'd been thinking — with her head that is. He folded the boots over and put them in a brown paper sack, then placed it on the bottom of a Saks shopping bag, adding some casual clothes on top: a pair of off-white wool slacks and boat-neck sweater, a pale pink wing-tip blouse with socks and hair scarf to match, and red gloves to go with the boots.

Then, because it was part of Imogene's modus operandi, he threw in three embroidered handkerchiefs. For a time he'd been frustrated when Imogene refused to blow or blot on tissue like the rest of the modern world. Tissues are for "stuffing things" she'd say. Now, he gifted her with hankies whenever he could find one as a memento of somewhere they'd been, or something they'd done together.

Mission accomplished, Wink picked up the Saks shopping bag with one hand and was about to set the lock with the other when Dory Davenport burst through the door, scaring the bejesus out of him. He squealed, grabbed his chest, and ran backwards on tiptoe.

"Eeek? That's what you say when someone frightens you? Eeek?" Dory laughed at him. "Did you piddle your panties, too, little girl?"

"Dammit Dory! What the hell are you doing here?"

"What the hell do you think?" She looked around the room and whistled. "Nice."

"Imogene wouldn't like you being here."

"So where is she?"

"I don't know. And even if I did — which I do not — why would I tell you?"

"You wouldn't, Wink. That's why I came on my own."

"Oh-h swell. Now you're stalking her? Hired a gumshoe to track her down did you?"

"Gumshoe? No one says gumshoe. Maybe if there's gum on your shoe — but not even. Regardless, I'm not stalking her, you moron."

"Then how did you find out where she lived?"

"She's listed."

"Not in Dial-A-Dyke."

"Try the Manhattan phone book."

"And you thought to look there all by yourself?"

"I'm not stupid, Wink."

"I didn't say you were."

"You call me Dory Dumbdyke behind my back."

Wink faked a fag-flabbergast. "Who told you that?"

"Everyone. They've been ragging on me for putting up with it."

"Re-e-eally? Well, did you ever stop to think, maybe it's my pet name for you?"

"Like me calling you Hood-Wink?'

"You don't!"

"I do!"

"How *dare* you?"

"Oh, I dare! I dare!"

The two were chin to chest, she looking up, he looking down —
both of them furious.

"Well," he seethed, "as much as I would love to stay here and duke
it out, I have a cab waiting, so you'll have to leave."

"You mean that one double-parked out front?"

"The same."

"I told him you were here for me and sent him on."

Wink dropped the Saks bag and ran to the window, opened the
shutter and peered out. Seeing no taxi, he slowly turned around and
took aim. "If you weren't a woman I'd pummel you for this."

"And if you weren't a pantywaist I'd shiver in my Timberlands."

It was a standoff.

Wink checked his watch and sized up the situation. He knew Dory
wasn't budging until he came clean, ending the façade between the two
of them and her obsession with Imogene.

"What is it you want, Dory?"

"Have you put in a word with Imogene on my behalf."

He'd already decided: not a chance in hell. "Yes."

"And?"

"No."

"That's it? No?"

"Yes."

"I don't believe you. She must have said something."

Wink dragged Dory by the arm over to the full-length mirror on
Imogene's closet door and asked, "Tell me what you see."

"Me. What of it?"

"I see a strange little, neurotic person dressed all in black, most of
it leather, with enough steel chains and keys dangling off her hipbone to
unlock Kingdom Come. I see a hairstyle with more wax buildup than
the biggest head at Madame Tussaud's. I see a ridiculous tattoo of a
heart and bleeding cross on your jugular and a tacky pair of blind-mice
sunglasses on your nose."

"So?"

"So? Think of who you're trying to impress!" He pointed to the
racks of Imogene's outfits. "She dresses in classic styles of bright colors
or pastels, regardless of the season." He forced her to examine the
room, focusing on items in plain view. "She reads three newspapers a

day and a book a week, listens to classical music when not dancing to rock, has a weakness for 19th century illustrators, is passionate about the theater, and loves animals. But what's most important is," he spun her to face him, "the first woman who caught her fancy after me carting her to your bitch-bar for a year is cast in her own image."

"Only because she's been brainwashed to believe all that lipsticker crap," Dory declared. "Deep down, I bet she's not that shallow."

"Don't say that. Don't use shame-slang to attack a woman who likes herself the way she is and prefers those who complement her. That's not shallow. It's her choice. And, honey, in the words of Cher — the *queen* of choice — it ain't you, babe!"

"Dylan," Dory corrected. "In the words of Bob Dylan."

Wink waved her aside. "A shorter Cher with bad hair. Close enough. The point is, I haven't time for this, so back off and face the fact that I know her much better than you know her now, or ever did, or ever will."

"In your dreams maybe."

"Meaning?"

"It means I'm on the inside of *every*thing."

"And what? I'm not? Name one thing."

"I'm betting you don't know my ex was Imogene's classmate and colleague and was cheating on me with Imogene's best friend."

"You idiot, I'm her best friend."

"You're Imogene's Manhattan weekdays best friend. I'm talking about her Island chums."

"I don't believe you."

Dory pulled a billfold from her hip pocket, flipped it open, unfastened an accordion of cellophane envelopes filled with faded photos and showed Wink a shot of two women, shoulder to shoulder, holding up tumblers in a sky-high salutation. He removed the photo and studied it before flipping it over. Scribbled on the back was: *Imogene LaPin & Annie O'Hara, AADA, 1966.*

"This photo is four years old and written in crayon."

"I like crayons. So sue me."

"It doesn't prove anything anyway. I spend lots of weekends with Mo."

"Fess up," Dory taunted him. "How long have you been seeing

each other on weekends?"

He handed Dory back the photo. "Since last year sometime. Early June."

"That's around the same time me and Annie broke up."

"It doesn't make sense. And even so, Imogene isn't required to tell me everything."

"Then what doesn't make sense?"

"I'm saying that picture doesn't prove anything! If she and Annie were as close as you claim, Imogene would have introduced us."

"People don't mix friends if they want to keep friends, Wink."

He knew that was true for him, but not for others. "If that's why you pretended you never met her, explain all your distant dyke drooling at Johnny's."

"I see her with you every Friday, but I've never actually *met* her. No sit down or real conversation," Dory admitted. "Annie always talked about her, that's all. Told me things. That's why I wanna bag her for my own."

Wink would have walloped her for that, but feared being walloped back. "She's not prey, Dory. And she's not an easy lay like what'shername."

"Who?"

"Imogene's 'supposedly' best friend that your lover was seeing on the side."

"No supposedly about it. Her name's Elaine."

"And you knew what was going on?"

"Annie cheating? In a way I guess. The triangle connection surprised me."

Wink felt his world crumbling. For a year and a half he'd hidden most of his past from Imogene, overlooking that she might be hiding hers, too.

"Do you think Imogene knew?"

"Would it make a difference?"

"Seriously? To be lied to by omission like that?"

"Annie and Elaine weren't cheating on Imogene, Wink."

"But they shut her out." He was thinking about himself now. "That's the same as a lie. It hurts as much."

EIGHTEEN
Late Saturday Afternoon, March 14, 1970
Triple Scoops

By the time Wink entered The Parlor at half past three, Imogene had finished recording what he'd required of her and, in doing so, made a decision. If anyone ever asked her to define a lesbian, she'd recount the story of her operator.

Imogene figured the operator must have been a lesbian, or a closet lesbian, or mother of a lesbian, or sister, aunt, or cousin of one, or a lesbian wannabe, or (at least) a lesbian sympathizer.

Or, maybe the operator wasn't lesbian-linked at all. Maybe she'd once been a damsel in distress like Imogene, and wanted to do everything she could to help a neophyte. Maybe she was an altruist doing unto others, or maybe she was making good on a soul debt.

Not that any of the maybes mattered. What mattered was, the determination of one woman to willingly guide another through a thorny rite of passage. What higher purpose was there for being female than that? What nobler cause could she hope to attain in life?

"You look like the wreck of the Hesperus!" Wink exclaimed upon seeing her.

"I do?" In the ninety minutes since they'd spoken, she'd gotten cozy, sitting with her feet up under her, drinking coffee and so engrossed in the task he'd delegated that her appearance slipped her mind. "Am I not up to par?"

"You're not even up to death-warmed-over. Go get gussied while I order."

Imogene stood for their custom cheek-to-cheeks before clutching the Saks bag Wink handed her and plodding off to the lavatory in her stocking feet.

"Mo, sweetie. Are you okay?" he called after her.

"No I am not. I feel like I've been beaten with an ugly stick."

• • •

In the world of waitress informants, Charlene was Wink's.

"I can't believe you didn't tell her," he admonished, halfheartedly.

"Uh-uh. Not only did she look like somethin' the cat dragged in, I be damned if she didn't drag one in! Has me kittensittin' in the restroom. She be lucky I'm a good ol' soul 'cause," Charlene poked him, "I'm sure you be tippin' me extra for that."

"A cat? Where'd she...?"

"Not my business, Mr. Wink. Kitty crawled outta her booby bin beggin' for mercy."

"A kitten then?"

"No, Mr. Wink. It'd be a full grown cat." She rolled her eyes. "Did I not say where I fetched kitty from?"

"Reached right in did you, Charlene?"

"Now you bein' bad," she cackled. "And, yessiree I did."

Wink laughed at Charlene's imitation of the commotion Imogene caused.

"Oh-h, you shoulda seen her sittin' here like a zombie behind glass, scarin' the livin' daylights outta people passin' by. They be walkin' up to the window like they do to check the place out, then be jumpin' back when her head bobbed up. Hah! 'Cept for them younguns. They be pointin' and laughin' at her 'til them mommies would slap their little fingers down and drag 'em off. Yessiree, Mr. Wink. You did miss some fun!"

"Sounds like it. But don't let on you told me. She's a bit bummed-out right now."

"Yessiree, Mr. Wink, and I be right sorry 'bout that."

"Sorry about what?"

Charlene froze. For a split second she flashed back to when the Georgia detective was pretending to be nice, plying her with questions she'd forever wish she hadn't answered.

"Sorry 'bout what you said s'all."

"What did I say?"

"Somethin' about Miss Imogene's bummy."

"I didn't say a word about her bummy, Charlene. I never speak of Imogene that way."

"Sorry, Mr. Wink. That be what I think I heard."

"You think? Or, maybe you think you're going to make me think you thought that by saying you think?"

"Now, now Mr. Wink. This keeps up, you best be readin' me my rights."

"Why is it you turn every conversation into an episode of Dragnet, Charlene?"

"Dragnet. That be a good one Mr. Wink." She chuckled. "You be orderin' now?"

• • •

Once Imogene emptied the contents of the shopping bag onto the sink top, it didn't take her long to do a complete makeover. Wink had chosen wisely and well, except for the high top, red rubber boots that weren't narrow enough to fit under her white wool slacks. She wasn't willing to wrinkle the pant-legs by stuffing them in. "I'll need to wear the fresh pink socks with my sneakers," she told herself, "even if they haven't dried out enough."

She thought about Charlene through it all and how sad the girl seemed to be. Contrary to the adage stating otherwise, Imogene believed she *could* judge a book by its cover, which was what 'reading people' involved. Years of discreet observation taught her that a garment's colors, condition, fit and how a woman carried herself were clear indicators of what was going on behind a woman's eyes and inside her heart.

Charlene's garments were always clean and crisp, with no trace of her white shirts graying, or her black slacks fading. Pride accomplished that. And, there was dignity in the manner Charlene strutted her full height, never slumping her shoulders in an effort to appear shorter, nor cowering to the little men that tall women were often deigned to date. But perfect posture could also be indicative of fear, especially in someone as defensive as Charlene.

On that morning, Imogene thought Charlene made a poor choice in wearing canvas shoes to work. Part of her assumed it was out of expediency and comfort, but a smarter part said the girl was working in them, wet, out of necessity.

"That's the biggest piece of the tattletale package," Imogene mouthed aloud to the mirror while applying her lipstick, "given that Charlene adheres to the Queen's code against complaining or explaining." She capped the tube and returned it to the makeup bag. "You give away as much in what you do say as in what you don't — at least to the few of us who listen carefully."

Imogene finished up by smoothing the sides of her hair and fluffing the fresh pink knotted scarf now holding it back, satisfied with the outcome, though drained of energy. Her droopy eyelids were evidence of both her lack of sleep and a scolding conscience.

On the one hand, she was eager to keep going until she found the woman who had hijacked her heart; on the other hand, she owed it to Wink to hear him out.

"I am hungry as all get out," Imogene told her finalized reflection as she filled the bottom of the emptied shopping bag with her cosmetics, then made a nest of her rumpled clothes for the sleeping kitten. She thought briefly about returning Charlene's pen before leaving it lying there, like an arrow under the washbasin.

• • •

"What a difference a face makes!" Wink marveled as Imogene slid into the booth opposite him after gently shoving the shopping bag under the table.

"Thanks for what you did, Wink. You're the best."

"What did I do?"

"Not much. The clothes. The cosmetics. The concern. Coming to my rescue."

"You forgot the food."

Imogene had already dug in but stopped to praise it all. "Scrambled eggs, dry; hash browns, blotted; orange juice, chilled; croissants, real butter; coffee, cream, cubed sugar...and wherever did you get this darling little bone china cup?"

"In the far back of your kitchen cupboard. Incidentally, you own enough china cups."

"I must if I don't recognize this one. Is that what took you so long? The care package?"

Wink looked down at his plate to hide his satisfaction, happy she'd opened the door to discussing her best kept secrets.

"No. I'd have been here sooner, but you had a visitor as I was leaving."

"Who?"

"Dory Dumbdyke Davenport. From Johnny's."

"Wink, I wish you'd stop calling women dykes. It's unkind." She took a sip of juice. "Say again. Which one's Dory?"

"The midget Elvis impersonator, minus the sequins, voice and any actual resemblance to the King other than the grease and jailhouse jacket."

"The girl who puppy-dogs you?"

"More like hounds! But yes, that's her."

"Why was she at my place?"

"To pledge."

"What?"

"Her undying love for your hand in matrimony."

"I don't follow."

"It seems, after your display on the dance floor last night the, ahem, lady lezzies took it as your coming out. It put you in play."

"In play?"

"Up for grabs."

"Grabs?"

"Available."

"Hold on. You're saying Dory wants to date me?"

"Yes, essentially, that would be the jump off point to jumping on."

"What makes her think I'd be interested? It might sound unfair, but I'm completely put off by what she exemplifies."

"Which is?"

"Men!"

"Present company included?"

"Oh, Wink. Knock it off. I no more think of you as a man than I do my brothers. Besides, even Dory's more butch than you."

"Are you opposed to that?"

"What?"

"Butches."

"It's none of my concern. If that's what she needs, or wants, or likes, go for it. I'm simply saying, it's not for me."

"And I'm saying, now that you've discovered your lesbian calling, you must be prepared to abide by all club conduct which includes embracing butches and everything gay."

"That's preposterous. I don't have to do any such thing."

"It'll be expected of you."

"By whom?"

"The powers that be butch."

"Look here, my darling boy, you know I don't do clubs, follow crowds, bow to peer pressure, or adhere to protocol of straight society. Ergo-o, I won't be intimidated by gays."

"You haven't a choice. You're either for, or against. One side, or the other."

"It's the law?"

"In a manner of speaking."

"And if I refuse? Will they stone me?"

"Sarcasm aside, no. But someday you could be profiled and arrested, or locked in a mental institution, or worse. That's when you'll want gays on your side."

Imogene pushed her plate away and motioned Charlene for more coffee. The Parlor had begun to get busy with early-birders. An upside-down reading of Wink's wristwatch showed it was shy of five. She knew they'd need to get going soon.

"Okay, Wink, I give. Why would I be profiled or arrested?"

"Being gay is illicit. Once you've taken the plunge, you're a criminal."

"In New York City?"

"Here. Nationwide. Worldwide." Imogene guffawed. "Why are you laughing?"

"Because that's ridiculous."

"Even so, it's true."

"Is not.

"Is too."

"You're trying to scare me, Wink."

"Am not."

"Are too."

"Hand to heart, I'm not."

"But why?" Imogene was confounded. "I don't understand."

"Psychiatrists say queers are mentally ill. Society says we're evil. So legally, you could be institutionalized where various treatments can be utilized in an attempt to 'cure' you. That includes legal rape by men. Or, you could be jailed, with guards eager to do the same."

Imogene's face turned ashen. She sat dumbstruck for a moment, absorbing his words. It made Wink fear he'd said too much and wish he could take the truth back to temper it with gentle lies. He never intended to scare her. (Okay, maybe he had, a little.) It felt like forever before she finally she spoke.

"Over my dead body."

"What?"

"I won't be forced to be part of any group, gay or straight, that assumes they can exert any kind of control over me. This is my life, Wink. *Mine!* And, I'm not living up to anyone's expectations but my own."

"I didn't make the rules, Mo."

He went back to eating what was left on his plate, cold by then. She stared into her coffee while stirring it. They remained quiet for a time. When she finally looked up at him he put down his utensils, looked hopefully back, and waited.

"Listen, Wink. I appreciate the pep talk."

"Pep talk?"

"I'm being facetious."

"Rats. I missed that one."

"The point is, I'm exactly the same person I was yesterday at this exact time. I have the same name, face, body, address, job, ethics, goals, dreams, bank account — the same everything. The solitary thing that's changed is, I've fallen in love. So, if you're saying that one fact makes me an outlaw with a mental disease, then I'm telling you — when ignorance prevails, you don't dumb down. You don't follow the leader. And you sure don't assimilate into any society that advocates doing the same."

"Imogene," he cautioned, "there's no other choice."

"There is. People live autonomously in this world. I'm living so myself, to some extent. We'll find a way to live autonomously, too."

"Tell me, what if this woman you're oh-so-certain will follow you into no man's land doesn't want to go?"

"Why wouldn't she?"

"Because it's your first time, Mo, and she knows first times don't last. Not for you. Not for anyone. She'll get in and get out with as little fanfare as possible."

Imogene leaned in towards him across the table. "Maybe you're right."

He leaned in, too. "I am."

She leaned further. "But what if you're wrong?"

He leaned close enough to touch her nose with his. "I'm not."

She sat back, shoulders straight, fists on her hip, head cocked upwards and her chin out. "What if I'm the one person in this room, or city, or world, or even this universe that gets to be the keeper? And I pass on the chance because I'm, what, afraid of failure, or of being wrong, or of a callous majority drafting moronic laws, or of getting my heart broken?"

Wink sat back and crossed his arms in defiance. "It will be."

"So?" Imogene closed her eyes and flattened her hand against her forehead, holding back a headache. "Listen to what I'm saying, Wink. I just found my heart last night and it already feels beaten and broken. Do you honestly believe coercion will heal it?"

"Fear might protect it."

"I've never been afraid of anything in my life!"

"Bugs. You're afraid of bugs."

"*Ugly* bugs."

"And, dirt."

"I most certainly am not afraid of dirt. Granted, I don't like getting my hands dirty. Or, being in a dirty place. Or, touching a dirty surface."

"And, dirty people."

"Oh, yes, that's true. Dirty people scare me. Well, not scare. Repel."

"Repulse."

"Better yet. Repulse."

"They do, me, too."

"It's the first thing that attracts me to someone."

"Clean?"

"The cleaner the better."

"So, Mo, you're saying, as long as a person is clean you aren't afraid of him?"

"Him? I'd be wary. But clean women don't scare me."

"Serial killers lean towards clean."

"That's your go back and collect two hundred dollars card, Wink?"

"Insofar as fear being a good thing in terms of protection from heartbreak and," he shrugged, "serial killers which, she could be, you don't know."

"Then let me rephrase. I'm not an imbecile. Maybe I'm naïve about some things, but I do have a keen intuition — which you might call fear — that makes me cautious and changes my direction at times. But until the hair raises on the back of my neck, I don't quit and run."

"You're quitting me."

"I'm not quitting you."

"You're quitting us, then."

"That's somewhat true," she conceded, "So, I stand corrected, because I won't marry you. But it isn't from fear. And, while I'm not altogether staying, neither am I running away."

"Could I be gettin' you two somethin'?" Charlene intruded, unable to eavesdrop in any other way. The place was filling up again and she couldn't dawdle long at the nearby booths, pretending to mix up orders.

"Charlene, go away!" Wink snapped.

"Oh now that be cold, Mr. Wink."

"I apologize. And you're right. Here." He handed her a crisp, clean ten. "Could you leave us alone a little longer? So we can talk. Man to woman."

"You be needin' any luck with that Mr. Wink?"

"That does it. Gimme back the ten."

"No. This is me be goin'. Watch me be wigglin' on away. But I be bringin' the check 'cause you can't be sittin' here 'less you be plannin' ta eat again. Sorry. Not my rules."

They both liked Charlene and continued to stare in her direction, filling the lull while calculating what to do next. Finally, Wink said, "It feels like I'm being gotten rid of."

Imogene looked at him with kind eyes, caring more deeply about him than she ever had. He'd been her protector and guardian, one of three people who helped shield her until her first love came along. "What's that mean — gotten rid of?"

"It's like Dory said to me earlier. She's alone after catching her girlfriend messing around behind her back."

"I didn't know. I'm sorry to hear that. I don't like cheaters." She paused. "Is that what you think I've done here, Wink? That I somehow cheated on you when I went searching for this woman without telling you first?"

"No!" He brushed off her remark before grabbing it back. "Okay, yes, maybe a little. But mostly I was thinking of what Annie-O did to Dory, that's all." Wink specifically said the name of Dory's ex, hoping it was enough of an enticement. He had no idea where sowing the seed might lead, but if it could return Imogene to him, it was worth his planting.

"Annie-O?"

"Yes." *Reel her in slowly*, he thought. *Keep the line loose.*

"Does Annie-O have a last name?"

"Something Irish I think. Like O'Sullivan, but not that. Not O'Grady, or O'Rourke. Not O'Malley. O'Brien, maybe. No. Not that."

"O'Hara?"

"That could be it." He pretended to think. "Yes, that sounds like it. Annie O'Hara."

Imogene was suspicious. It might be a small world — but it wasn't miniscule.

"I went to school with an Annie O'Hara."

"Really? Huh. You've never mentioned her to me."

"We both worked at the same ad agency before I changed jobs last year."

"That's right. I keep forgetting you're on the catwalk now."

"In the rag trade."

"Still, how well could you have known this Annie person? I mean, her name's never come up. And now that I think of it, you never said why you abruptly switched jobs."

Imogene stared hard at Wink, watching for some a clue to subterfuge. She told herself to wait for it until...there it was, the lean back look away with a nonchalant, one hand rub of his chin. It meant he knew all about Annie O'Hara and probably Elaine Trouvé, too. He was baiting her, but why? What did it have to do with them?

"It's a long story."

"Shorten it."

She sensed a showdown. He feared a setback. She faltered first.

"I'll make you a deal, Wink. If you'll accompany me to the hotel where this woman might be, and stay long enough for me to see if she is, I'll tell you about Annie."

"Oh now Mo, I would have gone with you anyhow," he bald-face lied. He'd no intention of joining her hunt and was trying his best to foil it, but was now caught in his own rat trap.

"We'll talk on our way uptown."

"Fair enough."

• • •

Charlene pocketed Wink's tip while clearing the table where he and Miss Imogene were sitting, piqued that they'd left without so much as a wave.

"It's not like I be owed one," she sulked. "It woulda been nice is all, seein' how I brat-sat Miss Imogene and did a mighty fine job at it, too!"

True, Mr. Wink forked over an extra five on top of the ten she'd weaseled out of him, so there wasn't reason to whine. But Miss Imogene left without a second thought about the kitten in the bathroom under the sink. Charlene was now stuck with taking it home, which didn't thrill her, sweet little thing that it was. She bet it was filled with a feverish disease that would make her sick, if not outright kill her.

"I be changin' the name from Petunia to Typhoid Sissy Mary," she griped.

Her anger turned to frustration when she checked on the orphan and found it missing.

"If that ain't my damn luck." She started stomping around in a fretful fit, worrying that Imogene might be back for it. "She best not be blamin' me for no kittynappin'!"

In fact, Charlene was in such a stew over not being told goodbye and having to report a missing kitten, she almost didn't see the blue Bic pen on the floor pointing towards a pair of shiny red boots sitting below the linen towel roll at the far end of the sinks.

She crept over, wondering if she was suffering from feline infectious delusion. It didn't prevent her from picking up one boot though. Turning it over, she squinted to read an inscription on the white rim of the sole: *This boot belongs to Charlene.* She quickly checked the sole of the other boot. *This boot belongs to Charlene, too!*

"Well, well," she said as she sat down and switched from her wet tennis shoes to her nearly new boots. "Lambs wool lined all the way to the tootsies. Don't that feel fine?"

For the balance of her shift Charlene strutted up and down the aisles in her red boots, even when she wasn't summoned and had nowhere to be.

"She might be Easter-lily-white and she might be rich," Charlene said to herself while handing a menu to the last diner on her shift, "but she best toughen up on her bitch-biz if she 'spects ta make it in this town."

"Who would that be, dear?" asked the early bird.

"That'd be Mo, mam. That'd be my good old friend, Miss Mo."

NINETEEN
Early Saturday Evening, March 14, 1970
Precarious Liaisons

Wink lucked out. The taxi he hailed outside The Parlor got stuck at an intersection on Sixth Avenue, halting traffic in both directions. It provided him with pry-time.

"Driver, could you stop the meter until this mess clears?"

"I could, but then you'd get the base charge for the first half mile again."

"How much would the fare be if we were still rolling?"

"The full forty blocks?"

"Yes."

"Maybe $2.75."

"If you stop the meter and don't start it again I'll give you a five now."

The driver saw the meter tallied $1.75, meaning he'd clear $3.25. "Make it six?"

"Done."

"Why not walk the two blocks over and flag a cab on Eighth, Wink?"

"At eighteen degrees out? At least we're safe and warm sitting here."

"You're right, of course. I feel I'm close to finding her, that's all. It's nerve-racking."

He settled back. "So what's this about Dory's ex, Annie?"

"Maybe it's not the same Annie."

"Sounds so. Why? Would you rather keep it secret?"

Imogene knew he was putting her on the defensive by acting innocent, as if they'd never played such games. "No secret. Pre-Wink is all."

"But if we'd gotten married I'd had heard the story eventually, right?"

"Hmm," she hedged. Imogene was a whiz at wheedling information out of others, but reticent about herself unless cornered, which she now was.

"So, spill."

"Her whole name is Anne Nancy Nicole Iris Eve O'Hara. The initials spell Annie-O."

"Catholic?"

"By birth. To her, the pulpit is a hideout for charlatans."

"Smart girl."

"But she still goes to mass every Sunday and eats fish on Fridays."

"Albeit conflicted."

"This will take longer than a traffic jam if you're going to sidebar every sentence."

"Sorry. Continue."

"We met at the American Academy of Dramatic Arts."

"Another thing you've never shared." Wink felt her glare at him.

"While there, we applied for two media openings at Mueller & Roth. She got hired on the spot. I got hired a week later because no one else answered the ad."

"You're kidding."

"Nope. I'd been a smart aleck during my interview with the department head."

"How so?"

"Her nameplate said Elaine Trouvé. Instead of looking up at me from her desk when I introduced myself, she just said she'd never heard of anyone by my name. So, I said I never heard of her name either!"

Wink laughed. "I can see you now. Was she an old prig?"

"No-o," Imogene answered warmly. "She was a beauty. She'd been a fashion model during the '40s and mellowed well. Had honed cheekbones and azure eyes that twinkled when she talked and crinkled when she laughed this slow, low, ho-ho-ho. And her complexion, oh my, like polished ivory." Imogene took a moment to envision Elaine. "She wore her hair in a bob, cut even all around and, instead of the normal graying at the temples, there were filaments of silver scattered throughout like little record needles."

"You weren't attracted?"

"Nope. So, how could I be a lesbian, right?"

Indeed, he thought. "Go on."

"But Annie fell. Hard!"

"Hold on. You mean you knew Annie was gay?"

"Suspected, let's say. I'd heard the word, but didn't understand the mechanics of it."

"You still don't."

Imogene reacted by momentarily shutting down. Being quizzed while stuck in a cab on a cold night was arduous and interfering with where she wanted to be.

"Sorry, Mo. Proceed."

"The thing is, Annie never mentioned a roommate. We bonded over our indifference to men. Even so, I was surprised to find her hung up on Elaine."

"Aside from her looks, was there reason to be?"

"I didn't think so at first. But Elaine intrigued me. She's much older but seems almost younger than us."

"Sounds pretty perfect."

"To Annie she was."

"Did they match?"

"How so?"

"Good-looking as a couple."

"Not at all. Annie was cute and homely, the same way that I'm pretty and plain."

"You're not plain."

"Yes, I am. If you take me apart, I'm quite plain."

"Where?"

Imogene turned to face him. "Look closely. My eyes are average, but my eyelashes are long. I capitalize on that. My nose is enviable, but it has a splash of freckles over the ridge. I cover those. My lips are kissable, but the fashionable red shades overpower them. So, I make-do with a less popular peach frost. My teeth look perfect, but two of my front ones are on a plate that, if I'm not careful, can pop out."

Wink leaned forward, then back to study her. "How is it I've never seen any of that?"

"Eh. It's probably because I like my face. I wouldn't switch it for any on earth."

"And, Annie?"

"Oh, well, Annie's another thing altogether! Her personality makes her. Without it, no one would give her a second glance."

"Be more specific."

Imogene dropped her head back and closed her eyes, visualizing her old friend's face. She described Annie's unbecoming tipped nose that forced one to look up her nostrils, and the heavy make-up base she wore that was two shades darker than her skin tone, producing a distracting borderline down and around her beetled chin from one ear to the other.

"Her hair is bleached flaxen and perm-burned. Her breasts are too large for her short-waist frame. She's got no butt. And the base of her neck has a dowager hump."

"She sounds like a fright!"

Imogene's eyes popped open as she reached over to touch Wink. "Yes, *except*, Annie distracts you with a gleeful gurgle in her voice, and these frolicsome eyes, and a dervish wit. It allows her to say the most outrageous things. I enjoyed Annie immensely. Her sassy bantering electrified any room she'd leap into."

"She leaped?"

"She was a leaper." They laughed. "Annie was my fun-fixation. Elaine was hers."

"Besotted by her, huh?"

"She even loved Elaine's addictions."

"A druggie?"

"No-no. But Elaine could swill gin like soda and stay perfectly poised, even when totally glazed. And, whenever she pucker-sucked Silva Thins, she'd rest her hand on the back of her hip so the smoke would rise into a halo over her head. It was amazing how she did that!"

"I dunno, Mo. Sounds to me, you were paying pretty close attention to Elaine, too."

"True, I was, but mostly through Annie's daily exaltations. I assumed she had a crush on Elaine, that's all. Both of us were still 'intact' as she used to say."

"How old were you then?"

"Nineteen. But if she was with Dory, the intact was an act."

"I thought women told each other everything."

"No. Everything we want others to believe, that's all."

By half past six their cab had managed to crawl up Sixth Avenue and hang a left on 42nd Street for a crossover to Eighth Avenue before heading uptown two more blocks.

Imogene was thinking the woman she sought had probably left for dinner by then. That is, *if* the woman was staying at The Royal Manhattan Hotel and *if* Imogene could find the room number and *if* the woman wanted to see her again.

Wink was thinking the woman had played Imogene and the hotel would be his salvation.

"If this turns out to be a wild goose chase, can we grab dinner at the Empire, Mo?"

"Yes. But only *if*, okay?"

The driver pulled the cab up close to the curb where the Royal Manhattan Hotel had rolled out a scarlet carpet from its beveled glass doors down a right angled ramp to the street. A white-gloved doorman in a gold buttoned, double breasted, bright red military greatcoat, black boots and matching brim cap stood eager to welcome guests and sightseers alike.

Imogene scurried past the mascot, into the lobby and over to the front desk, leaving Wink to wait in the atrium of ficus trees, stretched out on a salmon colored upholstered couch of an olive green palm leaf pattern.

"Can I help you, Miss?"

"I'm looking for a blonde lady who's about five foot six, with..."

The desk clerk cut her short. "She said you'd be dropping by, but I think she expected you earlier, even before they went to the theatre."

"They went to the theatre?"

"This afternoon. She and her three gentlemen friends are at dinner now."

"Three men?"

"Don't worry. Separate rooms. She asked that you please leave her a note."

Imogene wrote her name and number on a sheet of the hotel's embossed stationary the clerk provided, folding and placing it in a matching envelope before sealing it and handing it back.

"Thank you, sir. You have no idea how happy I am."

"Oh-h now, I might have an inkling. I'll be certain she gets this the minute she returns."

Plopping down next to Wink afterwards, she longed to spend the night right there on that sofa amid the fragrance of fresh flowers wafting, and tree leaves rustling in a fan fed breeze to the lullaby of piped-in music.

"How'd it go, Mo?"

"She was expecting me sooner."

It startled him. "What?"

"The clerk said so. She must have described me to him because he promptly handed me pen and paper to jot her a note."

"Seriously?"

"Dead."

"Impressive," he was loath to admit.

Imogene locked her arm through his, tilted her head, and cuddled up to his shoulder. "She and I must be carrying the same torch, huh?"

"Different torches. Same fire."

"The clerk was a little cheeky."

"How so?"

"He smirked the whole time."

"He's gay. That's why. He had her number and now he has yours."

"How can you tell?"

"It's a high frequency feeling you develop — appropriately punned gaydar — where you sense someone's in the life by looking at him."

"In what life?"

"The gay life. You should take notes."

"Why take notes when I have you as my gay guru?"

Wink thought about that, wishing it was true, accepting it wouldn't be much longer. He laid his cheek on the top of her head and closed his eyes as if to give her his blessing.

"So, dinner's on?"

"Yes." Pulling a hanky out of her pocket, she yawned into it. "Let's."

TWENTY
Saturday Night, March 14, 1970
Empire Empathy

For Imogene, returning to the Empire was like being locked in an Art Moderne time warp of stainless steel diners, each with a monitor roof and neon letters spelling out the eatery name. Inside, a wall of windowed booths with red laminated tabletops and red-cushioned seats was separated by a narrow, linoleum aisle and parallel line of countertops fronting steel stools where customers swirled while awaiting food chosen from an elongated overhead menu.

Unlike the encroaching trend toward haphazard splatter, Imogene favored the delineation, shapes and symmetry of the Moderne style. It was inspired, ingenious, candid and clean, similar to the qualities she sought in people.

Imogene and Wink rode to the Empire Diner in silence, a comfortable distance between them, lost in their separate thoughts.

She hoped to avert his further reexamination of her life, finding the practice of telling one's back-story laborious, preferring to quit a friendship rather than comply. Wink had proved an exception to the rule, as had Annie O'Hara, Elaine Trouvé, and Kirsten Sanderson.

But now she was on the verge of something delightfully different with someone altogether new. Being grilled to connect the dots from Annie to Elaine and onward felt extreme. She'd need to sort out which portions of her past to continue to conceal and which to divulge before they reached the diner. The contemplation was making her so, so-o sleepy.

• • •

April 1967

One glorious day Imogene LaPin was assigned an insufferable chore.

The Mueller & Roth agency was buried beneath a two-year buildup of media billings. Resolving the backlog required matching the minuscule type in Standard Rate & Data tomes to the figures on each statement before requesting payment. By the time the task became Imogene's, thousands of checking copies had accumulated.

"Why me?" she asked the company Comptroller, Joseph Brannigan, a towering Irish immigrant with an angular face and granite eyes who'd spent his stateside life ascending from interim mail clerk to corporate servitude. Imogene had the audacity to go over Elaine Trouvé's head and directly to him once she saw what the job entailed.

"Everyone relegated to this detail eventually quits," he answered without apology.

"If you think *I* will you can scratch that. Because I won't!"

Her attitude reminded him of his own youthful impertinence. "It must be done by someone in our media pool. You're it is all."

Imogene's bold stare was defeated by his neither looking up, nor saying more.

"Then you should have picked me to begin with," she crowed, snapping her fingers and exiting, adding, "piece-of-cake!"

The invoices were stacked ceiling high on five desktops in a dismal fifteen by twenty foot chamber where agency contract negotiations had once been hammered out. Whatever initial resolve Imogene mustered to master the undertaking quickly melted into the gloom of the room and manic monotony. She felt scourged, tackling the paper chase with crossed eyes.

After several weeks of repetitive tallying, she detected a pattern of error. For every one hundred invoices checked, an average of 3% were inaccurate by negligible amounts, most in the company's favor. As a result, she stopped examining the numbers and began mailing each invoice as accurate. Even so, due to the multiple duplicates of every bill issued after the original had been sent, it took her two months to sort, separate, and completely clear the billing backlog. A third month was frittered away to quietly reading behind the locked chamber door before the fertilizer hit the fan.

"What d'ya think you're doing?" spewed Ouzo McNoor, a caked-tooth accounts clerk angry over the influx of deposits Imogene's ploy had mysteriously required him to open, stamp, post, and file.

Imogene thought Ouzo was as plug ugly as a floating cigar butt in a mechanic's toilet. She might not have censored him for it, if his disposition allowed her that generosity of spirit. But his aversion to his own reflection left him targeting others as a means of feeding his self esteem. This time, he'd cornered Imogene on an end-of-day elevator.

"I'm doing my job," Imogene asserted, focusing on the strip of white lights flashing the floor numbers by.

"Your job is to *process* the invoices, not to rubber stamp them!"

"My job was to clear up the backlog. Which I accomplished after no one else could."

"We'll see about that!" He stood, stringent and seething while the elevator crawled to a stop, momentarily lodging the two of them alone between floors.

"Don't poop your pants, Ouzo," Imogene scoffed before shuddering at the thought.

By the time she was summoned into Joseph Brannigan's office the next morning, Imogene had her rationale rehearsed and memorized.

"What made you think you could employ dubious methods to circumvent company policy?" Brannigan boomed.

Imogene calmly explained her random selection of invoices and the error averages. "It saved you the cost of proofing, while generating a spiked cash flow resulting in a projected quarterly report with a strengthened bottom line."

Both stood silent and adamant as red blotches clawed up Imogene's neck, spreading like a lupus butterfly across her face.

He caved.

"In the future, Miss LaPin, you'll clear things through me first."

"Yes, sir," she exhaled.

"And you'll apologize to Mr. McNoor."

"Apologize, sir?"

"You insulted the nephew of a Vice President who then told his sister you'd be fired."

"I'm fired?"

"As a media clerk, yes." He dropped his eyes, letting Imogene wilt and begin to go. "But you're hired as our new Manager of Purchasing."

"I am?" She stopped without turning; waiting for her cue.

"You are."

With status came the cave as her new office, refurbished in icy pink walls, dark emerald carpeting, brass table lamps, chintz wing chairs and matching couch, fresh flowers and music filtered down through recessed ceiling speakers.

The promotion separated Imogene from Annie forevermore.

Her lunch hours became purchasing powwows and she was expected to mix with other department heads after hours, including Elaine Trouvé. The speed at which Imogene grew closer to Elaine mystified her. She would come to describe the transition as "something like chugging an emotional opiate that rendered me steadfast and ever at ease."

Nevertheless, when given the chance, she opted not to reveal Annie's hunger for Elaine.

"How well do you know Annie O'Hara?" Elaine chanced, once.

"Very. Why?"

Elaine didn't say.

TWENTY-ONE
July 1966 - August 1968
Kiss & Telltales

Elaine Trouvé lived in a Cape Cod styled house on Long Island Sound with her cousin, Kirsten Sanderson, an international airlines stewardess. As a towering Swede with sea green eyes, lanolin skin, and close clipped locks that felt like silk and smelled like lilacs, Kirsten proved a stunning presence, parading both brains and ambition up and down the aisles of the jumbo jets she was scheduled to manage for twenty-one days interspersed between every thirty. Together, Kirsten and Elaine had acquired all the amenities of seashore living, including the shared custody of a Pug named Peanut that ran freely about their fenced beachfront.

Imogene first met Kirsten after lungeing to stop the closing of elevator doors. When they popped open she was startled to see two women in the compartment standing uncommonly close against the back wall, looking caught.

One of the two was her former boss, Elaine, who'd been given a raise for clearing up the backlog in her department that Imogene eliminated, solo. Imogene hadn't seen her since being promoted, and was surprised Elaine hadn't called to thank her for the contribution her covert efforts made to both of their careers. She felt a casual acknowledgment would have sufficed. Even so, she offered a nod of respect towards both women as she stepped into the elevator.

In pivoting to face forward, Imogene caught the green-eyed beauty giving her a once-over, creating an uneasiness that was intensified by the woman's brazen introduction.

"I'm Kirsten, Elaine's cousin."

Imogene turned politely towards her and extended her hand. "How do you do? I'm Imogene LaPin."

"I'm well aware."

"You are?"

"Elaine's mentioned you many times. I pleaded with her to let me meet you, but you know how she is."

"Actually, I don't."

"She hates to intrude."

"That's admirable."

"And she's reticent."

"About?"

"Being attracted to you."

Slap her, Imogene thought. "You're mistaking attraction to with empathy for."

"Am I?"

"Your cousin helped me resolve a media concern that could have cost me my job. If it hadn't been for her understanding of my predicament, I might not be here meeting you today."

"Ah, yes, she mentioned that when it happened."

Imogene shifted her full attention to Elaine. "I was remiss in not saying thank you sooner. I hope you'll accept my apology and my appreciation that you intervened on my behalf."

The elevator eased to a stop, its doors sliding open to the main lobby. The three women exited quickly to keep from being trapped by a crowd seeking the express elevator reverting to up. As they turned to depart in opposite directions, Kirsten took hold of Imogene's elbow.

"We're grabbing lunch across the street at Schraft's. Care to come along?"

"Another time, perhaps. I'm meeting with a supplier now."

"We'll look forward to it, won't we Elaine?" Elaine remained mute. "Do you like the shore?" Kirsten continued.

"I can't imagine not."

"Our home has a private beach front."

"How fortunate."

"Why don't you come out this weekend? We'll have a cookout and chat. Elaine says you're clever."

Imogene's eyes met Elaine's again. "Oh she does, does she?"

"It's a date. You'll ride out with Elaine on Friday night and stay for the weekend." Taking Imogene's hand a second time, she held it longer than polite before adding, "Bring your suit!"

• • •

At noon the next day Elaine appeared at Imogene's office door. "Ordering in?"

"I did." Imogene pointed to the unopened bag sitting at the far edge of her desk.

"Me, too. Mind if I sit?"

"I'd like that."

Whatever past edginess either woman felt in the other's presence was gone. Now they spoke as if they'd known each other always and very much liked what they knew.

After finishing their sandwiches and second servings of coffee that Imogene perked fresh in the pot on a corner table, Elaine lit a Silva Thins and sat back. "This office is bigger than mine," she observed. "As a senior department head I'm entitled to more."

"Yours has a view of Central Park."

"For now. In no time it'll be blocked by a taller building." She looked around. "I like your office better. Why is that?"

Imogene opened a drawer to remove a glass ashtray, sliding it across the desktop.

"It's cozy."

"I'd say, intimate. And fancier." Elaine pointed to the deep cushioned couch. "Is there a fold out bed in there?"

"Well, rats, no." Imogene warmed to the notion. "It would make napping nicer, yes?"

"Napping wasn't the first thought that came to mind, but definitely, and at very least."

"I can redo your office if you'd like."

"The head honcho allows that?"

"It's totally my call now."

"Oh yeah? So. Tell me. Where do you bury the expenditure?"

"On the back of the beast. Whenever one account executive exits, another dilettante takes his place, brokering a different interior as a perk. It required us to keep a huge basement storage facility for castoffs, because the policy was to buy new. But now I recycle whatever's there. It's smarter, faster, and cheaper. Besides, most of these offices are for men. They see it's different and assume that equals new."

"I've never understood that interiors ruckus."

"Because you have no image problem."

"I don't follow." Elaine was blind to her charm, even when enticed to face it.

"Take this room. Before I redecorated, suppliers hustled me with inflated prices for stock and equipment we didn't need. They assumed I was stupid because I accepted a dark and dreary storeroom for an office. But now, they sail in, sit down, and gossip about what's going on at other agencies — then slash their prices just because they like coming back."

Elaine inhaled and held it before whistling out, "It's *you* they like."

"Thanks, but I'm the distraction proving the principle that perception is everything."

"Not everyone would agree."

"Au contraire, everyone agrees to a degree. We're all walking, talking examples of it, engaging in roles and routines to hide insecurities we can't cope with in any other manner."

"Are you suggesting life boils down to how hard, or easy we choose to make it?"

"No, not entirely. But I don't rule that out as part of the equation."

"So, you don't think being born diminutive and cute gives you an advantage?"

It pleased Imogene that Elaine thought of her as cute.

"Let's say, I use it my advantage, by not making it my disadvantage."

"I see your point. Still, I hate role-playing."

"Roles. One by day, another by night, one cosmopolitan, another country, one with family, another with friends, none totally honest, but all perfectly acceptable."

Elaine crushed out what remained of her second smoke and stood to go. "The thing is, kid, that seems too simplified."

"Life *is* simple. It's living that complicates it."

"True enough. I wonder though — are you as cavalier about love?"

"Hah! Not hardly, Elaine. I'm a complete novice in affairs of the heart. About life, too."

"You talk a good game."

"Isn't that what chats are all about? You throw something out there for a reaction that tells you everything."

• • •

Initially invited as their weekend guest whenever Kirsten was at home, Imogene was soon rewarded with carte blanche inducements to visit the cousins' compound at will, being treated more like a daughter of theirs than a colleague of Elaine's. She was designated a bedroom, a set of towels and linens, vanity space for essentials, a reserved spot in front of the television, and a permanent place setting at the table.

In exchange, Imogene surrendered her life to their private ties, readily responding to a mutual need for intense disclosure. Devotion became their lodestone; anticipation, their praxis.

The seasons glided by effortlessly for two years. Weekends began with Imogene's arrival Saturday morning in time for breakfast and proceeded through Kirsten's arranged Sunday night events, followed by Elaine and Imogene's Monday morning ride, side-by-side on the Long Island Railroad, a subway trip from the Madison Square Garden station to the Tishman Building stop, and a 37 floor elevator finale up to Mueller & Roth, concluding two days of potent fellowship.

Major holidays were enjoyed together. Road trips had Imogene seated between them up front. And, any party that the cousins agreed to attend required an extra invitation for Imogene from the hostess. The rare time Imogene was left out of the cousins' loop was when Elaine and Kirsten took their annual vacation abroad, entrusting their prized Pug to the care of their esteemed friend.

Upon return from one such venture, the three of them celebrated Imogene's twenty-first birthday at a seaside restaurant where Kirsten arranged to have Imogene's name put up in lights on the outside marquee. To Imogene, who couldn't recall ever celebrating her birthday as a child, the gesture seemed enormous and touched her deeply. Afterwards, they gave Imogene a kitten, intended to keep her mindful of them during their weekday periods apart. She tickled them by naming the tomcat, Pansy.

The trio stood out. Imogene was often mistaken for one or the other's daughter or niece. Not that the three looked even remotely alike, but they resembled each other enough in their mannerisms and camaraderie to make any visual error understandable. Some went so far as to say the three women embodied an ideal friends-forever milieu that children's programs invent; as if forever meant for always, instead of for now.

One summer afternoon while relaxing on the lanai and savoring a briny breeze wafting off Long Island Sound, Elaine positioned her chaise lounge directly behind Imogene's. During a lull in their conversation, Elaine's big toe wormed its way between the chair's webbing to caress the bared skin inside Imogene's bikini bottom.

"Not a goose," she'd later say. "A gander."

It got Imogene's attention, primarily due to the presence of Kirsten picking up shells on the shoreline, within toe-down visibility.

Imogene turned to Elaine and, acting more perplexed than offended, gently guided her foot away. But later that night, in the dark silence of suggestion that often wrestles sleep, a vague feeling of guilt beset her.

The following evening, Kirsten fled.

"I've been called to fill in on a flight to Paris tonight," she said, "then on to Berlin before heading to London. If it's okay with you, Imogene, I'll park my car at the station so you can drive it here next Saturday morning."

"You needn't." Imogene jumped up, eager to assist her. "I can wait for the train with you now and return your car tonight."

"No, no. If I'm back early in the week I'll want it sitting there for me." And like *that*, she was out the door without so much as a hug, a kiss, or further ado.

It left Elaine and Imogene alone.

For months Imogene had been pestering the cousins for a look-see at a stack of neatly labeled photograph albums stored atop a kitchen cupboard. Until then, Kirsten and Elaine had refused all her attempts at invading that one realm of their privacy. But on this tempestuous night Elaine was tippled, serving to cloud her judgment, dilute her resistance, and give her the courage to come clean. After some hemming and hawing she relented, on the condition she could hover while sitting on the arm of the easy chair Imogene rushed to, opening an album on her lap.

Elaine began the wistful process of putting names to faces as Imogene browsed through pages of women from out of their past, most of them friends, not all of them fully clothed.

"That's Corrine." Elaine's fingertip lighted on a back row image near the crimped edge in a black and white snapshot showing a group of girls gathered at an outdoor café. "My first."

Imogene missed the clue. "Was she French?"

"Oh, yes!" Elaine alluded. "Very Voltaire in our clandestine culture. As every woman there would tell you."

They remained silent for a moment, each in her own private world, Imogene transfixed in musings and Elaine in memories.

Neither of them heard the key in the lock.

Kirsten's return to the sight of Imogene and Elaine sitting together caused voices to be raised and callous accusations to flow. It began with Kirsten objecting to their close proximity, followed by allegations of hanky-panky while she was away. But rather than flat-out denying it, Elaine counterpunched.

"It sounds to me," Elaine slurred with booze-diffused logic, "like the pop calling the kettle black."

Imogene looked up from her browsing long enough to insert, "Pot."

"That, too!" Elaine added.

"You've been devising this all along," accused Kirsten.

"Oh no, here we go with you shifting your titty flings with crew chicks onto me sitting home alone until you return to say you're always too tired."

"You've no proof of that! Besides, this isn't about me, or what you think I might have done. This is about what's going on right here under my nose."

"You haven't allowed anything to go on under your nose for a year now. Or should I say — that included *me*!"

"Well, maybe if you didn't drink so goddam much all the time."

"Well, maybe if you didn't bitch about my drinking so goddam much all the time."

"And stink from those goddam cigarettes you're always sucking on."

"Sucking that I'm forced into doing to calm my nerves."

"Forced into, my ass! No one ever forces you to do anything, including cheat on me!"

"I'm forced to put up with you giving me crap all the time."

"I see you're not *denying* what's going on here."

"Why bother? You're gonna believe whatever you want, so you can cover up your own pussyfooting around."

"With whom?" Kirsten fumed.

"You tell me! You're the pussyfooter!"

The blame and condemnation continued for a full five minutes before ending abruptly when Kirsten harnessed the frantic dog (that had run to and fro trying to calm them) and raged out, slamming the back door, cracking the glass in the process.

During the cousins' fevered face-off, Imogene remained puerilely focused on their trinity, blind to any bitterness and deaf to all discord. Even after Elaine staggered out to pursue Kirsten, Imogene blithely continued looking at photographs, "La de-da de-da," with a whistle here and a hum there. It wasn't the first time the two had bickered in code around her; she couldn't foresee it as being the last.

But when Elaine returned with her lip split, Imogene darted to get a soft, damp cloth.

"What in the world, Elaine! Did you fall?"

Elaine eased herself into the vacated chair and pressed the cold cloth to her lip before handing it back to Imogene and lighting up. "Sort of. But not hard. And not for long." Leaning back with her leftover tumbler of scotch balanced in one hand and a lit butt dangling in the other, Elaine looked up at Imogene, woozily. "Long story or short?" she offered.

"Short and quick."

"Me and Kirsten are lovers. Not cousins. The end."

"Lovers. Uh-huh. That's more of a short-short."

"Kirsten thinks you and I are doing it."

Imogene pushed a hassock up closer to Elaine and sat. She leaned forward with her elbows on her knees, making certain not to miss a word.

"Kirsten thinks we're doing, what?"

"Which I was," Elaine continued. She gulped the scotch and winked. "But! With Annie."

"Annie? My Annie? Annie O'Hara?"

"Shh! Kirsten doesn't know about Annie, and you can't tell." Elaine grabbed Imogene's hand. "Swear."

"Yes, I swear. I guess. It's...I'm confused. Where? When? You're always with us."

"At work, mostly," Elaine divulged. "In your office. Whenever you left the building. It was the lure of lamplight and locked doors. You almost caught us once."

"Caught you?"

"Remember the time you couldn't get your key to work?"

Imogene did. She'd raised hell about it when the locksmith finally arrived, then looked like a dolt when he easily opened the door.

"We were jamming it from inside until you left for help. Then we slipped out."

"What were you doing in there?"

"Geez-Louise! You're such a dumb little kid sometimes. What'd'ya think?"

The sneer stung, but discovering that Annie was closer to Elaine's heart than she was brought Imogene nearly to tears. "So, you two limited your rendezvousing to my office?"

"No." Elaine was blasé. "Whenever I visited my mom, Annie rode along."

"What did your mother think?"

"Dunno. She's comatose. But mother wouldn't have approved," Elaine scowled. "She wasn't ever keen on Kirsten, even back when I needed her most."

A disquieting awareness came over Imogene: she'd been engaged in a tender tug-of-war with this much older woman for a very long time

— perhaps, from the moment they met. Yet not once had she realized, it didn't matter that nothing carnal had occurred between them, because flesh could no longer shield her from a smoldering intimacy, nor protect her from the unbridled sorrow of saying goodbye.

TWENTY-TWO
Saturday Night, March 14, 1970
Elucidation

"What are we doing here?" Imogene yawned.

"The kitten woke up while you dozed. Home was the better choice." Wink bent back into the cab to thank the driver for turning his radio off while they sped uptown to West 85th instead of down to the diner on West 22nd.

"Was I out long?" She clutched his arm as they walked into the whitestone and up the stairs, he carrying the shopping bag of spent clothes and she carrying the kitten.

"About twenty minutes. You talked some."

Wink entered the apartment ahead of her, checking the rooms and turning on lights. Even though the first block off the Park from Columbus Circle to West 86th was deemed safe, he took no chances with her well-being.

She placed the kitten on the floor calling out, "Pansy! We have a daughter for you."

"Don't you think you should drop the little darling into the litter box first?"

Pansy jumped from his perch on the sideboard and crept over to the moving bundle of fur, hoping for a bug to bat at, bite into, and trot around in triumph. Instead, he began sniffing the kitten and cleaning it.

"Damned if you didn't make a fairy out of that cat, Imogene."

He picked the kitten up and carted it to the bathroom with Pansy tagging along while Imogene put an aluminum percolator on the stove, filled it with water, inserted its stemmed metal basket, added Maxwell House grounds, capped them with a strainer, secured its glass knob lid, adjusted the blue flame of the gas burner beneath it, waiting long enough to hear the gurgle and see a first perk before setting an egg timer for six minutes.

"You want something with this?" she offered as he passed behind her on his way back to the living room. "Sandwich? Doughnut?"

"You have doughnuts?"

"Plain and powdered."

"Both!"

Wink arranged some kindling and enjoyed the whiff of sulfur from the Diamond match as he lit a fireplace log and became engrossed in watching it burn, undisturbed by the chime of the timer. Imogene transferred the boiling brew into her grandmother's Barvarian chocolate pot and served it to them in matching china cups balanced on a tin tray.

The room felt toasty with its soft-pink 3-ways set on low, a period portrait of a young woman positioned over the mantle, two floral pattern rugs on the parquet floors, and a wall of shelving holding hardback books intermixed with figurines, each one with a story attached to a special time in Imogene's life. The scene was set.

"So, who's Kirsten?"

Imogene hadn't intended on revealing any additional Elaine chapters of her life, deleting Kirsten altogether. He'd caught her unawares. "Kirsten?"

"You mentioned her in your sleep."

"I did?"

"Distinctly."

"Anyone else?"

"Nope. She was the one mystery Miss."

"It's because she's BW." He looked puzzled. "Before Wink."

"That would include pretty much everyone, wouldn't it?"

"I suppose."

"So, again, who was she?"

Imogene groaned. "Someone Elaine introduced me to."

"Dory's-Annie's-Elaine?"

"Kirsten is Elaine's cousin."

"Errrrnt! Lesbians."

"What?"

"Cousin is code, honey. Anytime a woman introduces another woman as her cousin, that woman is probably her under covers lover."

"Well, I didn't know that at the time." She refilled their cups, exasperated. "Honestly, Wink, you should write a book of queer catchalls. I predict a bestseller."

"How couldn't you know?"

"Okay, maybe...*maybe* there was once a teensy inkling I knew without knowing. Like I know that light will turn on when I flip the switch." She pointed to the Stiffel candlestick lamp next to the wing chair where he sat with his legs crossed and his cup resting in the flat of one hand like a model posed for a photograph. "But it's not a sure thing until *after* I flip it and the room lights up. That kind of unknowing. Elaine was my colleague and Kirsten was her cousin. It's what they told me. It's what they wanted me to think. And it worked for me."

"Then Elaine was nothing more than a colleague?"

"Elaine was my best friend," she answered, reluctantly. "As a kid I never had one. So she was my first real friend."

"And by 'friend' you mean...?"

"Oh for crying out loud, Wink. Is that word code, too?"

"Unless 'girl' is prefixed. Look, I've been taking you to a dyke dugout for a year without you showing any hint of being one. Now you're saying your best friend was a lesbian all along, plus your classmate Annie, plus Kirsten." He began imitating a newscaster at a crime scene. "Will the body count never end? Film at eleven."

"Fine, Wink," she laughed, appreciating his parody as the best cure for crankiness. "It's no to the use of cousin. No to the use of friend."

"No to the use of pussy."

"I can't say pussy?"

"Every time you say it I snigger, waiting for you to let it loose in public."

"One of my pet poems of the 19th century is *Faithful Pussy*. Have you heard it?"

"Ah-h, no."

"Would you like to?"

"Again, no."

"But I've always been fond of that word."

"Why am I not surprised?"

"Can I say pussycat?"

"No."

"Pussy willow?"

"No."

"Pussyfooting?"

"No."

"Puss-in-Boots?"

"If you must. But never without the galoshes."

"That really rots my socks," she protested. "I bet men are the ruination of this."

"Indubitably."

Upon hearing the repetitive mangling of his nickname, Pansy pranced in carrying the kitten by its neck and jumped up on the couch to settle down. Imogene and Wink stopped conversing long enough to delight in Pansy's demonstrative love for Petunia. He saw it as between two tomcats. She saw it as between mother and daughter.

"Hold on, Imogene," Wink snapped back. "You never had a friend growing up?"

"No friends. We were one of those picture perfect families with elephantine skeletons in the closet. It taught me to be an avid listener only. I never shared anything personal about myself. Until I met Elaine and Kirsten, I never fit in. Elaine was the first person I told the truth about me to. The first person I truly trusted and cared about."

"When did you find out about Annie?"

"At the very end. Annie was the proverbial fat lady singing."

"Are you still angry at them?"

"Who?"

"Elaine and Annie. For their betrayal."

"No. I was disappointed," Imogene pouted, "and felt wretched over it. But not angry. Because the adage is true — that you never forget your first."

"Love, Imogene. You never forget your first *love*."

"That remains to be seen. But I'll never forget Elaine. She genuinely cared about me. She watched over me, same as you do, Wink. She helped me get to here. Elaine was my first, in that respect. So no, I wasn't angry. But when I walked into her office one morning and found her gone — I was crushed."

TWENTY-THREE
Wednesday, August 21, 1968
All Sorts Of Sisters

Three weeks after the Kirsten debacle, Imogene learned that Elaine and Annie had jumped ship without giving notice.

Annie pinned a note to the needlepoint pillow on Imogene's office couch that read: "I'm inconsolable. My Laineylips left me. I can't be anywhere we've ever been together. Forgive my omissions. Forget my admissions. Adieu!"

Elaine just left.

As a low level clerk, there wasn't a way to learn where Annie went, but as a corporate executive, Elaine could be tracked by agency headhunters. They said she made a lateral move to a Madison Avenue firm, accepting a modest office for a larger salary and fancier title. Imogene obtained her new number within minutes.

"Is she in?"

"No," her secretary said. "Who's calling?"

"Imogene LaPin."

"Is there a message?"

"Lunch tomorrow, your choice, my treat, call to confirm."

"I'll see that she gets it."

Imogene hung up, determined to salvage whatever she could of whatever they'd once had. But by the time she left work that day, Elaine still hadn't checked back.

She knew she could find Elaine standing on the LIRR platform where the bar car halted for those catching the 5:35 to Oyster Bay. And, as much as she wanted to do that, she also knew better than to force a confrontation.

Yes, Elaine's indebted to me, she thought to herself as she walked home through Central Park, hiding her tears behind the faux tortoise shell Foster Grants that Kirsten took off and gave to her after Imogene casually mentioned liking them. *But feeling beholden breaks many a bond.*

• • •

Her lingering hope that Elaine would call stretched into weeks before the hurt in her heart forced Imogene to examine her new awareness of female familiarities. She decided she'd need to understand their actions and emotions, even if it encumbered the burgeoning intensity of her own.

Jump-starting this quest meant scouring the classifieds of The Village Voice, a newsprint tabloid popularized by its inside back page of quirky things to do. It was there she found a listing for the monthly meeting of The Daughters of Bilitis. Being a bona fide Daughter of the American Revolution, she assumed the Bilitis ladies were similar and safe.

"First I'll qualify for admittance," she predicted to Pansy, "whereupon they'll welcome me into their inner sanctum."

August is a wicked month in Manhattan. The heat oozes upwards from the pavement to sodden the fresh and sabotage the fashionable by smearing skin with a wet, itchy film likened to congealed bacon grease.

It makes being stylish challenging, but Imogene thought a club with as prestigious a name as The Daughters of Bilitis would require it.

For the occasion, she selected a sleeveless, lemony linen dress and matching collarless coat; a wide brimmed, satin-sashed, Anne of Green Gables bonnet; a pair of English, double woven, white cotton gloves; white patent leather pumps and a singular string of pink antique pearls — convinced her outfit would defeat the late-day swelter of the city streets.

Instead, it proved a dead-duck-walking suit to those curb sitters seeking a diversion from their suffocating tenements near the Ninth Avenue meatpacking district where the meeting was to be held. After much misdirected fun played at her expense (turning her seven block walk from the subway station into a fourteen block trek), she finally wised up and reached the rundown fifth floor walkup posted with a handwritten *DOB Meeting Upstairs* handbill.

The meeting room was nothing more than a gutted loft stretching for a half city block with windows painted shut on the street side. Overhead lights producing harsh beams fevered the space to stifling while freestanding industrial-size fans whipped it in four directions. The noise made from the rotating blades required hollering in order to be heard.

To one side, a portable microphone connected to mismatched speakers was mounted on a tripod and arranged on a makeshift platform opposite refreshments spoiling on plywood and sawhorse tables. Folding chairs filled the center area with seating for fifty where seventy had already gathered.

"Hello," Imogene radiated, her outstretched, thumb-cocked hand aimed at the foursome crowding the door. "Could you gentlemen direct me to the Daughters of Bilitis meeting?" Her entrance created a creeping hush as all eyes converged on her. "Please?" she added, unaware she'd mistaken the suit and tie, Florsheim shod, flattop boogie semi-ducktailed daughters for sons.

"Bitch!" one spit, still reeling from the fractious coalition aimed at ousting proclaimed lesbians from the equal rights movement. "Snooping bitch," she added, taking to the stage, calling for a rant against the "yellow turd feminist infiltrator and all patriarchal societies bridled by propriety and plucked body parts." A ruckus erupted.

Imogene might have heard the jeer and the gargantuan gaffe might have registered as blundering to her, if only the long taunting walk, the odious multistory climb and the oppressive heat hadn't coalesced to make her queasy and on the brink of fainting.

The moment the guest speaker (who bore a remarkable resemblance to Beryl Reid in *The Killing of Sister George,* appropriately costumed in an identical belted raincoat and black fedora) seized the mic to insist the audience quiet down, an elfinesque, tousled mop, cat's-eyed blonde hovering craftily close grabbed Imogene's arm and dragged her from the den, down all five flights of stairs and out onto the pavement. The sky was black by then. The streets, quiet.

"I'm Lindsay Briggs," the girl huffed, squeezing Imogene's hand in both of hers. "You're a brave woman to show up here. Were you sent to incite us? Because it definitely worked!"

"Sent?" Imogene reeled, still woozy.

"By the National Organization."

"Of?"

"Women!" Lindsay began guiding Imogene back towards the Klein's Square station, trying to distance them from any chance of being chased.

"No. No one sent me. Certainly not them." Imogene barely kept pace, answering out of a sense of obligation.

Staying several steps ahead while walking backwards, Lindsay asked, "Why?"

"For suggesting they change the equal rights amendment text from one gender to none."

"Again, why?"

"I thought it would sell better."

"I don't get it."

Imogene stopped to catch her breath and remove her coat. "Rats. My hat. Where's my hat? My gloves?" She looked back on the hatless, gloveless sidewalk.

"You can forget that hat. It was either you, or it. Anyway, Alexander the Great said the spoils belong to the victor. You know he was gay, right?"

"Alexander didn't say that."

"No?"

"A 19th century senator did."

"I'm pretty sure it was Alexander."

"Regardless, it doesn't apply because the actual saying goes, 'To the victor belongs the spoils of the enemy' and I wasn't the enemy."

"Trust me, you were. And they got your hat to prove it."

Imogene motioned Lindsay to a stoop. She needed to recharge and make sense of the melee. A stoop seemed as good a place as any. "Sit?"

"Sure. But I had the gay part right, right?"

"Technically? No. He was married three times and fathered children, but Mary Renault wrote about his preference for men in general and his best friend, Hephaestion, in particular. Although, I don't see what his personal life has to do with anything."

"It's what we do," effused Lindsay, hoping the Bilitis incident hadn't soured Imogene on her. "We stake claim to everyone of influence who was gay. It validates gay as good. If you hate gays, you hate Alexander the Great, Joan Baez, Tallulah Bankhead, Leonard Bernstein, Lord Byron, Truman Capote, Willa Cather..."

"Wait. You memorized their names in alphabetical order?"

"More than three hundred so far. Joan Crawford, Quentin Crisp, Marlene Dietrich, Isadora Duncan..."

"Crawford? Duncan?"

"They were bisexual."

"So-o, what? You get half of them?" Imogene turned her head in all directions.

"What are you looking for?"

"Making sure you're for real."

Lindsay stood and stepped away. It gave Imogene the opportunity to study her. The girl was impishly cute, even though her large breasts were out of proportion to her nearly nonexistent belted waist. A glance below the hemline of her khaki shorts revealed the common characteristics of an athlete's legs. She wore mahogany, penny-loafers with neither pennies nor socks, a white cotton shirt with the long sleeves rolled up to the elbows, a red bandana looped around her neck and wood rings on three fingers, like those found in beach resort gift shops. Imogene had never been to a resort, but people she knew who lived on the upper east side often sported such rings.

"I'm betting you made enemies at NOW, too."

"Does shunning count?" Imogene started to feel better.

"I can't pretend I'm surprised."

"I wouldn't have believed you if you tried."

Lindsay looked bit by her words.

"Listen, Lindsay. There's no excuse for rude and I'm being that. I'm sorry."

"S'ok." They shook and began anew. "So, what's this about a genderless proposal?"

"It's pretty simple. We're all single from the time we're born until we're married, if we do. Then single again between divorces and the survivor half of us before we die."

"So?"

"So, the equal rights amendment pits women against men. I have no qualms about that in general. But in this instance, if they'd replace the women's rights requirement with singles' rights wording, we'd get all the privileges due us and the protection needed, without a gender war."

Lindsay studied Imogene's features while absorbing her thoughts. She liked what she saw and heard, enough to ask her on a date if she dared.

"That would work especially well for lesbians."

"Yes." Imogene stood and took one last hopeful look behind them for her hat before starting towards the subway again.

"What did the leaders say?"

"They joined in booing me out the door."

"Us, too. Our kind," Lindsay owned up. "They think they'll get it ratified without us."

"With or without, it won't ever be ratified as currently worded."

"You could be wrong."

"I'll clap the loudest if I am."

"For being wrong?"

"Naturally. If I'm wrong, we all win. But if I'm right, everyone loses. No good comes from my being right."

"Say, do you feel like drinking to that? My treat."

Imogene imagined the piano bar at The Drake, or maybe a deep, soft couch in the lobby of the Algonquin. She didn't think Lindsay meant then and there, at a grim looking bar where a menacing sentry kept watch. The name scrawled on cardboard over the door read: COOKIES.

"It's okay," Lindsay told the guard. "She's one of us."

Once they cleared the double door entry and started up two levels of stairs, Imogene nudged, "What kind of place is this?"

"A lesbian club. That's the last man you'll see again before leaving here."

"Oh swell. Another club. What's it take to be a member of this one?"

Lindsay flashed a look back at her. "Are you putting me on?"

"Yes," Imogene lied, having cursory thoughts of Elaine and Kirsten, Annie and Dory, Lindsay, the den of daughters, and now, herself — all awry.

There was an acrid aura about Cookies, murky and smoky and sordid with moaning music. Shoddy café tables secured from former establishments were spaced close together, each encircled by shortened ladder-back chairs. The walls were papered in brothel-red flocked flowers. The stemmed glasses hanging from a rack over the jerry-built bar bore visible fingerprints on most and lipstick imprints on some.

The bartender was woeful: the type of woman whose eyes lay bare a heart older than her head and grayer than her hair. Behind her, a mirrored wall reflected melancholy. Women mingled, mostly in shadows.

As Imogene stood silent, wishing for lightning to strike her, Lindsay hurried off with a dance offer, promising to return. It left Imogene temporarily trapped between courtesy and calamity. In the damp hot she felt a weary chill.

"Is this your first time here?" came a soulful voice.

Imogene looked around to her left where a woman sat alone in a booth bordering the back wall. Her hands rested lightly in her lap. Her eyes were blurred from imbibing warm wine. A dribble of Burgundy remained in a glass on the table before her. Imogene visualized L'Absinthe by Degas, saturnine and resigned.

"Yes, it is."

"I'm Marie. We're here for my birthday."

"How old?"

"Thirty-one," the woman groaned.

"Nine years older than me," Imogene calculated while looking around for Marie's party, seeing no one nearby. "I'm sorry. That slipped out. I'm nervous."

"You needn't be. My friend will be right back. Would you like to join us?"

Imogene suspected she'd been intentionally left as bait in a dive she'd never return to again. But the woman was being kind.

"I would," Imogene offered, wanting to simply sit there for a minute to satisfy an odd craving for the nearness and pretense of protection. "But I can't. I need to go. But thank you. Marie, is it?" They matched each others fixed look for a moment longer than felt safe before Imogene added, "Happy birthday!"

Once back on the street Imogene slipped into her coat before hailing a cab. It was still early for a New York night and she was hungry, but decided against stopping for takeout before heading home. She felt tired and tarnished from risking her life twice that day, or so it seemed.

As she peered solemnly out the window, flashing by people standing on street corners, she began dreading the arrival of a Friday without somewhere to go and someone to belong to. She searched unfamiliar faces for encouragement, but saw none. She listened for the voice in her head, but heard nothing. She sought celestial guidance in a new direction, but was heading back from where she began hours earlier and every bit as lost.

There was no way she could have known — nor was there reason to imagine — the first lines she'd pen in her journal once the weekend arrived would be: *Saturday, August 24, 1968. This morning I met the nicest fellow. Her name is Wink.*

TWENTY-FOUR
Saturday night, March 14, 1970
One Ringa-dinga-ling

Imogene bolted from where she was stretched out on the couch across from Wink and flung herself towards the sideboard where the hefty, black Stromberg-Carlson 1230 phone with its enamel dial plate and steel retainer barely rang once before she answered it, "Hello!"

"What took you so long?" came a warm-taffy drawl from the other end of the line.

Covering the receiver with one hand, Imogene did a little in-place jig, flashing a giddy look at Wink and bouncing a thumbs-up before taking a deep breath and making a halfhearted effort to sound nonchalantly.

"You're lucky I found you at all."

"I knew you would," the voice boasted back.

"Golly," she caved. "Did you? How's that?"

"Because of how we met. And how meeting you made me feel. I didn't doubt that you'd find me. Not for a minute."

Imogene lifted the phone off the sideboard and, turning the bottom side up, pressed it to her heart as she eased herself down onto the floor where Pansy was now rubbing up against her. "Meeting you made me feel special, too."

"Okay. Enough chitchat. When can I see you?"

"Ah-h...it's...8:26 now. How's does 9:31 sound?"

"Thirty-one?"

"Is that too late?"

"For a Saturday night? Hardly. Make that, perfect. Thirteen is my lucky number, so I pay attention to any variation of it, like forty-nine, fifty-eight, sixty-seven. I combine numbers for everything I do. It makes 9:31 perfection."

"That's incredible."

"I'm told, odd. But you're my first incredible."

"No, I mean, thirteen is my lucky number, too. I do the same. Make lunch dates at 12:19 and schedule appointments for 1:03, or 2:47, or 3:55. If I can't leave work at 4:54, I wait until 5:08. Or, I settle for two numbers adding up to 13 in a sequence of three or more. Even my birthday totals 13."

"Mine, too!"

"Oh *no* it does not!"

"Oh *yes* it does too! This is blowing me away."

"Then, I hope you're sitting down."

"Will lying down do?"

"It will."

"Done. Now tell me, why?"

"A split-second before you came through the door at Johnny's last night, I glanced up at the clock behind the bar and it was 11:58." Imogene sensed the woman's awe before adding, "on Friday the thirteenth."

For a moment the two of them seemed suspended as one in space.

"Is it Twilight Zoney on your end of the line?" Imogene finally asked.

"I was beginning to think I was alone in that." Another silence slipped by before the woman suggested, "Maybe you should hang up and hightail it here to me."

"I will. But tell me one thing, first?"

"Shoot."

"What's your name?"

"Izzy."

"Izzy." Imogene said the name aloud while standing back up and turning towards Wink, who'd been watching her every move and listening to her every word. She spoke the name again for him, "Izzy," while holding the phone high, unaware that her eyes were as happy as his heart was glum. "Is Izzy short for Isabel?"

"No. Worse. It's a nickname for Eloise."

Two things happened, instantly.

First, the line went dead. Imogene was so stunned to learn the woman's name was Eloise, she inadvertently disconnected the call when she dropped the weighted phone base on her left baby toe and collapsed to the floor, yowling. Second, Eloise tried calling her back (over and over again), but all she got was a busy signal.

"What the hell!" yelled Wink, rushing to her rescue as Pansy leaped on and off her in a panic, meowing.

"Ow-ow-ow-ow-ow-ow-ow!" she cried in a crescendo of misery. "It hurts. It hurts. Ow-w-w-w, it hurts! Oh Wink, oh Wink, oh Wink! It hurrrrrts!"

"Easy, Mogy. I'm here. Let me look at it. Easy. Easy. Calm down, calm down."

"I can't calm down," she bawled. "It hurrrrrrrrrrrrrts!"

"I can see that. The nail is bleeding. But you just nicked it."

"It's squashed. *Squashed* I tell you. It's squashed. It's squashed!"

"I'll get some ice."

Imogene beat the floor with her free fist. "Ow-ow-ow, Wink. It hurts, it hurts!"

Wink ran to the kitchen, emptied ice cubes into a large stainless steel bowl, filled the bowl with cold water, returned to where she was sobbing, wrapped his arm around her waist, lifted and swung her around and into the wing chair and plunged her foot into the ice water. It caused her to cry out even louder.

"Quiet down, Mogy," he hushed. "The neighbors will think I'm killing you."

"Not me. My toe. My poor little toe," she whimpered as the ice water began to slowly numb the pain.

"Why did you drop the phone, Mo?"

Imogene picked up the kitten that had fallen off the couch during the commotion and gestured for Pansy to hop on her lap. "Cats are so sensitive, Wink. Did you see how she came to my rescue?"

"No. I was a little busy." Wink placed the phone base back on the sideboard and set the receiver in its cradle. "You're lucky you didn't break your foot with this thing. It's heavy as hell."

"See that book?" She pointed to the one he'd retrieved off the floor when he was there earlier that morning.

"Yes."

"Pull the photograph out of it and tell me what you see."

He did. "I see you being hugged by...is that your mom?"

"Yes."

"She's a good-looking woman."

"True. But what else do you see?"

"You mean the doll you're holding?"

"A blonde haired, blue eyed doll. The first doll my mom ever gave me. Read the back."

Wink turned the photograph over and read the penciled scribble aloud. "It says, mary elloeez. 12-25-51." He looked at Imogene, puzzled. "Who's Mary Elloeez?"

"That's the name of my doll. Eloise. I was five. I wrote it phonetically. Same with marry. When she gave me the doll, I told my mom that someday I'd marry Eloise."

"I don't understand."

"The woman I'm meeting tonight. Izzy."

"Yes."

"Izzy is short for Eloise."

"No way."

"It is."

"No. No. That can't be."

"Yes, it can be. It is. Her name is Eloise."

Wink dropped the photograph onto the book and stepped away from the sideboard. "That's too, too extreme, Mo."

"Hello," she sing-songed. "I know. It's cost me a toe!"

Recognizing the unintentional rhyming of words, they each air-spit in one palm, then fist-hit it with the other and said, in unison, "Make a wish."

"I wish this wasn't happening," he said.

"I wish it was happening to both of us," she said.

"Take it back, Mogy. This is crazy. It's not to be believed. If you saw it in a movie, you'd boo. If you read it in a book, you'd burn it."

"Not if it was in *Ripley's Believe It, Or Not.*"

"Even if!"

"You're part of this, Wink."

"Not anymore. I'm bowing out. I'm stepping aside. You're on your own little girl."

"Great! Here I am, crippled for life, and you're sending me off in the dark of night to a hotel with no eyewitness for what very well could be a love affair that rivals that of...of..."

"Gertrude Stein and Alice B. Toklas."

"Right! Gertrude and Alice!" Imogene exulted. "And they are...?"

"Dead dyke doyennes. One baldish and the other mustached."

"That's it? They're the brass ring?"

"As far love and devotion goes? Yes. Stein was a writer. Toklas, her muse."

"Fine! We'll rival them, then. Do you have any books by her?"

"No. And I don't intend to read one. Frankly, I'm surprised your Island lezzies didn't turn you on to them."

"Why would they?"

"Because that's what your tribe does. You rule the bookstores, we rule the baths."

"Is that a fact?"

Wink looked at her through his hand-me-down, castoff eyes and patchwork heart, wishing that the life befitting of him would not begin for her. He hoped, if there truly was a Goddess nicknamed God nicknamed Betty as Imogene decreed, She would bypass Mo, allowing her life to be unblemished by betrayal and disappointment. He would willingly air-spit dual rhymes a trillion times if he thought he could make love go easy on her.

"Yes."

"Then I'll need to get to it. But right now we're going to meet Eloise at the hotel." He'd dried her crimson foot by then and she grimaced before hobbling to the closet and disappearing inside. "Would you feed Pansy and Petunia for me?"

She asked it of him as if nothing had changed, like they'd already been married for years and at each other's beck and call.

"I'll ride to the hotel with you," he agreed from the kitchen, "but I'm not staying for whatever's after."

Imogene emerged in a violet turtleneck and matching wool pants, primrose scarf tied in a square knot, and fleece-lined cuddle boots. She pocketed a handkerchief embroidered with violas before choosing a charcoal grey, Nehru collar, snap-front wool cape and matching gloves.

"I depend on you staying for whatever we do."

"Even hanky panky?"

"Oh, Wink. Isn't that jumping the gun a bit?"

"Not for anyone but you." He grabbed his coat. "Are you dressed warm enough?"

"As long as I don't walk the width of Manhattan, I'll be fine."

When they caught a cab from the exiting passengers heading into Imogene's building, she interpreted it as a favorable omen; he interpreted it as doom-laden. To support both theories, the cab caught all the green lights from where it turned south onto Columbus Avenue to where it crossed over to Broadway in transit to Columbus Circle and Seventh Avenue.

"How's your toe?"

"Throbbing, but bearable."

"Does that mean you won't be crippled for life?"

She laughed. "This time, anyhow."

"Good. Because there's something I need to say, Mo." She took his hand as if she knew what was coming, hoping her touch would somehow be enough to change his mind. "This is our ride into the sunset. Whatever we had, or hoped to, is done. It's over."

"It doesn't have to be, Wink."

"Yes. It does. This began as a game for us. Two people adrift who didn't want to end up alone. But the closer we became, the more I wanted our ideal to be real."

"I know."

"I don't think you do, Mo. You can't love someone you don't know. It's discovery that leads you to liking and loving in spite of your differences."

"You don't believe in love at first sight?"

"No."

"Because it hasn't happened for you?"

"Because it doesn't happen for anyone. If you don't believe me, look at all the books devoted to debunking it."

"It's not that I don't believe you. It's that books are penned opinions formed by personal experience. Those who fail claim others will as well, asserting their own history of failure as expertise. Then the selfsame experts get together to create trends supporting failure as a fact for all, encouraging and excusing it like an infantile game of follow-the-leader."

A traffic standstill on Seventh Avenue at 45th Street briefly delayed them. They watched from afar as couples gathered under Broadway theater marquees during intermissions of plays about finding and losing love.

"Tell me, Imogene, do you see all people with broken hearts as know-nothing failures?"

"No. But the ones choosing the hogwash of experts over their own intuition are."

"Well, you might be right." He sighed. "But I refuse to lose you in bits and pieces. I'm making a clean break."

The taxi started up again, turning right on West 43rd Street for a block and then north on Eighth Avenue to the hotel.

"Will you call me, Wink?"

"No."

"May I call you?"

"Don't." He squeezed her hand.

Upon reaching the entry of the hotel they'd visited together as best friends hours earlier, Wink ended it with a simple, "Goodbye, Mo."

She stayed put for a moment, staring out the window, torn between his heartbreak and her happiness, focusing on the fellow in the chesterfield coat with his gloved hand on the door handle, eager to claim their cab.

"See you all of a sudden, Wink," she promised as she slid out, intending to tell the man the cab wasn't available. Instead she looked up into his face, dumbfounded.

"Ronald Newman?"

"Imogene?"

"I thought you moved to England."

"I did. I'm in town for a week visiting Patsy."

Wink stepped out of the cab and called out over it. "This cab's taken, but I'll share it if you'd like."

Ronald Newman turned toward Wink. "Andy? Andy, is it really you?"

"I'll be damned! When did you get back in town? Where you headed?"

"The Kitty Hawk."

"Jump in. We'll go together."

Wink blew a kiss to Imogene as Ronald took her place, asking in passing, "You know Andy Wink?"

She nodded.

When shutting the door she heard Wink say, "You know Imogene? How? Where?

TWENTY-FIVE
Saturday Night, March 14, 1970
The Second Time Around

Sitting on the couch under the ficus trees in the lobby of The Royal Manhattan Hotel clutching a nosegay of lily-of-the-valley, Imogene thought Eloise resembled a cross between Lee Remick and Anita Page, typecast there as a character of quiet elegance that passersby yearn to meet.

Well, thought Imogene, *it's clear she'll be the social butterfly of the two of us.* Pleased by the notion, she waltzed over and plopped down on the couch beside Eloise, so close, they meshed from shoulder, to hip, to thigh, to knee, to calf, to ankle.

"Have you been waiting long?" Imogene cooed.

"Would it sound corny if I said all of my life?"

"Corny is good."

"All my life," Eloise twinkled.

"And, was it worth the wait?"

"For your sake, it better be!"

"Ah-ha! The woman tries sweet-talking me by ultimatum."

"Judging from the way you take to a couch? I'm thinking I'm batting a thousand in that department."

They remained silent for a moment, astonished by the odds against ever meeting again and grateful to have beaten them. Imogene thought Eloise looked delicious in her turquoise cashmere turtleneck, chosen for the ardor of her eyes. She resisted an urge to take her fingertip and run it along the ridge of Eloise's nose, from the parting of her warm golden eyebrows to the gently bent button of its tip. She admired Eloise's exaggerated cheekbones creating a subtle edge for the length of her eyelids, expanding upwards when she smiled, which she readily did; basking in Imogene's overt attentiveness and obvious approval.

"You have a gap between your two front teeth," Imogene noted.

"I hate it."

"You shouldn't. It's the mark of a beautiful woman."

"I told someone that once. Who told you?"

"My mom. She says it's been a good omen for centuries."

"For whom?"

"Omenites."

They laughed appreciably.

"Hey," Eloise spotted, "you have a gap, too!"

"It's my one claim to glamour fame. Besides, no one looks better twiddling a stem of sweet grass than gals like us."

"Becky Thatcher, eat your heart out."

"You betcha!"

"Speaking of sweet grass, I hope you like these." Eloise gave Imogene the nosegay. "It's not much, but the best I could do in a jiffy. I rescued them from a room service tray and added the used doily myself."

"Lily-of-the-valley is my favorite springtime flower."

"Mine, too."

"How about that?"

"Yeah." Eloise felt their happy-dippy-dopey thoughts collide. "How about that?"

"Okay you two, break it up! This is a respectable establishment. No doting allowed on our premises."

Imogene turned to see a lanky young man strutting towards them, his thick, sandy hair hiding his eyes in the seductive style mainstreamed by male models. He had a high pitch to his boyish voice belying most young men his age.

"Imogene, meet Martin."

"Marty, if you don't mind," he said, offering his hand to Imogene, then lifting her up by it and twirling her around when she took hold. "How do you do, my lovely?"

"Marvelously, thank you."

"I can see you've broken the spell."

"What spell might that be?"

"The one Izzy cast on herself to never again become involved with a pretty woman. How you managed to nab her will be the sizzling of our dinner conversation. May I?" He offered Imogene his arm to escort her towards the hotel's dining room. In turn, Imogene offered hers to Eloise.

Once the maître d' had seated their party of five, Imogene excused herself on the pretense of freshening up when, in truth, she needed to breathe. The jubilation she felt in the presence of Eloise coupled with their bewildering commonalities made her tremble.

She asked herself what the chances were of their meeting, falling in love, being torn apart without first exchanging names or numbers, losing each other in a city of eight million and finding each other again in less than twenty-four hours.

She factored in Eloise having the same name, hair and eye color as the doll she planned to marry at age five, added their shared quirk for deducing numbers to equal 13, the same sort of gap between their front teeth, having button noses, a fondness for specific flowers, and being slaves to color coordination.

The odds were incalculable, implausible and uncanny, yet, so. It both boggled her mind and flooded her heart with arrant joy.

Nothing Wink had harangued made sense now. Nothing she'd become privy to as Elaine's confidante equated. Nothing she heard at the Daughters of Bilitis gathering, or dodged at Cookies, or observed in all her year long trips to Johnny's even remotely compared.

As she faced her reflections on the walls of ceiling-high, gold framed mirrors stretched over white marble sinks, Imogene hoped for a sign.

She understood the ramifications of the decision that was now hers alone to make. She could follow her heart by accepting a dinner invitation, without knowing how it might end. Or, she could walk away and not look back, thereby sacrificing a short term memory of a life she imagined with Eloise for the long term certitude of what she knew of Wink.

Imogene picked up a miniature bar of soap in a turquoise blue wrapper nestled in china dishes flanking the porcelain handle faucets of each basin. She unwrapped it, flattened it out, and read the centered white lettering:

Royal Manhattan Hotel
44th to 45th STS., AT 8th AVE.
NEW YORK, N.Y.
CASHMERE BOUQUET

"Her cashmere sweater is turquoise blue and she gave me a bouquet of lily-of-the-valley," Imogene said aloud to herself.

Placing the wrapper in her pocket, she straightened her shoulders, pressed both hands over her heart, inhaled deeply, closed her eyes, exhaled sweetly, opened her eyes, turned, and strode out the door.

TWENTY-SIX
Saturday Night, March 14, 1970
Two Man Minimum

The Kitty Hawk on Third Avenue was as much of a Mecca for straight men on the make as gay, although gays would argue that all the purported straights were bisexual, and once they whisked their lady dates into the turn-of-the century renovated taproom, the action sought would be as focused on gent-gent scoring as otherwise.

At least, that was Wink and Ronald's known history at the Hawk, a loud, festive, upscale watering hole of fetishism in Brooks Brother's attire where every Hamilton changing hands had a phone number inscribed.

The old friends hadn't had time to talk. They'd been too busy holding on as the cab driver barreled recklessly across town before stopping short in front of the bar. Wink jumped out.

"I got it," said Ronald, remaining long enough to pay the fare and get the driver's name off the hack license. "Hennessey," he threatened, "if I ever have the misfortune to hail you again, you better slow the fuck down, or be prepared to pull that steering wheel out of your ass."

Once inside the barroom they sought refuge at a high circular table for two, perfect for chatting over and cruising around. Wink and Ronald had been lovers for a time, but never lived together. Theirs was a hashish pipe dream in that respect.

"How do you know Imogene?" they chimed together before Ronald went first.

"I swear, I had no idea she was a lez. I'm so *verklempt* about it. Can't wait to tell Patsy."

"Slow down buckaroo," Wink suggested, motioning for vodka

martini refills. "Pasty, as in your former fag hag best friend? *That* Patsy."

"Yes. She's going to plotz!"

"Patsy knows my Mo?"

"She's Imogene's boss."

Wink was astounded. "Oh...my...God."

"What?"

"You're the rude, crude, arrogant jackass Imogene carped about every night for months until you moved to England."

"Yes, yes, yes! That's me to a tee," he agreed. "That's the cover I used to discourage women from hitting on me. Handsome man that you know I am."

"I do," Wink lied. Ronald wasn't handsome, pretty, or cute (the ranking prerequisites of the trick-trade). What Ronald had was a boyish look beyond his actual age, with a weakness for button down collars, crew neck sweaters, khaki pants, and penny loafers. He was tall, sinewy and pale with thick sandy hair that he parted from left to right in perfect creases resembling the width of comb-teeth drawn across his head. His eyes were a Caribbean green, with a bedroom bag beneath each one. He had a cleft chin, and dimpled cheeks. Charming? Ever so!

"To retain my cover and keep from being pursued," Ronald continued, "I wasted the first fifteen minutes of every morning telling Patsy about my conquests of the night before, in full earshot of Imogene. Of course, I made the men women to *revile* her."

"I'm surprised she let you get away with it."

"Trust me, she didn't. She doesn't cower. We bandied barbs upon sight of each other. She declared me disgusting, wicked, fiendish, Neanderthal, scum — I swear, Wink, she was a veritable walking thesaurus of derogatory terms to describe me." He gleamed. "But always in a witty way. Her zingers are sidesplitting."

"And Patsy?"

"In on the ruse. It made our side of it all the funnier."

"Wait. It's coming back to me now. Mogy told me about a promotion at her new job and mentioned Patsy. It seemed like a step down from her ad agency gig, so I never pushed for more."

"Can't prove it by me. She was hired because she went to the same alma mater as Patsy's boss, which pissed Pats off."

"Because?"

"She and her boss are tight."

"As in?"

"Rumored affair."

"For real?"

"Dunno. Patsy's as sex crazed as any man I ever met, that's for sure. Ribald, too."

"Unusual."

"Not in the garment industry. If you can't cuss and be crude at the top of your lungs you're *bupkes*. Patsy's a pro at both. She intends to rule that roost someday."

"None of this sounds like Mogy's thing."

"Not the talk, but a whiz at biz. Before Imogene, Patsy was tethered to that place. Now she takes long lunch hours, vacations — even goes home early if she wants. Not that she wants."

"This is wild."

"It *is!*" Ronald punched Wink in the arm. "Okay, your turn, Sister Mary. What's the deal with you and Imogene?"

Wink hesitated. For more than a year he'd thought of Imogene as his best friend. It made him wish Ronald had appeared two days rather than two hours earlier to see it for himself. Now, Imogene wasn't his and might never be again.

"We're neighbors."

"Same building?"

"She's on 85th. I'm still on 86th. We met in the park one day and clicked."

"Not the Rambles!"

"Honestly Ronald," Wink looked at him in disbelief. "What would she be doing there?"

"Hey, for all I know there was a tit-takeover after I left. So, purge. You clicked, how?"

"Wavelengths. We laugh at the same things."

"Then I'm betting she doesn't know you hustle."

"No."

"And deal. Do you still?"

"Recreational stuff for a few private clients is all."

"Where?"

"Financial district."

"Still baggin' Wall-balls, huh? You're too much, man."

"Not that," Wink protested. "I manage keypunch operations for a major house there."

"How very stick-in-the-mud. Have you sworn off priests, too?"

Wink felt uneasy. He and Ronald had met on the street outside a Park Avenue high rise, each mistaking the other for a rich trick's son that might work into something more permanent than the unadulterated sex life supporting them. "I'm trying to make the break, okay?"

"Answer me this, then. What's she doing with the likes of you?"

"Damned if I know!"

"Well, all I can say is she's been in threads for over a year now and Pasty likes her a lot. I think she might have filled the void I left there."

"She never mentioned you by name. Patsy was mentioned maybe once. Twice at most."

"Regardless. She and Pats are glued." He ordered another round. "But I swear, I thought Imogene was the straightest, most prissy person I ever met. The kind of girl my folks always hoped I'd bring home. Christ, Wink, I've never even heard her curse. She's a paradox among piece goods salesmen. Even the old coots cool it around her."

Wink knew 'paradox' was the perfect word to describe Imogene now. Not that he faulted her reticence. She'd followed his lead on that. If he'd inquired, she would have been forthright. If she'd inquired, he wouldn't have.

"Something amazes me about her."

Ronald lit a Dunhill and inhaled deeply before exhaling, "What?"

"It's the knack she has for things falling into place in the nick of time. She sets her sights and makes it happen, against all odds. Nothing fazes her."

"That's what I finally did by moving to England after meeting the *one*."

"Seriously?"

"No lie. He's an antiques importer from London. He's teaching me the ins and outs, gives me a percentage of the profits, and I get to fly here in January for the Winter Antiques Show at the Armory and for the Philadelphia Show in the fall."

"So, what are you doing here in March?"

"My old man died. I'm here to sit Shiva. Then I'm off again."

Wink wasn't sure how to react. He'd never known his birth parents and felt contempt for the cold-blooded brutes that had absconded with him. It always seemed unfair, that boys like Ronald got the whole wax candle while he was denied even a flicker of wick.

"I'm sorry, Ronald."

"Don't be. That showboat sunk long ago."

They'd settled the tab and were pushing out the exit now, through the partnerless crowd of desperate eyes seeking cold comfort as midnight struck; boisterous to mask their dismay.

"But," Wink stumbled for the right words. "I mean, weren't you his first born son?"

"First born?" Ronald buttoned his coat, turned up the velvet collar, and whistled for an uptown ride. "That's rich, Wink. I was his *only* son. My mother almost died having me, with no hope for another. I'm his dead brother's namesake. Can you believe it?" He shuddered. "In that despicable, depraved echelon of self-righteous indignation my father emanated, he spawned me, sanctified me, gave me everything money could buy, shunned me," Ronald paused to ground out his cigarette with his sole, "and then he died."

TWENTY-SEVEN
Saturday Night, March 14, 1970
Nobody Pinch Me

The Playbill Lounge at The Royal Manhattan Hotel was everything one might expect of a freshly renovated building bordering Tin Pan Alley. Program covers of hit shows were enlarged, framed, and affixed to the walls. A ticker-tape printout of who was starring in what, where, and when ran as instant information. Menu entrees were named after famous thespians; ticket holders engaged in chatter sparked by show-stopping performances; agents, producers, publicists and columnists congregated there as trendies.

Imogene thought the Lounge a perfect milieu for the first time she and Eloise appeared as a couple together, in a place neither had ever heard of, nor seen, nor been with any other.

"Do you live in Manhattan?" began Freddie Fata, a mega man who'd been ridiculed by his tony classmates for being tall and fat with a last name easy to lampoon. Having made millions in polymers, Freddie selected the unseemly avocation of lavishing cash and gifts on much younger men, expecting a corporeal return. He fancied Martin, and Martin's price was an all expense paid trip to Manhattan for himself and two friends. George and Eloise were his tag-alongs.

"Uptown off Central Park West." Imogene was wary, but polite. In his Scottish tweeds and silk shirt with a neck so thick he couldn't button his collar or tighten his tie, Freddie appeared ostentatious to her. He wore a different gem on each of his stubby fingers, a gold choker around his neck and a tiger's-eye lapel pin woven through his blazer in the middle of his breast pocket securing a jam-packed bundle of new, neatly folded hundred dollar bills.

"Sounds expensive, living in the city solo."

"For the wealthy-wannabe, yes." She knew this fishing game and played it, well.

"You sayin' you don't wannabe rich?"

"I'm saying I am rich. I don't want to be wealthy."

"Why the hell not?"

"Don't you find it requires keeping one eye on your money, and the other on those who conspire to take your money away?"

"You got that right, little lady."

"I knew she would," touted Eloise.

What began as gentle prying turned into comfy conversation once Freddie found neither Imogene nor Eloise were kowtowers.

"George is my reluctant intended," volunteered Marty.

"He thinks I'm going to make an honest woman out of him," George winked through horn-rimmed lens that magnified both the size and vigor of his koala grey eyes.

Marty was petulant. "Well, you promised."

"I did no such thing."

"You promised to be honest. And, you promised I could be the woman."

"Oh, I see. Then all I need do is remove the nouns, pronoun, preposition, verb, adjective, conjunction, and modal verb from my promise to get a declaration not yet in evidence as fact."

"Which makes you, what?" Imogene cut in. "An English teacher, or a lawyer?"

"He's the teacher," Marty winced. "I'm studying to be a paralegal, so I understood part of his fancy-pants way of saying..."

"Now boys, let's not sulk over impossible dreams," Freddie scolded. He returned his attention to Imogene. "*That*, incidentally, is the musical I wish we'd seen instead of the one we ended up at. Have you seen it?"

"Impossible dreams as in *Man of La Mancha*?"

"Yes. It's at the Martin Beck. I tried to get tickets earlier today, but it was sold out."

"I saw it three years ago at the ANTA on a thrust stage. The most thrilling production I've ever experienced. I can't imagine any musical ever surpassing it. The acting was exceptional. The score was phenomenal. The lyrics were brilliant. The staging was superb. It's one of those rarities where you're compelled to buy the cast recording and learn every word of every song. What's more, you leave the theatre giddily exuberant. All you want to do is hug someone. Anyone!"

"Dammit," snapped Freddie. "Waiting to see it will be all the harder now."

"It might not be as good at the Beck, or without Richard Kiley and Joan Diener in the leads. Her voice is mesmerizing. And his delivery had such passion and precision, even the men in the audience wept openly."

"That thrust stage sounds wicked," joshed Marty. Imogene looked so puzzled by his remark that he backtracked. "I mean...what kind of stage is it?"

"The platform extends into the audience on three sides, with all entrances and exits coming from either the back of the stage, or from under the tier of seats. It feels like you're sitting *on* the stage and that you're part of the show."

"So, why not keep it at the ANTA?"

Imogene noticed Eloise eyeing the bread, so she removed a roll from the basket and buttered it before handing it to her. "Broadway is the heart of New York with bigger theatres generating more money. To me, they sacrificed art for economics by moving it to the Beck."

"What'd'ya say we see it someday soon boys? Next trip, I'll get us orchestra seats at the Beck and reservations at Sardi's for the best Italian food in town."

"No, not Italian. Not at Sardi's." Imogene hated to dampen his spirits, but he deserved forewarning.

"The name isn't Italian?"

"The name is, yes. But the food is of an English pub variety. Good enough for gawking at celebrities, but if you want great Italian food, you go to Mulberry Street in Little Italy." Imogene was in her glory talking about the City with out-of-towners.

"You've been to Little Italy?" George piped in. "My parents emigrated from Sicily, but once they landed in Boston during the forties they never ventured further west than Lawrence. My mom was the cook and my dad was the gardener for a rich family there." George said he'd heard about Little Italy and dreamed of going, as if it were an actual country instead of an ethnic area.

"I've been many times, George. When I first moved here I crashed for a few weeks at a friends apartment. He lived in a fifth floor walkup facing Prince Street. One day I heard a loud commotion, so I opened the window and looked down to see a slew of men carting a huge gold statue of the Virgin Mary anchored to a platform that had hundreds of streamers of dollar bills stuck to it. And from as far as my eyes could see were throngs of people lining the street, crying out at the tops of their lungs and throwing coins at the statue as it was paraded up Mulberry to the church on the corner. I swear, it scared the bejesus out of me!"

Eloise continued dining through the entire conversation. It struck Imogene as enchanting, how Eloise savored everything placed within her reach, seemingly unaware of the table talk. So when she stopped long enough to comment on the golden calf-like story, everyone gave her their full attention. "Was it the Feast of San Gennaro, Imogene?"

"It was."

"Scared the bejesus out of me, too. Had to be calmed down with a calzone."

"When was that?"

"Must have been '41 or '42. I was three when we moved away."

"I thought you were born in the Midwest," Marty said.

"Nope. I was born a New Yorker. Raised mostly in the Midwest though."

Imogene and Eloise locked eyes, causing the room and everyone in it to momentarily fade away. Marty brought them back.

"So, what'd'ya say, Izzy? Club 82?"

Eloise shrugged, "Why not? As long as Imogene's game."

"I am. What's Club 82, Marty?"

"A drag show. You know, where men dress up like women and sing songs."

"Like Milton Berle?"

"Better than Berle. I hope someone does Carol tonight. It was a gyp getting Phyllis Diller instead of her."

"I'm confused," Imogene admitted. She was offering a taste of her apple pie à la mode to Eloise while turning her head towards him. "About the Diller part."

"That's where we were today while Miss Izzy here was squirming in her seat, fretting that you might not find her. We saw *Hello Dolly*."

His words jolted Imogene. Her fork went flying and her elbow knocked over an ewer of ice water that sent Marty scrambling to lift the cloth, hoping to stop the flow from running off the table onto their laps.

"What is it? What'd I say?"

"Nothing, Marty, I'm so sorry. Oh what a mess!" Imogene used their napkins to help sop up the water. "It's...you...oh my...you saw *Hello Dolly*, that's all. Fifty-nine plays on Broadway and you went to *Dolly*. This entire day has been one incredible coincidence after another. Borderline scary. Like being caught in a euphoric fantasy that could turn into a chimera at any time."

"What'd she say, George?"

"Don't pinch her because — if this is a dream — waking up would be a nightmare."

TWENTY-EIGHT
Late Saturday Night, March 14, 1970
Second Nature

It's odd, thought Imogene, *how it doesn't require being alone with a woman to learn intimate details about her.* Eloise was thinking the same about Imogene as Marty and George hopped into the back of the taxicab, requiring Freddie Fata to sit up front.

"It's not allowed, so face ahead at all times," demanded the driver. "No turning to talk. No causing a distraction. Deal?"

"Deal, deal," Freddie waved off the terms. He wanted to be in the back holding Marty on his lap like Imogene was perched on Eloise's. It was the one thing he envied about women: their ability to touch like lovers and be perceived as innocent in plain sight.

"Where to, then?"

"Club 82."

"Didn't I pick you up from there last night?"

Savvy hack drivers were invaluable in a city the size of New York, so Freddie rarely forgot the name of one. He studied the license sealed in the clear plastic nicotine stained envelope glued to the glove compartment. When nothing registered, he marked the lapse to inebriation on the night before and the lateness of the hour, which also made receiving any quid pro quo from Marty impossible. Freddie wasn't about to miss out again. One hour at the Club, then back to the hotel before the clock struck two.

The cab driver remembered Freddie because, not only was he an extravagant tipper, but also a homely old brute in the company of a handsome young man, an Italian looking dweeb with an oversized head, and a standout blonde babe. He'd wondered what she was doing with the two hustlers and their mark last night. Now, the old fart had added a younger redhead. The men were definitely faggots, but the ladies

166

weren't hookers. So why were the two slumming? It didn't add up to someone who prided himself in making sense of stories he overheard from those he herded. He was silently cursing his last fare for closing that damnable privacy partition when Freddie begged, "Can I slide this open so I can listen to what's going on in the back?"

The driver checked his outside mirror, slid his gears into first and pulled out into traffic. "Suit yourself, fella."

"So, Imogene, how is it you haven't heard of drag queens?" George queried.

Imogene was positioned on Eloise's lap with her knees up tight against the front seat, creating a spoon effect while making more room for the boys. "Why should I?"

"Because it's a big part of living openly."

"Again. Why?"

The two boys stared at her. Finally, Marty spoke. "Are you playing us?"

"No."

"But you're gay, right?"

"I'm crazy for this lady here, if that's what you mean. But I'm new. Haven't memorized all the lingo yet."

"And by *new* you mean..."

"My first."

"Your first?" Marty tried to compose himself. "Or, first time with a woman?"

Imogene furrowed her brow. "That question feels...uncouth."

George punched Marty. "It is, and he's sorry. But there's a line drawn in swishland sand. Once you step over it, you need to name what position you play."

"Position?"

"So everyone knows your cruising status." George looked at Eloise for help, to no avail. Eloise wasn't one to tell on herself, let alone expect it of another. "You want it spelled out for you, Imogene?"

"Yes, George. I'd appreciate it."

"Okay. If you're strictly into women, you're a lesbian, dyke, lesbos, lezzy, Sappho, diesel, lipsticker, femme, bulldyke, or butch. If you're into both men and women, you're bisexual, bi, swings both ways, play for both teams, AC/DC, tutu, binary, flip-flop, dual, twofold, or flipper.

Men into men are faggots, queers, sissies, Marys, puffs, queens, tops, bottoms, dandies, and *faygeles*. At least we were. Now, guys are just gay."

"Lesbian sounds a lot like 'less being' doesn't it?"

"Yes. We all hear it that way."

"Intended as derogatory?"

"All the lesbo names are. Gay is more carefree."

"So, how is it male homosexuals are now generically gay, but lesbians are branded with slurs in addition to the female standards of whore, tramp, bitch, and slut?"

"Maybe because men fight for change. Women get a free ride."

Marty felt the scorch Imogene's look gave George and intervened. "What word would you prefer, Imogene?"

She twisted her head around to adore Eloise's face. "Dame," she suggested, partly to diffuse the conversation, but mostly because she saw the two of them as superior in their newly founded Queendom. "Dame Eloise and Dame Imogene."

"No fair," griped Marty who'd readily adopted the idea. "That makes *Nothing Like A Dame* your instant anthem. Can we have an anthem, George?"

"Sure. How about, *A Wonderful Guy*?"

"Perfect! Let's get a tranny to sing it tonight." Marty turned from George to Freddie. "Can you Freddie? Can you arrange that for us?"

"I can," Freddie connived, banking on a later-night reward. "And, I will."

"Both songs?"

"Both of them."

Thud!

The taxi came to an abrupt stop in front of Club 82, hurling the boys against the back of the front seat and Freddie into the dashboard.

"What the hell?" Freddie exploded, checking to see if his nose was bleeding. He hadn't hit it, but the violent stop scared him so much he thought he had.

"Cat in the road," the driver lied.

"Cat in the road my ass!" Freddie blustered.

Imogene's position on Eloise's lap kept them from being hurt, but the men were all now irate and itching for a fight. She tapped the window near the driver's right shoulder. "Sir? Sir!" she said. "Did we ruin a special song for you. Is that it? Maybe one your wife likes? Or, one your girlfriend sings to you on occasion?"

He caught her reflection in the rear view mirror as his embarrassment eclipsed his anger. "Maybe my wife," he grumbled. "Maybe, that."

"Then I apologize. We were having a little fun at the expense of *South Pacific*, that's all. We didn't intend to diminish the joy you feel when your wife sings. I bet she means it, too. I bet you are a wonderful guy. Because, clearly, you are *nothing* like a dame!"

The laughter was spontaneous; everyone felt vindicated.

Despite it all, Freddie gave the driver a generous tip. Imogene misread the looks on the faces of the two men when it occurred by surmising it made a big man of the one, and a better man of the other.

Once inside the Club, Eloise slipped her arm around Imogene and spoke low. "Would it also be rude of me if I were to ask my place on your dance card?"

"First card," Imogene murmured. "First dance, ever."

TWENTY-NINE
Late-Late Saturday Night, March 14, 1970
Kind Of A Drag

Freddie Fata was ready to bribe whomever it took to buy the favors he needed at Club 82, and the headliner, Onthelam Chopp, was eager to pocket Freddie's cash.

"But you must understand, Mr. Fairy," Chopp pacified.

"Fata!" Freddie corrected. "It's my name, not my definition."

"Yes, darling," Chopp drawled in his best Tallulah Bankhead voice, "but you're not the first Sugar Pops in here tonight offering me enough cash to float a year supply of Slo-Pokes."

Every female impersonator at Club 82 was required to adopt a farcical wordplay stage name as outlandish as Onthelam Chopp, but none lived their roles to the extreme that he did, dressing and playing the role of Tallulah since he was a boy growing up in Montgomery where the Bankheads had a distinguished political cachet. Tallulah made it legendary.

It helped that Chopp was thin, with an oval face, high forehead, and narrow nose similar to the film star who'd died of hard-living a year earlier. In tribute, he did his utmost to appear as her clone. His wig was a knockoff of her sleek, shoulder length hairstyle parted on the left with a soft, wide, reversed flip at the bottom. He mirrored her large, eyes encircled in eyeliner, her relaxed upper 'm' of a lip, and always bared one shoulder when performing in an elegant little black dress.

"Understand, Mr. Fata, our ladies — and I take tremendous leeway with the term — our ladies have a rehearsed show that simply does not dock in the South Pacific tonight."

"How about just the one, corny in Kansas tune then?"

"That's still in the South Pacific sweetheart."

"How about if I said Annie G. sent me?"

Had Chopp owned the joint he'd have butchered the varmint on the spot, convinced such pantywaist attempts to impress chicken-bait would prove the death of him someday anyhow, all over a get-sex song that would be sung and forgotten in less time than it takes to crack an ass.

"Let me see what I can do."

Freddie slipped a Franklin down the front of Chopp's dress.

"My dear, the twin is going to want one, too."

Freddie slipped a second hundred in before turning around, catching Marty's eye and indicating the fix was in.

"Hey, Tubbs!" Chopp called to the ticket taker who was stuffed into her tuxedo like a penguin in a red bow tie with a black bowler hat balanced on its head. He pointed for her to meet him and her lover, Stout, at the far side of the stage. "Listen you two," he mumbled, "I can't tell if the guy over there at table eight is vice, Fed, or asshole."

"There's a difference?" jabbed Stout. She and Tubbs had served as substitute staff at the club from day one in the early '50's.

"How many times do I have to tell you, Stout, *don't* jab me! I bruise."

"Tallulah was a bruiser, not a bruisee, Miss man."

"That's the inner butch of her I haven't mastered."

"Well, don't get your tits in a twist over it. What gives?"

"See the codger over there?" muttered Chopp. "He dropped Mrs. Genovese's name in trying to get me to add a couple hits from *South Pacific*."

"Clearly," Stout concluded, "he's an asshole. A Bonanno boss put a hit on her eons ago and Dom Vito turned to ghost toast last year."

"Was she ever whacked?"

"The toe tag's still out on that one."

"Maybe," Tubbs added, "but everyone tied to her is already worm-eaten."

"That's what I thought. So, get this. He called Mrs. G, *Annie*, as if she were still alive and knowing her couldn't get him five in the back of the head."

Chopp was alluding to Steve Franse, the original manager of Club 82 who was saddled with keeping an eye on Anne Genovese while her husband, Vito, dodged authorities in Italy. A lesbian by reputation,

Anne gained her freedom from her first marriage to Girad Vernotico after Vito saw her, wanted her, murdered Girad and married her two weeks later.

"That guy picked a bad name to drop," said Tubbs. "I mean, Franse was no friend, but he never gave us grief, and he didn't deserve the brain drain he got when Anne sold Vito out."

"Not our call," Chopp admonished, fearing the place was still bugged.

Tubbs looked towards Freddie who was waving at them, thinking his request was being slated. "Doesn't the creep know most all of that's over? How dare he even try a con like this?"

"I don't have time to care," fluttered Chopp. "But let's play safe. Break open a bottle of whatever he's drinking. No bar brand. Nothing watered down. And, deliver his drinks on the house with regular refills. Get him drunk and get him out of here, pronto."

"Done," said Tubbs. "Whose tab?"

"I'll cover it. There's a Hamilton in it for each of you if he's gone in less than a Franklin."

"I'll do you one better," swore Stout. "He'll be gone in a Grant."

• • •

Club 82 was what one might expect of a cabaret located in the seedy neighborhood of 4th Street on Manhattan's lower east side near Second Avenue. It had a vertical red neon sign glowing BAR in white lights against a backdrop of dirty windows with oilcloth blinds tied down tight to hide the hardship behind them. Beneath the sign was an unmarked arched entry partygoers were paraded through before maneuvering a steep staircase leading down to the old brick building's basement. On the way, they were treated to dimly lit walls plastered on both sides with framed, black and white glossy photographs of every entertainer getting his start in drag society, starting in 1953 when the place went gay.

By the time Imogene was escorted into the lore-lair, the secrecy and shadiness of trannie entertainment was fighting to survive. Celebrities who once visited the Club during its 24-hour daily zenith gradually ceased to exist, and packed houses of conventioneers, sailors on furlough, and college boys who came to razz and ogle had dwindled to strictly weekend attendance.

The demise was attributed to the Stonewall Inn uprising (also alleged to have been owned by the Genovese crime family). It launched the first faction of heralded queers to storm out of the closet and onto the streets, serving as a green light for transvestites to appear in public places during daytime. The new view shared by past patrons was, "Why pay the price to sneak a freak peek now that the sidewalks are free-for-all sideshows?"

"Remind me why I need a file on drag queens again, George."

He had seated her away from Eloise and next to him at one of three bistro tables arranged in a clover to accommodate their party of five. She asked because she'd always been wary of masculine girls at Johnny's and still harbored some resentment for being treated as an enemy by the Daughters of Bilitis who'd taken her hat hostage. Here, the waitresses were all decked out to look like men. Was there any expectation of audience participation beyond watching the show?

"Because Freddie says this club is on a short list of famous places that will close their doors within the year. Two years at most."

"So?"

"Now that you're lesbian, drag is part of your world. You need to be cognizant of it, so when you get old and look back on these days you can provide an oral history."

"But it *isn't* my world, George. I don't even know what the word 'drag' means. And my personal history only began at two minutes before midnight on Friday. It's not a day old yet."

George checked his watch. "Yes, it is. You're thirty minutes past your coming out hour. And, drag is an acronym for dressed resembling a girl."

"Then what's she?" Imogene pointed at a waitress. "Drab?"

• • •

They'd been seated on bentwood chairs at tables covered in starched white linen cloths, near a stage constructed like a catwalk in front of a long mahogany bar lining the back wall. A trellis extending across the top of the stage was covered with a rainbow of flashing rays under a large strobe of mini mirrors twirling from the center of the ceiling, casting sparkles of light that fell like flickers of confetti over the audience.

"See that baby grand over there where the extras are lining up?" George asked.

Imogene leaned over to peer past the people seated beside them. "Yes."

"Errol Flynn once played a song on those very keys with his penis."

Imogene cringed. "Eloise! George needs you to change places with him right now."

But before she could, the lights dimmed, the music began, the emcee strutted to his mark, a solitary spotlight found him and something extraordinary transpired.

As tacky as Club 82 was and as ridiculously dreadful as many of its best impersonators proved to be, Imogene was bewitched by their performance. She laughed. She hooted. She stood and cheered after every solo. She clapped when Freddie was singled out and mocked for being in the audience with Oliver and Dodger the night before, then hooted for adding Little Orphan Annie (her) to his entourage. And she beamed with pride when Eloise cried, "Hey!" over the raucous caused when she was left out of the limelight. "What am I? Tuna fish?"

"Chopped liver!" the chorus of queens sang out.

Eloise stood and raised her glass, shouting back, "I knew that!"

Applause.

Applause.

Applause.

THIRTY
Earlier Saturday Night, March 14, 1970
Whims & Acronyms

Eloise's insides were tap-dancing between fright and euphoria. Her hands appeared calm, but the muscles were crawling around under her skin. She felt her eye twitch.

After Marty paid the drag king for five admissions and collected their stubs she called out to him, "Hold on!"

"What's up? Scared your girly-friend is going to panic?"

"No. She's not the type. She didn't flinch when the desk clerk told her I was here with three guys."

"You checked?"

"He bet me five there wasn't a chance I'd ever see her again. I bet she'd find me. I even told him to ask what took her so long. Believe me, he was tickled to deliver the full report."

"Did you take his money?"

"No. But I did take him up on a hot caramelized pecan roll slathered in cold butter from Stouffer's. I'm telling you, they're to die for."

"Remind me to order some for breakfast. Meanwhile, what gives?"

"My eye. It's twitching like two-forty."

Marty looked hard at her face. "Which one?"

"The right one, below the eye. Can't you see it quivering?"

"My right, or your right?"

"Oh great. Now they're both going at it. You're telling me you don't see movement below my eyes?"

"Nope. No tics. No twitches. Nothing."

"How can that be?"

"Dunno. But don't worry," he giggled. "I won't let on you're getting weak in the knees."

175

"Eyes," she mumbled, although her knees felt wobbly, too.

Eloise knew the reason she felt her heart thudding like a banshee on a timpani inside her chest was because it had been nine years since her fresh-out-of-high-school crush crashed and burned and she swore, come hell or high heels, she'd never trust her heart to anyone again.

Even so, her mind and body were now making it clear she'd never felt the ferocity for Gail Parkerson that compared to the emotions she was hiding for the fledgling sitting across from her.

When Freddie fell asleep at the table, George switched seats to help Marty with him. It gave Eloise an opportunity to marvel at the pinkish glow (produced by reflective light from one of the floor spots) encircling Imogene. She reached over and ran her fingertips lightly up and down Imogene's arm before asking, "How old are you?"

"Twenty-three last October. Seven months shy of twenty-four. And you?"

Eloise removed a pink-papered, gold filtered Fantasia from the silver case she carried in her pocket, bought to deter flirts from perilous pursuit. She'd had it engraved with the words *Night & Day*, pretending it was from her lover and that the song sealed their hearts forever; a lofty ideal she didn't believe in. Now, the case was something she'd be forced to explain without sounding pathetic. Or, ditch the case? Not likely.

"Eighteen days into thirty-one. First week Pisces."

"Second week Libra."

"I've never known a Libra."

"I've never known a Pisces."

Freddie interrupted. "What are you drinking, Eloise?"

She hesitated to answer, half tempted to order the Bolla Soave shared by the others over dinner at the hotel. "Canadian Club and 7up."

"And, you, Imogene?"

"I'll have what she's having."

"I'll have what she's having," parodied the boys in high voices.

The drag king taking the order was sizing up both women, trying to figure out if the men had rented toy wives for the evening. But once she saw Imogene bat her eyes at Eloise she knew all gay was in play.

"Make that five C.C. and 7's and five stemmed glasses with a bottle of Dom Pérignon and a tray of hors d'oeuvres. Some brushetta or crostini maybe?" He stuck a twenty in her cuff.

"Even if I have to bake it myself. How's that?"

Eloise lit her cigarette from the candle centerpiece and sat back, grateful for Martin's attentiveness to Imogene. It gave her time to relax and quietly ponder the circumstances.

She found herself grappling with the possibility of being tagged as the love of Imogene's life, in the way she once believed Gail Parkerson was the love of hers before discovering she'd been nothing more than one of Gail's many discarded amenities. Gail had cheated her out of four years; the first two disguised by deceit and the last two entrenched in treachery. After months of exhaustive brooding she finally buried the betrayal by packing up her two Pekingese and moving to Florida, landing a bar job on Clearwater Beach, and eager to spend the rest of her life partying.

The fact was, she hadn't thought about Gail Parkerson since reclaiming her heart in 1961. Yet the laceration left by lies hadn't healed. Eloise wasn't inclined to trust again. She often wondered if she hadn't lost the will to.

"This is what I think." Freddie directed his prediction to them all. "If those two ever do make a go of it, Miss-Been-There-Done-That is bound to let something slip to Miss Greenbean. Something she shouldn't. Something she can't take back."

"Or, worse," added Marty. "She won't reveal bits she should about her intimate past, so when Miss Greenbean finds out, even tears won't wash the sins of omission away."

"Intimate past?" Eloise chided. "Isn't that kind of a big term for you to be using?"

"Would you prefer it in four letters, Izzy?"

"Not even in hand language," Imogene scolded.

"Hey Imogene," George pestered, "couldn't that be an acronym, too?"

"Could and was. Early slave ship logs listed the initials only next to the names of crew members caught and punished for — wait for it — fornicating undesirable Christians of the King."

"Well hell," said Freddie, moping. "That ruins it for me." He chugged a glass of champagne, belched, and added, "Oh what the fuck. Set 'em up!"

Behind the laughter, Eloise wondered if Freddie had intentionally exposed her alter ego to examination. She wasn't promiscuous, but she did have a tendency to let women perceive her as so since free love was all the rage. Plus, there was that 'big-shot' gene compelling her to appear as a Donna Juan. She'd flirted herself onto numerous slippery slopes requiring fast-talking escapes, embellished in the retelling to sound more like escapades.

"Big-trouble gene is the better name for it."

"I heard you." Imogene squeezed Eloise's hand. "That's the problem with conversations going on inside your head. Sometimes you answer yourself out loud."

"Huh?" Eloise raised her eyebrows real high and opened her eyes real wide, looking all around like someone else had spoken and Imogene was targeting that elusive person. But inside, she went right on thinking: *Look at her, so self-assured. I wasn't that bold at her age. And totally innocent at eighteen when I was seduced. I hadn't a clue as to what Gail was doing until after it was over. And now, here I am, the older one with the chance to do it right by not repeating the wrongs done to me.*

"I think we'd better go," Imogene repeated to her.

"What?"

"Freddie is looped and the boys are restless. Don't you think it's time?"

Eloise looked over at him, slumped in his seat. "How did that happen?"

George was distressed. "Freddie insists he's staying until they sing our songs, but he's already passed out twice. I'm scared he'll fall out of his chair."

"If he wakes, tell him they sang the songs," ordered Eloise, "and let's shag this place."

"You help George and Marty," Imogene insisted. "I'll flag a cab."

THIRTY-ONE
Early, Early Sunday Morning, Match 15, 1970
Connecting The Magnetars

Stepping out into the crisp morning air stirred up a sense of déjà vu for Imogene. All she'd seen when they arrived at Club 82 was the sidewalk beneath her feet and the opening of the maroon cabaret door as she was ushered through it. Upon exiting, she faced the opposite side of the street and automatically turned towards Second Avenue.

It wasn't the bone-chilling air that made her freeze in her footsteps, but a familiarity from having been an actress at the La Mama Theatre two doorways away. The proximity to her past crossing paths with her present (yet again) alarmed her.

Her eyes veered upward through the arctic air to catch a parting cloudscape exposing clusters of lemon ice stars sparkling against an onyx sky. For a moment she felt trapped within a trompe l'oeil, one that had charted the energy of her own life with the energy of Eloise's and, one by one, a magical map had formed to connect the dots, pulling those energies together until the layers overlapped. It was as if they'd been arranged on an invisible grid that was dropped down like a delineated destiny around them, treading time until being individually summoned as a pattern of luminous points to be fixed in eternity upon their inevitable demise.

"Hey, lady! You need a lift?" A cab had pulled up to the curb with its motor idling and window rolled down.

"We're here!" struggled Marty from behind her. He'd directed Freddie up the stairs and out into the street as George and Eloise followed. Recognizing the driver as the same one who'd dropped them off earlier, he opened the door and balanced Freddie up front, "Back to the Royal Manhattan, please."

This time, instead of Imogene sitting on Eloise's lap, Marty sat on

George's, leaning forward to hold Freddie's head up while chattering about what a terrific time they'd had.

Imogene was in the middle of the back seat sitting as close as possible to Eloise, their hands locked and her nose nuzzled near Eloise's ear.

"Will you check on Freddie," Imogene asked softly, "to make certain he's all right once the boys get him to his room?"

"Yes. I just wish we'd met without all this fuss, so not a second was lost to us."

"Nothing was lost. It's all going as it should. Someday, we'll look back on this night and be grateful for it."

"I'm grateful now."

"Me, too. What a splendid ending to the day. I had a terrific time."

"Didn't we though?"

"Indeed we did."

"I'll call you."

"Take good care of your friend first."

"He's Marty's friend, not mine. I tagged along for the free food, that's all."

"Regardless, he's a link to us being here."

The trip back to the hotel was quick. When they arrived, George hopped out and asked the doorman for help at getting Freddie onto his feet and up to his room while Marty dealt with the fare and tip, adding enough to more than cover Imogene's ride uptown.

Eloise turned, tipped Imogene's chin upwards and gave her a tender, gracious, breathless little kiss; the kind of kiss that leaves a lady longing.

"Where now?" the driver asked.

"Twelve West 85th Street."

They rode in silence, he glancing over to where she leaned against the far side window watching the tree tops sway above the long, stone, western wall of Central Park.

She was feeling favored, comparing the belief Jews avowed as being the chosen people with her new awakening. She finally understood the tribulations of being blessed as the cost of being consecrated. It was the price Jews paid for 'getting to be' Jewish.

Whether the epithet was true, fair, right, or wanted was no longer an issue. It had been inscribed in the annals of time, and nearly everyone on earth had heard of the anointment to be accepted, or believed in, or not.

Now, the act of being chosen was the basis for the conviction she'd hold as theirs alone to revere. Seeing Eloise for the first time proved momentous. Searching for her proved monumental. Finding her proved the benison for her heart's devotion. And being lesbian would prove the price they'd pay for love everlasting.

A block before reaching her destination, the driver raised his voice to disrupt her musings by admonishing her. "You should steer clear of those people."

She turned to address his profile. "What people?"

"Queers. Steer clear of queers."

It prompted a droll, "How alliterate of you."

"No, it ain't schooling. It's common sense, is all."

THIRTY-TWO
Early-Early Sunday Morning, March 15, 1970
Happy Daze

Imogene was surprised to see the hallway lights on and Charles Frank halfway up the stairs.

"What's wrong?"

"That's what I was going to find out, Missy," he yawned, pointing upward.

Imogene tilted her head. "Is that my phone ringing?"

"Nonstop. Been going on like that for fifteen minutes. Thought I best check. Wanted to see you safe before suggesting you answer it."

"I'm sorry for waking you, Charles," Imogene blushed. "It's probably my mom. I've been so busy I haven't had time to call her this weekend." They passed each other on the stairwell, she scampering up and he shuffling down.

"If you say so, Missy. But it doesn't sound like that kind of ringing to me."

Imogene leaned over the banister to offer up her finest Scarlett O'Hara impression. "Why Charles Frank, I do declare, what*ever* do you mean?"

"Happens to the worst of us," Charles warned. "And the best. Night, Missy."

Once inside her apartment, Imogene hastily pushed the wing chair nearer to the phone.

"I'm here, I'm here! Hello?"

"What took you so long *this* time?"

"I thought I did good." She checked her clock. "By my count I dropped you off barely twenty minutes ago."

"Seems like twenty hours."

"You missed me so soon?"

"That's an understatement."

Soothed by the sound of Eloise's voice and the serenity of being home, Imogene motioned for Pansy to jump up and touch noses before the cat ensconced itself on her lap. "Such a good pussy you are."

"Pardon?"

"I'm talking to my kitty, Pansy. She's feeling neglected. As is my new little earth angel, Petunia, who's crawling up my leg — *ow* — wanting equal time."

"You have cats?"

"Two. You?"

"Dogs. Pekingese. Lucy and Gracie."

"Do Lucy and Gracie like cats?"

"Yes. I'm staying at a gay guy's place right now. I helped move him north from Florida after his transfer a couple months ago. He has a Blue Point that gets along fine with them. Maybe because they're all Chinese."

"Neighbors anyhow. Siamese cats are from Thailand."

"How is it you know these things?"

"I had a Siamese as a kid. I read everything I could find on her."

"I'm not much of a reader."

"That's okay. I'm too much of one. We'll balance each other out." She yawned. "Sorry."

"It's allowed. I'm tired, too. I just needed to hear you got home safe and to ask you to dream of me."

"I'll dream of you always from now on."

"You think so, huh?"

"I do."

"Imogene?"

"Yes?"

"I had the *best* time tonight. I can hardly believe how good."

"Me, too. Tenfold. Can I see you again later today?"

"I'm stuck having breakfast with the boys before checkout at noon. We're booked on the dinner flight out of LaGuardia. After stashing our bags at the shuttle I'll have six hours for you."

Both knew six hours wasn't nearly enough but neither wanted to dampen anticipation by saying so.

"I'll swing by and pick you up at 11:58."

"Promise?" Eloise was fading. She'd begun dozing off with the telephone's mouthpiece burrowed into the pillow near her ear.

"Promise," quieted Imogene. "Star-of-David my heart."

She could not bear to hang up the phone, fearing the sound of a busy signal would startle Eloise. Instead, she gently lifted the cats down off her lap before standing to place the receiver on the chair. Then she tiptoed to the couch, removed the cushions and arranged them on the floor nearby, fetching additional pillows from the bedroom. Once arranged, she threw a quilt on top before feeding the cats, taking a long shower, and slipping into a collarless red flannel nightgown that reached to her ankles.

Finally, she switched off all but one night light casting a low ray from her bedroom, and snuggled up with the phone receiver near her ear, trying to tame the utter excitement swirling inside her by matching the rhythm of her own breathing to that of the sleeping Eloise.

She must have napped for all of three minutes before jumping up, flipping on the lights, and heading to the closet where she selected a shoe box from a top shelf and emptied it onto the floor. Then she pulled out the sliders on her 1920s' secretary, flipped down the slant desktop, selected a red felt marker from a compartment of pens, aligned a metal ruler to one edge of the lid and carefully printed H A P P Y B O X as one word in bold letters.

While the ink dried she scavenged the pockets of her coat and clothes to rescue the petal and stem remnants of the yellow rose, a matchbook cover from Johnny's, the blue soap wrapper from The Royal Manhattan Hotel, a napkin with The Playbill Lounge logo that a waiter placed under Eloise's glass, the Playbill fork that flipped on the floor after feeding Eloise pie, two ticket stubs from Club 82, the photograph of her as a child hugging the doll she'd said she'd marry one day, and the cork Freddie popped from a bottle of Dom Pérignon.

She placed all these keepsakes in the H A P P Y B O X and kissed the lid before closing it inside the desk, turning off the lights and settling down to sleep, dreaming of Eloise; the two cats cuddled together at her feet.

THIRTY-THREE
Early Sunday Morning, March 15, 1970
The Eyelids of March

Imogene awoke with a high fever and angry cough. At first she blamed it on the room being hot and dry, a condition familiar to occupants of old buildings heated by cast-iron radiators. She hoped putting a pot of water on to boil would moisten the air and help clear her congestion, but all it did was create a clammy film of condensation on the cupboards and appliances.

She glanced at the calendar taped to the side of the Kelvinator. It was the Ides of March. "Figures," she sneezed, then sneezed again, seven consecutive times in all; an inherited idiosyncrasy. *I feel like Caesar warmed over*, she thought. *The pain in my chest might not equate to the daggers by Brutus, but it's brutal. And being betrayed by my body two hours before I need to dazzle Eloise? For once I can relate to today's date.*

Imogene wasn't surprised that her lack of sleep and long search in the bitter cold put her at risk. And somewhere along the way she must have inadvertently stuck her contaminated finger in her mouth, nose, or eye; an error she rarely made. It was the first rule she learned as a toddler: Never touch your hands to your face.

Regardless, her immune system had been compromised. She dragged herself back to her makeshift bed, stretched out and, finding the line to Eloise disconnected, dialed.

"Hiya, mom."

"Dolly? Is that you? I was sitting here asking Amos and Andy where you were. We were worried about you. Dear little Dolly. You didn't call me yesterday. Why?"

"The cats didn't say?"

"Amos had an idea. But I told him, no-no-no. Not my Little Dolly." Imogene could see her mom batting an eye at the cats over her obvious innuendo. She wasn't certain whom her mom enjoyed making laugh more, herself, her daughter, or her cats.

Imogene was in the habit of calling her mother daily since her father committed a socially accepted suicide on her twenty-third birthday five months earlier. Not that her mom knew the whole truth about how her husband died, and not that her father had ever gotten Imogene's birth date right, and not that it was of any consequence.

What made it memorable was, on the day he died she'd been celebrating on the Island with Elaine and Kirsten. It was their first get-together after the blowup of '68, followed by an eleven month scabbing over period. Imogene fully intended to share the interim details of her life, but they each had too much to tell in too little time for telling before the last train back to the city.

Arriving in Manhattan that unusually beautiful Indian summer night, she dawdled some to people-surf and eavesdrop in the Madison Square Garden Station before making a quick stop to pick up a dozen Chock full o'Nuts crunchy-fried donuts and sharing them with stoop sitters along the way. Once home, she eagerly called her mom to recount her delightful day, never expecting to hear her brother's accusatory voice on the other end of the line.

"Where have you been, dammit?"

Normally she'd ignore his bluster by requesting he put their mom on. But Imogene felt brother-proof that night, so instead of a rebuff, she answered cheerfully.

"I went away for my birthday weekend. Why?"

"Dad's dead. Get home. Mom's too distraught to come to the phone. I'll tell her you're on your way." And slam, he hung up on her.

All of this mishmash past began invading Imogene's thoughts while her mom rattled on about the antics of Amos and Andy, causing Imogene concern. What would she be expected to tell Eloise about her father? How much and when? Should it come out in drips and drabs over a lifetime so they could die of old age (together, at the same moment, in the same place) without ever discovering all there was to know? Or, should they reveal their past in marathon style, burying it behind them like old mobsters sealed in new cement with only a jackhammer chance of their bones being resurrected?

"Dolly? Are you still there?"

"Yes, mom. I was saying, I was out and about and waited to call you from home."

"That's fine, as long as you stay safe. I'd prefer you not use a filthy pay phone anyhow. The contaminated things."

Uh-oh and bingo! Imogene thought. "I feel infected, mom."

"Oh no, Imogene, don't tell me you're sick." Imogene braced herself for the rehash. "After your bout with pneumonia as a baby we were told you could never, ever get it again and survive. The doctor was very specific about how much damage your lungs had suffered and how vital it was for you to stay well. He said 'dead' dear. Dead! Weren't you listening?"

"I was a year old, ma. If I'd been two I might have listened. But I was one. And I was dying, if you recall."

"Recall? Dolly, not a winter goes by that I don't recall and worry about my darling little girl. Oh-h." By now she was past the sentiment of fret and nearing the cusp of an ongoing whine.

"Mom, snap out of it! My throat is raw. My head and lungs ache. It hurts when I cough and my nostrils are clogged. Tell me what to do."

"Do you have any chicken broth?"

"Maybe a cube or two."

"Cube?"

"Freeze dried."

"Oh for heaven's sake! Well, it'll have to do. Dissolve it and drink it hot, like coffee. And, suck on some horehound. Do you have any horehound?"

"No."

"No horehound?" She was flabbergasted. "Why, when I was a child my mother wouldn't be without horehound in the house."

"Grandma never mentioned horehound."

"I miss those days. Being little. Sitting on my dad's knee while he plunked on that banjo of his. My mother fussing in the kitchen, trying to keep the wood stove burning hot enough to..."

"Ma-a, you're digressing."

"Oh? Well! Hello? Where was I?"

"My throat."

"Better Made potato chips and Vernor's ginger ale. No daughter of mine would be without both in the house. Vernor's will settle your stomach. The chips will scrape your throat. Ice cream after will soothe it. But not too much ice cream. You don't want to get fat like your mother." Imogene's mom always spoke of her own weight in the third person.

"Egad, Ma. I weigh all of ninety-four pounds."

"It adds up fast. I'm telling you, lay off the ice cream!"

"Fine."

"Oh Dolly. I'm so sorry you're sick. Do you want me to come and take care of you?"

"Thanks, but not necessary."

"Because I would."

"I know."

"All right then, dear. You get in bed and take some Bayer and go to sleep. Sleep is what you need most. And when you wake up, call me."

"I will."

"Don't forget."

"I love you, Mom."

"I love you, too, Dolly."

"Bye."

Imogene's mother was a practical and conventional woman with a love of literature and a flair for drama that Imogene admired and respected. But in order to meet Eloise by noon, Imogene knew she needed something more radical than ginger ale, chips and soup cubes.

She needed drugs.

Not that Imogene ever took drugs or had a desire to. Moreover, if she wasn't so hopelessly in love and so wretchedly ill on a morning requiring physical flawlessness, she would have done as her mother directed.

Instead, she donned a floor length quilted robe and matching scuffs, stuck a handkerchief in each pocket and climbed a flight of stairs to see if the resident drug dealer could provide her with a quicker fix.

• • •

Steve Stein was an endearing wastrel with a goofy grin plastered to his chipmunkish face clouded by a chronic five o'clock shadow. Pale and puny, Steve spent his days and nights dressed in a black Munsinger t-shirt and black Levi jeans with a scuffed brown belt riddled of ice-picked holes to get the leather tight enough to hold his pants up, leaving the excess tongue to droop down. Imogene thought it must have been his short, corkscrew curls and sleepy, spoon-sized eyes that attracted the coterie of girls, eager to engage in free love with him. Or, maybe it was the hollowed out White Owl blunts stuffed with weed he provided as an incentive.

Imogene liked Steve. They'd chitchat during chance encounters while trapped like rats on stalled subway cars, or carry on as yentas arrogating a neighborhood stoop on midsummer nights, or mimic seasoned shoppers sampling kosher foods at Zabar's.

During the five years she'd lived at 12 West, Imogene heard of how Steve was chastised for being an indolent child prodigy expelled from numerous prep schools before becoming a New York University delinquent paying exam takers with pot in order to obtain his bachelors degree in applied mathematics. He'd subsequently been fired from every job his parents procured for him, cited for shiftlessness and causing mayhem by providing marijuana to file clerks.

The final straw came when Steve was hired as an insurance adjuster for his uncle's agency. Instead of investigating, he rubber-stamped each claim, endorsing instant checks from a desk size book intended for dispensing petty cash.

Now, his parents paid him a princely sum to eschew their Armonk home except on Yom Kippur when the interchange of forgiveness was necessary to those with hopes of being written into the Book of Life.

Steve drifted through a cloud of smoke towards the knock on his door. *It must be cops,* he thought. *Or, could it be my titty tribe? Or, is it my supplier? Welcome world!* Steve was magnanimous when stoned. In fact, the sole person he never anticipated to come knocking was the redhead from downstairs.

"Steve, thank goodness you're here."

"Come in, man. Enter. Peace, man." *She sounds raspy. I like that blur on her. Don't I?*

"I need your help. I've got some sort of bug. I'm not sure what.

But I can't have it right now. I can have it — sa-a-ay — seven hours from now? Just not now. Can you help me?"

Steve often hallucinated about the day the girl from apartment 3 would loosen up and smoke some bhang. *Am I hallucinating now?* He sucked on the roach pinched between the two orange stained fingers of his left hand, gulped the intake of smoke, held it, and was about to offer her a hit when he zoned a bit. *Do I have a sister? Is this my sister?*

"Big bug?" he exhaled.

"Probably. Listen, do you have drugs I can take? Something that will pep me up and help me appear function? Does marijuana do that? Does it come in capsules?"

He stood and studied her for almost an hour, or maybe an elongated minute before he felt himself floating over to one of the four deep cushioned, bright colored couches arranged around an oversized coffee table littered with hashish bongs, joint clips, and other drug paraphernalia in the middle of the room. Once there, he dug deep between the tie-dyed pillows, put his head down to rest, felt someone in the room, and saw a huge hand pull a pillow size glassine envelope of blue pills out of the mouth of a gnome. After envying its hat, he meandered over to his kitchen and selected a mug inscribed *World's Greatest Dad* from a foldable bamboo dish rack. He filled the mug with the little blue pills, swung around to face the stranger staring at him, held the cup up high, waltzed back over to where Imogene stood and presented it with grandiosity.

"How many do I take?" she sniffled.

Silence. Thinking. His eyes coasted closed until a clue popped them back wide open. "One. Two." *Button my shoe,* he thought.

"And, then?"

"Wait." He was trying to remember what came next.

"I take one or two now? And again in maybe, what, three or four hours?"

Steve's expression became intense, like his hearing was on a six second delay waiting for the sound to travel the interminable foot between them. "That's it! Shut the door."

"Okay," she heaved. "I will. I'm going. Thanks. How much do I owe you?"

"For what?"

"These." She held up the cup.

He took a doobie hit before studying the inscription. "Cool man," he snorted, bobbing his head in approval. "I didn't know you were a dad."

By the time Imogene returned to her apartment and stood swaying over her kitchen sink with a glass of water in one hand and Steve's drugs in the other, she understood her predicament perfectly. If she was incredibly stupid, or undeniably desperate, or both, she'd down the little blue pills and wait as Steve directed. If she was sensible and smart, she'd flush the pills down the drain and return to bed, canceling her date with Eloise until — possibly — never again.

THIRTY-FOUR
Late Sunday Morning, March 15, 1970
Departures & Arrivals

Imogene heard ringing in her ears. She'd fallen into one of those desirable deep sleeps where her lips parted and saliva slipped out, dribbling off her cheek to dampen the white pima cotton pillowcase beneath it. She took comfort in the purity of white terry towels and cloths, white cotton blouses and eyelet dresses, white summer nightgowns and matching robes, white table coverings and napkins, white gloves and hankies, and pristine white panties. She slept best on white sheets, cocooned under a white down comforter where she often dreamed of looking polite in white.

But in a flash she was on her feet, embracing denial. Her nose wasn't as clogged. Her head didn't spin. Her eyes had dry seepage near the tear ducts, but appeared clear. Her lungs whistled and body ached, but not to the breaking point. And, although her throat still stung, it felt more like a twinge than a raw gnawing.

As for the ringing, it was the phone, set down on the floor and shoved under a chair so the cats couldn't knock the receiver out of its cradle — a game of Kill Ma Bell that Pansy was fond of playing. The cat was now stretched out on her back, tangled in the cord, slapping at the base, teaching Petunia attack tactics.

"Eloise!" Imogene answered.

"Oh good, I caught you. Change of plans. Logan Airport is closed."

Imogene checked the clock and saw the two were due to meet in less than thirty minutes. "What? Why?"

"Um. Something about an early Easter?"

"Nor'easter, maybe?"

"What's that in Florida-speak?"

192

"Freezing hurricane. Blows off the ocean from the north. Dumps large amounts of snow. Shuts down towns and stretches of highway. You're staying over?"

"No. If it weren't for my Pekes I would, but James is unreliable. I was skeptical about leaving them to begin with so I gotta go. Otherwise, you'd have me here, ready or not."

"I'm ready," she lied. Under no circumstances did she want their romance to be rushed. It required looking and feeling her best, with emphasis on the looking part. "How are you getting back to Boston?"

"Freddie tried to rent a car, but they wouldn't take cash. It looks like we're busing it."

"When do you head for the Port Authority?"

Imogene waited while Eloise sucked on her cig. "Port what?"

"The bus depot."

"Oh, right," she exhaled. "Soon. Freddie's at the desk tallying up the damages now. Then he'll get our fares and stash our bags 'til departure."

"You're three short blocks north of there. I can catch the subway and get downtown in a jiffy. How about, I meet you inside the 41st Street entrance in 49 minutes? Does that work?"

"Perfect."

"I'm half way out the door."

"I'll wait for you."

Imogene was about to hang up when she heard Eloise yell.

"Hey!"

"Yes?"

She wavered before asking, "Do you?"

Ah-h, Imogene thought; *my first test.* "Yes. Yes, I do."

"Ditto."

Imogene took pride in being a 'clean machine' ready to roll on three hours notice, but this time she went for 'clean enough' and a roll of the dice. She slipped into a matched set of Dietrich-style dark chocolate, pleated wool trousers and turtleneck sweater, chose cream colored knee socks flecked with the identical shade of brown, and added a deep pocket, camel hair stadium coat with a hidden closure that, when zipped all the way up the front, formed a high collar to protect half of her face from the wind and cold. Start to finish she was out of her apartment, down the stairs and through the front door in under six minutes.

She was back up the stairs and inside her apartment in another two minutes, taking time to slip into the brown leather ankle boots she'd forgotten altogether, wrap an ecru scarf around her neck, grab a pair matching mittens, and pocket a tube lipstick, eight transit tokens, a hanky, and some folding money.

"Pansy and Petunia," she saluted before locking the door behind her, "woman the fort!"

• • •

The 42nd Street IND subway station was a block from the mammoth tawny brick Port Authority Bus Terminal: a long, rectangular base that had a cracker box tower bordering the Hudson River to the west, and a half-moon upper storied front facing Eighth Avenue to the east, all anchored between 40th and 41st Street.

Inside and out, the terminal stood as an Art Deco beacon of big city style that wowed the weariest of world travelers and comforted the downtrodden by providing temporary refuge.

The first time Imogene LaPin arrived at the terminal was a nippy afternoon in 1965 after winning a national talent search sponsored by a major network in conjunction with The American Academy of Dramatic Arts; a watershed moment for her, launched on a lark.

Weeks before, she'd been a freshman attending Wayne State University as a theatre major when George Romney was installed for his second term as governor of Michigan. One morning she was summoned by a University liaison asking that she recite *The Highwayman* as part of the program presented during a dinner given for dignitaries attending the Governor's Ball at Cobo Hall in downtown Detroit. Imogene had won the American Legion Oratory Award during her senior year of high school for the delivery of that Alfred Lloyd Noyes masterpiece and assumed she'd garnered the honor as an indirect result.

Her presentation to an audience of three thousand went well enough to earn her a standing ovation. Afterwards, when leaving the

Hall alone and wishing she had someone in her life to share the excitement of the moment with, a dapper man with a high forehead, conspicuous widow's peak, salt and pepper sideburns and steel framed glasses approached her.

He identified himself as Leonard Lyons, handing her a business card with the address of a television studio jotted on the back.

"I want you to repeat that performance here, by noon tomorrow," he said with the clear expectation that she do so, offering no explanation as to why she should. "Don't be late. You're a shoo-in."

Imogene couldn't say if it was because the Cobo Hall audience had left her on a huge high, or she felt a need to oblige the fellow for praising her, or that his request seemed compulsory. She complied, that's all, by getting up early the next morning to take three different city line buses to the designated Dearborn address.

The trip was longer and took more time than guesstimated. She caught the Woodward Avenue bus at the edge of the Wayne State campus to travel downtown past the Bonstelle Theatre (where she was earning apprenticeships in set-design and greasepaint), past Greenfield's Cafeteria (where the family dined whenever visiting Detroit), and Hudson's Department Store (where she and her sisters once sat on Santa's lap).

Of those few people on the bus, most got off at the Penobscot Building, Detroit's tallest skyscraper at forty-seven floors with its 1920s relief sculptures of Penobscot Indians chiseled into the stone facade. The bus then circled around the courthouse on Griswold, where she'd once read Mae West was put on trial for public indecency. Imogene intended to ask the bus driver if he knew the details of that before he began railing against the decades-old decision to tear up the trolley lines. She listened without interest until catching a needed transfer where another driver expounded on his years maneuvering the outlying Avenue lines. Imogene escaped his jabbering via a second transfer exposing her to yet another thirty minute spiel.

By then she didn't know where the hell she was, or what the hell she was doing and was about to wail, "let me out, let me out" while pounding on the slide down dual glass windows and yanking the overhead cord until she dinged the driver to death. But before she could, the bus stopped a block from the television studio, minutes before the noon deadline, opening its doors to the onset of a sudden downpour.

As the final person to appear, Imogene stood dripping, drenched and dismayed, under a hot spot, center stage. There was no audience, save for an emotionless voice behind an overhead tinted window in the control room saying, "Thank you." It made her execution of the poem nothing short of remarkable.

Before beginning the dreaded trek back she approached the fellow striking the set.

"By any chance, can you tell me who this guy is?"

The weary intern looked at the business card Imogene handed him. "For real, lady? He's the best known theatre critic in New York. America, even."

It was her mother who informed Imogene of the unforeseen news during a phone call to her daughter's cold-water flat near the Wayne campus where Imogene barely made ends meet.

"Imogene, why didn't you tell me about this? I'm so proud of you! But heartbroken you didn't tell me. Dolly? Are you there?"

Imogene was busily counting pop bottles scavenged from weekly frat parties to return for the deposits, and combining the partial contents of booze bottles taken from their ad hoc bars. When she had enough liquor to refill a bottle she'd sell it back to the boys at half the price of one sealed as new. The dual operation provided her with funds to buy staples for the week.

"Tell you about what, mom?"

"About you going to New York!"

"I'm going to New York?"

"It says it right here in today's *Free Press*."

"Honestly mom, I have no idea..."

"Oh for goodness sake, Imogene. Papers don't make stories up. I'm reading it right here!"

"Then read it to me mom. Because you're not making sense."

At a scant two inches, below the fold, on an inside page, among other fillers deserving a smidgen of the public's attention, Mrs. LaPin read a clip that stunned Imogene.

"My little Dolly won the Midwest Regional ABC Talent Search and chance at a full scholarship to the American Academy of Dramatic Arts in New York City. Imagine that!"

"Honestly ma, I didn't know."

Imogene recounted the event-turned-ordeal from being summoned to speak at Cobo Hall, the ovation, the debonair man, the grueling Dearborn trip, getting soaked, the recitation and her cold return to campus. Except for an initial tweet of excitement, her mom seemed to be listening to every detail until the very end, when Imogene realized Mom never left the starting gate.

"You spoke at the Governor's Ball?"

It was just as well.

A month earlier Mrs. LaPin had eagerly cosigned the three hundred dollar student loan Imogene needed to complete her third semester at Wayne State. But her father refused, fully aware his signature was required for the loan approval. He didn't care that she'd worked as a sales clerk for five hours five nights a week and another twelve hours every Saturday from the age of fourteen to earn her freshman tuition, room, board and books.

"What a stupid waste of time and space," he derided her, "sending you to college."

"You didn't. *Me*. I sent me to college."

The news of winning a contest she'd inadvertently entered encouraged her to promptly pack all of her belongings into a borrowed red Tourister Tiara hardshell, board a prop at Willow Run, fly to Newark Airport, and take a shuttle into the nation's largest bus station of the greatest city in the world to embark on an accidental adventure.

Arriving without a job, a place to live, and all the money she had left to her name (one hundred and thirty-one dollars and thirteen cents sewn inside her coat pocket), Imogene tarried long enough to pay homage to The Port Authority of New York for delivering her onto the streets of Manhattan.

Five years had whooshed by. She'd not been back inside its unhallowed walls, since.

• • •

Imogene made it down to the 42nd Street subway station in record time, pushing past the throngs of visitors before bounding up the tiered staircases. Once outside she walked swiftly to within sight of a wall of windows and swinging doors exposing the ground floor of the terminal to the periphery of Times Square. There stood Eloise near the 41st Street entrance.

"Simmer down my heart," she ordered, savoring the moment before crossing through traffic and dodging the crowds to reach Eloise's heroine's hello. Imogene looked up the full five inches into her eyes. "How long do we have?"

"Less than four hours. We were lucky to get seats on the 3:45."

"Where's your bag?"

"With George. He'll put it on the bus. Until then, I'm all yours."

Most of those sidestepping them with luggage, duffel bags, or carts of boxed belongings winked and smiled.

"That's odd. What do you suppose all the friendly is about, Eloise?"

"They probably think we're sisters who haven't seen each other in ages. People relish the look of love on faces strangers."

"Now I'll never view two women hugging quite the same."

"It's more because we look like two all-American girls next door. In the real world, if we appeared or behaved the least bit butch, the gloves would come off."

Imogene rose up on tiptoes to bestow a quick, slick, bliss of a kiss. "I'm not interested in the real world. I'm interested in *our* world, exclusively."

It was the nudge Eloise needed to relax her grip long enough to button up her navy blue cargo coat that (not coincidentally) matched the shade of her boots. "Good! Because I can do *our* world standing on one foot with my eyes crossed and wrists tied behind my back."

"Dibs on the tying," Imogene teased, clasping Eloise's gloved hand and leading them out into the high noon sun as one.

THIRTY-FIVE
Sunday Afternoon, March 15, 1970
Tour d'horizon

Imogene knew Eloise had already chowed down with the boys, but the Empire Diner was close by and would provide them an opportunity to begin a conversation of mutual discovery. Sitting and staring at Eloise would be enough to fit the bill, but if her stomach could tolerate it, she wouldn't push away poached eggs on dry toast to quell a queasiness the drugs were causing.

"Are you hungry?"

"I can always eat, but I'd rather sightsee some." Eloise pulled a silver and black camera out of her coat pocket. "I want proof of you."

"Holy-moly, a Kodak Instamatic 100!"

"You've never seen one?" Eloise handed it to her.

"I wanted this the year before I ran away from home, but couldn't afford it."

"You ran away from home?"

Imogene peered through the viewfinder and spun around. "Some call it going off to college." She snapped a shot of Eloise. "The best way to see this town is to walk it, but we haven't time. What-say we take a cab to Fifth Avenue and hop a bus to the Village?"

"Lead on!"

The two women strolled arm in arm north to 42nd Street and far enough east for Eloise to see the full spectrum of prostitutes, porn shows, panhandlers, and drug paraphernalia plaguing the district before flagging a cab.

"Whenever my Aunt comes to visit, the first thing she wants to do is drive around this area. She finds it fascinating."

"Your uncle doesn't mind?"

"Never married."

"Well, well."

"Her looks and voice have always reminded me of Snow White, with the same dark hair and doughy complexion. Each word she speaks is pronounced perfectly, soft with Monroe undertones. The voyeurism is completely out of character."

"Any love life?"

"That depends on who's speculating and what you need to believe. She never tells on herself. Points towards the possibilities, but in opposite directions to different people."

Imogene had instructed the driver to take the Columbus Circle loop before crossing to Fifth Avenue on Central Park South so Eloise could see the entrance to Central Park and Lincoln Center, the gathering of horse drawn carriages waiting for visitors leaving the Russian Tea Room and Carnegie Hall, the storefronts of Bergdoff Goodman and Tiffany's before dropping them at The Plaza Hotel, a stone's throw from the 56th Street bus stop.

"This takes longer but we'll treasure the memory more," Imogene assured, dropping coins in the fare box for them both.

"It's more romantic," added Eloise.

Imogene liked hearing that. It scored as yet another match between them.

As the bus lumbered down Fifth Avenue, she pointed out the Tishman building. "That's where I work, and if you look back to your right when we pass the next street, you'll see cast iron lawn jockeys on the balcony of The 21 Club." When Eloise turned, Imogene leaned in and rested her chin on Eloise's shoulder in order to share the view.

"I see them!" Eloise exclaimed. "What's their story?"

The bus stopped to accommodate tourists waving for the driver to wait.

"They represent the stable colors of wealthy horse farm owners who made the place a famous drinking spot in the 1930s."

"So, there are twenty-one jockeys?"

"A misconception. There are thirty-three outside and two inside. But that isn't how the place was named. During Prohibition it was a speakeasy called Jack and Charlie's 21, with fake walls, conduit chutes, and hidden vaults. The owners could render the place lawful by flipping a switch that revolved the walls to hide any illegal apparatus. Even the floor opened to upend the bar and slide the booze into the sewer. Once Prohibition was over, the owners' names were dropped, but the 21 remained."

"That is so-o cool. Have you ever been inside?"

"Twice."

"Is it true movie stars go there?"

"Stage and screen stars."

"Did you see any?"

"Not while there. But I've seen my share of them around town."

"Were you ever as close to one as you are to me right now?"

"Many."

"Tell me?"

"All in good time, woman. Look! Look through there." The bus had begun rolling again and Imogene pointed to a bronze statue of a nude woman with flowing hair riding a fish in the promenade. "That leads to Rockefeller Plaza and its ice skating rink and, look," she took Eloise's hand and pulled her over to the east side of the bus, "that's St. Patrick's Cathedral and — more important — Saks Fifth Avenue across the street."

Eloise laughed as they moved to a forward facing double seat. "Saks over Saints, huh? From a redhead that sounds almost sacrilegious."

"Why? Do I look Catholic?"

"You look Irish."

They both sat back, Eloise watching Imogene's eyes flitting about, looking for other landmarks to point out as the bus chugged through traffic.

"Well, gee, that suddenly explains a lot," mused Imogene.

"Like?"

"Like being singled out in crowds to be kissed by Irish politicians."

"Anyone I've heard of?"

"Probably. Last year John Lindsay kissed me during his run for Mayor as a Liberal. Our picture made page two of the *Post*. I wish I'd kept a copy. Another time Bobby Kennedy kissed me. You can't get more Irish Catholic than that."

"You were kissed by Bobby Kennedy?"

"Yes."

"Where? How?"

"Here. Eighty days before he was assassinated. He was riding in the St. Pat's Day parade and spotted me while I was trying to get through the crowds in front of where I work."

"And?"

"He jumped out of the car he was in, grabbed my arm, turned me around and laid one on. Then his people hustled him right back to his car and off they went."

"That would have blown me away."

"It was actually kind of eerie. I was working at an ad agency handling Nixon's voiceover tapes at the time and was exposed to some murky media tactics. So when Kennedy was killed I was aghast. A friend even suggested, if Kennedy hadn't dallied by kissing me, he might have been several minutes earlier everywhere and missed being shot. I know that's silly, but it played with my mind for a time. Anyway, I ended up quitting that job. Now, I ignore politics altogether."

For the first time, Imogene had temporarily lost her sparkle. Eloise likened it to watching the blood draining out of a person's face right before she keels over.

"It's still pretty ironic," she ventured, still unwilling to let the story go, "especially where he kissed you."

"On my lips?"

"No, in front of the building where you work. The address is satanic." Imogene gave her a perplexed look. "You mean a preacher never tried to scare you with the 666 symbol?"

"No. But then, I gave up Christianity for Lent when I was ten."

"Honestly?"

"Even earlier, but officially, I used Lent as my key to flee, yes."

Eloise found Imogene's nonchalance charming, becoming so immersed in their conversation that they missed ten blocks of Fifth Avenue before she jumped up to yell, "Stop!"

Once off the bus, Eloise whisked Imogene across the street and posed for a photograph of herself in front of Arnold Constable's.

"You know, Eloise, you nearly shattered my perfectly good eardrum for this shot."

"Sorry. Had to. My mom was working here when she was carrying me."

Imogene stepped forward and gave her a playful push. "Get out!"

"No lie. I've heard endless stories about how well she was treated here."

"I meant it as, I'm so very jealous of you being born in New York."

"Way up town, but still." Eloise peered into the windows before asking, "Take another of me?" So Imogene did, and another, and another.

"Did your mom mention the clientele to you?"

"Hoity-toity."

"To say the least. I've never even stepped inside," admitted Imogene. "Too intimidating."

"Somehow, you don't strike me as the intimidated type."

"I'm mostly not. But condescending people make me claustrophobic. Does that count?"

"If so, they do me, too."

"In its heyday," Imogene spoke on the sly as if she were spilling classified information, "those who frequented here included Vanderbilts, Rockefellers, Carnegies, Morgans, Presidents, Congressmen, movies stars. Even Thomas Edison."

"Really? She left that out."

"What did your mom do?"

"Sales. It was after she gave up being a surgical nurse in the mid-30s. Is Doctor's Hospital near here?"

Imogene saw another bus heading towards them so she took Eloise's hand and ran them back across the street to get on board, talking along the way.

"It's across from Gracie Mansion, where the Mayor lives, on East End Avenue and 87th Street. Also *très* upscale." They took the first seat facing the front window.

"Makes sense, then. She was working there when she fell in love with Dr. Mell."

"First name?"

"She's never once said. Dr. Mell is all. An obstetrician. She still lights up every time she speaks his name. Back then she was dating him and seeing my father on the side."

"Foxy momma! But your dad won out."

"Kind of. Mom and Dad lived on bordering farms in rural Alabama. She had a kid crush on him, but he was seven years older and engaged to a girl named Sarah Lou."

"Go on."

"That's where it unravels. Dad and Sarah Lou were in a car crash. He was driving and she was killed. He came here to start over. Later, mom moved here to attend nursing school. They ended up looking out for each other."

"Then she still had a thing for your dad?"

"No. But they were best friends. One Friday night, when Mom was off for the week and expecting Dr. Mell to take her out and propose, he didn't show up at the hospital, he didn't meet her at the restaurant, and he didn't call. It made Mom so mad, she eloped with Dad."

"No!"

"Yup. And when she went back to, there was Dr. Mell full of apologies. He'd gotten held up with an all night breech birth of a destitute woman on the Bowery."

"He couldn't phone?"

"It was the Depression. The woman had no phone. Both the mother and baby died. He told her he was beside himself, saying all he wanted to do was get back to her and how he didn't want to ever be without her. Then he got down of one knee and begged her to marry him."

Imogene pulled out a handkerchief and was set to use it. "What did she say?"

"Um, no-o!"

"That's such a sad story."

"It really is. She quit, took a job at Arnold Constable's, and never worked as a nurse again."

Imogene looped her arm through Eloise's and hugged it, riding along in silence afterwards, past 34th Street where the front doors of the Empire State Building could be seen on their right, and on towards a landmark dear to her heart.

When the structure was still blocks away, Eloise spotted it. "What's that?"

"My favorite building in all of New York."

"Make it mine, too. Does it have a name?"

"The Flatiron Building. At twenty-one stories, it was once the tallest edifice north of 14th Street."

"When?"

"Around 1900."

"Too bad every building in New York isn't as beautiful. Can we get off here?"

Imogene checked Eloise's watch. "We can't if we're going to visit two more places. Next time. How's that?"

The bus approached the intersection where the road diverged, veering toward Broadway, past 22nd Street and on to the Village. Eloise turned and continued to look at the Flatiron from the side and back until the bus had completely gone by.

"Recognize this area, Izzy?"

"Should I?"

Imogene pulled the cord and the two of them got off, scurrying down Broadway to 19th Street and on to the front of Johnny's.

"Egad," Imogene reacted with dismay. "This dive looks even sleazier in daylight."

"Don't they all?"

"Can't say," Imogene confessed. She positioned Eloise for a photograph, framed by the reinforced steel entry door, incorporating the littered sidewalk and tawdry sign. "I've been to exactly two girl bars, but I can tell you the other one, Cookies, is much worse than this."

Imogene snapped the photo before switching places so Eloise could take a shot of her.

The day was frosty, but the brightness of the sun and the joy they felt warmed them as they huddled close, hurrying towards Fifth Avenue to hail an uptown cab.

"We have time for one last stop," Imogene let on as they slid close to each other in the back seat, looking like two giggling schoolgirls in town on a holiday from the heartland.

The cab driver was Bunyan-burly in a buffalo plaid shirt, Levi's, red suspenders, and Barrier boots, citified by his Yankee baseball cap. "Where to, ladies?"

"Serendipity's, please."

"Hold tight. I'll have you there in no time," he winked.

They did as told and held tight, chitchatting with him all the way, mostly about where he was from in Alaska.

"Women are scarce up there as it is," he confirmed, "but pretty misses like the two of you would be a rare-stare."

Arriving at the acclaimed East 60th Street address with it's sepia tinted exterior, big black door, cast iron lamp post, flower box steps and red satin curtain confectionary window display, the driver refused to accept either the fare or the tip. "Spend it inside instead. My treat."

Imogene thanked him. "How is it a lucky somebody hasn't snapped you up by now?"

"Oh, I can be snapped up easy enough. It's the tying down I resist."

Once inside the parlor, Imogene and Eloise were inundated with the aroma of chocolate permeating the air. They were seated under a stained glass chandelier at a marble topped bistro table and given a checkerboard menu that was, to Eloise, "dizzy with desserts."

Imogene stopped the waitress from leaving. "I'm sorry, but we're already late to catch a Boston bus, so could you bring us your biggest mug of hot chocolate to share with two spoons, two straws, and the check?"

"You bet," the girl said, jotting it down as a special.

Once she was out of earshot, Imogene apologized to Eloise for ordering without first consulting her. "This is pretty much a rich kid's hangout and tourist trap. I find it daunting."

"Why?"

"Don't get me wrong. I've no misgivings about wealthy people. It's money that's scary."

"You're scared of money?" Eloise had never heard of such a thing.

"Not of making it. I've always liked making it. When I was seven I passed as four. My brother dressed me up like a waif sending me door-to-door to sell Christmas cards."

"He didn't."

"He did. And I was *good* at it, too!"

"What was your pitch?"

"None. First he'd target the few, upper class, high-rise apartment buildings. Once inside he'd knock and hide. When the door opened I'd be standing there in my tattered costume acting poor and pitiful, offering a box of cards. The person would look around and invariably ask, "How much?" I'd hold up one finger and they'd pay me my dollar and watch as I trudged to the next door on the floor. I gave a grand performance every time!"

"Didn't anyone ever wonder where your mother was?"

"Nope. Where I'm from, rich people prefer the poor to be invisible. A buck was a trifling price to pay for my disappearing act. I never spoke. I just kept that one finger held high until I was paid."

"That's a fun story."

"And a fond, fond memory. How about you?"

"I sold illegal fireworks to truckers."

"Hah! Cherry bombs trump Christmas cards any day."

They both had their arms folded on the table, leaning forward, eager to catch every word of the other's contribution to the conversation, deaf to the influx of noise by children's parties occurring all around them.

"So-o, Imogene, what is it about money that frightens you?"

"Having it, holding it, spending it, keeping track of it, paying bills with it, carrying it, washing it so I don't get my hands dirty touching it. You know, the ordinary things. I'm hoping, once we're officially spoused..."

"Spoused?"

"Whatever the word for it, you'll handle the finances. I'll add your name to my bank account and you can take it from there."

"Are you nuts? You can't hand your money over to me and trust I'll do right by you. What if I wiped you out and ran off, leaving you with nothing?""

"First of all, you won't. And, even if you did, I'd start over. I love working, and the solitary thing I like about money is earning it. The rest is of no concern. So. Deal?"

Eloise was skeptical. She'd never heard of anyone who was afraid of money. She, herself, loved money; loved having it, looking at it, stacking it, rolling in it, collecting it, counting it, and framing it. She loved hearing coins jingle. She loved the feel of folded bills. She even loved the smell of money, and dearly loved spending it. Furthermore, it didn't even have to be *her* money. She was happy to spend anyone's money available!

"Most couples divvy up expenses. Even my folks keep separate stashes."

"Do you want to be your folks?"

"Perish the thought."

"Then it's a go. You can keep your own account, but I'm putting your name on mine."

"Wouldn't that depend on when this...spousing...takes place?"

The waitress delivered their quart size cup of hot chocolate and left the check without intruding further. Imogene took the two paper sealed straws and unwrapped them.

"I've always dreamed of doing this," she giggled.

"What?"

"Share a drink through matching straws."

It surprised Eloise. "You've never shared a soda with someone before?"

"Purposely not."

"Why?"

"Because I wanted it to be with the person I knew I loved. I wanted to know, when we gazed into each others eyes, the moment wouldn't be wasted on someone I couldn't remember, or someone I wanted to forget." She paused long enough to stick the straws through the high, thick swirl of real whipped cream decorated with shavings of bittersweet chocolate, topped by two maraschino cherries. "I wanted it to be you."

THIRTY-SIX
Sunday Afternoon, March 15, 1970
Am I Blue?

Imogene assumed she was on a happiness high. Before leaving the parlor she'd snuck a blue pill down with her last gulp of cocoa and all the way back across town her head was in the clouds, her heartbeat was galloping like a polo pony, and it felt as if bliss had been permanently chiseled onto her face. Could the fabled Good Fairy have rendered her lovesick by smacking her silly with that legendary wand?

"Wan," Eloise was saying. "You look wan. Pale. Are you feeling all right?"

They'd made it back to the Port Authority with little time to spare, jockeying through the huge main chamber, dodging daytrippers and long distance travelers wrestling bulky backpacks and cumbersome satchels. They bounded past rows of beechwood benches filled to capacity and around glass kiosks, out the ticket-numbered door, onto the cement sidewalk, and up the ramp where Eloise was due to board a bus for Boston.

"I'm fine," Imogene huffed, barely making it. "Why wouldn't I be?"

"Water is streaming from the corner of your left eye."

"Oh. That."

"And out of your right nostril."

Imogene blew her nose in her mitten, then stared in disbelief, as if she saw, not herself at all, but a *dybbuk* as the culprit.

It prompted Eloise to reach into Imogene's coat pocket to retrieve the handkerchief she'd seen put there earlier, then gently tilt Imogene's head upwards to dry her face before pressing their cheeks together. "You're burning up."

"Maybe I'm hot to trot."

Eloise laughed. "Do you know what that means?"

"Not really. But I always wanted to say it. Does it apply?"

"No." Eloise wrapped her arms around Imogene and hugged her harder than she'd ever had anyone. "And, yes."

"So, does this mean next weekend is good for you?"

"Good?"

"For me flying up to Boston."

"Of course. Yes! You'll fly up? You mean it?"

"Are you surprised?

"Surprised? I'm thrilled!"

They did not kiss goodbye.

It was either due to a sudden fit of awareness, as if anyone looking at them could tell by their faces something intimate was imminent, or Imogene thought she could give Eloise a bout of drug addiction.

Whichever, when the driver made his last call, Imogene dropped her arm around Eloise's waist and used it to guide her on board before the doors swung shut.

For a brief moment, Imogene knew it took all the strength she had not to get on the bus, followed by all the strength she had not to pass out and fall under it.

Marty motioned for Eloise to take the window seat he'd saved for her. She squeezed into it in time to raise her hands in mimicry and mouth the words "I'll call you" to Imogene, who had followed the ramp along from the outside as Eloise walked down the inside aisle.

Imogene stood as close to the window as possible, one hand raised in the air, fluttering her fingers as more of a provisional 'see you' than a waved goodbye.

Eloise lip-read the words "I love you'" from Imogene.

Imogene lip-read the word "ditto" from Eloise.

And then she was gone.

THIRTY-SEVEN
Sunday Afternoon, March 15, 1970
Secrets & Guys

Eloise kept her eyes glued on Imogene as the bus backed out of its berth. She continued staring aimlessly once it rolled down the ramp of the Port Authority, under the overpass of the Henry Hudson Parkway and headed uptown to the Cross Bronx where it would turn east to Connecticut, picking up I-95 all the way to Boston.

Even under ideal weather conditions and no traffic at maximum speed, it would take five hours to get back to Portsmouth where she'd temporarily set up house as a favor to James Ellis, a two-tour Vietnam vet and career Staff Sergeant stationed at Pease Air Force base with his wife, Sherry. Getting married had allotted James the pay upgrade he needed to live off base.

However, unbeknownst to the military, Sherry got an annulment after learning James was gay on their wedding night. He failed to inform the military of his marital status change, knowing he'd be drummed out of the service if there was even an inkling of him being homosexual. Instead, he hoped to be lucky enough to coast through this final tour of duty undetected. It's why he lied to Eloise about Sherry's absence (saying she was in Ohio caring for her ailing parents).

The presence of Eloise provided James with the perception of husbandhood.

• • •

James Ellis first met Eloise Fitz in 1966 when he visited the Clearwater Beach Tiki Bar she managed. He was stationed at MacDill in Tampa back then and got it in his head he'd be safe from being outed if he crossed the causeway to drink at the popular gay-friendly place.

"Safe for knuckleheads maybe," Eloise told him, serving up shots of ouzo.

James was a short, thin, balding fellow of Greek descent with bull-breathing nostrils, a smile forming dimples that could pick up nickels, and a deep, mellow voice that even his worst critics found beguiling.

One weekend, he and his fake-straight base buddies were heading to Manhattan to visit Byron Steele, a wealthy market research analyst who once paid James a Franklin for a quickie near the downtown Dunedin docks, then tipped him with four round-trip, first class plane tickets to New York, suggesting he bring three friends along for wrestle and relaxation.

Eloise deduced the much older Byron intended the freebies to be given to young men, but James only had two other friends, so she took him up on his offer to tag along. It proved a gold mine for her. She and Byron clicked and stayed in touch. Riding on the tailcoats of rich gay guys became routine for her after that.

On the upside, both of Byron's parents were high priced lawyers living in St. Petersburg. She'd met them soon after the New York trip when Byron was down visiting for a month. Like his father, Byron was a Stetson Law School graduate , was generous to a fault, and knew people in both high and low places who could get him pretty much anything that needed doing, done.

On the downside, Byron was a pathological liar. He'd lie about being late, which he invariably was, often by hours. He'd lie about the weather outside, even if you were out in it, standing next to him. He'd lie about the price of purchases while showing you the contradicting receipt. Basically, he was on lie-automatic, even when his lies were vacuous and transparent, even when the person he was lying to said, "I know you're lying." He'd even lie about lying.

Although Eloise recognized Byron's mendacity as a colossal character flaw, she made it work to her advantage. Whenever she visited New York City she had a penthouse on East 48th Street to stay in (gratis), a driver and limousine at her disposal, and plenty of petty cash left under her breakfast tray napkin for padding her pockets.

In exchange, whenever Byron was in Florida on business, she'd be his plus-one. He'd provide her with the appropriate couture (she was allowed to keep), travel and accommodation expenses to all the date destinations, dining at the finest restaurants, and orchestra seats to opening nights at gala events, third row on the aisle.

"Who am I to nitpick?" she asked when Byron offered her his Eloise-friendly terms.

James knew Eloise had scored big with Byron after he'd introduced them, so it came as no surprise to her when he bargained for a sizable favor in return.

"Come to New Hampshire and stay for a few months. Sherry won't be there before June, and I sure could use a friendly face around until I establish contacts. It won't cost you a cent."

Eloise's beach side bartender gigs were seasonal and she wasn't keen on spending her off time managing the gift center of a Palm Harbor orange grove. The job itself was fun; she enjoyed meeting tourists and cajoling them into buying tacky souvenirs. But she had a tendency to draw cash from the till, leaving a note for it and closing up early so she could go bet on Tampa's jai alai, straining her ties with the grove's owner. Never mind that she limited her unpaid leave to when business was slow, and always returned the funds the following morning. And never mind that during her off hours she baby-sat the woman's kids for free. It wasn't the principle, but the principal; eight hours of a calculated lost interest on the borrowed money was valued more by the grove owner than their friendship.

The chronic animus made the timing right, along with a nibbling need at the edges of Eloise's party girl personality to find somewhere to be needed and belong. She was sixty-seven days shy of turning thirty-one and — while any state with snow would be her last choice of venues during winter — she felt a sliver of obligation to James.

"I can't go without my peke's."

"No problem."

"And, we're agreed it's temporary."

"Absolutely."

So, in early December of 1969, Eloise left the free room and board, laundry service, car care, paid insurance premiums, allowance, and gamut of security at her parent's home within walking distance of the sugar white sands on the Gulf of Mexico, for the sleet and snow at sea level in Portsmouth, New Hampshire.

• • •

"Hi, my name is Izzy," Eloise said to the young man standing behind her at Elroy's, an old gypsy caravan converted to a mobile hamburger stand that parked itself near the wharf every Friday after sunset and stayed open until two in the morning on Monday. It served as both a fun food source and last chance place to cruise after the local hot spots closed at 1:30.

"Marty," came his fast, friendly reply. "You're the doll living with James Ellis on Market Street, upstairs over 107."

"The doll part is debatable, but the rest is right. Are you two friends?"

"Like Leviticus and salt water taffy."

Marty worked as a teller and general clerk at the bank where Eloise cashed a stipend from her parents each week. He was popular for his playfulness and the joy he spread among the lady account holders there, as well as being a different variety of pleasure for many of the male depositors. It helped that, for all of his whoring around, he didn't look a day over 17.

Yes, Marty knew James. Everyone on the sly seemed to either know him, or *of* him, because James was the town's go-to-gay-guy, profiting by arranging play dates between "local queers and visiting closeteers" who couldn't chance being outed in their faraway hometowns.

By comparison, the friendship between Marty and Eloise hadn't been a long one, but it had been instantaneous and true. He served as her escort around town, and she played den mother to his sophomoric friends.

"Ours is a match made in homo-ven," he'd said to her. "Get it?"

• • •

Snow was accumulating at a dangerous rate. It made peering out the bus window at the landscape impossible, but was perfect for daydreaming, which Eloise did as she as rode along, contemplating the fiasco she'd made of things by getting herself involved with James. Not that it was the first time she'd made the wrong choices to appease the wrong people, but she wanted it to be the last.

"I phoned for James to pick us up at the Boston depot," Marty interrupted.

"What did he say?"

"The standard. Always wanting you to wait on him, but bitchy about reciprocating."

"Why is that, do you suppose?"

"It's because you're female. If you were a man, and he thought he had a chance to score, he'd jump through hoops to grant your every wish."

"Did he ever tell you about the time he loaned his car to a trick he met while stationed in the Philippines and never saw either again?"

"Hell yes. Me and everyone else who asks to borrow his Bug."

"Once burned twice selfish, I suppose. What time did you say we'd be there?"

"Seven, and to bring a bottle. That way, if we're delayed, he can get drunk while waiting and you'll drive us home."

"If he's not soused already." James' daily drunkenness disgusted her.

"Has he been doing that again?"

"You mean he stopped?"

"Apparently not."

Eloise nudged Marty. "Did you mention to James I'd met someone?"

"No-o. And I don't want to be within rampage distance when he finds out!"

"Rampage? Why?"

"Because he needs you right where you are until his tour is up."

"He hasn't so far. I haven't been summoned to any of his official functions. But I'm sure his wife can come back for a weekend if necessary."

"You mean Sherry of Tampa fame? Sherry left him."

"No, you're mistaken. Sherry's in Ohio taking care of her parents."

"Is that what he told you? How he got you to help him commit fraud?"

"Fraud? What fraud?"

"Once Sherry knew he was gay, she had the marriage annulled and married someone else within months of them tying the knot."

"Whoa! He didn't tell Sherry he was gay going in?"

"Nope."

"So, it was never a toy marriage?"

"Nope."

"Are you serious?"

"Serious as Satan in a San Francisco bath house, honey. Unlike back at MacDill, no one at Pease has ever met Sherry. So he's been showing your photo around, saying you're her. On the base, on the streets and even when he came into the bank to get a loan to buy that custom car from Germany last December. You endorsed it as his wife."

"I most certainly did not."

"Then he did. I typed up the papers and processed them."

Eloise was momentarily taken aback. She was angry to have been played yet again but knew she'd have a hard time getting out of Portsmouth with all possessions if James discovered she was onto him.

"Oh-h, right," she opted out. "That loan. I'm so focused on thinking about Imogene it slipped my mind. So-o, you thought buying the Volkswagen was a bad move?"

"Oh come on! Custom stereo speakers installed in the front and back seats, a sunroof *and* extra vents for air conditioning piped through?"

"Extravagant, yes. But I must admit, the black dash and carpeting contrasting the red leather seats and door panels make it a mighty fine looking Bug."

"True."

"Remind me. How much did that cost?"

"Three grand. I couldn't believe it. That's nearly twice the price of here."

Eloise was silently fuming, but knew if she brought the fraud to the bank's attention, James would be arrested and court-martialed at forty-three with no job, no pension, a felony record, and nothing to show for service to his country.

"Listen, Marty, let's not mention this conversation to James. He'd have a hissy-fit if he knew we were discussing him behind his back."

"My lips are sealed."

Eloise returned to looking out the window. All she could make out were headlights from cars pulling off to park on the interstate in both directions. They'd be late getting back to Boston..

THIRTY-EIGHT
Sunday Night, March 15, 1970
Boys Will Be Toys

James Ellis had no intention of meeting Eloise and her boys at the Boston bus depot. He wouldn't have objected to her taking off if they'd asked him along. Not that he could go. Duty calls and all. But they hadn't the courtesy to include him. That ticked him off to the bottom of the bottle.

Then there was the expectation that he transport her and three guys who couldn't fit in his Bug even if the seats were taken out and the top was sawed off. Fetching them would require he drive Eloise's Buick Electra 225 to Boston. Seriously?

Wasn't it demeaning enough when the Air Force denied him pilot training because he couldn't meet the sitting-height requirement? So why would he ever condescend to drive a car the size of an airliner down the highway, primed for people to take potshots at him? And what about the gas bill, huh? Even on a cloudless day her jetmobile needed at least one fill-up before the three hour round trip was over. Plus, the way the snow was coming down? He'd be lucky to get there, get them, and get them back in four hours. At any rate, he had better ways of spending his time and money than chauffeuring Eloise and all her little hangers-on around.

"Oh stop!" lisped Larry Dee in a pell-mell Boston accent that all within earshot found so delightfully engaging they became transfixed.

As a born and bred Beantown barber by day and crackerjack cruiser of bikers by night, Larry Dee met James on Daytona Beach during the Fairy Fling of '67, where a cigarette sticking out of the waistband of tighty-whities served as the come-on code. Larry was the one and only trick who'd ever remained true to James

"The trouble with you is, you think fairies should remain friends

— like we're all members of some silly swish sorority."

"Marty and George were my friends before she moved in," James glowered into the phone. "Now, whenever a guy calls, he wants her instead of me."

"First of all my darling sweetheart, they weren't your friends. They were your slam-bam thank you plans. Secondly, you still have me — sing it! — I made a rhyme."

"Hell, you even prefer her, Lare!"

"Only after I'm done with you, bambino, which I will be, if you continue on as heinie whiney tonight. Where is Izzy Fitz anyhow?"

"Waiting for you at the Boston bus depot."

"What?"

"She and her prissy-posse were due there from New York 45 minutes ago."

"Jesusmaryandjoseph!"

"I told her you'd pick them up in your dad's Caddy because my ride isn't big enough."

"Thanks a lot for making me the bad baboon, Ginny!" Larry knew James recoiled at the Jimmy-joshing, but hated being called Ginny even more. "Why didn't you take her blue-magoo?"

"I didn't, okay? She's with two studs and their sugar daddy in tow."

"Say no more Pouty Patty. I'm on my way." Click.

It worked like a charm. James knew Larry could be lured into doing almost anything by the mention of studs. Having that ace up his sleeve pleased him.

In truth, James hadn't told Marty anything. He'd simply hung up the phone. If Larry hadn't checked in when he did, the four would still be waiting for him to show. They could have waited all night for all he cared. He felt pretty smug about the whole subterfuge shebang for thirty seconds before the phone rang again.

James assumed it was Larry getting back to apologize for abruptly hanging up.

"No apology needed," he answered in lieu of hello.

"No apology offered," came the girl's voice on the other end of the line.

It irritated James. "Get lost. This number's for men only."

"Does your mother approve of the way you answer the phone?"

It struck him that his mother would not. Instead, she'd be appalled. She'd say she raised him better and he should be ashamed of himself. *Wait a minute*, he thought. *What gives this bitch a right to tell me how to answer my own goddam phone?*

"No, she doesn't."

"Then at ease solider. Mom isn't calling."

"Who is this?" James snarled.

"Imogene LaPin. I'm calling for Eloise Fitz. Is she there?"

"That figures."

"It does? Why? Who are you?"

"I'm her husband. And, no, she's not here. She's gallivanting in Boston instead of being home where she belongs, taking care of me!"

"I see." Imogene paused. "Will you take a message?"

"Do I sound like her secretary, lady?"

"I'll settle for a good trooper who doesn't forget to tell her."

"I might."

"You won't."

"You think not?"

Imogene spoke slowly and enunciated so he couldn't miss either the message or the intent. "Our eventual in-person introduction will be less *painful* if you tell her Imogene called. Ta-ta!"

James slammed the receiver down on kitchen's wall phone, threw open the refrigerator door, removed two six-packs of beer and retreated to a wrapback bamboo swing hung from an exposed 18th century rafter in his living room. He would still be sitting there, surrounded by empty cans, when she walked in at 9:40 that night.

• • •

Larry Dee never met anyone who didn't like Eloise Fitz. Within two months of living in Portsmouth she'd easily established herself as one of those soft spoken, Southern style, ladylike, lipstick gals who was always polite, endlessly gracious, and ever willing to welcome others into her good-times world. That included James Ellis — although he didn't know why.

Larry liked James because their tricking styles matched. It made for happy camping it up and around. Too, Larry was a sympathetic sort who'd identified James as a Powder Puff Profile anomaly; he wasn't tall and dark, or blonde and buff, or young and hung, or handy and handsome, or filthy rich and able to purchase any or all of those gay guy partialities.

Neither was Larry. At five foot six inches, he had a huge head set squarely on a short neck above wide shoulders, a massive chest that triangled downward to a slender waist, flat ass, and stout legs possessing the style of a traipsing peacock.

But unlike James, whose fruitcake personality fluctuated between martyrdom and misfit, Larry was a generous, kind, thoughtful, gut-bustingly funny bon vivant who didn't let anyone interfere with who he was, or what he chose to do with his life.

True, he restricted his weekends on the wild side to far off places and kept closeted for the comfort level of his family, whom he loved dearly. But even if they did think the worst and agree with the law of the land condemning gays as heinous and subject to arrest, they never admitted anything out of the ordinary about him. And, the fact that his two sisters were lawyers, his three brothers were cops, his father was a union boss, and his Sicilian mother had all of them living beneath one roof probably had nothing to do with their absence of acrimony and presence in being enamored of him.

It was nearly eight when Larry roared up in front of the bus terminal on St. James Street in the Back Bay section of Boston with the windows of his parents' black Eldorado open and *A Boy Named Sue* blaring on the radio.

"Have you been waiting long, sissy?" he yelled.

"Are you kidding?" Marty opened the door and slid in. "We got here seconds ago. It was by far the best bus ride of my life. Man, did our driver ever know how to muscle his way through — even when tractor-trailers were pulling off by the droves!"

"I thought there were four of you."

"There was, but Freddie had his limo waiting and took off the second I said we had a way home. Hell, if he'd told me sooner I'd have had us all in the limo and saved you the trouble. The bus trip totally did him in. I think rich guys never ride buses and don't want to be seen when forced to. George said he was one big fidgety-fag the whole trip back."

"Freddie? Not Freddie Fata."

"Friend of yours?"

"Oh God, yes! He's every whore's worst habit. And by whore I mean the front and center stand-at-attention type. I had the old hag. It must have been..." Larry caught himself a hair's breadth shy of revealing his true age. "Where's Izzy?"

"In the lady-loo splashing water on her face. She dreamed the whole way home."

"You mean slept?"

"I mean *dreamed*!" Marty poked at Leo's heart. "You can always tell when they aren't alone in there."

"What aren't you saying, Hedda Harlot?"

Marty slid over closer to Larry. "She met someone."

"Don't kid me now."

"I swear. The woman's been bitch-bitten by a bitch-kitten."

"Izzy? I don't believe it! I've been out with her and James at the Barnyard every weekend and she never looks at women. Never dances with anyone either. I mean, yes she's a fag hag but, as God is my witness that I am Mary Sunshine, I don't buy it."

George hopped into the front seat and corroborated the news, complete with the name of Eloise's new lady-in-dating and even more details of the troupe's Big Apple escapades.

"We're clucking like little old ladies over lemonade," Larry cautioned. "Better change the topic before she gets here."

"Wouldn't this make a great car ad?" Marty suggested. "Queens in a Cad." They each lifted their right hands up in unison and did the 'S' wave three times.

THIRTY-NINE
Sunday Afternoon, March 15, 1970
I Do Ado

Consumed with longing, Eloise intended to close her eyes for (at most) a minute to envision the face of Imogene and imagine what she was doing while alone in New York without her. She felt exhilarated, experiencing every cliché of being in love she'd ever heard of, but with a tirade of emotions that were totally foreign to her. So, how could she sleep, and why would her dreaming take such a drastic detour?

Was it because, on just such a long ago Ides of March snowy night, when sheets of sleet formed layers of black ice camouflaging the tar top roads outside of Mayview, Missouri, Barbie Brown was driving the green and cream color coupe given to her by her parents as a high school graduation gift six months earlier when it skidded off the road and headlong into a tree, killing her upon impact.

Barbie and Eloise had been on the same basketball team during their senior year of high school, playing different positions and partying after home games with different people. Each went off to a different college the first week in September and each dropped out on a different day in October after securing a job at Hallmark in Kansas City.

It was on the card counting production line that they'd met again and, while sharing their similar stories, decided to pool their paychecks, get out of their parents' homes, and move into an enviable apartment over a retail shop near Troost Avenue.

But Barbie Brown died on the day they'd returned home for the Thanksgiving holiday, two weeks after they'd moved into their new home, and two minutes after she dropped Eloise off at her parents' place.

The news shocked Eloise, who couldn't deal with Barbie's death even though her mother tried to sugarcoat it with happier thoughts and comfort foods.

"Things happen for a purpose, Eloise," her mother would say. "Have a donut."

"What possible purpose?"

"To prepare you for life."

"Oh, great, this life lesson was brought to you by *m-y-y* Mom, paving the way for more instant death to come, with donuts no less. Waytago, Ma. I feel so much better."

Here's the rub: Eloise's despondency wasn't limited to the loss of her close friend. It also centered on them being the same age, making the same choices, while doing virtually the same things, at the same time. When Barbie died, it removed death from Eloise's friendly file of denial and planted it firmly into her reality where it wasn't wanted, needed, or appreciated. Eloise could easily rip that weed up by its roots and dispose of it during her daydreams, but every night it would come barreling back as a nightmare.

Eloise never returned to the Kansas City apartment she and Barbie shared. She didn't go back to work either. Instead, she phoned and said she had appendicitis, prompting her coworkers to send flowers, cards, and personal notes of cheer. Her employer continued to mail paychecks.

Eventually, it forced her mother to dig out a three-cent Florida postcard left over from their snowbird days, address it to the personnel department, print a resignation and forge her daughter's signature. The card read: I won't be back. The checks are in the mail. Thank you for everything. Eloise Fitz.

• • •

"How would you like this packaged, Mrs. Fitz? Is it for someone dear to you?"

"Yes," Eloise's mother told Mrs. Parkerson, manager of gift-wrapping at Harzfeld's Department Store where she'd taken the grey mink pillbox hat purchased in millinery minutes earlier. "It's for my daughter. She'll turn nineteen in two months and I'm praying the hat will inspire her to leave of the house."

The word 'prayer' was like music to Gail Parkerson's ears, having been the proud daughter of a Pentecostal upbringing, a religion she professed to love more than Jesus-himself-say-amen. She had, after all, been made a medium when she was baptized as a child, the same as Christ was a medium to receive the Holy Spirit. And then, after being baptized a second time into the body of Christ, she was immersed a third time with the Holy Spirit.

Granted, she never understood how all this was achieved since immersion was involved only once, assuring a thin white sheet would cling to the shadowy triangle and feisty nipples of her perfectly shaped body as it was led up out of the water. But the successfully staged show made the fervor of embracing the other two baptisms cogent. She was regenerated and justified, selected and sanctified, and *nothing* could take that away.

So what if she slipped a little now and then? Slipped so badly she fell on her back and, while bending her knees to stand up, they became weak and split apart like cheerleading triggers. Who's to say it wasn't the presence of the Holy Spirit making her go boom-sticka-boom, or that she yielded herself, not with more water, but with whatever provision readily available? Hadn't such preordained thinking gotten her to where she was, doing what she was doing? Wrapping presents for customers at the finest store on the Plaza in Kansas City was her *métier*.

"Are you saved, Mrs. Fitz?"

"Oh my yes! I wouldn't have bought it otherwise. It was half off and marked down another 15% when I showed the floorwalker some soil on the satin lining."

Gail inspected the hat. "I don't see any soil."

Mrs. Fitz, who spoke in a fast Alabaman accent at all times, pursed her lips and declared, "Well, I-be John Brown." She looked at Mrs. Parkerson with an impish glint in her eye and got a twinkle back.

"What I mean by saved, Mrs. Fitz, is do you walk in the footsteps of your Savior, Jesus Christ and hold His Word in your heart?"

"I attend church when I'm not working if that's what you mean." This was technically true. Once she and her husband began opening a string of diners after leaving New York sixteen years earlier, she'd worked every Sunday. But prior to then she attended church with irregularity, continuing to do so, sporadically, albeit vicariously, still.

"Then your prayers will be answered."

"Oh you think so, huh?"

Mrs. Fitz was a good woman — a kind, hardworking, well-intended woman. But she was also commonsensical. Yes, she believed in God. No, she didn't fear Him. It was more like she worked with Him as closely as was practicable to get the things that needed doing, done. If the rules had to be bent, or the truth stretched to fit, so be it, as long as no one she cared about got hurt in the process.

Oh, and one more thing. If you so much as dared to breathe a negative thought in the direction of her daughter, she'd grind you up and serve you as grits to guests at your own memorial service, collect compliments for the tasty recipe after doing so, and pocket the tips.

"Do you carry a picture of your daughter, Mrs. Fitz?"

She answered by opening her green leather clutch and pulling out a wallet size graduation snapshot of Eloise Fitz wearing a custom-made, off-the-shoulder, baby blue taffeta dress to match her merry blue eyes, details Mrs. Fitz added aloud after handing the monochrome print to Mrs. Parkerson.

"She's very pretty," praised Mrs. Parkerson, lingering over the girl's face. They were words Mrs. Fitz was accustomed to hearing.

"My Eloise was voted Queen of her prom."

"Then we have the tiara in common."

Mrs. Fitz felt pleased by the way the conversation was progressing, pushing it a bit in a certain direction by presenting the photo of her daughter, seeking to benefit by association. Because Mrs. Fitz thought Mrs. Parkerson was about the prettiest woman she'd ever seen north of the Mason-Dixon, having observed her from afar in Harzfeld's many times, paying acute attention to how Mrs. Parkerson garnered glances from every man she pranced past.

When Mrs. Fitz asked the millinery clerk who the woman was, the tattletale told her it was Mrs. Parkerson, twenty-five and already divorced with two children to support, ages three and five. Rumor had it the oldest girl resembled, not her ex-husband, but a high school sweetheart who could often be seen lurking from a safe distance during holidays.

"Well," Mrs. Fitz offered Mrs. Parkerson sincerely, "I'm not one bit surprised you were prom queen, too."

"Oh gracious me, no, Mrs. Fitz! I wasn't. I was a runner-up for Miss Kansas."

You couldn't fault Mrs. Fitz for being impressed. She had, herself, been the belle of the ball as a younger woman, capturing the attention of the cream of Manhattan's most eligible bachelors and almost landed one before ending up with Padraig Fitz.

Few knew she was twenty-five by the time they married, or that she spent the next six years being begged by Padraig to start a family. She'd refused, fearing childbirth would ruin her figure and spoil the pleasure of being flirted with and fawned over. For, in addition to possessing a sophisticated style and bodacious bosom, Mrs. Fitz had gams that made men melt whenever she entered a room, or walked down a street, or put up her feet.

The fact is, if she hadn't had an afternoon fondness for fooling around, Eloise might never have been conceived, or raised as the focus of her father's attention and joy forever after.

"I was told you posted a room for rent on the employee bulletin board."

"I did indeed," said Mrs. Parkerson, certain Jesus had sent Mrs. Fitz to her. Silently, they were both thinking the same thing at that very moment: Eloise would make an ideal roommate.

"Of course, my daughter isn't an employee of Harzfeld's, so maybe she would need to secure a job here first?" Mrs. Fitz knew that wasn't so. She was merely trying to move the idea towards an ideal conclusion.

"That's not required." Mrs. Parkerson spiraled the last ribbon, putting a final touch on the gift-wrapped box. "But there is an opening for an assistant in my department."

Mrs. Fitz looked around. "How many people are in your department?"

"Counting myself and your Eloise? That would make two."

Hence, a plan was hatched. Mrs. Fitz would leave the wrapped hat for Eloise to pick up on an arranged date, after which the charm of

Mrs. Parkerson and the power of prayer would take control.

• • •

It irritated Eloise, to be expected to drive forty-nine miles into Kansas City to pick up a gift forgotten there by her mother. She didn't care whose gift it was, knowing it could have been for any one of her many relatives. Each parent had siblings, all of whom were married with children, except for her Uncle Lester who died of a heart attack when skinny-dipping with his best friend, and her cousin Billy who had a tutu hidden under his bed, and her Aunt Edna who was widowed with money and a fetish for fun times. Her mother hoped Eloise wouldn't take after her Aunt Edna; so she did.

At least once a week Mrs. Fitz hinted how nice it would be if Eloise would marry and give them grandchildren. And at least as often, Eloise would counter it with, "Like mother, like daughter," as yet unaware she was not and would never be.

All she knew at nineteen was, had it not been for a pact her mother made with her father that her mother never intended to keep for a conception never meant to occur, Eloise wouldn't have stepped off an elevator in Harzfeld's Department Store, or plodded over to its gift-wrapping desk to pick up a package containing a pillbox hat that she'd never wear in a gazillion years.

But she was born. She did go. She would step off the Harzfeld's elevator. And once she locked eyes with Gail Parkerson in the gift-wrapping department, any vestige of annoyance she felt disappeared, and the rancor she harbored at being ill-conceived vaporized.

It was not love at first sight.

Indeed, it was not love at all. It was more like shock and awe that struck Eloise, making the rapidity with which hers and Gail's friendship developed nothing shy of remarkable.

Naturally, Eloise was hired on the spot, and as naturally (or so it seemed to her at the time) she invited Gail and her daughters to her parents' home for Sunday dinner after the church services Gail required Eloise attend, having learned she'd ceased going at age eight because (she said) her dad needed her to pump gas and clean windshields on weekends. It was an argument Mrs. Fitz finally conceded. At least, if Eloise was in overalls helping her dad, she needn't wonder nor worry where the girl was.

During the Sunday family dinner following Valentine's Day, 1958, Mrs. Fitz made a spontaneous-sounding suggestion.

"Mrs. Parkerson, I'm told that you have a room in your home for rent."

"Why yes, Mrs. Fitz, I do."

"Might you be inclined to rent it to Eloise? Mr. Fitz would guarantee her monthly rent and offer you an additional ten dollar stipend to cover gasoline if she could also ride into work with you each day. Is that fair?"

"Fair and generous, because there's no one I'd rather rent my extra room to than your lovely daughter."

The Parkerson home in Lee's Summit, Missouri was a 1925 bungalow with a broad and deep front porch sheltering a wood-slatted swing suspended from its teal blue wainscoted ceiling at one end, and a pierced-metal glider set perpendicular to the street at the other. The whitewash clapboard exterior exhibited two tall windows on either side of a centered front door that, like the shutters, was painted loden green. It wasn't a fancy home, but it had the charm that small vintage houses invariably do when complemented with the ivy covered gated trellis and weatherworn brick walkway that this one did.

Initially, Eloise slept in the guest bedroom with a view of the shaded back yard where she could watch over Gail's daughters at play. Gail slept in the master bedroom on the opposite side of the house, next to the girls' room and single bath.

One night as Eloise drifted off to sleep wearing only a tee shirt to keep her shoulders warm, she heard her bedroom door open and detected the sweet scent of Gail's Gigolo cologne.

Eloise had been thinking about Gail, intending to recreate the day they'd spent together in her dreams. She felt fortunate for their friendship, which could be perceived as a godsend to those who believed in such. Eloise neither believed, nor disbelieved, but was willing to string along with whatever others needed in order to survive in a world that often bewildered her.

Yes, she went to church every Sunday, but more for the sustenance than the sermons. As someone reared in restaurants, she'd developed a preoccupation with food and the joy it brought to people — friends, family, and truckers alike. And to her, there was no better food to be had than fresh-made meals by Midwest church ladies.

So when Gail crawled into her bed and began lightly scratching her back with her long, slender, red-polished nails, Eloise felt more relaxed than riled; more comforted than coerced. It seemed normal. And, when Gail's hands slipped, first under the T-shirt and then slowly lower to where Eloise was bare, she became curious as to what was Gail was doing, but not enough to doubt the motives of this woman she trusted and admired.

But when Gail began exploring the area of Eloise's torso that she herself had only visited hygienically, it made her anxious.

"Haven't you ever done this before?" Gail spoke softly.

"No."

"Never?"

"Never."

Eloise could feel the moistness of fresh lipstick as Gail kissed her back, saying she was giving Eloise a secret gift that belonged to no other two people on earth. She said they must treat it as divined, never to be shared with anyone, either in words or in actions, lest it be taken away and their love for each other be lost forever and ever, amen.

To Eloise, that sounded as if the two of them had somehow been ordained to do whatever it was that was about to be done.

"Okay," she said.

• • •

Three years later Eloise became enraged after Gail told her how silly and ridiculous she was acting. "Grow up, Eloise. "I have two girls to rear and they've begun questioning me. Think about what's best for them."

"Haven't I helped you raise them like they were my own sisters? What's wrong with what we have? What's changed?"

"What we had was temporary."

"That's not what you said."

"What we had is frowned upon by Jesus."

"That's not what you told me. You told me Jesus never said a word about it."

"Eloise, I need to think of the future. I want the girls to go to college."

"I'll get a second job."

"I'm pregnant."

"You're what?"

Gail was blasé. "I'm pregnant. I'm going to have a baby."

"But how could that be?"

"I've been seeing someone for a while now."

"What do you mean, seeing? How long?"

"A year. Eighteen months, maybe more."

"Why are you telling me this?"

"He's the tax accountant lawyer for the church. We're having an affair."

"Wally? Wally Ashland?"

"Walter. He prefers Walter."

"When? Where?"

"Where what?"

"Where have you been having your affair?"

"Here, of course."

"In this house? In our bed? Oh my God. *Here*?"

"Now, Eloise, you mustn't take the Lord's name in vain, dear. Besides, it's *my* house and *my* bed. We shared it, yes. But if you'll think back to when I rented you the room, it was the bed at the other end of the hall I offered. That was your bed. Anyhow, Walter proposed and I've said yes. So, you'll need move out. Right now would be best for me. I've already packed your things."

And it came to pass, the conspiracy that took Mrs. Fitz and Mrs. Parkerson twenty minutes to hatch, and two months to hammer out, and caprice to alter, and eighteen months to unravel, and minutes to confess, and seconds to dismiss, died.

Instantly.

• • •

"Wake up, we're here," said Marty, rousing Eloise from her deep sleep.

"What! I'm up. What?"

"We're here. We're in Boston. We're pulling into the depot. We're back."

"Yeah, yeah," she yawned, dabbing her eyes. "I knew that."

FORTY
Sunday Night, March 15, 1970
Any Port In A Storm

Eloise was too tired to talk, too contented to fight and too intent on calling Imogene to bother with James that night. Their arrangement had been as a favor, for a temporary time. Any obligation she might have once felt was now fulfilled. End of discussion. During the final leg of a long return to the place she'd soon be leaving, she resolved to remain calm and play along until the moment she walked out.

James Ellis had lucked into the apartment he rented on the top floor of a former colonial era town house harboring an attic stairwell that was converted to a numbered address nailed above an added arched entry. Once inside, the narrow plank steps led up to a four-room flat, anchored by an expanse of windows filling the width-wall from floor to ceiling at the eastern end. James had arranged pillows on a quilt covered mattress parallel to it, providing a place to take in the lights of Kittery, Maine across the harbor and marvel at tugboats moored in the choppy waters below.

Inside the apartment to the left was a wall of hooks to hang coats and a wood rack to set wet boots during inclement weather. A narrow kitchen measuring eight-by-ten was refurbished in chalk white and updated with new appliances, cupboards, countertops, and a bistro set.

At the opposite end of the windowed wall in the main room were bedrooms separated by a full bath with a large porcelain basin, clawfoot tub, beveled mirrors, and a hexagonal tile floor. The larger, master bedroom to the left belonged to James. The guest bedroom to the right with a porthole looking out over Market Street was Eloise's.

Except for a bamboo swing hanging as its centerpiece from one of the ceiling rafters, the apartment was decorated in an eclectic mix of period pieces and complementing accessories that included an armoire, a Hepplewhite camelback couch, two overstuffed chairs, built-in bookcases, and a long credenza below a sizable reproduction of *Bathers* by Renoir that was tastefully framed and mounted. James had purchased the lithograph to give the perception that he was cultivated and straight in the event any flyboys dropped by unannounced.

The feminine touch to James' den was Eloise's room, dominated by an early 19th century pencil post canopy bed adorned with long panels of organdy across its overhead frame. The delicate fabric swooped down for tying back from the mainstay during daytime, and left loose like a bride's veil at night, encouraging her to sleep as if enveloped in clouds.

"Imogene called," said James as Eloise tiptoed into the dark apartment. "Twice."

"Twice?"

"I answered one. The second time I let it ring."

"Then how do you know it was her?" She switched on a table lamp before going into the kitchen and flipping on the overhead.

"I was her. I've got that ring down pat."

"Any message?"

"Call her. She was quite clear about it."

In a flash, Larry made his familiar flamboyant entrance by exploding through the door like Ethel Merman on meth, talking a full body mile a minute.

"Why the hell did this place look so dead from the wharf? I could hardly see to park the Cad behind the building." He waved to James. "Hi homo, we're home! Move your bustle and rustle us some food. We're starved. Never mind! I'll cook, you do the dishin'. Get it? Oh little twinkletoes, you shoulda been with us on that ride back here. Am I right Izzy? It was a trip! And, by trip I mean a terror. May I be frank? You woulda shit bricks all the way there and back if you'd been with us, Jimmy. And, by Jimmy I mean Ginny as in gin. Where's the goddamn gin? Eeek! There's not enough macaroni in this box to Yankee my doodle."

Eloise discreetly backed out of the chatter and closed her bedroom door before dropping down on the floor to greet her happily yapping, dancing Pekingese.

"Hello, my darlings. Hello, hello. Well yes," she kissed Lucy and Gracie, "I missed you, too. I'm sorry I left you. Yes I am! Oh yes I am! I won't ever do it again, ever, ever. Come give your momma more kisses. Yes, yes, yes. I love you, too. I do. Oh yes I do!"

Once the pups settled down, Eloise cracked the door. "James, did you feed my kids yet?"

"Fed and walked."

James had joined Larry in the kitchen by then, putting the final touches on his Poor Pitiful Pearl routine and starting in on his Dave Garroway persona, adding local scoops to the latest gossip Larry was letting loose about the boys of Beantown.

Eloise decided to give the dogs a final piddle before retiring, changing into a pair of red flannel pajamas, matching robe and leather sole slipper socks first. Afterwards, she lifted the pekes up onto the bed, dropped the drapes around her, burrowed under a white goose down comforter with her pink Princess phone in one hand and a scavenged Girl Scout flashlight in the other, eager to dial Imogene and hear the cheer in her voice.

FORTY-ONE
Sunday Afternoon, March 15, 1970
The Book of Dory

By the time the bus pulled out of its berth and she'd watched the last fumes of exhaust dissipate, Imogene's body was begging her to go home, go to bed, and soak up the next few hours of much needed sleep in anticipation of being awakened by the phone ringing and Eloise's voice carried back to her from some three hundred miles away. Maybe more. Maybe less. What did the number of miles matter? Any was too many.

She popped in another little blue pill and thought she heard Alice (of Wonderland) singing *Very Good Advice* dancing through her ears. As a child, she'd played the little golden record often, long after the lesson was ingrained and melody memorized. Alas, this day, taking her own advice was not on Imogene's short list of things to do.

Instead, she returned to the 42nd Street subway station, boarded a train for Union Square and focused on staying alert until the doors opened onto the 14th Street platform. Taking a firm hold of the railing, she pulled herself up the cement steps to the sidewalk and looked around to get her bearings before trudging over to Broadway and down two blocks to the Pensée Bookstore.

Imogene had been a regular at the Pensée when she first moved to New York, coming upon it while wandering the streets alone one afternoon. For a month of Sundays it was her sanctuary, a place where she could lose herself among the rows of tomes piled so high, the ceiling light from one aisle was often blocked by the well stocked shelves in the next. Browsing the Pensée was her day at the beach and trip to Disneyland rolled into one. Not that she'd ever been to Disneyland or desired to go.

Once inside, Imogene went directly to the checkout where she saw the backside of a boy crouched down on the floor, his head hidden inside the lower shelf of the counter.

"Excuse me, sir?"

"What?" the guy grunted.

"Do you have a section on divergent lifestyles?"

"Lady, can't you see I'm busy down here. Spit out whatever it is you want."

"Lesbianism."

"Doing research I suppose?"

"Yes. Yes, I am."

"That's what every closet case coming in here says." His voice became high and jeering. "I'm writing an article and I need to research queers."

"Did your mother teach you to talk to others like that?" Imogene knew, each time she utilized the rearing ploy she sounded more like her own mother. The thing was, it worked.

"Sonofabitch!" bellowed the boy, hitting his head on the shelf he was under when jerking up to lambaste her. "What friggin' business is it of yours what my mother taught?" He'd popped up like a freshly wound Jack-in-the box, coming face to face with Imogene who stared, amused, before calmly extending her right hand.

"You're Wink's friend, Dory Davenport, aren't you? The person who slipped me a Mickey Finn at Johnny's."

"That was Wink's drink," she quickly tattled, embarrassed. "Bombay Gin on ice, only."

"Finn, gin, it did me in. I'm still suffering the side effects."

"And you're wrong about Wink being my friend."

"Come now. I see you party with him every Friday."

"He buys. I deliver. What's it to you?"

"Hey," Imogene yielded, "I'm here to look for books. That's all."

It forced Dory into the awkward choice between shut-up or showdown. *I might as well shake,* she thought. *Apparently the offer isn't going away until I do.* "Aren't you worried about dirtying your hand by shaking it with a dyke?"

"What? There's no washroom in this joint?"

Dory was still attracted to Imogene, true. But after watching

Imogene crumble upon sight of the blonde marauder at Johnny's, lying in an attempt to gain a bogus advantage, being given the evil eye by the cab guy and talking to Wink in private, her conscience finally caught up with her. She now understood her aim to get even with Annie was reprehensible. What's more, it backfired.

Guiding her through the store, Dory singled books she thought Imogene sought.

"That section's on sex. Over there are the Banyon paperbacks. Here you'll find a few on fetishes, gay history, nonfiction, poetry and pulp. That's the psychology and psychiatry sector. Most those studies deal with men. What are you looking for, specifically?"

Imogene scrutinized several titles. "How specific can it get?"

"That depends on what you and your partner are into." Dory couldn't judge how much Imogene knew, or didn't, of her and Wink's tête-à-tête at her apartment, or of the cab-con she played on Imogene's intended. She hadn't believed it possible for Imogene to find the woman, but nixed the idea of confessing all the same.

"How complicated can it be between two women?"

"Two women? Two what kind of women? Are they butch or femme? Is one bi? Will there be role-playing? Are they into experimentation and toys? Is it a fling, a one-nighter, a wide-open free-for-all, a ménage à trois, polyamorous, monogamous..."

"Slow down, Cleopatra! I'm talking Romance 101 here."

"You mean it's the initial voyage for you? Or her? Because, trust me, there's no way the woman you were eyeballing at Johnny's is amateur status. Her age, alone, brings baggage, same as breeder world."

"Breeder world?"

Dory stalled, suddenly seeing herself as Imogene-green. The two were about the same age but Dory knew, ten years in the life had hardened her. She began again, slower and gentler.

"Straights are baby makers. Breeders. The experts say you bring all your past lovers to bed with you at all times. You consciously, or subconsciously compare everything about their bodies both inside and out. The noises made, the odors emitted, likes and dislikes and even the count of their heartbeats. The skills and hurt you acquire converts into baggage carried from one lover to the next. The more partners the more baggage. Sex stats are like sports stats. When you break up you can compare notes with anyone who's had her before you. Basic locker-room."

"I see," said Imogene. But she didn't. Not really.

"For example, if your woman is bi, she's bringing her stable of men into bed with you, even acting the part, or expecting you to, based on what she likes men to do to her. Pure lesbians limit their desire to the female perspective. They shy away from sex toys since nothing phallic is wanted or needed, unless one of the two has been with a bisexual woman, which could influence her by that kind of experience. We might have a clinical book with a chapter dissecting that."

"Egad."

"What?"

"The tawdriness of this baggage business."

"I guess."

"Tell me, if a woman is coming out of a bad relationship, and what you're saying is so, is that burdensome for the new person whenever something innocently said strikes a bad memory chord?"

"Oh, absolutely! Former lover issues cause relationships to fester and shatter all the time, which serves to prove the Lesbian Idiom."

"That is?"

"Lovers are a dime a dozen, but friends are friends for life."

Imogene tsk-tsked. "Sounds more like an *idiot*-um to me."

"Huh?"

"If you elevate your partner to the proper place of adoration and respect from the onset and keep her there for the duration, wouldn't it ensure a lover for life?"

Dory left Imogene alone to read new jacket covers and thumb through dog-eared pages of used books until she lighted on two volumes to her liking: a 1933 hardback edition by Gertrude Stein entitled *The Autobiography of Alice B. Toklas*, and a recent release that even Dory hadn't yet read, *Patience and Sarah,* by Isabel Miller.

"Why these?" Dory asked before bagging the books.

"Wink said Stein and Toklas were elementary."

"And, the other?"

"The jacket says it's a love story taking place in an upstate New

York area my ancestors helped colonize in the 1600s."

"Come-on. This is all you were looking for in lesbian literature?"

Imogene laughed. "Let's say the books reached out to me. If that makes sense."

Dory studied Imogene as she removed a Marine Midland checkbook from her inside coat pocket and wrote out the amount, then flipped a few pages to record the transaction and bring forth a balance. The contradictions she saw in Imogene bugged her, like how Imogene appeared as articulate and poised and shallow and silly simultaneously. Maybe Wink was wrong?

"Imogene, has anyone ever told you you're pretty enough to stop wearing makeup?"

"Thank you and yes, but I'm not. I need a light base to smooth out my skin tone and mascara to enlarge my eyes." She handed Dory the check. "The lipstick speaks for itself."

"But why bother? It's a conspiracy thought up by men as a turn-on and way to improve us, as if we needed fixing."

"Who in the world fed you that malarkey?"

"It's not malarkey."

"Yes, it is. Makeup has been used for 4,000 years by both genders. Egyptians began using eye makeup in ancient times to ward off evil spirits. They even thought eyeliner could improve their eyesight. I bet there's a book in this place that'll verify cosmetics as a staple to enchant women for thousands of years. Men capitalized on it, sure. But women wear makeup for other women, not for men."

"That's not a very feminist way of thinking."

"Look, if you don't want to use makeup, don't. But draw the line at berating women who do. Cherry-picking the feminist agenda shouldn't define or sway you, no matter how good the intentions. I like the way I look in makeup. I do it for me. Same as how I dress. Same as how I wear my hair."

Dory handed Imogene her purchase along with two Pensée advertising bookmarks. "I'll be damned if you don't make sense. It's annoying. But come back and see me anyhow."

"I'll do that. By the way, do you ever go to The Parlor on 8th Street off Sixth Avenue?"

"The ice cream place? Why?"

"There's a liberated young woman working there who's single. She has a crusty exterior hiding an earnest heart."

"I don't need any fix-me-ups."

"I'm sure you don't, Dory. But if you drop by there, tell Charlene I said bye for me?"

Imogene felt Dory's eyes on her as she walked away. When she reached the door she added, "I appreciate your help, Dory. Especially the way you always looked out for me at Johnny's. I never forget a kindness."

FORTY-TWO
Sunday Night, March 15, 1970
For The Record

Whenever Imogene fell asleep in a fetal position, Pansy would stick his nose into her ear and sneeze to wake her up. If she lay asleep on her back, Pansy would put his paw on her eye and press to pop it open. If neither the eye nor the ear tactic worked, Pansy bit Imogene's nose.

From the looks of it, one would have thought Pansy targeted the nub of Imogene's nose as his primary means to teach Petunia how to get fed, fast. But no, Imogene was simply sick with a fever nudging 102° and a flow of nasal glue clogging her windpipe. Her cough fluctuated from a wheeze and a whistle to a rumble and a choke, depending on whether she was lying down or sitting up, and her head felt like it had been jackhammered.

She'd fed the cats the minute she got home — then collapsed into a deep sleep until half past seven when she jerked awake and wobbled up to call Eloise, whom she was told wasn't there. She returned to sleep and awoke a second time at nine, due to difficulty breathing. This time she struggled to dial Eloise. When there was no answer she became anxious over whether Eloise had made it home safely, or if the dour man claiming to be her husband gave her the message she'd left.

The notion that Eloise might have a female partner sprang to mind, making her wonder if adultery was in play? Imogene disdained adultery, due mostly to her father's fondness for it.

She thought back to a time he jam-packed the glove compartment with condoms before taking her, her mom and sisters for a summer trip. After the driving got underway, he ordered her mother to hand him a map. The second she opened the compartment door, he slammed on the brakes and hundreds of condoms tumbled out onto her lap,

241

bruising her soul.

Not that Imogene knew what the white 'rollables' were at the time. It would be years later and only in retrospect that she felt the melancholy such daily displays of callousness caused her mom. But then, Imogene learned most of her life-lessons upon a reflection.

The couch in Imogene's apartment was still near the radiators by the windows where she'd dragged it the day before and, although she seldom let clothes lie long wherever she dropped them en route to relief, this day she was too weak to worry. She'd somehow managed to cover the couch with clean sheets, a hill of pillows, and a tea rose print flannel blanket with pink satin trim (thinking it prettied up the place a bit in case she died there) and moved the hassock next to the couch for easier access to the phone. The balance of her energy was spent crumbling half a sleeve of Ritz crackers into a cereal bowl before pouring Campbell's cream of tomato soup over them and eating it as gruel, washing it all down with water and another blue pill.

By the time the phone rang at half past ten Imogene was lightheaded. Eloise's voice was her one saving grace.

"What took you so long?" she answered. It made them both, "Hah!"

"Oh, babe, the trip back took forever. The storm delayed us. Cars were stranded all along the interstate. The streets in town are even worse. Did you get hit by it?"

Imogene zoomed in on the 'babe' word. No one had ever referred to her as that. Could it mean something different in the gay world than in the straight? Babe!

"Imogene?"

"We got the cold. And, I'm lonely."

"I hear that. I dreamed about you all the way back."

"You did not."

"But I intended to."

"It's been a long weekend for you, huh?"

"Not long enough and worth ever second." Eloise's sincerity shifted to concern. "How are you? Do you still have a fever? Did you get any rest?"

"Fine, I haven't checked it, and some. I keep thinking of how we didn't kiss goodbye."

"Me, too. Martin razzed me about it some. Says I'm so old I've forgotten how to woo."

Imogene had tried to forget what Dory told her about baggage and bed stats. It seemed so sordid and sad she'd have preferred not knowing.

"Have you wooed much? Or, should I say, many?"

"No. Until I met you I didn't do woo."

"Really?"

"You'll see. I plan to make you woozy."

Dual smiles.

"Eloise?"

"Yes?"

"It's my fault we didn't kiss. I rushed you onto the bus."

"It's nobody's fault. I was stunned by the sight of you, right off. Then to have lost you before you found me again, only to say goodbye. It was almost too much for me to bear."

"Me too."

"I wasn't even looking."

"Me neither."

Eloise reached under her pillow, pulled out a box of Fantasia gold tipped cigarettes and lit a hot pink papered one with the Zippo she kept in an ashtray next to her bed. "Tell me, what's the other number you scribbled down on my bus schedule?"

"Work. Dial me there if you'd like. I share the room with my boss and a numbers clerk, but it's a large space and I can talk easily. I think so anyhow. No one's ever phoned me before."

"Never?"

"Not in the year and more that I've been there."

"So, I'm the first?"

"Again and again...yes."

Eloise stole a drag after feeling a tingle race through her body lighting up every inch of it, thinking she and Imogene were a natural together — like warm water flowing into a scented bath. "I won't call you at work unless necessary. We'll need a code name for that."

"Code?"

"A man's name you can say while talking to me. Like Elmer."

"What's wrong with me saying Eloise?"

"You don't want your coworkers to find out about me. You could be fired."

"I don't think so," Imogene scoffed.

"No, it's so, sweetie. Technically, we're female felons."

"I keep hearing that, but I can't comprehend it. I mean I *can*, but not to the degree it makes any sense. It computes more along the lines of a Blue Law with me."

"The ones keeping stores closed on Sunday?"

"And the ones saying you can't wear a striped shirt with plaid pants in public."

"There's such a law?"

"It's still on the books. Funny thing is, at least *that* law is understandable."

"As opposed to..."

"Any stupid restriction I can get away with ignoring. I don't even pretend to respect authority when it peddles inequities."

"Well, this law's a biggie. We aren't allowed to be in love. It truly can get us arrested."

"You sound like Wink. I thought he was trying to scare me."

"Honey, I wouldn't scare, hurt, or harm you in any way for any reason. But we *must* keep what we have strictly between us."

For a split second Gail Parkerson flashed into Eloise's mind. It irked her to know she acquired these truths from someone who'd betrayed her and cast her aside in favor of those who'd happily burn her at the stake.

"Imogene, are you listening?"

"Yes."

"I'll never lie to you. I'll never betray you."

"Nor I, you. But everyone lies at times. I accept that as inherent. Nevertheless, I'm holding you to the betrayal part."

Eloise was grateful for the clarification. It corresponded perfectly with her concept of honesty and matched her declaration of allegiance. "Deal."

"But Elmer is out. I once had a teacher named Mr. Elmer with Eddie Cantor eyes and Mick Jagger lips, more purple than red."

"It was as close to Eloise as I could think. I hate my name."

"Do you?"

"Yes."

"I don't. Someday I'll tell you why I love your name. But for now, let's stick with Izzy. It's short for Isidore, Isaac, Isaiah. My firm is Jewish. No one will be the wiser."

"Works for me."

"Listen, listen!" Imogene placed the mouthpiece of the phone under her breastbone and held it there. "That's the sound of my heart beating with you inside it."

Eloise lit up. "Are you always so open with your emotions?"

"Syrupy? Sentimental? Happy-dippy?"

"Something like that."

"It's one of my many character flaws."

"I see. Then, I'll just have to suffer the consequences, won't I?"

"Hold that thought for a minute, will you?"

"Uh-huh." Eloise knocked the ashes off the end of her cigarette, then inhaled a deep final fix before squashing it out. She listened to Imogene walking across what sounded like a bare wood floor, and opening what must have been a console because music began playing.

"Can you hear it?" Imogene shouted out on her way back to the phone. "It's Frankie Valli singing *Can't Take My Eyes Off You.*"

"I can!" Eloise answered.

Imogene flopped back down on the couch and cuddled up to the phone. "On my way to the subway station there was a pawn shop that had one of those hard cardboard portables in the window with this record on the turntable."

"No kidding?"

"I'm not. So, I marched in and said to the old guy there, 'Sir, I looked across a crowded room Friday night and fell in love for the first time in my life and that record,' I pointed to player in the window, 'that record was blaring on the jukebox.'"

Eloise tittered. "What'd he say?"

"Not a word. Imagine an Orthodox Jew in a shiny black suit with a black satin yarmulke bobby-pinned to the back of his head and the stump of a wet cigar weighing down his lower lip, looking at me over his glasses, all gruff like. He got up slowly, unlocked the door of the little cage he was in, plodded over to the window, removed the record, and handed it to me."

"No."

"And before I could ask him how much he wagged one finger while opening the door and shooing me out. If only you could have seen the joy fill his eyes when I said *mazel tov*."

"What a great story."

"*Our* story, Ms. Iz. It's all part of our story now. Oh-oh-oh! I meant to say. Save your bus ticket for our happybox."

"What's that?"

"Right now it's a Keds shoe box with the word on top. I'm placing mementos of our times together in it. I've put in the rose you gave me, a soap wrapper from your hotel, the key to your room, matches from Club 82, the cocktail napkin from under your drink at the Playbill Club, our straws from..."

"Imogene? Imogene?"

"Yes?"

"Sweetheart, you're gonna need a bigger box."

Imogene closed her eyes. "As big and as many as it takes for the rest of our lives, Iz. You'll help me make it fanciful, right?"

"I will."

"I want us to live a romantic life in a romantic home, preparing romantic meals while listening to romantic music, and never again walk away, wake up, or go to sleep without kissing and saying I love you."

"Can I say, ditto?"

"Ditto works. Ditto's fine."

"Then it's a deal." Eloise blew a kiss. "Sleep sweet," she added. "Dream of me."

"And you of me."

Imogene returned the receiver to its cradle and stared at it, half-hoping Eloise would call back. When she didn't, Imogene opened their happybox and removed the Royal Manhattan Hotel soap wrapper, wrote on the inside flap, folded it back up and slipped it into the breast pocket of a blazer she was to wear to work in the morning. Then she hung a fresh gown on the back of the bathroom door, perfumed the bath water with Devon's eau de violets, and relaxed in a long, hot bath before returning to bed and to sleep.

In her pocket was a wrapper from the hotel soap she'd taken

on the night she said she loved her from the start.
And the record of their meeting was inscribed there
as a greeting to her heart.

~

3-13-70

FORTY-THREE
Monday Morning, March 16, 1970
Unorthodox Jews

Rita Renwyck had the insolence to monitor every outgoing call Imogene LaPin dialed, and had done so from Imogene's first day at Jerome Brothers Menswear.

On Monday, March 16, 1970, Rita began monitoring her incoming calls, too.

Rita Renwyck never had a kind word cross her lips or generous thought pierce her heart for longer than it took to accept a compliment with the bat of an eye, then dismiss it with a sneer. Why she was hired to greet department store buyers and juggle piece goods suppliers for one of the nation's largest designer label menswear manufacturers was a mystery to all, including the office staff and hundreds of salesmen seeking appointments during the thirty years she sat behind the JBM front desk, pulling and plugging phone cords.

Best guess? The garment industry was predominantly male, notorious for coarse language, vulgar innuendo, angry egos, preposterous deadlines, cutthroat competition and rollercoaster costs. Rita was the one woman the Jerome brothers could find who didn't care if your wife died and your cat was killed and your car crashed and a mugger knifed you in the elevator and the chair she assigned you to bleed-out in was on fire — you either followed her rules, or you didn't get buzzed through the door.

Some claimed Rita was a concentration camp survivor who'd appropriated the attitude of her captors. Others pretended she was the product of abusive parents, or a sadistic marriage, or a dominatrix after hours. But most every man muttered "get laid" under his breath, blowing it out the edge of his mouth in her direction before taking a seat to suffer her authority.

Being detested by Rita didn't bother Imogene. It eliminated expectations. In the fourteen months she'd worked for Jerome Brothers, Rita had never once responded to any of her arrival greetings. It suited them both just fine.

"Good morning, Rita," Imogene shot by, late.

"You have a message."

By the time Imogene stopped in her tracks and slowly pivoted, Rita had turned her back, leaving a pink "While You Were Out" slip on the front desk with a New Hampshire number inscribed; no date, no name, no message.

Imogene felt vulnerable.

• • •

January 13, 1969.

"Call me Myron," he said, standing to greet Imogene as she walked through the door. He had a rash of grey ringlets covering his head, a wide open smile dominating his face, lively green eyes and towered over her by more than a foot. "Sit, sit. I understand you recently left Mueller & Roth. On 31 here, is it?"

"I did. It is. They occupy two floors, actually. Thirty-six and thirty-seven.

"Did you clerk there?"

"Manager of Purchasing and In-House Production." She handed him her résumé.

"Impressive."

"Basically I spent money and disbursed funds while dodging propaganda."

"Still, it was a ton of money and the spin worked." He sounded wary. "Why leave?"

"I didn't like what went on around me."

"A conflict of principles then?"

Unemployed for two weeks, Imogene had the need, but no real desire to get hired. If she hadn't craved a Primeburger from it's 50th

Street lunch counter near Madison Avenue and read the *New York Times* Help Wanted ad while waiting for take-out, she wouldn't be sitting where she was sitting, or wishing she wasn't. Exhibiting an attitude was no way to get hired. And yet...

"There was that," she permitted.

"I see. Well, the opening we have is for an assistant manager."

"Okay."

"It probably doesn't pay as well."

"Okay."

"Are you familiar with the manufacturing end of menswear?"

"No."

"Any background in merchandising?"

"None."

"Why are applying for this job?"

"I've worked in this building for three years. I like being able to catch the train downstairs without going outside on cold, or rainy days."

Myron rubbed his forehead with his fingertips. "That's not exactly the answer I was looking for."

"It's the truth." Imogene never expected to get hired. It was only her third interview for a job after moving to New York and she wasn't good at it. She'd gotten her first job as a magazine artist on her looks alone, and her second in advertising by default. "All I can add is that I'm quick study. It would take me a week or so to get up to snuff, but I can and I will."

Myron was dismayed. They needed an experienced person, preferably male. It was an all male office except for a secretary to the president, the receptionist, and his protégé, Patsy Wolfe, who would be her boss and had specifically asked that he ignore any plea for female equality. Patsy reigned as manager of two manufacturing departments and preferred to train a man to split her duties — eventually — but wouldn't budge on ever relinquishing control of either division.

And who could blame her? Patsy was hired as a clerk fresh out of high school, putting her hooks into Myron early on. Her rise to the middle was rumored to be payment for lying down on the job; scorn fed by envy. Few knew Patsy worked the late shift in one of the JBM factories during her junior and senior years of high school to supplement her mom's meager income after her father was killed in the

Korean War. She had earned her place in a profession controlled by men. If anything, Myron was the father figure Patsy lost, and the role model she found.

"Unfortunately, we can't wait. We need someone who can hit the ground run..." Myron stopped mid-sentence and looked up. "This says you went to Wayne State University?"

"I did. In Detroit."

"I went to Wayne State University!"

Imogene's jaw dropped. She'd never met anyone else who'd been to the school, generally ignored by locals because it had no football team. She'd chosen Wayne for its superb prelaw and theatre programs, but couldn't imagine why he did, unless it was his height.

"I can see how that could be. The one sport they cheered was basketball and you're sure tall enough."

He threw his head back and laughed hard. "A Jew walks onto a basketball court. That's a good one!" Jumping up, he reached out and shook her hand. "You're hired. When can you start?"

"Um-m," Imogene was flummoxed by the offer. She thought, *did I just score 3-out-of-3 in landing a job after clearly flunking another interview?* "How's right now?"

"Great. Follow me and I'll show you around on our way to personnel."

Patsy Wolfe was livid. The young woman Myron hired was at least four years younger, five inches shorter and thirty pounds thinner than she, with auburn hair rivaling her sandy blonde and chestnut eyes to her blazing blues. The girl wasn't as buxom, but neither were her hips as wide or butt as big. Patsy had a perky nose and pale skin that identified her as Swedish or Irish, whenever she wanted to conceal her Jewish heritage, while Imogene looked sheer shiksa. If she was, hiring a gentile for a management position would be a Jerome Brothers first.

Forget the job specifics. Patsy concluded Myron had hired her equivalent instead of her inferior, requiring them to compete for the attention of the corporate executives, sales staff, shop jocks, and factory liaisons.

"I need to break that bitch fast and get her the hell outta here," she told her best friend, Ronald Newman, on the sly. "She knows zero, zip about this business and I'm not about to play fucking nursemaid. Did you see her all but curtsying behind Myron when he introduced us? Like he was her protector for chrissake. Where did he dig her up anyway?"

"Same alma mater," Ronald snitched. "It trumps nepotism."

"She went to college? I am *not* amused, Ronald."

"Dropped out."

"You've talked to her?"

"Hell no. I snuck a peek at her work history while it was being transferred to steno and get this — she was the drama counselor at Kadima in '65."

"Kadima's a kosher camp."

"Yep."

"So score another point for being a princess. Where is she now?"

"Myron let her leave after she finished with Mordie in administrative."

"Perfect. Gives me time to get it in gear. Tomorrow I'll start driving the little suck-up so hard, she'll call it quits before sundown Friday."

Patsy's fears proved premature. After escorting her into one of the company showrooms for a face-off the next morning, Imogene made her intentions clear.

"I left a better position making more money because I'm not interested in being a boss, or privy to what goes on behind closed doors. If that's what you're training me for, fire me now."

"I don't buy it," Patsy dared, wary of women without motives. "Why take a job if your five year goal isn't climbing all the way up the ladder?"

"Five year goal?" Imogene whinnied. "Each new day is an eight hour goal for me. Better yet, two four-hour goals split apart by lunch, making the latter half tentative. All I want is the pleasure of tackling something new without the responsibility, or headaches of being in charge."

Imogene had pegged Patsy Wolfe as a formidable woman with big ambitions who demanded excellence, sought confrontation, and showed no mercy for the weakness of others. She respected tenaciousness and Patsy for having it.

As for Patsy's alter ego of acting raunchily, regardless of who was in the room, or how high up on the tactical totem pole? It was a swaggered bawdiness that escaped Imogene's interest. She tuned it out.

In stark contrast, Imogene neither cursed nor told off-color jokes in mixed company. She didn't dress provocatively, or behave inappropriately, or conduct herself in any manner viewed as unladylike. It made her every bit as unorthodox as Patsy.

One primary difference manifested itself: Patsy preferred being one of the boys to one of the girls, whereas Imogene sought kinship with neither. Imogene was a maverick.

• • •

"Your phone rang but I was on the other line so couldn't get to it," Pasty apologized.

"S'ok. I should have been here. Got caught on an elevator coming up that switched to express midway, so I had to catch another back down from the Top of the Sixes."

Patsy gave Imogene the once over. "You look like puke."

"I do?" Imogene promptly checked her outfit for creases, wrinkles, or spills, and her nylons for runs.

"Not what you're wearing, Einstein. Your gills look green. Rough weekend?"

"Actually, Pats, the weekend was magical."

"Oh really." In all the time they'd worked together, Imogene never used a word more descriptive than 'fine' to indicate how her weekend went. "Is it anybody I've met, or want to do?"

What did I say? Imogene wondered. *Did Ronald blab? Or is this Patsy's standard Monday morning routine of prying? She knows I never discuss my personal life.*

The reality was, if Patsy hadn't seen her dining with men on numerous occasions, she'd have sworn Imogene was a closet nun. That's what made Imogene's "magical" admission an information breakthrough.

Until recently, Patsy saw herself as the shrewd, entertaining type of woman every man wanted to bang, and Imogene as the prim and proper type they wanted to marry.

Now, she conceded Imogene was also as bright and as witty as she, upping the ante of general attraction, but not competition. They'd become such an invincible office duo after a year of solidarity, Patsy told Myron it was time to let Imogene take control of the subsidiary division (secretly hoping the promotion would open a door into Imogene's sub rosa life).

"No, you've never met," Imogene assured, "but I'd like you to, someday. How's that? It'll be awhile. Maybe a month or more."

"Seriously?"

"About the meeting?"

"No, I mean, are you *serious* about this someone?"

"Oh, that. Yes."

Patsy took the top half of her bagel and heaved it, hitting Imogene in the back of her head. "Fuckorama, it isn't fair! I'm older! Slightly. That means I get married first."

"Slightly older?" Imogene spun her chair around and rolled over to Patsy's desk. "As in, sour milk is slightly older than fresh?"

"Shut up." She smothered the bottom half of the bagel with cream cheese and offered Imogene the first bite.

"I guarantee, Pats, you'll marry before me. I'm more the extended engagement type of person. Besides, it's long distance right now."

"How long distance?"

"About three hundred miles."

"I wish you'd mentioned that before I pitch a perfectly good half a bagel at you."

Imogene's phone rang. When she spun herself back, Patsy overheard her say, "Imogene LaPin. Hi, sweetheart. Did you miss me?"

So did Rita Renwyck.

FORTY-FOUR
Monday Afternoon, March 16, 1970
With This Ring

Imogene feared she was delirious. She'd been taking Steve Stein's magic blue caplets for three days and was running low. Initially, they'd quelled her cough by making her too relaxed to expel secretions. She likened it to serenely choking to death and, although the prevailing aches subsided for a few hours of ecstasy after popping a pill, the agony gradually crept back until she was shaking again. Clutching the glassine envelope in her pocket and needing a fix, it was proving a real effort to get home from work and near the phone where she and Eloise longed for the sound of each other's voice to keep them close.

It didn't help that she'd stopped to pick up prints from the roll of film she'd stolen from Eloise's camera and paid a premium to have developed overnight — but how she'd mistakenly boarded the IRT Broadway uptown line was unclear. Fortunately, she realized the error in time to get off at 79th Street. It meant a longer walk to her apartment than she thought she had the strength to complete, but she had no other choice.

"At least I'm safely past Needle Park," she said aloud to embolden herself, adding, "I wonder if that's where Steve buys his stash."

Once out of the station and onto the street she longed to linger at Zabar's but felt too feverish to try. Instead she began tromping towards home, doing her best to keep from slipping and falling in gutter slush.

It was slow going, each block requiring a stop to catch her breath. Leaning her forehead against the cold and frosty window of David's Jewelry store during one such break, she saw something that made her flutter with excitement. There, in a display featuring estate jewelry, sat a charming antique ring tagged as one-of-a-kind.

Imogene used the plate glass to steady herself as she slid sideways to the shop's door, applying the full weight of her body to push it open and stumble inside.

The clerk came quickly to her aid. "Are you all right?"

"If I can have some water to take a pill, please? Then I'll need to see that amethyst ring you have in the window."

"The estate piece?"

"Yes."

He guided her to a slipper chair so she could sit comfortably and lean back and provided her with a disposable wax cup of water before disappearing to the rear of the store, returning shortly with tea.

"It's rooibos from Africa," he offered. "Red tea. If you sip it you'll soon feel better."

Imogene loathed tea, but she drank it, finding it warmed her, soothed her, and helped the double dose of drugs go down.

The clerk was an urbane young man about her age, small and thin with spirited eyes and a full head of tobacco-brown hair. He wore a dark blue suit with a barely visible vertical lavender hairline stripe and a tailor made companion shirt, to which he'd added a purple bow tie with matching silk hanky flopping from the breast pocket. By the gentleness of his voice, the delicacy of his manner and an epicene beauty, she hoped he was the son of wise and loving parents who took pride in him. But she kept her thoughts to herself, in case they were misconceived.

"Thank you," she said, instead. "That was good of you."

"Oh dear, think nothing of it. The water had boiled. It simply took an extra tea bag and china setting."

"All the same. And the porcelain cup! I never drink a hot beverage out of anything but. I have one at the office. I even carry one with me when I go out to eat."

"I do, too! How scrumptious." His voice became higher and more animated. "You must be a Libra."

"I am."

"Well, there you have it, then. All lady Libra love those little amenities of life. I include myself, naturally."

"But of course."

The two sat sipping and chatting until Imogene couldn't suppress her need to know a minute longer. "Might I still see the ring?"

"The ring! The ring!" he said, jumping up and fetching it from the window case. "May I recite the narrative?"

"Absolutely."

"It is 18 karat gold dating to 1870. We weren't able to find the name of the goldsmith, but we do have the provenance. It came directly from the estate of the deceased, whose grandmother was the first to own it. I have a sepia cabinet card of her wearing the ring as verification. The family wants that returned, but I can make you a photocopy of it if you wish."

"I'd appreciate that, yes."

"The price is seventy-six dollars, but I can let you have it at my employee discount rate of sixty-seven. That includes the tax. Let me do it for you in friendship, please? It's an exquisite ring, even if the price seems high. Gold fell to thirty-six dollars an ounce but it's due to double soon."

Imogene studied the band, cast like daintily pruned tree branches; two v-shaped twigs on each side of the setting with a slender stem dividing them. The oval center had a pattern of intricate prongs all around with four of the larger tines balancing the solitaire inside the center space. "It's precious."

"Would you like to try it on?" he offered. She held out her hand. "Oh my, it fits your finger beautifully. Your hands are so dainty. A perfect size six?"

"Yes. But the ring isn't for me."

"Are her hands as small?" He wasn't being presumptuous. She was being open.

"Larger."

"Could she wear it as a pinky ring?"

"She'd have to."

"Would you like me to put it aside until you can bring her in?"

"No, no. I want to give it to her this weekend. To slip it on her finger myself and see if it lights up her heart the same as it has mine."

"It will. It's a mystical ring."

"Mystical?"

"Now, mind you, this is nothing more than what I was told, but I'm inclined to believe it's true." He poured them each a second cup of tea, sat down on an adjoining stool, and crossed his legs. "According to

Greek mythology, the amethyst is said to foster sobriety. But lore states it has protection and healing powers as well. In some European countries, warriors wore ankhs made of amethyst into battle."

"Interesting. An ankh is the Egyptian symbol of life, isn't it?"

"It is. And, when worn close to the heart, it carries the energy of fire and passion to stimulate emotions and ensure faithfulness. The ring finger is connected to the heart, making the powers the same, but stronger, because the blood bond between the two is unbroken."

"What's the pinky connected to?"

"It's the guardian and true measure of the heart," he winked and purposely raised his pinky while drinking his tea. "For me, that is."

Imogene reached out and touched his arm. "What a pleasure you are."

He blushed his thanks. "This stone was brought back from Brazil by the mother, who had the band and setting custom made for her daughter and gave it to her as a forget-me-not before the girl left on a summer trip to the country. That's all of the story I'd tell to a straight spirit, but because we're of the kindred kind, shall I go on?"

"Do."

"The girl was riding with her best friend in the back of a two horse buggy driven by a hired hand who'd been tippling. Well! About halfway along, lightning struck from out of a cloudless blue sky, startling the horses. Naturally, they took off, and when the buggy hit a ditch in the dirt road, it flipped over and all three passengers were thrown."

"Oh my! Was anyone hurt?"

"The driver was killed. The girls were badly bruised, but survived. And until her last breath the mother credited this amethyst for protecting her daughter from death."

Imogene was enthralled. "What do you think?"

"I like to imagine a little mischief was going on in the back seat and the ladies were so-o relaxed that love saved them when they hit the ditch. It's the romantic in me."

The two sighed and sat and sipped for a minute more before Imogene asked, "Will you take a check?"

Later, as she trudged along home, Imogene thought the ring in her pocket made the distance seem shorter, the wind seem warmer, and the wrong train taken seem purposeful.

But mostly, she believed the ring made her and Eloise seem destined.

FORTY-FIVE
Saturday Morning, March 21, 1970
Emergencies Room

Imogene was lying on a hospital gurney in the emergency room corridor of Mt. Sinai Hospital with a clear liquid drip connecting a tube stuck in her arm, waiting for the police to arrive and arrest her for illegal drug possession. She was contemplating whether to give up the name of her supplier, or take the rap herself should a deal be offered. It was just a thought. She knew the answer to that (clean) hands down.

The doctor, who had confiscated the last of Imogene's drugs before stabbing her with a needle the size of Staten Island, slipping an oxygen mask over her mouth and letting her be wheeled away for x-rays, said she'd be back. That was around 10:20 the night before, shortly after being admitted because she couldn't stop coughing.

It was now nearing four in the morning. She'd been thinking about Eloise the entire time, of how they'd talked on the phone from six to ten every night, sharing all those tidbits two people long to know about each other. She wished she could call to mind some specifics but try as she might, she was drawing blanks, except for the fact that Eloise was looking forward to picking her up at Logan Airport in seven hours.

Imogene hadn't told Eloise she was doing drugs, or that she'd overdosed. It didn't seem fair to spring it on her so early in a love affair that hadn't technically reached the affair stage yet.

"Are you feeling any better Miss LaPin?"

Imogene refocused her eyes on the doctor (who had apparently snuck up behind her for the sole purpose of scaring the other half of her to death). "A little woozy."

"I'm not surprised. You had a temperature of 102.9°, but we've got it under control now. The antibiotics kicked right in."

"Antibiotics?"

"You have pneumonia. Walking pneumonia in layman terms.

"Why?"

"Because people persist in walking around with it. It's a milder form of the full blown."

"Then it wasn't a drug overdose?"

"Drugs?"

"The blue pills."

"Pseudoephedrine? Hardly. You might have sought medical help sooner if you hadn't taken them. They mask symptoms. I was vehemently opposed to them when they first hit the market five years ago and you're a perfect example of why."

"Against what?"

"Over-the-counter cold meds."

"Cold pills? That's what I took?"

"Essentially, yes. I kept you overnight so we could get a second look at your lungs and make certain you're stabilized. But once that's done I'll write you a prescription for the cough and you can be on your way. You'll need bed rest. Eat soft foods, and drink plenty of liquids including chicken soup. We tend to push the soup around here."

"So does my mom."

"How long have you been fighting this?"

"I woke up sick last Sunday."

"Six days. Then you should be feeling better in another five. A virus normally takes ten to run its course. Yours will take longer and your energy level will be low for another month or more, so I want you to check back with me when the prescription runs out."

"I need to fly to Boston today."

"No planes for at least a week. Two would be better. Unless you want your eardrums to feel like your chest and risk a full blown case of this."

"I don't."

The doctor stopped writing on her clipboard long enough to reach out and take Imogene's hand, much like her mother would if her mother were there and thirtyish and tall and wore a pixie hairstyle and had black horned rimmed glasses and was a doctor. "Your chart says you specified being seen by a woman doctor?"

"Yes."

"That's not always possible. We're scarce, especially in the ER."

"Thanks for the heads-up. I'll take it to my grave."

"Not on my watch, Miss LaPin."

• • •

Andy Wink's phone rang, and rang, and rang. He was still wearing the watch Imogene gave him so he opened one eye to see if it was working, listened for ticking, and then checked it again.

"It's after four in the morning," he shouted. "Who the hell?" He grabbed the receiver and sunk back into his eiderdown pillow, pulling the blue wool cover up over his head, fully prepared to sleep through any conversation that didn't include a proposition from Rock Hudson. "What!"

Imogene coughed his name out. "Wink?"

"Mo?" He was suddenly awake and speaking rapidly. "Mogy, are you okay sweetheart? Talk to me. I'm having trouble hearing you. Speak up."

"I can't, Wink."

"Can't what? Why not?"

"Help."

"Omigod, what's wrong? Imogene, are you hiding? Is the closet door locked? Has someone broken in? Is he there now? Have you called the cops?" He was already half way to the wardrobe where he hung his pants in perfect sequence, according to shade from chino to black, suits the same from dark blues to medium greys, ironed jeans from bleached out blues to new denims, blazers by solids, stripes, plaids, and jackets of corduroy, leather, and suede.

"I have pneumonia."

"Pneumonia?" He sounded disappointed. She didn't need a hero for pneumonia. Or, did she? "How? I bet you got it from looking for your dream dyke." He returned to sit on the bed, leaning over and listening.

"Wink. I need you to do me a favor. Our Rave Day is this weekend."

"Run that by me again, what Rave Day is."

"Rings and vows exchanged. Eloise's and mine. In Portsmouth,

New Hampshire."

"Portsmouth's a long, cold distance from here. If this is to invite me to your..."

"But I'm sick, Wink. Terribly sick." Her voice was low and weak.

"So it seems."

"And if I don't show up she might think it's an excuse not to come." She sneezed a loud, high-pitched, whistle-snot sneeze. "Oh-h, Wink. I can't believe it. After being alone for so long. And now this, when I'm finally..."

"Calm down Mogy." *She needs me,* he thought. *Deep down, isn't that all that counts? She's in trouble at four in the morning and she called me.* "Tell me what to do."

"Take my plane ticket and go see her. Explain. Give her the gifts I bought. Tell her I'll be there next weekend. Do that for me Wink. Pleeeeeeeeease?"

He couldn't believe she asked it of him. After he'd specifically warned her against calling. After he banned her from his life. And still, she ambushed him by trusting he'd help snag the woman who'd taken her from him. The woman he damned every minute of every waking hour of his life. Well, maybe not every minute of every hour, but some hour of one day for a minute or two. The stupid named, stupid woman whom he hated most in the whole stupid universe.

"Yes, Mo. I'll go."

Wink quickly regretted his decision. He knew he'd spoken too eagerly to take it back, or even establish terms. At least, that's what he was berating himself for later the same morning as he held his breath when the turboprop prepared to land at Logan Airport, where his nemesis wasn't expecting him.

But before leaving New York, he stopped by the hospital to check on Imogene.

FORTY-SIX
Saturday Morning, March 21, 1970
The Ghost of Mistress Past

Eloise was edgy, concerned that the conversations between her and Imogene each night might be too revealing and could scare her off, or dampen a spirit that appeared ever lively and optimistic. She'd once been every bit as innocent and effervescent, before having the sanguine sucked out of her by one woman and nearly submitting to the advances of a second who'd been stalking her for several months before she fled Florida. Both discerned loneliness in her and aimed to exploit it. The one who'd been ruthlessly triumphant was now clouding her thoughts and darkening her drive from Portsmouth to Logan Airport to pick up Imogene — the girl Eloise wished she'd met first and known only.

• • •

"Gimme a Dewar's, neat, will ya Izzy?" summoned Dr. Adelaide, a regular at the Beacon where Eloise worked six nights after closing the beach bar at dusk. "The bottle stays."

"This isn't the Long Branch, Doc," Eloise reminded her after transferring a double shot to a tumbler, "and I'm not Miss Kitty."

"Nah. You got it all over Miss Kitty. And I'm better looking than Doc."

Dr. Ada Adelaide was an Armenian who'd flown to America to study, and stayed for the promise of equality. Tall and slender with smooth, saffron skin burnished brown by the Florida sun and onyx eyes matching the luster of her thick, short, layered hair, Ada often endured the unsolicited attention of straight women and gay guys, both of whom mistook her for a pretty boy.

The doctor grappled with other issues, as well.

Behind closet door number one was her homosexual self, identified as a person afflicted with a mental illness by the American Psychiatric Society.

Behind closet door number two was her heterosexual self, empowered with credentials to diagnose and commit self-number-one to an institution, where she could legally prescribe shock treatments and surrogate sex as a means of curing herself, of herself.

Behind both doors was a respected dual-doctorate psychologist and shrink bisexual who drank to excess from having too many doors with people ringing her bells, day-in-and-night-out.

Eloise and Ada were formal friends with informal feelings, to the extent that Eloise was willing to file a missing persons report if, after having asked around, no one had seen or heard from the doctor in 48 hours. Whereas Ada was willing to answer Eloise's call for help if need be, 24/7. In the three years Ada had frequented the Beacon, neither emergency ever presented itself. The two never mingled outside the tavern, but each had the others back within those walls, built on an easy rapport involving quiet speculation about the bar's patrons.

"Bad session was it, Doc?"

Ada never discussed a patient per se, but she'd transfer the general diagnosis of one onto a patron exhibiting similar tendencies at times.

"More like a bad sessions week. You'd think rich bitches who wake up to sunshine every morning in beach houses on the Gulf coast would be happy, wouldn't you?"

Eloise didn't entirely qualify. She wasn't rich, but she did live within walking distance of the surf. And she wasn't sad, but did fluctuate between 'leave me alone' and 'a good time was had by all' with no discernible difference. Ostensibly, she was more good times than not, disguising any regret that festered or pestered her.

"Most folks here are trying to get away from some*one*, Doc, not the sunrise."

"I expect so," Ada conceded after honing in on a woman about the same age as herself at the opposite end of the bar. "What's her story?"

The woman was a visitor at the end of her last night in town, waiting for a ride to Davis Islands for a seaplane flight from Peter O. Knight Airport to her home in Key West. At any other time, Eloise would have told Ada that.

But on this night Eloise needed some free advice of her own. By doing a little transference like Ada had often talked about, maybe she could get some insight on a personal problem without exposing herself to examination.

"Her? She's a sterling in recovery from being with a woman who cheated on her."

"A sterling, huh?" It was Ada's technical term for women who were pure lesbians. The distinction was needed during their barroom diagnosing. "The cheater with another sterling?"

"No. A man."

"She was with a bi-broad then?"

"Afraid so."

"Hmm. Time was when sterlings would shun bisexuals and bi's would stick to those in their open-marriage coteries. What is it with bi's scheming to infiltrate sterling world these days? And why the hell did she mess with one?"

"That's your gig, Doc. You tell me." Eloise poured Ada another double.

"Know anything else about her?"

"Not much. I heard she was seduced right out of high school by the woman though. A beauty queen."

"True competition?"

"Certified. State level."

"Tiara tootsie?"

"Fourth runner-up."

"So, we understand the allure. What else?"

"Let's see." Eloise paused to pretend to think while topping off all the glasses at the bar, including that of the woman being used as her decoy, exchanging a few words with her out of earshot of Ada before returning. "Where was I?"

"Details on the bi."

"Oh yes. Um. Divorced. Two preschoolers, I think."

"She was down with that?"

"In a sisterly sense. Thought she'd spend her life with them. Once wanted to."

"How long did it last?"

266

"Three years was it? Mentally more than physically." Eloise looked at her stand-in, then back at Ada. "Turned out her lover had been fishing for a husband the entire time."

"Interesting."

"What?"

"Your need to substitute 'fishing' for fuck." Ada tapped for another drink. "See, that's why I'm intolerant of bisexuals, present company included."

"I'm not bi, Doc."

"Me. I'm bi. Not you."

"Are shrinks supposed to do that? Be bias that is."

"To be bias for, or against people, places, things and behavior is a natural tendency found in everyone. I remain impartial with patients, but I can be bias on my own time. "

"Then why a bias against bi's? Is it because you all go back to men eventually?"

"No, we don't all go back. But we have that capability. Always. We pretend otherwise and can even make ourselves believe it depending on whom we're pursuing, but it never goes completely away. At any time we can choose to switch and many of us do. It's part of our brain biology."

"Not mine. I never had any interest in men."

"And therein lies the prodigious difference."

"What?"

"Sterling homosexuals find heterosexual sex as unnatural to them as sterling heterosexuals find homosexual sex unnatural. Neither would ever willingly engage in it. They'd violently oppose it if necessary. Be honest. Could curiosity make you have sex with a man?"

"No."

"Peer pressure?"

"No."

"A million dollars in tax free money?"

"No, Doc. Nothing could get me to vomitville."

"Because you're incapable of it — unlike a bisexual, who can choose to flit back and forth, even if it only happens once. We open ourselves up to it. We justify it happening. We seek validation. A pregnancy becomes a miracle. Ours is a third dimension, natural strictly to us."

"Then what's the point of being bias?"

"There's no point. But we're all bias to different degrees. Honest people own up to it. I guess my biggest qualm comes from the tendency for bisexuals to use religion to cover their tracks and make sterlings their scapegoat."

"They do?"

"I've known bisexuals who'll leave a gay relationship to commit to a straight marriage, then campaign against gays by insisting, if *they* gave up the behavior after finding Jesus, all gays can."

Eloise was surprised. Up until then, she thought no one had ever been duped by someone like Gail but her. "Why do they do that?"

"To gain praise from other religionists. No such person was ever gay. They're all bisexuals capitalizing on their standing by willingly endangering the unadulterated homosexual community."

"All of them?"

"Let's say, way too many. Of course, the reverse is also true."

Eloise stopped what she was doing to lean on the bar, cupping her chin in one hand so she could look directly at Ada and better understand what she was saying. "You lost me there."

"It's like this. Bisexuals who settle on a straight lifestyle will gripe the loudest against homosexuality, pointing the finger away from themselves."

"Go on."

"Bisexuals who settle on a gay lifestyle will gripe the loudest about all the rights they lose once they come out."

"Hmm."

"The reality is, those on the front lines creating an uproar represent a melting pot of bisexuals taking sides against themselves, while sterling homosexuals are targeted to suffer the hate and take all the heat."

"Tell me, is that you, or the scotch talking?"

"Probably both. I'd be drawn and quartered if I said it in a public forum, that's for sure."

Eloise respected the Doc's opinion. It always left her with something to ponder. Besides, she'd been a bartender long enough to know, every person lives some size of lie. "Well," she offered by way of escape, "I reckon bisexuals haven't cornered the market on fishing, regardless."

It made for a hearty laugh, but failed to provide the diversion Eloise needed; pretending the talk was about the woman down the bar had become discomfiting for her.

"True enough, Izzy. But now there's a bigger threat looming."

"Threat?"

"Have you read the recent study out by Masters and Johnson?"

"Can't say that I have. Or, ever will. Why? Should I?"

"They've found there's never been an outbreak of sexually transmitted diseases among lesbians."

"That's good, right?"

"Very! But with more bisexuals infiltrating the herds, I predict it won't last."

"Oh, we're herds now, are we, Doc?"

"Don't be cheeky. What I'm saying is, STDs will begin popping up, slowly but surely. Lesbians have always been sexually safe, but that day is coming to an end."

"Gee, I hope you're wrong," Eloise cringed. She knew nothing about sexually transmitted diseases, except that she'd heard gay men got them all the time.

Ada tapped the bar with two fingers. Eloise poured her another double.

"So, that's the gist of it, Iz?"

"Of what?"

"Her, doofus. The lady down the bar we're scrutinizing."

"Oh. Her."

"What happened after their breakup?"

Eloise purposely bided her time, careful not to give herself away. She'd excused herself to walk the length of the bar and back, wiping it down, attending to all of her customers including the woman on whom she was transferring her personal past. Upon returning, Eloise leaned even closer to the Ada so she could speak in a more subdued manner.

"She swore off all relationships, but is thinking about getting mixed up with someone who's pursuing her."

"Does the second one have kids, too?"

"Two teenagers about to graduate."

269

"Regardless. It serves her right if she gets betrayed again."

"Why's that?"

"Because she should have learned the lesson about bisexual women bringing our baggage to bed the first time."

"Like?"

"For one thing, even if we don't return to men, we fantasize about them and expect to be simulated with sex toys."

Eloise jumped back. "Dammit, Doc! You're creeping me out."

"You, but not her." Ada pointed to the innocent woman. "What do you think the biggest beef is I hear from straight men?"

"Spare me."

"Kids! Men feel neglected when the kids always come first. It's the exactly the same with bi moms. Kids will always come first."

"I suppose."

"Whereas, that one? She might be lonely and feeling vulnerable, or desperate, or maybe she's a masochist. You can't always tell."

They both then looked at the unsuspicious woman, who caught their glances and raised her glass to them.

"What's a masochist, Doc?"

"Someone who gets pleasure from pain. It's not uncommon. Female victims like her tend to fill voids with carbon copies. They spend their lives blaming themselves for losing someone they never truly had."

Eloise had washed and dried all the stemmed glasses and hung them one by one in the overhead racks while taking in the doctor's assessment of her, disguised as the woman at the end of the bar whose ride finally arrived. They waved good-bye. Eloise felt beaten.

"Never truly had? Gee, Doc. Is that what you tell all your patients?"

"Hell, no. Well, not for the first year or two. But after that, I get impatient with patients. If they refuse to face life with my guidance I'll pull their heads outta their butts."

Eloise poured Ada a round on the house. Then, for the first time while on duty, she poured herself a shot and the two clinked glasses.

"Bottoms up!"

Several weeks later Eloise told Ada she was taking an indefinite leave from the Beacon to help a fellow move to New Hampshire. After the last call for drinks, the doctor paid her tab and the two women hugged, wishing each other a heartfelt best. Then, a second before the doctor went out the door, she turned back to say, "Hey, Iz."

"Yes?"

"Pledge you'll dodge the switch-hitters?"

"Except for you, Doc. How's that?"

"Not to worry about me. I'll always be there for you. Just give me a call and we'll chat."

It left Eloise wondering if the doctor knew the truth about her all along.

FORTY-SEVEN
Saturday Morning, March 21, 1970
On My Honor

As Eloise parked her car in the short term lot and went inside the terminal to check the arrivals and departures, her thoughts remained dominated by Dr. Adelaide's words from their last chat together.

What she felt for Imogene bore no resemblance to her former self, yet she heard herself tell Imogene, "You can do better than me. I'm trouble."

In fact, Eloise had so berated herself out of fear of proving a disappointment to Imogene that, directly after hanging up the night before, all she wanted to do was call her back to speak the truer words gnawing at her heart, the ones she hadn't yet allowed past her lips. Regret kept Eloise tossing and turning all night. Intent on making amends before Imogene left for La Guardia at ten, she was up by five, watching the clock on the windowsill tick away, cigarette by cigarette, until she finally phoned Imogene when the hands struck seven-after-six.

No answer. She dialed again, and again, thirteen times, for thirteen rings each, once every thirteen minutes and still, no answer.

At 10:03 she gave up and began to agonize over the final words they'd spoken to each other the night before, afraid that they might have been their last if Imogene was still in New York and purposely not picking up? She revisited their last conversation.

"Can we have a ceremony?" Imogene pleaded. "Just the two of us. With oaths."

"I'm no good with gush," Eloise let on, unwilling to put anything into writing. It was part of her decision to not be vulnerable again.

"That's okay. I'll write a poem for us."

"Oh, no, not a poem! Spare me."

"Will you hate it if I do?"

"Hate is a strong word."

"Hate is great. I'm dreadfully bad at composing poetry. Hate guarantees you'll give it the review it deserves. Boo me if you want. But write it, I must!"

"You're so corny."

"Maize is my middle name."

"Now that's something I can believe."

Although the talk was delightfully flirtatious, Eloise thought she heard Imogene cover the mouthpiece at intervals, as if someone was with her in the room, saying something she didn't want Eloise to hear.

"Are you alone, Imogene?"

"Unless you count Pansy and Petunia. You're not allergic to cats are you?"

"No. Why?"

"I'm coughing some, that's all." Imogene hadn't told Eloise how dreadful she felt, careful to cover her cough-tracks. She couldn't know the many fade-ins and fade-outs made Eloise wary.

First Eloise thought Wink was there. Then she thought it was someone else, possibly another woman. Then she scolded herself for being suspicious and feeling jealous. But it didn't occur to her that Imogene might be even sicker than she was when they parted, because Imogene was upbeat.

"So, it won't be long now. In a few hours I'll be getting on a plane and, lickety-split, I'll be in your arms for the entire weekend."

"What about after? Then what?"

"Why? Are you staying in New Hampshire?"

"I was thinking about returning to Florida, or Alabama. My folks have moved back to Montgomery, but the Crystal Beach house hasn't sold yet. Anyhow, I cashed out my bank account here today."

"Is there a chance of you choosing New York instead?"

"I don't think I have what it takes to live there. It's so big."

"I've never been to Florida."

"Impossible. Everyone's been to Florida at least once."

"Not me. Regardless, I'm required to stay here for six more months."

"Why?"

It was an impulsive lie that Imogene might not have told if she hadn't felt like road kill. "A book I'm writing takes place here." *Egad,* she said to herself. *Where did that come from?*

"You're writing a book?"

"Um."

"You're a writer?"

"I guess I'd have to be."

"In addition to your day job?"

"Oh sure."

Eloise could hear Imogene wilting, no doubt exhausted from working all day, writing at night, and spending hours on the phone with her. She assumed Imogene must feel at least as drained as she did from being madly in love while trying to deny it. Except Imogene wasn't the one trying to deny it.

"Six months, huh? That's all it'd be?"

"Think about it?"

Now it was Eloise who lied. "I will."

"Listen, sweetheart, it's ten, and as much as I'd like to talk to you all night, if we're going to be bright-eyed tomorrow we'd better get off the phone and into bed."

"I'm already in bed."

"As am I. So close your eyes and dream of me as us. I love you, Eloise."

Eloise thought about saying ditto — and would have — but she dilly-dallied too long before the line went dead and regret set in.

FORTY-EIGHT
Very Early Saturday Morning, March 21, 1970
Knight & Gay

Imogene wasn't surprised Wink still had a key to her apartment, or that his returning of the phony first one while pretending to end their friendship was done for effect. She knew she deserved the payback, so said nothing, forcing him to bring it up on his own.

"I am, after all, a queen," he declared. "Drama should be a great expectation."

"You're certainly good at raising the dickens!"

Point and match.

On his way to the airport via her place, Wink stopped off at the hospital where nurses mistook him for her fiancé because he said he was. Regardless, he didn't disapprove of such assumptions. Toy marriages were an established pretext among homosexuals wherever you lived. He'd been with numerous rural gays who had flocked to New York thinking life would be better and easier. It wasn't. True, there were more places to hide and people to protect you. But if you wanted to succeed, Wink knew the safest route remained through the closet.

Imogene must have counted on him helping her because she'd left a pre-packed Bantam Flower Power suitcase ready for him to deliver on her behalf, saying there was no need to open it. Naturally, he opened it because — c'mon — what self-respecting best friend wouldn't?

"Oh, for the love of Sal Mineo would you look at this!" Wink said to Pansy who had jumped inside the bag as soon as the cat heard the sound of the zipper. Wink hadn't seen as mishmashed a package since Imogene wrapped a shirt she'd given him for his birthday and he nearly threw it out, mistaking the mess for bundled waste.

This time she'd misjudged the size of the paper by cutting it too short. Then she patched over the bare spots with ragged edge pieces;

none of the folds were equal or creased, cat hair clung to all the tape and the knotted ribbon was plainly pitiful.

He removed the package and stripped the wrappings, intending to sneak a quick peek at its contents. Instead, it changed his plans altogether. He made himself a pot of coffee, fed the cats, cleaned the litter, washed his hands, and set down with the open box on his lap for a more thorough examination.

Buried under red tissue paper at the bottom of the box were two early Edwardian era ankle-length nightgowns made of crisp, heavyweight cotton in remarkable condition. Easily a century old, Wink contemplated where Imogene had snagged them and for how much. Except for slight yellowing of the fabric, they looked as if they'd never been worn. Surprisingly, the two gowns were so much alike, Wink thought they must have been made at the same time, possibly for sisters.

Each gown had an embroidered cuff, collar and hemline. Stretching down the front from the collarbone to the breastbone were layers of quarter-inch, flattened pleats. The yoke opening was fixed with mother-of-pearl buttons fitting as pistils through flower-embroidered buttonholes. The purity and delicacy of the construction made Wink wish he was svelte enough to try one on and gambol around.

Tucked inside the neck of each garment was an unsealed white envelope. The envelope inscribed *Eloise* had a color photo of Imogene taken outside of Johnny's. Imogene used pinking shears to serrate the photo's edges. The envelope marked *Imogene* contained a matching photo of Eloise. Both were dated March 15, 1970.

Between the nightgowns Imogene placed lily-of-the-valley sachet bags tied through the opening of a Phillips labeled Frankie Vali 45, *Can't Take My Eyes Off You*.

As for the gray velvet ring box, Wink dared not open it, believing it would be bad luck to do so. But he did read the handwritten card attached to it.

Dear, I love you. I do. There is not another way that I can say the words to make them sound more beautiful, more true, more meaningful to you. So when I whisper them, remember, from December to December our whole life through — there will never be another who will hear from me these words: Dear, I love you. I do.

After returning the gifts to the box in the order Imogene had placed them, Wink rummaged through her desk drawers to find remnants of the *toile de jouy* fabric he'd used to wallpaper his bathroom. Imogene said the cloth was too *Français-fabuleux* to discard. Now he was thankful she'd kept it.

The background was ecru with the imprint of a dark red 18th century pastoral scene. He wrapped the box in the *toile*, following her lead by scalloping the edges when cutting the cloth to the proper size. He rubber cemented one edge to the box for positioning and glued the other on top, burnishing both together to create the perfect seam. It made the gift look fancy-schmancy.

In place of a ribbon he tied the box with a long, gold, curtain cord and tassels Imogene salvaged from under the cushions of a couch left on the street. He attached little brass bells to the tassel that he didn't think Pansy's collar would miss, and removed both cats from the suitcase, whisking out the interior out before dropping the freshened gift box in and zipping it up.

Finally, he took time to tidy up the place. Imogene deserved clean sheets on a freshly made bed and all her clothes hung, especially after the ordeal she'd put him through. Oh, and a dusting of flat surfaces. And the dishes washed. And the cats nails clipped before combing them and leaving them extra dry food and fresh water.

But he didn't return the furniture to its original positioning, or place the phone back where it belonged. Those changes he had found heartwarming.

FORTY-NINE
Saturday, March 21, 1970
Exit & Entry

"Your vitals are good. No indication of a fever. Your color is back. There's a negligible shadow on your left lung near the heart, but I don't think it's anything to be concerned about. I need to listen, so take a deep breath. And, exhale. Again. Now cough. Sit forward. Again, deep breath. Exhale. And cough."

Once the doctor finished her routine, she hooked her stethoscope around her neck and sat down on a stool beside the transient bed reserved for Imogene earlier that same morning. "You don't list a family physician, so I'd like you to come back here for a follow-up x-ray in two weeks as a precaution."

Imogene still felt terribly tired and would have preferred staying put with aides attending to her, nurses checking on her and comestibles delivered. But she'd already been out of contact with Eloise and away from Pansy and Petunia for twelve hours. She thought Pansy would be fine, but Petunia was still new to their home and must think her a terrible mother.

"I'm better." It was the most she could muster.

"You sound better. Nowhere near well, but much better. The nurse says you slept soundly. You'll have to keep that up for as long as your body insists."

"I try not to let my body push me around, Doc. But if you say so."

"I do. Tell me, what's your secret to bouncing back from the brink? Your tests were off the charts several hours ago. Now you're stabilized."

"Me? I'm a ninety-four pounds of blue twisted steel," Imogene wisecracked. "My lungs and my legs might not have gotten the message yet, but my heart has."

"I see. Well, I'd say by the glow in your eyes and on your face...wait a second." The doctor peeked under the sheet covering Imogene's feet. "Ah-ha! You're glowing all over."

"I'm in love."

"I thought as much. I think I might have even made a note of it." She removed Imogene's chart from its holder at the foot of her bed and pointed to clipboard scribble. "Yes, there it is. Heartthrob-itis, right next to bed rest." She replaced the chart. "So? Tell me?"

"My first. I think that's what's sucking the air out of my lungs. It might even account for that shadow on the heart side."

"First time is momentous. You're sure it isn't a crush?"

"I am," Imogene assured, adding, "Although, I've never had a crush."

"Not even in high school?"

"Not even."

"Well then, Miss LaPin, I'm happy for you." The doctor stood to go. "But that doesn't mean you can ignore my directives. Take your meds. Get plenty of rest. Drink lots of liquids. And, don't forget the chicken soup."

"I promise."

"Then I'm hereby releasing you. A nurse will be by with paperwork and two scripts. One's an antibiotic. Take it all, exactly as directed. The other is a codeine based cough medicine to ensure sleep. You're already slated to come back to see me. Don't forget."

"I'll be here."

"Take care of yourself Miss LaPin. And, *mazel tov!*"

This is no way to begin the first day of spring, Imogene thought after being wheeled out the hospital emergency exit and into the bright sunshine. *The clock at the nurse's station said 1:39. That means, if Wink's flight from LaGuardia to Boston takes 90 minutes and the drive from Boston to Portsmouth matches that, Eloise should be getting home at about the same time I get back to 12 West.*

Imogene hoped Eloise's shock and dismay at Wink as her emissary would be tempered by the gifts she'd sent, ending any anxiety created by her no-show. She needed Eloise to know how deeply she regretted not being able to call her from the hospital, and understand there wasn't a way to reach her until they'd both returned to a home base. Regardless, she'd never be using another public phone ever again.

• • •

Eloise was aggravated at the tall, blond-haired man striding towards her who kept waving and intentionally blocking her vision as she searched for Imogene among the passengers arriving from New York. The fellow looked familiar. She hoped it wasn't someone from out of her distant past longing to talk over old times. It was 11:30 and Imogene's return flight left Logan at 6:30 the next night. That meant too few hours to spend together.

"Eloise! It's me. It's Wink. Hello! Don't you recognize me? Hello!"

She felt a crushing blow. Instead of Imogene, the annoying blonde approaching her was Andy Wink. That meant Imogene wasn't coming. She held her breath, beating back her disappointment, wanting to turn quickly, run fast, and hide.

"Imogene couldn't make it," Wink goaded, fully aware it wasn't what Eloise wanted to hear; knowing it was mean of him to make her wait. "She sent this as a peace offering instead." He handed Eloise the suitcase bearing Imogene's box of gifts.

"But...wh-why?" Her words were barely audible.

"Oh, right, silly me, you haven't heard. Imogene has pneumonia. She was still in the hospital when I left New York, but should be released today, barring complications. I saw her this morning on my way to the airport. She was wheeled into emergency just after ten last night, but the doctor was satisfied by Imogene's progress."

"Pneumonia? Hospital? Emergency? Doctor?"

"Yes, yes, but don't concern yourself." Wink took Eloise by the arm and began ushering her out of the terminal. "She sent you her heart and some trinkets. Say, I have a swell idea! Why don't you let me drive so you can sit back, relax, and open your gifts while I tell you the whole story? Come on now. Shoulders back. Chest out. Chin up. Which way to the car?"

FIFTY
Saturday Afternoon, March 21, 1970
Close Calls

If Eloise had been looking for a sign that she'd fallen in love, it came in the form of Andy Wink. The second he told her Imogene was sick, Eloise tuned him out and focused on returning to Portsmouth, packing up her pekes and all of her belongings and driving as fast as possible to New York to take care of Imogene for the rest of their lives.

It was Imogene who convinced her to do otherwise when — without introduction or explanation — Eloise dumped Wink on James, locked herself in her bedroom, and phoned ahead.

"I'll be asleep every minute I'm not working," Imogene stressed. "And as much as I want you here, it wouldn't be a pretty time for me, or a quality time for us. That's no way to begin our life together."

"Work? You shouldn't be going to work!"

"We'll see how I feel about that come morning. Fortunately, I have one of those bosses who is not keen on delegating responsibility. She's quite capable of handling the whole shebang herself, if it comes to that."

"But what if you go in and a crisis crops up and you're expected to stay late?"

"Darlin', it's not my style. I've been working forty-hour weeks since I was fourteen and in all that time, I've never worked late, not even once. After five is Patty's party. Her true love is that company. I'm nothing more than her hired right hand, with no desire to change that."

"So, you expect me to worry and wait?"

"No-o," Imogene imitated Garbo. "I vant you to pine for me until ve meet again."

"No sweat, Greta. That I can do. Tell me when and where."

"It's already a go. I land in Boston at 8:50, Saturday morning,

March 28th. My travel agency has confirmed the ticket."

"I seem to have fallen for that line once before."

"It was as sincere then as now. But it comes with a hitch."

"Uh-oh. What?"

"Can this be our last call tonight? And, no more than a one hour call a day until then?"

"That feels harsh."

"On me, too. I'm sorry. The thing is, I picked this bug up when I tracked you down eight days ago. The diagnosis is, the worst of what I have should be lessened by Saturday if I sleep as much as possible until then. Doctor's orders. Say you understand. Pretty please?"

Eloise didn't want to understand. All she wanted was for them to be together without further ado or delay. "What about that cough you keep covering up?"

"I swear, one swig of my prescribed syrup and I'm down for the count."

Eloise had nestled down with the pekes asleep on two pillows nearby, a comforter pulled up close to her chin, and a Cheshire cat smile gracing her lips. "Say the word and I'll be there. I've already got one foot out the door."

"A thousand times over, I want you here, believe me I do. But, don't."

Once they hung up, Imogene hoped Eloise would defy her. She wanted her to call back. She wanted her to say, "I'm on my way and nothing can stop me!" Tears filled her eyes at the prospect of all the things that could prevent it from happening. Not in a morose way. She didn't do glum. She was mushy to a fault, yes, but never maudlin. Yet there she lay, weakened with walking pneumonia, leveled by lovesickness, desperately pleading for Eloise to call back.

"Ring phone. Ring!"

It did.

• • •

Imogene's mother had been trying to get in touch with her for most the morning. Early on, there was no answer. Afterwards, the line was busy for nearly an hour. She began by blaming the weather as the culprit, but reconsidered when recalling Pansy's penchant for answering the phone with mewing after knocking the receiver out of the cradle. Why Imogene hadn't taught the cat to hang the phone back up mystified her.

She elected to try once more before checking with the Red Cross. Getting through on a half a ring startled her.

"Sweetheart?"

Mrs. LaPin remained silent, half-thinking she'd dialed wrong, but certain she hadn't. "Izzy, is that you?"

"You have a sweetheart named Izzy?" Mrs. LaPin asked, mischievously.

"Oh, Mom, you surprised me. I thought you were someone else."

"Named Izzy?" It left Imogene at a temporary loss for words. "Silence won't make me go away, Dolly. You might as well tell me now as never. Who's Izzy? When will we meet?"

"Oh, Ma."

"Don't oh-ma me. I've never known you to show any interest in anyone. Suddenly you have a sweetheart?"

"We met a week ago. But it's what you'd call a long distance thing, so let's let it go for the time being."

"How long distance, Dolly?"

"Portsmouth long."

"New Hampshire?"

"Yes."

"Careful, Dolly. Portsmouth is where your grandmother got married."

That news was a whammy. "You never told me Grandma got married in Portsmouth."

"What's to tell? Your grandfather was a marine and stationed there."

"Granddad was a marine?"

"Handpicked by Teddy Roosevelt to 'Speak softly but carry a big stick' worldwide!"

"Hold on, Mom. He was part of the Great White Fleet campaign?"

"He was."

"How could you not tell me that?" Imogene knew she'd come from secret keepers because it was the American way. No airing of dirty laundry. No discussion of what went on behind closed doors. Skeletons trump truth. The past was history, pun intended. But this wasn't classified. Was it?

"The subject never came up."

"How could it without you bringing it up, Ma?"

"Well I'm telling you now aren't I? Geesh."

As much as Imogene loved her mom, she found her exasperating at times. This was one of those. "So, why Portsmouth?"

"Oh, dear, now let me think. It was after your Great Aunt Anna threw Momma out for having an affair with her husband."

"Grams had a sister?"

"Oh my yes. She was the last of ten children. Aunt Anna was the next to youngest, but there was a twenty year age difference between them. They're all dead now."

"This is beyond belief."

"Why, dear? We all die."

Imogene gritted her teeth. "About the affair, Mom."

"Well, Momma *said* Anna's husband forced himself on her, but he was more than fifty by then and Momma wasn't long off the boat from Sweden. Orphaned at fifteen, the poor dear. Still, I hardly think an old man would have dallied after a young girl without cause."

It baffled Imogene. She'd long ago accepted her mom's second-class citizen status as voluntary, ready to comply whenever a man entered the room. But this seemed extreme.

"Skip to the marriage, Mom."

"I don't see the point of it."

"Yeah, well, Pandora has left the box."

"Oh for heaven's sake," she relented. "She was working for a family in Portsmouth when Dad's ship docked. He was originally on the S.S. Alabama but ended up on the S.S. Maine for his final tour of duty. Portsmouth was his last stop before being sent home. Now where did I put Daddy's document with the ship names? Amos? Get down from there! You naughty pussy."

"Mom! Stop with the cat and continue. Please?"

"It was all so long ago, Dolly. Daddy said he was about to return to Grand Ledge, over in western Michigan where he was born, when he met Mother. They wrote to each other after he got home. He proposed. She accepted. He sent money for the train here."

"Then how...?"

"You know your grandmother."

"I kinda thought I did, but I kinda think I didn't."

"She squandered the money! So, by golly, he got on a train and went to fetch her. The train trip back was their honeymoon."

"It doesn't sound very romantic."

"Oh, no-no-no. It wasn't. Your grandmother hated the sex, hated the pregnancy part. That's why they got the divorce that ruined my life."

"Why doesn't the divorce surprise me? And, how did it ruin your life?"

"I was a child of divorced parents, Dolly! It was a disgrace! People didn't get divorced in 1938. It was unheard of." It put Mrs. LaPin in a huff.

"But Ma-a, weren't you twenty-five in 1938? Didn't you get married in 1938?"

"Who's telling this story?"

"You. Sorry." The conversation had thoroughly drained Imogene. "Listen, Mom, if I say we'll do details when I get there for Mother's Day, can this be the end of that until then? I'm feeling wilted and need to hang."

"Will you be bringing Izzy along with you in May?"

"I will."

"Then it's definite? I can tell the cats?"

"You can."

"We're holding you to that, Dolly. I love you."

"I love you too, Ma. Bye."

Mrs. LaPin hugged her handset before she hung it up. Then she patted it on the top like she would a puppy. *To think*, she thought, *my little Dolly has finally fallen in love with Izzy. Izzy? I bet it's short for Isaac, probably a nice Jewish doctor. Or, a banker!* She clapped, *goody-goody. That is, unless my Dolly is pregnant. Pregnant is no way to start a marriage if you need the love to last. But then, if she's pregnant, so what? She can move back home to live with me when things don't work out. We never had the mother-daughter talk. We can have it now.*

"Oh, Amos and Andy," she bubbled. "I'm going to be a grandmother! Isn't it exciting?"

FIFTY-ONE
Saturday Afternoon, March 21, 1970
Gift Rapt

When Eloise finally emerged from her bedroom after talking to Imogene, James and Wink were putting a meal on the table; potato salad, baked beans, olives, apple pie, coffee, and sliced chicken breast sandwiches on pumpernickel with lettuce, tomato and Russian dressing.

"Here she is," Wink trumpeted upon seeing her. "I was on my way to get you, woman!"

Eloise now knew how Wink had come to Imogene's aid without waffling. She said he fed her cats, vacuumed her apartment, hung up her clothes, and even changed the linens on both her bed and couch so she could return to tidiness and spend all her time recovering.

"Thanks, Wink," she said, squeezing his arm before she sat down.

"For what?"

"For being a class act, including your trip here. I won't soon forget it."

"Honeychild, you won't *ever* forget it! I'll never stop cashing in those brownie points."

"Who is this Imogene?" James carped. "Wink won't blab a thing."

That came as a relief. Eloise didn't want James knowing what she was up to. His probing proved Wink was both a gentleman and a friend for not divulging whatever he knew about hers and Imogene's involvement. She followed Wink's lead in answering.

"Imogene's an old friend."

"How old?"

"Seems like always."

"Is she as butch as she sounds on the phone?"

"Butch, no," Wink chimed in. "Tough? Absolutely! You don't want to get caught in her crosshairs." He turned towards Eloise. "But when she likes you, she doesn't disappoint."

"So how do you fit into it, Wink?" James didn't really give a rats-ass about the phantom woman as long as he had a boy toy sitting at the table. "Are you staying with someone in Portsmouth, or moving here, or what?"

"Pretty little ol' me?" Wink batted his long eyelashes in James' direction before reaching out and swatting his hand. "Why, Miss Eloise here begged me to tag along on your behalf. You mean you didn't tell him, Miss Eloise? Did I go and spoil the suu-prise, suu-prise?"

Eloise delighted in James' reaction. "Don't gape James. And, answer the fellow. Do you like him? He's your New York souvenir."

"Very much!" James offered up his best Greek grin. "You're welcome to stay here with us, Wink. With me."

"Why Mr. James, do tell. Of course I'll stay." Wink helped himself to seconds from every dish on the table. "Mercy-Mary-me, it's the least I can do for love."

Over the next week Eloise focused on Imogene's arrival. They'd each been sending the other a card daily, enclosing a tender note. The first one arrived unexpectedly on the Wednesday after they met; neither imagined the other would think of doing it. Eloise selected hers from a rack in the hotel gift shop on the Sunday morning of her departure. Imogene hand crafted hers that same Sunday evening from cardboard and silk scraps she kept in her desk. Both posted their cards to each other early Monday.

Because each conspicuously added S.W.A.K. to the back of her envelopes, they'd rush to their respective community mail delivery foyer tables, search for a familiar handwriting, feel giddy upon finding it, and inhaled a whiff of the scent sent lingering therein.

"I'm like a silly schoolgirl getting mail from you," Imogene enthused during a phone session. "My fingertip follows the line of each letter of your handwriting. I hold your card next to my heart. I kiss it, as if it were your cheek."

Eloise felt the words Imogene spoke and wished she could say them as easily.

"Ditto."

• • •

Blue laws required most stores be closed on Sundays, but that didn't stop Eloise from getting her friend, Moose, to let her in the back door of his Kit & Caboodle Shop located at the far end of Market Street.

Moose was a towering, broken-nosed, hulk of a fellow with steely gray eyes and a wavy white ponytail fastened with a red, Andy Boy broccoli rubber band. A black brier pipe was always clamped in his nicotine stained teeth that he'd stop to light every few minutes, leaving a puff of charred Middleton's Cherry tobacco smoke trailing behind.

He and Eloise had done daily business in the four months since she moved to town. While Moose attended his nine-to-five retail six days a week, she was out rummaging the streets for sellable discards and attending estate sales, ever seeking that elusive sleeper to buy for a farthing and turn into a fortune. Moose told Eloise she had a real feel for what people collected.

"For every twenty quick-sale things you bring me, you snag one of true value. That's persistence. That's how you learn the biz."

But this day, Eloise wasn't selling. She was looking to buy.

"What's your price range, Iz?"

"No range, but whatever I find, we might need to trade at least half the cost."

The Kit & Caboodle was a ground floor warehouse filled high and deep with rows and rows of antique and collectible furniture, decorations, glass, pottery, books, paintings, ephemera, household goods, and all the gimcrackery imaginable dating between fifteen years to more than a century old. It would take an avid shopper a week, just to do a three second glance at every item in the place, but Moose knew his inventory by heart and where he put each item — as long as he was given a hint.

"I need a unique gift for a girl who's sort of engaged and starting a new home."

"What kind of house?"

"A New York City whitestone. Whatever that is."

"They're 19th century townhouses, usually three to five stories, with fifteen foot ceilings, oak floors, and a hallway staircase leading to each level of living area. Most have been hacked up into apartments by now. Is she a connoisseur?"

"Like me?"

Moose tossed his head back and hooted. "You're not a connoisseur. You're an accumulator. Huge difference."

"Okay, okay. Don't rub it in. It's a simple, special gift is all."

"Right, for an engaged girl who makes you blush."

Eloise leaned over to catch her reflection in the steel framed mirror affixed to an oak and porcelain shaving stand. No use denying it. She looked positively tickled pinkish.

After spending the better part of the afternoon rejecting suggestions and being distracted by clever things, Eloise saw something her heart knew it sought.

"This is it! This is perfect. What is it and how much?"

Moose ambled over to look inside the bottom drawer of a blanket chest. "That? That's a hooked rug from the mid-19th century. Not popular right now, but if I keep it long enough I'm betting these bad babies will be big sellers someday."

The rug had the scene of a thatched roof cottage with a white picket fence, a black dog, an orange cat, a yellow bird, a fruit tree, and little red flowers scattered around on a forest green background.

"I can let you have that for ten," he offered.

"I can pay you five," she wangled.

"I can keep my mouth shut and give it to you as an engagement gift."

"Sold! As long as you won't up the price ten dollars on the next thing I buy to cover what I didn't pay for this."

"Sounds reasonable enough."

By Tuesday Eloise had bartered Moose out of an antique wholecloth quilt constructed of twenty-five hand worked line-stitches of thread for every inch of woven white cotton fabric. It had a four-inch appliquéd border in pink with matching binding all around, a two-inch appliquéd sash of lavender separated from the pink by a quarter inch of green, and motifs of lavender and pink triangular baskets on beds of little green leaves spaced five inches apart. Between each basket were embroidered two, small, fulvous rings, interlocked to symbolize wedding bands.

On Thursday she went through eleven boxes of newspaper-wrapped porcelain figurines before finding one of a young, redheaded girl sitting at a typewriter with a pencil clenched in her teeth and wadded up paper at her feet. Eloise hoped Imogene would understand it meant she supported her dreams of becoming a writer, but she had no intention of moving to New York, or anywhere else until she knew how to deal with her list of what-ifs and resolve James' loan scam before it became a scandal.

Finally, on the day before Imogene was to arrive, Eloise ferreted out the ring.

She had planned to buy a purple amethyst to closely match the ring Imogene sent to her. But after visiting every jewelry store and pawn shop within twenty miles, she couldn't find a style of ring to compare, or cut of stone to compete. It took moving aside the last crate of books from the last of the many showcases at Moose's and peering down through the dusty glass onto a shelf jam-packed with trinkets before she spotted it.

There, among a jumble of costume jewelry, rested a fluted gold band set with an oval blue opal glittering sparks of frenetic reds each time her penlight beam bounced off it.

No haggling, no discount, no expectation of favoritism was involved. Eloise checked the price listed on the tag, slapped down her cash, gently pocketed the ring, and floated out the door.

She had nothing left to do but get herself to the airport on time.

FIFTY-TWO
Saturday Morning, March 28, 1970
Waiting Games

Imogene was lost.

Her flight landed on time thirty minutes earlier. She checked her wrist out of habit from not wearing a watch. Watches made no sense to her, the same way Eloise not being there to pick her up on their RAVE day made no sense to her, the same as choosing the right word in her head to describe the feelings in her heart made no sense to her. Regardless, the foremost word she felt right then was concern.

The arrival area was deserted. The last of the plane crew trudged by, frowning like they'd assumed she'd been left at the altar. The lights dimmed. It was cold. She was alone.

Inwardly, she was singing the Dusty Springfield song, wishin' and hopin' Eloise's dogs hadn't broken loose. That's as negative an image as Imogene could conjure up as a reason Eloise was late. Even then, she loved dogs too much to hold onto it.

She considered calling Eloise, but that would involve using a pay phone, which wasn't possible without a rag and bleach to wipe down the box, dial, cradle, and receiver. She might be able to locate a janitor's closet somewhere that could provide her with the cloth and bleach, but would it also have unused rubber gloves available? And, how far would she have to walk to look?

Oddly enough, Eloise's being disconcertingly late was not what mattered most. It was more important to convince herself to stay put, like she was taught to do as a child: When lost in the woods, sit still, and stay put.

She'd gotten lost a lot as a child.

She was incapable of sitting still and staying put.

It was a good thing, too, because no one ever noticed her missing.

If she'd stayed put all nine times she got lost in the woods as a kid, she'd still be sitting and waiting to be rescued. She bet some Cub Scout would have tripped over her remains by now, called dibs on her bones and crammed them into his knapsack for third grade show-and-tell. Programming would have been interrupted: Breaking News From Huntley and Brinkly. Brinkly would have reported it, pithily. And, wasn't that just like a boy? Touching bones that didn't belong to him. Getting a badge for it.

"Imogene!" yelled Eloise, tearing headlong down the darkened corridor towards her. "I am so, so sorry I'm late. We had a flat tire on the way here and the boys had to change it." She swept Imogene up into her arms and hugged her. "You have no idea what it's like to watch two fags trying to change a flat tire on the side of the highway. If someone hadn't stopped to help, we'd still be stranded there."

Imogene didn't care. She'd been found.

The return to Portsmouth was joyful despite the ordeal of letting James drive. He'd felt guilty about intending to leave Eloise and her friends stranded at Logan Airport before Larry Dee unwittingly came to their rescue. James let this slip after downing too much Mateus Rosé on an empty stomach. The uproar it created somehow worked itself out.

Eloise had been both eager and anxious about seeing Imogene again. To calm her nerves she invited Wink along to pick Imogene up, who invited James, who insisted on driving after bemoaning Eloise's big bad Buick made him appear dwarfish to those in passing cars. Somehow, having Wink in the dandy-candy seat made all his namby-pamby insecurities vanish. But they resurfaced the minute he saw an ice patch in the road, panicked, braked and turned the wheel towards near disaster, spinning them four times before hitting a snow bank and tearing a tire. Eloise couldn't tell which was worse, the near fatal whirl, or the hysterics of James and Wink when they jumped out of the car and raced around like guillotined hens.

By the time they finally got to Logan, located Imogene, left Logan, and pulled onto the interstate heading north it was nearly noon. Eloise recounted the torn tire tirade from the back seat where she and Imogene sat, shoulder-to-shoulder, hand-in-hand.

"Thankfully, men on motorcycles rode to our rescue."

"Oh, we could have changed that tire," Wink bragged, "if we hadn't seen those cycles coming and wanted the view of butts bending over."

"And grunting going on," added James.

Once into New Hampshire, they left the interstate to travel the more scenic Route 1. Eloise hoped to sell Imogene on the beauty of the ocean and how living near the coast could be as romantic a place as anywhere else on earth. To advance her agenda the foursome stopped at a Hampton Beach diner and chatted like old married couples, until everyone was up to snuff on Eloise's New York trip, and the who's-who list of Imogene's Manhattan life.

"Patsy was intent on me seeing her apartment in Brooklyn. That's where I was when I dialed Eloise Thursday night."

"We talked for an hour long distance on Patsy's dime," Eloise added.

"What's the deal with her apartment?" Wink was always on the lookout.

"A great place. She has the upper two floors of a duplex in Brooklyn Heights. Eat-in kitchen, separate dining and living rooms, a bath and a bedroom on one floor. Then two big bedrooms upstairs and a walled porch roof the width of the house and ten feet deep. And, get this — she pays one-sixty a month, utilities included!"

"It still doesn't explain it," stressed Eloise.

Wink reached out and grabbed Imogene's hand. "It? What, Mo? What it?"

"Oh-h, nothing," she scoffed. "I was still pretty shaky from fighting this virus, so when it got late she suggested I stay over."

"And? And?" He milked her for details.

"Tell him!" insisted Eloise.

"And nothing. She came in the room after I'd turned the light off and was nearly asleep and asked me if I wanted her to sleep in there with me."

"She was coming on to you!" the boys blurted in unison.

"See?" Eloise added.

"She wasn't!" Imogene discounted. "Was she?"

"Oh-h, wait a sec," said Wink. "Have you told Patsy about Eloise yet?"

"Not really."

"I bet that's it. I bet Ronald ratted and she was putting a move on you to see if it was true. That's how straight people think. To them, if you're gay it means you sleep with *all* men. Selfsame rule applies here."

"Who's Ronald?" Eloise and James asked in unison. It called for air-spits, wishes, and more coffee.

They took a roundabout way into Portsmouth via the historic district where structures dating from 1630 to 1900 were built around a waterway that had been drained dry seventy years earlier. Wild berries growing in the field gave the neighborhood its name: Strawberry Bank

"Living here must be sublime," said Imogene after wandering the area a while. She was already charmed by Portsmouth, busily snapping photos for their Happybox. Standing by one dilapidated house overdue for demolishing, Imogene promised Eloise a similar structure someday.

"You can keep the picture for posterity," chided Eloise, "but I'll hold you to the house."

By the time they finally arrived at the Market Street apartment, twilight descended. Wink and James took off across the harbor for an all-nighter at The Barn, a gay nightclub in Kittery, Maine. It left the two women to themselves.

"Before we climb these stairs and go into the apartment there's something you need to know."

Imogene geared up. "Lay it on me."

"I have two Pekingese."

"Lucy and Gracie. I know."

"Lucy is perfection. She loves everyone, behaves beautifully, and is so gentle that I swear, I've never even heard the dog woof more than once. Maybe twice. But very softly."

"And, Gracie?"

"Gracie doesn't like anyone but me. James walks and feeds her, but she hates him."

Imogene was unperturbed.

"I love these dogs, Imogene. They're everything in the world to me."

"I understand."

"That is, before I met you."

"Of course."

"And I love my folks."

"Dogs. Me. Folks. Got it."

"And donuts."

They heard Gracie scratching and barking wildly from the bedroom as Eloise entered the apartment first, turning on the lights. Imogene scrambled to position herself on a chair in the center of the living room, letting her coat slide off her back onto the floor.

"Ready?" Eloise crossed two fingers for luck, opened the door and let the pups out.

Both dogs did a whole body wagging dance towards Eloise, stopping for hugs and kisses as she dropped to her knees and held them close, rubbed their backs, and returned their affection. In the jubilant process of twirling around, Gracie spied Imogene.

At first the dog froze in her tracks and stared. Slowly and cautiously she lifted her head high, sniffed at the air through her flat-faced nose and stared some more before waltzing over, rising up on her back legs, putting her front paws on Imogene's knees and gently scratching to be picked up. Imogene obliged her. To Eloise's awe (and later to James' chagrin), their mutual adoration was instantaneous.

"Did I mention?" Imogene remarked. "I'm the Chinese sign of the Dog."

"I'm the Chinese sign of the Rabbit," Eloise beamed. "I'm so-o lucky."

The women leashed the pekes for a jot down the street, letting them loose in a nearby grassy area to tinkle before returning to the apartment for the night. It was eight by then.

While Imogene busied herself in the kitchen preparing a carafe of Hershey's cocoa and a plate of Big Top peanut butter toast, Eloise put on the reel-to-reel tape she'd made especially for them from her Webcor recorder hooked up to the high fidelity console she used to copy music off single 45's and long playing disks.

The first song drifting into the kitchen was Roy Orbison singing *Pretty Woman*.

"This is what I thought when I first laid eyes on you," Eloise said, standing in the doorway, watching Imogene as she measured the sugar, salt, and cocoa powder into each cup before blending it with a splash of milk. "It's one of the songs I selected from Johnny's jukebox while I pretended to ignore you."

"Really?"

"Really. I'm ruined for thoughts about anyone else whenever it plays now."

"I dare you to come over here and say that."

Eloise did, remaining until Imogene transferred the smoothed contents of both cups into a pan of more milk, beat it with a rotary wheel and set the fire on low to let it warm.

Only then did she turn to embrace Eloise, placing her face against Eloise's shoulder as they swayed slowly to the second song on the tape — the one playing that enchanted evening when Imogene used hand language to ask the blonde haired, blue-eyed stranger for a dance from across a crowded room; the song they first trembled to.

It was *Something*.

FIFTY-THREE
12:13 Sunday Morning, March 29, 1970
Overture

Eloise carried a pair of blue fluted, onion pattern china cups and saucers into the living room and placed them on a low table next to a bowl of miniature marshmallows and a porcelain chocolate pot, so the two of them could sit on the mattress in front of the windows overlooking the harbor and take in the moon's reflection, dancing like skimmed pebbles on the bay below.

They shared their mutual esteem for Venus, wished on first seen stars in the sky, and relaxed to the music flowing softly as symbolic of their heart-to-heart; noshing a little, dancing a little and discussing the songs Eloise had chosen for their RAVE Day medley, to which they both knew all the lyrics.

Pretty Little Angel Eyes: Curtis Lee

There's A Moon Out Tonight: The Capris

Brown Eyed Girl: Van Morrison

"I know the words don't relate much, but you are my brown eyed girl, Imogene."

"And you're my Angeleyes. One word. Not two."

"Must say, I'm not keen on that name. But you tagged me right off, so I knew you'd want the song on tap."

"Face it. Those baby blues make you look angelic." Eloise was about to say 'angel-ick' when Imogene pointed, "See that moon?"

"I do."

"The Capris captured it perfectly. I've been mesmerized by that moon from the very first time I saw it rise in the sky. Some nights it was the one thing I could count on to be there for me. Spectacular, always, no matter partial or full. But now — with you — I feel the ardor of it, too."

What A Difference A Day Makes: Dinah Washington
You're All I Need To Get By: Marvin Gaye & Tammy Terrell
Do You Believe In Magic: The Lovin' Spoonful
Can't Help Falling In Love: Elvis Presley
Then He Kissed Me: The Crystals

They slowed to the sonorous sound of Washington, bopped to the beat of Marvin Gaye, shuffled to the Spoonful, crooned along with Elvis and emphasized 'she' while singing backup for the Crystals.

"That's just how it was, too," Imogene nudged, "if you count me falling on my face as the walking up part, followed by an intoxicated pantomime to dance. Granted, I was already yours. But the kiss clinched it."

"As it should be," observed Eloise, caressing the nape of Imogene's neck, awakening her every nerve.

Hooked On A Feeling: B. J. Thomas

"Which reminds me. I have a sussie for you."

"What's a sussie?"

"A surprise." Eloise jumped up, disappeared into her bedroom and returned with a large, meticulously wrapped package.

"Wow! You do gifts like my mom, almost too pretty to open. Me, I'm terrible at it. I commit a crime by trying."

"What'd'ya you mean?" Wink hadn't told either woman of his intervention. "The gifts you sent were exquisitely wrapped."

"How sweet." Imogene tapped Eloise on the nose. "And kind. And blind."

"Rhyme!" they squawked, air-spitting followed by a right fist hit.

"Make a wish," Imogene urged.

"You're my wish."

"No fair. I had dibs on that!"

"You didn't call it."

"In that case, I'm goin' in!" Imogene ripped the package open with a vengeance, finding her earlier wished upon a star had come true: a cottage with a white picket fence and pets in the yard. "Oh-h, Eloise. It's divine."

Removing the hooked rug from its box Imogene laid it out flat.

"It's too fine for the floor. We'll need to hang it." It made them misty-eyed. "How did you know I'd want this for us, Iz?"

"It's what I want it for us, too."

Teach Me Tonight: Dinah Washington

Imogene intuited Washington's sultry voice as the tip to it being time. She slipped off the mattress and excused herself by improvising a dance to the torch song request for a tutor. In doing so she realized, it wasn't just the moon that suddenly made sense to her now, it was also the lyrics to songs. Before, she'd understood the definition of words as surface sentiments. Now, she assimilated the amorous elements as well, aroused by having fallen in love with Eloise.

I Second That Emotion: Smokey Robinson

My Girl: The Temptations

Once inside the bathroom, Imogene saw that Eloise had hung their Victorian nightgowns on the back of the door. She took a quick shower, singing along with all the Smokey stanzas streaming in through the air vent, toweled off, slipped into her gown, combed her hair, and pinched her cheeks to the Temptations before returning to Eloise.

Come Softly To Me: The Fleetwoods

Happy Together: The Turtles

Eloise followed Imogene's lead by rhythmically rotating across the room to the beat of the Fleetwoods before disappearing to duplicate Imogene's routine (except she smoked while brushing her teeth and added a smidgen of Shalimar behind her ears, neck, and knees).

While Eloise primped and the Turtles sang, Imogene retrieved a brown paper bag from her suitcase that sat near the door where she'd dropped it upon arrival. The bag had a wrinkled red bow stapled to its folded over top. Once both women were back scrunched up together, Imogene gave Eloise the package.

This Girl's In Love With You: Dionne Warwick

"Where in the world did you find pink silk sheets?"

"Cloth is my business, lady. Favors come with the territory. Will they fit?"

"They're perfect." Eloise looked dotingly at her. "Perfect."

Her response elated Imogene. "Tell me something, Eloise?"

"Anything."

Imogene cast her eyes on the bedroom door. "Have you shared the bed in there with anyone? Say yes, or no."

"No."

"Are you just saying that?"

"No. The bed's an 1810 four-poster, but the mattress is new. No one has slept on it but me, Gracie and Lucy."

"So, this is a first for both of us?"

Cherish: The Association

"Listen to me, because I barely say things once, let alone again. You're the first person who's ever been exclusively in love with me. And I'm in love with you in a way I've never, ever felt for anyone else. I never even knew feeling like I do was possible." Eloise held up one finger. "Now hold that thought. I'll be right back."

She disappeared behind her bedroom door for several minutes. Upon returning, she glided over and took Imogene's hands, helping her to her feet.

Chapel Of Love: The Dixie Cups

"Keep in mind, you were supposed to be here last weekend, on the first day of spring."

"Disclaimer noted," said Imogene as the two did the Stroll to where Eloise stopped and stepped aside so, as she opened the door, Imogene's view wouldn't be obstructed.

The period room, with its tester bed blanketed in the antique quilt, was lit by three pink candles inside glass globes arranged on candle stands at each corner of the four bedposts. A fifth stand set near the window held a single globed candle burned to welcome Imogene's arrival — thirteen candles in all. On the chest at the foot of the bed, Eloise placed a cut glass vase filled with a bouquet of thirteen daffodils nestled in sprays of baby's breath.

It was too idyllic for words. "Oh-h, Eloise!" was the most Imogene could muster.

1-2-3: Len Barry

"See here?" Eloise led Imogene to the bed and ran her hand over the quilt. "I don't know what the baskets mean, but the two gold rings represent wedding bands. And, look!" She pulled out the bottom edge of the quilt from where it was hidden behind the footboard. "I had our names embroidered."

The letters were a half-inch high and stitched in white within the pale pink appliqué centered in the border of the quilt; a smaller red heart separated their names from the date:

Imogene & Eloise March 13, 1970

Imogene put her arm around Eloise's waist and pulled her close. "We're going to have the most marvelous life together, Eloise Fitz."

Eloise raised her arm around Imogene's shoulders and hugged. "Indeed we are, Imogene LaPin."

The Very Thought Of You: Doris Day
Bewitched, Bothered, & Bewildered: Doris Day
I Only Have Eyes For You: Doris Day
I've Never Been In Love Before: Doris Day

Together they stripped the mattress and remade it with the new silk sheets, turned down the quilt and released the sheer organdy panels that curtained the bed.

Eloise told Imogene to close her eyes. Once she was certain no peeking was going on she opened a drawer in one of the candlestands, removed a purple felt Crown Royal bag and quickly slipped it under Imogene's pillow.

When Imogene opened her eyes they stood, face-to-face. Each slowly undid the mother-of-pearl buttons on her own gown before letting it drop to the floor.

"Pretty lucky timing," Imogene noted when *I Only Have Eyes For You* began playing.

"Yes. But not entirely luck. These songs are meant to be the overture to the soundtrack of our life together. I've never made a medley for anyone before."

"Well," confessed Imogene, "I've never seen anyone nude before."

"Not even your sisters?"

"Not like this." Imogene reached out to caress the curvature of the underside of Eloise's jaw line inward to the center of her chin, then ventured down her neck to her collarbone and outward to her shoulders. A reverence overtook her. "When growing up we bathed alone and pretty much dressed in the dark." Imogene ran her palms down Eloise's arms as she spoke. "The rules were pretty puritanical in that respect."

"You didn't peek at other girls in the showers after gym class?"

She held and kissed the back of Eloise's right hand. "After the first day, I played hooky from gym all six years." She held and kissed the back of Eloise's left hand. "May I?"

"Yes."

Imogene cupped Eloise's persimmon size breasts. She looked at her own, then back at Eloise's. "They're not much bigger than mine. Just prettier."

"They're not prettier."

"They are. And I am adamant about it!"

Imogene stepped back, looking down. She noted that both of their frames were thin, their skin, the creamy pale pink of magnolias, their stomachs, flat. "If I took a photograph of your belly, close up, it would look like the surface of the moon with one little crater."

"No pictures."

"It's a creative thought. I've been known to have them out loud." Imogene spun Eloise slowly, purposefully. "You're so-o beautiful."

Eloise spun Imogene around the same. "You're more beautiful."

"No you are."

"No you are."

"No you are."

Eloise pulled Imogene close and held her tight. "What I am is cold."

Can't Take My Eyes Off You: Frankie Valii

The last song on the tape began as they climbed into bed and covered up. Imogene felt a lump under her pillow and pulled out the purple felt bag. Inside were two ring boxes — the one she'd given to Eloise and the one Eloise was now giving to her. They opened the boxes and each slipped the intended ring on the other's left hand.

"What we feel now will last within us forever," pledged Imogene. Her eyes crinkled and cheeks ached from the joy on her face that spoke for the whole of them.

• • •

It was nearing sunrise when they finally drifted off to sleep, although neither ever wanted to simply 'sleep' again. Intimacy had given them energy and inspiration, but sleepiness overcame them in spite of all efforts to resist it.

"I still can't believe how you matched those songs to the feelings in my heart," murmured Imogene. "Flawlessly."

Eloise's cheek rested against Imogene's back with one arm draped across her waist and the length of their torsos touching, their legs and ankles entwined. She was reluctant to utter the worn out cliché, but couldn't resist.

"Was it good for you?"

"It?"

Imogene turned over, so they faced each other.

"*It?* Are you kidding me?" She pressed her lips against each of Eloise's eyelids. "It was a tango. A ballet." She kissed each of Eloise's cheeks. "It was a fox-trot. A mambo." She kissed each of Eloise's ears. "It was a fandango. A tarantella." She kissed Eloise's forehead. "It was a waltz." She kissed her nose. "A minuet."

Lastly, Imogene kissed Eloise's lips — twice — as delicately as a finch feather floating on a spring breeze.

"It was an aria. It was an acclamation!"

FIFTY-FOUR
Sunday Evening, March 29, 1970
Winterizing

Eloise resisted change of all kinds. She'd eat almost anything put before her, so it didn't exactly include food. And it didn't always apply to clothing or shoes.

What she resisted was the idea of changing to a healthier way of eating, preferring a circus diet comprised of the same daily sweets interspersed with small side dishes of necessary nutrients.

As for her wardrobe, although extensive, she resisted trends. Instead, she wore the same combination of expensive turtlenecks and straight-leg slacks in the winter, Levi denim jeans and trademarked sweatshirts in the spring and fall, light tan khakis and camisoles under linen shirts in the summer, and snazzy blazers whenever she wanted. She'd often wash whatever outfit she took off at night, intending to wear it the next morning rather than change altogether.

Shoes were treated similarly. She'd wear the same pair daily until the heels wore down and soles split and sides gave out. She preferred to leave most of her thirty-one pairs of shoes in their boxes with the price tags intact because, for Eloise, it was having the options to create the perception of change that counted, not the change itself. She applied that concept to all aspects of her life. It made sense to her.

Whereas, falling in love as a forever commitment didn't. Eloise witnessed that oath taken too often, by too many, who had invariably failed. She had dismissed the possibility of 'till death do we part' as fallacy. Now, although bewitched by Imogene, a part of her still refused to accept the 'ever after' of it.

The 'happily' portion remained in play. She was deliriously, overtly, aggressively happy — haunted by the bane of her once being passively, submissively, supposedly happy. Who could honestly say she wouldn't be superficially happy again if her current ecstatically-happy ended someday? That statistical safety net was pervasive.

Eloise hoped she and Imogene would last forever. But her need to remain independent trumped that; her vow to never again put anyone first in her life was written with pain on a petrified part of her heart. The very idea of uprooting herself to move to Manhattan would be like changing from cotton tees to wool turtlenecks for a hike in the sun on sand: challenging, but unrealistic in her estimation.

Yes, Eloise told herself as she packed the Electra with Imogene's things, she had moved to New Hampshire for a few months as a favor to a gay guy. That wasn't change. That was a long vacation. That was relinquishing a beach life that had begun to get old. That was escaping parents who wanted marriage for her and grandchildren for them.

So what if it gave her folks false hope when she trailed along after James? Deep down they knew. At least, they must have sensed it by the way she spent her school years in the company of girls. They must have discussed the possibility of it by her failure to connect with anyone since being blindsided with betrayal by Gail.

Sure, she'd have friends over for dinner. And, yes, her mom was cordial in a Southern hospitality kind of way that got everyone through a 'fine' evening feeling welcomed, but never asked back when shown the door.

Regardless, that was then and this was the morning after. Eloise had watched Imogene sleep sweetly, and awaken joyfully, and dress dauntlessly, and eat with abandon, and laugh with a gusto that a woman in love does.

She wrestled with how to tell Imogene she preferred Portsmouth, that she'd find a place to move the belongings she'd bought for shipping to Florida, and make a home for the two of them there, near Strawberry Bank instead. The question was, would someone like Imogene ever sacrifice her big city security for a town scavenger who got by on a stipend from home?

It brought to mind the one gift she hadn't yet given to Imogene: the porcelain figurine of a girl sitting at a typewriter with edited versions of a novel wadded up on the floor. She'd secretly packed that with Imogene's things, as a kind of going away gift.

Imogene said she needed six months in New York City. Eloise

consented to think about it. She had. She decided, not now. Not ever.

By twilight they were on their way to Logan, where Imogene would catch her return flight to New York. Neither of them had brought up when to meet again, not wanting to be the one to ruin their glorious weekend and nonpareil coupling of body and soul.

The pups were asleep on pillows in the back, guarding a crate containing a large thermos of coffee, sandwiches, chips, donuts, packets of sugar, Peke treats, utensils, cups and saucers. A glass bottle of milk, a jar of water, and four baby Cokes in green bottles sat in a metal bucket of ice. The two needed one final fond moment together before parting. They chose a picnic in the back seat of the Buick as the best way to let go.

"What's that you have?" Eloise pointed.

Imogene had disappeared into a shop on Saturday and emerged with something like a bigger, thinner, bendable book. It was left in a sack on the front seat between them.

"Oh! You know, I meant to show you." She pulled out a calendar of reproduced 19th century lithographs featuring little girls in seasonal settings and opened it to March.

Snow had begun falling in big, fat, wet flakes within minutes of them getting on the road. It became concentrated so quickly, Eloise was forced to flip the windshield wipers and headlights to high before glancing over at the calendar, long enough to spot the thirteenth circled in red and the twenty-ninth with two hearts added.

"Shouldn't the hearts be on the thirteenth when we met?"

"Nope. The thirteenth is the anniversary of our falling in love. The twenty-ninth is our Diditday. We'll be celebrating both."

"Diditday, huh? That's original. Too bad anniversaries are limited to once a year."

"Well, snap out of sad, sister, because we'll be celebrating them every month. Also, in addition to the 13th and 29th, every diditday gets a heart on our calendar. Hearts are a fitting form of keeping track, don't you think?"

"Yes." Eloise was leery.

"Ours is not going to be a life of pent up emotions or neglect. If sullen sneaks in, we'll check the layout of hearts on the calendar as a go-to reference of possible reasons."

"I like that idea, I do. But where will you be hanging the calendar?"

"In our kitchen, of course. Why?"

"Seems a little obvious don't you think?"

"No-o-o, silly. It's our secret code! Nobody will figure it out."

By the time they'd reached the outskirts of Boston, a flashing sign on the shoulder of the interstate indicated Logan Airport was closed. Imogene fussed with the radio until she found a travel advisory had been issued for all of New England urging drivers to seek shelter. A perilous spring nor'easter had whipped in off the Atlantic catching forecasters by surprise for a second time that month. Cars were pulling off and piling up at an alarming rate.

"I'm not turning around to strand us in this. I'm taking you to New York."

Imogene made no attempt to dissuade her. Instead, she gingerly slid across the seat to snuggle close, grateful that the density of the snow provided them with privacy in their very own winter wonderland.

It took them nearly six hours to reach 12 West. Although treacherous at times, the massive downfall created an aura of dreaminess, turning the trip into a sentimental journey where each recounted memories of winters as children growing up in the Midwest. Except for gas, they didn't tarry along the way, happy to plow on in the shadow of big rig tire tracks until the sky cleared near Bridgeport and it proved smooth sailing for the final sixty-seven miles.

FIFTY-FIVE
Early Monday Morning, March 30, 1970
Propinquity

When the lights in Imogene's apartment didn't go off for two nights in a row Charles became concerned. He knew if she was in there and in trouble Pansy would be caterwauling at the door. The critter was more canine than feline in that way.

"I'm in good paws with Pansy," Imogene maintained.

Nevertheless, he'd ascended the stairs and walked the hallway several times, tapping on the door and pressing his ear flat against it, trying to discern movement or moaning inside.

On Monday morning, after being given a low growl by Pansy when he passed Imogene's door on his way to the roof, he decided he'd wait one more day before dragging out an extension ladder and climbing up to peer through her window where a shutter was cracked open. He was still on the roof checking for the source of a water spot forming on the ceiling of a top floor rental when he saw a 1965 Buick Electra 225 edge its way into a parking spot across the street.

"That's a mighty fine car," he whistled. "None better in my book."

Charles had never contemplated buying a car before that distinct make and model rolled out of Detroit, all two plus tons of it. He thought it more elegant than the 1965 Eldorado and sleeker than the '65 Town Car; more affordable, too. Not that he had any need for a car in the city, but he'd find one if he got the chance to own that superior four-door sedan.

When he saw Imogene slip out the passenger side of the Electra his heart did a jig of relief, the kind a proud dad might have while watching his child from afar. She was safe and sound and looking euphoric.

That buoyancy was an important indicator to Charles, who'd

grown accustomed to her always seeing more to life than what he'd surmised. She got him to contemplate trifles like how a rose petal fits the curve of a thumb like a hat. She said songbirds are as crucial to nature in making morning minuets as tree frogs are for evening symphonies; the buzz of a bee is a language humans are too dismissive to decipher; each wing of a butterfly depicts an empyrean route, and all pets are earth angels.

"Do you suppose they're trying to tell us something," she'd propose when the robins arrived each spring, "or are they talking about us? Birds can do that you know. Crows can even recognize your face." He didn't know any of it, but when she said it was so, he believed.

Imogene looked up and, seeing him standing there on the roof with his calloused hand held high in the air, poised to welcome her, she responded with a huge wave.

Charles detected a difference in her, even from that angle and at that height. Imogene was sparkling! It wasn't until the driver stepped up out of the car and turned to follow Imogene's wave upwards that he identified the source of Imogene's energy.

She was sparkling, too.

"Oh, Missy," said Charles turning away and shuffling back to minding his manners. "Oh Missy, Missy. I sure am gonna miss you when you're gone."

• • •

Eloise had never been to Central Park. She saw it looming up an embankment within a hundred feet of Imogene's apartment and suggested taking the pups there for a quick tinkle.

"It's unbelievable. We're in the country in the middle of Manhattan."

"This is a smidgen of it, Eloise. That leads to the Shakespeare Garden where I can't wait to walk with you. Six blocks down is the Delacorte Theater. The Rambles is a fairy-tale trail ideal for birding. We'll make wishes on the Angel of the Waters at Bethesda Fountain, rent a boat for a row on the lake, hold hands on the carousel." She hooked her arm through Eloise's as they headed back to 12 West. "Or, we can sun on the Great Lawn and cloud surf."

"Great Lawn?"

"Sheep's Meadow. It was named after herds grazing here until the 1930s. But after Streisand appeared there a couple years ago to throngs, they dubbed the Great Lawn."

"Did you go?"

"To hear Streisand? No. I'm not into watching women through binoculars late at night. But I'm open to the possibility."

She's charming, Eloise thought, captivated by Imogene's every word. "Do you get to come here much?"

"I did walk from here to the zoo's cafe for breakfast with the sea lions every workday morning."

"But you stopped?"

"As of today."

Before opening the door to Imogene's apartment the two discussed the possibility of problems erupting between Eloise's dogs and Imogene's cats. For safety sake, they carried the pekes into the flat, finding Pansy and Petunia lounging on the sideboard showing a slight disdain, but mostly disinterest in their arrival. Imogene hurried to pick Pansy up, hugging, petting and apologizing to him for being away so long. She did the same for Petunia.

"I should have named Petunia, Copycat. Their love was instant, too."

After a quick tour they collapsed together on the couch.

"Great place, Imogene."

"It is, isn't it? A tad small for two people and four pets, but cozy-small. Kissable-small."

"There's no place for you to get away from me here."

"A good thing, 'cause all I'll ever want to do is get closer."

Eloise glimpsed the old brass clock sitting on the mantelpiece. "That thing right?"

"Afraid so. I need to be at work soon."

"Is there cuddle time?"

"Always, Iz, even when there's not. You'll always come first. I promise."

• • •

Imogene was running on adrenaline. She didn't know how to convince Eloise to move to New York, but now that they'd christened the place, she couldn't imagine Eloise ever leaving her.

She'd crept out of bed to shower and dress, leaving Eloise sleeping soundly for what she hoped would be most of the day. Her work number was clipped to the phone in case Eloise had forgotten it (after dialing it innumerably in the past seventeen days). The cats' names were taped to the cupboard where their food was stored. Love notes were taped to every piece of furniture, the mirrors, the mantelpiece, the fridge, and inside the hi-fi.

With forty-five minutes to spare, she crept out of the apartment and hastened down the block to the Associated market on Columbus Avenue for bialys, onion rolls, cold cuts, mayo, milk, eggs, a tomato, butter, two apples, a bunch of grapes and cheese. The person checking out in front of looked familiar. She tapped gently on her shoulder.

"Lady of Absinthe?"

The woman ignored her, clearly annoyed by being touched.

"Sorry," Imogene offered, "but you remind me of Degas."

"Why? Do I look like a ballerina to you?"

"Same artist, different setting. We met last June at Cookies. On your friend's birthday? She'd left you alone. You invited me to join you. It was my first time there. Your name is Marie. Does any of this ring a bell?"

"My name, obviously." Having paid for her purchase, she condescended to look Imogene up and down, remembering the style of meticulously matched attire seldom worn by Lezlandians. "Okay, yes," she mumbled. "How are you?"

"I'm in love!" Imogene sang. "Would you like to meet her?"

Marie scanned the storefront for an alternate escape route but saw none. ""Uh-huh," she sidestepped, backing away until out the sliding doors. "Sure."

Imogene raced to catch up to Marie, delayed at the corner by a flashing Don't Walk.

"What are you doing in this part of town anyway?"

How absurd, Marie thought, *to be accosted so early in the morning by someone I met a year ago while under the influence of cheap rosé.* "I live here."

"Where?"

"On 85th."

Imogene remained frozen in place for a moment after the light changed and Marie started. "I live a 12 West 85th Street," she hollered.

It brought Marie to a halt in the middle of Columbus Avenue. She wheeled around looking as if she hadn't heard right. "I'm at 15. You live across the street from me?"

"Evidently."

"Well that's just weird."

By the time Imogene slipped back in and out of her apartment to deliver the groceries, she had twenty minutes left to get to work on time. Four of those had her bustling to the subway and down the stairs to its southbound platform.

She was grateful to catch an express that deposited her inside the belly of her building in fourteen minutes, leaving two to get upstairs by nine.

Unfortunately, the elevator up got stuck for three minutes going up.

Fortunately, her boss, Patsy, was on it, flattened within two people of her against the back wall.

"Christ, Imogene, I swear you look like you finally got some," Patsy trumpeted for all to hear. Some turned to catch Imogene blossom like a Confederate Rose from cream into crimson. The rest held their collective breath, intending to make the indiscretion their water-cooler hearsay of the day. "Oh my God, I was pulling your chain," Pasty continued, looking over at Imogene, as did those standing near to her. "Look at you!" More eyes followed. "You're bright as Borscht!" Laughter erupted. "Damn, it's true. You finally got laid!" Imogene heard one faint 'yay' before an alarming chug jumped the elevator up two feet and it coasted back down to their floor.

She did not get off, waiting until she could step forward and push the 'close' button once Patsy and the others were clear of the doors.

Instead, she rode up to the Top of the Sixes, down to the lobby, and back up again, repeating the ride until she was certain her face had drained of embarrassment and she was prepared for whatever awaited.

"It was during this ill-fated elevator mishap," she'd write that night in her journal, *"that it dawned on me: I know the intimacy Eloise and I share is sacrosanct, beautiful, wholehearted and fun, but — APPARENTLY — we didn't invent it. We weren't the first to do it. How could I have hoped we had, or thought we did?"*

FIFTY-SIX
Monday, March 30, 1970
Out Standing

Eloise remained in bed after Imogene returned to the apartment and left again.

The first time Imogene exited Eloise was semiconscious, aroused by the same sensation she'd enjoyed earlier that morning when being kissed all over. No one had ever kissed Eloise all over before; she was grateful for that. There would be no comparisons to quash and no one to think about ever again but Imogene.

The second time Eloise only pretended to sleep as Imogene planted a little kiss on her lips saying "I love you" very softly before leaving her to drift off again.

It wasn't until late afternoon that she was finally fully awakened by the phone ringing. It took a second for her to get her bearings before she scrambled to answer it.

"Hello?"

"Hello." The woman's voice was low, calm, and suspicious. "Who's this?"

"This is Imogene LaPin's residence. May I ask who's calling?"

"Momma LaPin." She heard Eloise gasp. "You sound surprised, dear. Are you?"

"No, I'm nude. I mean, I'm...um...I ran to get the phone."

"Nude."

"Yes. I'm sorry. It slipped out. I don't know why."

"Don't worry, dear. I've probably talked to nude women on the phone before. Not that any of them ever told me so."

"Could you excuse me for a second?"

"I'm not going anywhere."

Mrs. LaPin had always been devious. She knew her daughter

314

wouldn't be home from work before 5:30, so calling her earlier carried the clear intent of meddling. If Imogene ever brought anyone home with her, she might catch that person unawares.

She'd been dialing Imogene at odd hours for years, beginning her ruse when Imogene went away to college and continued it after she'd moved to New York. It was the first time anyone picked up (nude or otherwise). Mrs. LaPin had hoped for a male voice.

Eloise scooted to the bedroom, slipped into her clothes, lit a cigarette, and returned to the phone, jittery.

"Mrs. LaPin?"

"Yes, dear. I'm here."

"Imogene isn't home from work yet."

Mrs. LaPin puckered up at hearing Eloise call her daughter's apartment 'home' as if it was her home now, too. "My mistake," she fudged. "I meant to call my son and dialed Dolly in error."

When Eloise didn't question who 'Dolly' was, Mrs. LaPin interpreted it as the woman being nickname savvy. Time to intervene. "Do I hear you smoking?"

"Yes."

"My husband smoked. I hated it until the day he died. Now, I miss it. We inherit regrets from people, don't you think?"

"I hope not."

"Imogene shouldn't inhale smoke. Her lungs are weak."

"I won't smoke around her."

Gotcha again, Mrs. LaPin noted, the 'won't' word indicative of an intent to stay around.

"Imogene mentioned she was going to Portsmouth for the weekend. Are you from there?"

"Yes. There was a blizzard. I drove her back here after her flight was canceled."

"That was good of you, dear. Thank you for helping out." Mrs. LaPin felt relieved. The woman had done her daughter a kind deed, that's all.

"Honestly, it was my pleasure."

"Well, I can't see how driving from Portsmouth to New York in a snowstorm could be a pleasure, but it's nice of you to say so."

"Yes, ma'am." Eloise couldn't believe how she was cowering, as if she were coming apart.

Eloise's nervousness puzzled Mrs. LaPin. Of course, deep down, she knew why the girl was skittish, but she wasn't willing to shift from her preferred state of denial to that dreaded quagmire of reality quite yet.

"Her grandmother once lived in Portsmouth."

"Yes. She mentioned your mother was married there."

"She did? Already? I only told her a few days ago."

"Maybe because we were there and..."

"Yes, dear. That makes sense. Silly me."

Dual pause.

"Is there a message I can give her, Mrs. LaPin?"

"Yes, Izzy."

"Will I need a pen?"

"Oh, I'm sorry. I inadvertently called you Izzy."

"That's fine. Most people do."

"I see," Mrs. LaPin said and saw, perfectly. Not surprisingly or happily, but not unhappily, since it wasn't altogether unexpected. More like, she saw disappointedly, in a waving white flag way.

"You'll tell my Dolly that her momma called?"

"I will."

"Bye-bye, dear."

"Bye."

Mrs. LaPin had been leaning forward in her rocking chair as she talked to Eloise, her eyes studying the floral pattern of the carpet, counting petals as a way of ensuring calm. She dropped the receiver into its cradle and stared at it for a minute before sitting back and summoning Amos and Andy. The two old, roly-poly, red tabby cats lumbered over and hopped up, one nestling in her right arm and the other in her left. Once ensconced, Mrs. LaPin began to rock and sing, "By-o, by-o, by-o, by-y. By-y-o, by-o, by-y-y," over and over, as if she were clutching babies to her breast and offering up a farewell lullaby.

• • •

Eloise wondered if she'd outed the two of them to Imogene's mother. She lit a cigarette from the one she was smoking before snuffing out the old butt. They hadn't gotten around to discussing their relatives yet, or what their families did, or didn't know.

She'd been willing to act the pretense-hetero part in order to spare her own parents the shame of having a lesbian for a daughter, even though she'd always been a daddy's girl and he'd made it clear that nothing she could do would change that. His declaration diluted the risk but didn't erase it.

Her mother remained an uncertainty. After retiring, she'd become a church lady, a bridge club member and a social whirlwind about town. More than likely, her mother wouldn't want others know of her daughter's lesbianism, since some had already flagged Eloise as an old maid (the solitary acceptable alternative to marriage and children) and her mom had done nothing to deny it.

"Perish the thought," Eloise told the pekes, leashing them up for a trot to the subway to greet Imogene while thinking of how she'd intended to do more than get up and get dressed that day. She wanted to surprise Imogene by sweeping the fireplace ashes down the chute, making the bed, washing the coffee pot and cups left in the sink, and straightening up a bit. One person living in a one bedroom was doable. But two people in the same space made tidiness more of a necessity.

If only Mrs. LaPin hadn't called.

FIFTY-SEVEN
Monday Evening, March 30, 1970
Table Talk

Eloise was stumped. "What are all of these dishes and pans doing in the fridge?"

"Throw them out," ordered Imogene from the front room. She was busy selecting outfits for them to change into before catching a quick meal at O'Neal's. Imogene swore they had the best burger basket in town and an amusing ambiance.

"Trash them? Why?"

"I don't do dishes much. I buy them secondhand and use them a time or two. But once they pile up I chuck 'em. Except for cups and saucers, everything else goes. The fridge serves as bug free storage 'til then."

"Pots and pans too?"

"The whole megillah."

"Have I fallen in love with a lunatic?"

Imogene came up behind her and shut the refrigerator door.

"Do the math, milady. A plate costs a penny. Pans are a nickel. The time it takes to wash them, dry them and put them away is worth more than that to me."

"Finally, I know why people throw good stuff out."

"As a kid I was stuck doing dishes for eight every night and hated it." Imogene raised her fist in the air and repeated, "Hated it!" She turned back to Eloise. "Now I do away with them."

"Well, I *like* doing dishes."

"Get back Jack!" Imogene pushed Eloise out of the kitchen.

"I do."

"Now look who's in love with a lunatic."

"Maybe. But it gives me time to smoke and think about things. So, let's deal. If you do all the cooking and stop hiding dirty dishes in the fridge, I'll wash, dry, and put away."

At that juncture, Imogene's culinary efforts included sandwiches, leftover sandwiches, takeout sandwiches, and TV dinners, all transferred onto an eclectic collection of china plates. "Deal. But I can think of *much* better ways to spend your time." She handed Eloise an outfit. "Here."

"What's this?"

"Your size. Everything I buy is too long. These haven't been altered yet. I have others, too, and sweaters to fit us both."

Eloise welcomed the change. Since leaving Portsmouth, all she had were the clothes on her back. It pleased her to find they both favored classic styles, and the Orlon rainbow in Imogene's sock drawer made her salivate at the prospect of matching them to her wardrobe.

• • •

O'Neal's Baloon appeared longer than wide. It had the traditional tavern charm with a narrow linear patio of two person tables arranged single file and an awning equipped with clear plastic panels that zipped together and reached to the sidewalk, serving as a substitute for the glass wall yet to be installed. Diners sheltered there could both sit on display for passersby and fraternize with the dancers from Lincoln Center that frequented the place.

They'd been seated on the 63rd Street side of O'Neal's with partial views of Central Park and the New York State Theatre, all bordering Columbus Avenue Circle dispersing traffic in every direction.

"Hoofer, as in...?" Eloise asked.

"Dancer. Most of the waitresses her are aiming for stardom. This has become a late night hangout for ballerinas and Broadway-bounds."

"That explains the legs on these ladies."

Imogene looked up from her menu and around at the help. "You know, Iz, before tonight I..."

"Never you mind."

"Gee whiz. Spoil all my fun."

Once their orders were taken, Eloise surveyed the place. "It's an odd name isn't it?"

"O'Neal's?"

"Baloon. Spelled with one 'l' instead of two on the awning."

"Another example of man-made morality forced upon the majority by a minority."

"I don't follow."

"It was originally named O'Neal's Saloon. But after it opened, someone cited a blue-law that forbade the use of the word 'saloon' on any New York City marquee."

"No!"

"I kid you not." Imogene opened the paper napkin table setting, removed the plastic utensils, and began dipping them in her ice water, then drying them before use. "The law was enacted during Prohibition. So, rather than remake the awning they changed the 'S' to a 'B' and *voilà!* O'Neal's Baloon was born."

"That's ridiculous."

"It is. But as long as pulpits divert donations that pay politicians to push a self-righteous agenda, they'll continue to control these issues."

Eloise frowned at the suggestion of moralists having the upper hand. Her reaction wasn't lost on Imogene. Both knew the subject of religion could be a bone of contention eventually, but hoped for later than sooner.

The waitress delivered dark green plastic lattice boxes of burgers and fries and a pitcher of beer with two frosted mugs that they clanked together before digging in.

"To be honest," Eloise ventured, "religion and I don't mix."

"Great!"

"You say that now. But will it be a problem down the line?"

"No."

Eloise stared at Imogene, the woman whose face she adored and attitude she admired. So decisive. So assertive. So-o naïve. "I saw a prayer book on the mantle in your apartment."

"*Our* apartment. And, so?"

"Are you Jewish?"

"Most Jews would say, no. If your mother is Jewish, you are. If she isn't, you can't be. It's strictly a matrilineal thing. Of course, if I went back a generation and uncovered records proving my maternal grandmother was Jewish, my recognition as Jewish would be compulsory. That could happen. But for now, I'm Jewish by choice."

"You can do that?"

Imogene laughed. "You can do anything, darling. Focus and storm forward."

Eloise came from a long line of people telling her otherwise; that the best a woman could hope for was to marry rich and obey the rules. "Tell me, how?"

"Well, for openers I was never baptized. I never believed the dogma and refused to sing the John 3:16 song. I began studying Judaism solo in 1956 and enrolled in formal studies after moving here. In '66 I became the first to complete the Temple Emmanuel conversion program who wasn't marrying into the religion. At least, that's what I was told. I was bat mitzvahed three years ago at the Village Temple on 12th Street."

"So-o, do you believe in it?"

"Literally? No. I don't believe in any male divinity, or anointed authority. Although in some ancient Jewish texts God is female. I like the idea of that." Imogene shrugged. "It provides me with an ethical code of conduct. I'm not enslaved to Judaism. I'm not devout about it except for the High Holy Days that I enjoy as a period of contemplation and gratitude. It's kind of like in politics, when I vote against candidates. In this case, I voted against all other religions, but I espouse the principles of Judaism, most."

Eloise felt safe.

"How about you, Izzy? What's your mantra?"

"I'm reluctant to discuss it." She touched on being raised by the Golden Rule and of her disingenuous adherence to Pentecostalism to appease a former friend. The flashback upset her, so she spoke low and left out the details. "That was long ago and far away. I don't want any of it resurrected."

While the waitress cleared their table she suggested possible desserts. They both favored warmed apple pie à la mode and more coffee. After she left, Eloise leaned forward, reached under the table and rested her hand on Imogene's knee.

"I need to tell you something."

"I'm all ears."

"Your mom called today."

"She did? I didn't hear the phone ring."

"Around four. Maybe half-past."

"The sneaky-Pete. She knows I'm never home at that hour."

"I thought it was you, so I picked it up."

Eloise proceeded to tell Imogene the entire conversation. Upon finishing, Imogene, who'd been listening intently (except for laughing at the nude part), was befuddled.

"I'm sorry, sweetheart. Did I miss something? What part of all that worries you?"

"I outed us to your mom."

Imogene shooed it away. "Nonsense. Mom knew this day was coming long before I did — probably when I was five and told her I was marrying my blonde haired, blue-eyed doll." Now it was Imogene who leaned in and spoke low. "It was the only doll I ever loved."

Eloise sat back and stared at her. "You aren't trying to spare my feelings?"

"Listen, sweetie, all through high school Mom created drama by choosing boys for me to marry, and every single one of them was a version of her preferred first choice, Saul Gold."

"So?"

"Saul was short, rich, fastidious, terribly bright, and known for wearing a shower cap to gym class. In the rain, too."

"No."

"Mom's a lodestone for Nancy-boys."

"Maybe she didn't know. Maybe it was a coincidence."

"Number one, there's nothing Mom doesn't know. Number two, there's nothing Mom admits to knowing."

"Then she won't have a conniption about us?"

"The topic will never come up."

The waitress delivered their dessert and coffee. They lingered before paying the check.

"How about when I meet her?"

"Act normal. Outwardly, we're no different than two best friends on a sleepover, or sisters who lock arms when walking together."

"Your mother might not see it that way."

Imogene reached out, took hold of Eloise's hands and squeezed them. "If she thought I was lying to her she'd raise Cain. It's what all moms do when their kids act like they're hiding or ashamed of something. But that's never been me, and it's never going to be me."

Eloise wasn't arguing with Imogene. She was trying to understand her strategy. She'd heard stories from friends about their coming-out brouhaha. It seldom went smoothly.

They left O'Neal's and were heading towards the Central Park underground terminal. The evening was menthol cool and calm.

At any other time, Imogene would have suggested walking the distance home, tickled by the closeness of their shoulders, the clutching of their hands, and the bowing of their paired heads immersed in conversation along the way. But she was weary. She hadn't had but two hours' sleep in the past twenty-four and needed to be up early in the morning. She ached for home and hearth. The intent of logs burning in the fireplace and them entwined in each other's arms nearby it was foremost on her mind.

"One last question, Imogene. What if you're wrong? What if your mother sees us as criminals?"

"That's two questions."

"It won't upset you?"

Imogene stopped under the glow of an overhead street lamp, turned towards Eloise and looked deep into her eyes.

"Look, hon. Mom gave me life. Maybe that was her destiny. Raising me was the responsibility she accepted and reveled in as a mother. But you're my destiny. And your life is a responsibility I accept and will revel in as your partner. Period. Exclamation point."

When the women got back to 12 West and entered Imogene's apartment, they found the cats lying best-friends-close to the dogs, all four looking innocent.

The cats were black with soot, as were the paws and skirts of the dogs. Every book, box, bag, magazine, photograph, candle, dish and decoration from every shelf and piece of furniture was either out of place or on the floor. The pillows were off the couch, the phone was off the sideboard, the blankets were off the bed, and there were paw prints everywhere, even on the walls. It looked as if the dogs and cats had been at each other from opposite directions until they either wore out, or found enough common ground to establish a bond that would last a lifetime. The truce required a communal nap.

It was too funny to feel furious and too late to care.

"Don't worry. I'll clean it all up in the morning," Eloise offered.

Imogene stifled a laugh. "Be my guest, babe."

FIFTY-EIGHT
Tuesday, March 31, 1970
Taking Up Routes

Eloise and Imogene got up early so they could take their time showering and dressing together before leaving for work; Imogene to her office and Eloise to borrow a bucket from Charles, one with a more substantial mop than the squeegee Imogene was accustomed to using.

But first, the two dunked buttered bialys in cups of hot coffee while sitting on the edge of the bed with opera glasses, peering out from behind cracked-open shutters onto the street below, watching neighbors confront the circumstances of a new day.

"There they are." Imogene pointed to Marie Moss and her partner, who appeared several years younger, five inches shorter and twenty pounds heavier.

"Voluptuous."

"She is, isn't she? A real life Rubens."

"The sandwich?"

Imogene elbowed Eloise. "I was thinking more in line with the Flemish fellow who painted big busted nudes."

"Do you know this Miss Rubens' name?"

"Lisa Colt, I think."

"She's acting awfully seductive for someone on the streets this early in the morning."

"Yes, she is. Why isn't Marie responding? Unless ignoring counts."

They watched as the two stood fidgeting before Marie went east up the block towards the subway and Lisa went west down the block towards Columbus Avenue.

"Look!" Imogene pointed towards a woman glancing at Marie when walking by, turning to keep an eye on her until Marie disappeared around the corner. Then the woman raced to the redstone where Lisa had doubled back to greet her.

Imogene and Eloise matched raised eyebrows when Lisa kissed the other woman a little too long and touched her way too low before they climbed the buildings steps and disappeared inside.

"And to think," deduced Imogene while closing and locking the shutters, "a month ago I'd have mistaken that whole fanfare as a reunion between old friends."

"I bet you'd have been leery at very least."

"Any chance Marie knows?"

"Yep."

"How?"

"The defeat was all over her face. Lisa might make her feel like she's doing her a favor by being with her. She may even flaunt her flings."

"I despise cheats. My dad was one. He stood for everything I vowed never to be."

"Was it difficult?"

"Nah. I only make vows I can keep."

"That's not what I meant."

"I know."

They stood at opposite ends of the bed, pulling it out from the wall, flattening the sheets, fluffing the pillows, and adding the marriage quilt that Imogene had wisely taken along with them for the drive from Portsmouth to Boston that ended in New York.

"Why do people put up with infidelity, Iz?"

"It's a game. Marie plays victim to Lisa's coquette. I've seen it a lot, mostly when one is much prettier than the other, or smarter, or richer. But if it's chronic, coupled with Lisa's act of irresistibly cute, it could mean she got too much of the wrong kind of adult attention as a child."

"Touched?"

"Or worse."

"And, Marie?"

"Hmm. A lack of affection from the mother often makes grown women feel like they don't deserve to be loved. That could be it."

"So-o, you're a purple-people-reader, huh?"

"Strictly of those who kept coming back to the bar, girl after girl. We can socialize with Marie and Lisa for fun. But real friendship requires honesty. That's not them."

"You *do* know Marie's a connector, right?"

"Connector?"

"In chaos. Which is what life is, kind of, I think."

"Tell me more."

"Connectors are people who, by accident or design, help you speed up, slow down, change directions, or turn around — all in an effort to get you to wherever on time. I met Marie, seemingly on a lark, twice. Yet there she was all along, living across the street from me for four years. Someday I'll connect the dots of where we all started from before getting to here. I'll find the why. But for now, I'll accept her as an obscure point of light drawing me towards you. Like a magnetar. "

"Magnetar?"

"It's a neutron star with an extremely strong magnetic field."

• • •

Imogene sat in the seat nearest the sliding door between train cars, studying the entities of passengers. She didn't detect any pride in their postures or flickers of passion in their eyes. Instead she discerned a mixture of weariness, woe, and acquiescence; full body stares riding silently, swaying with the rhythm of the subway car as it sped them all in one direction.

The commuters were nameless, yes, but not entirely unknown. The same familiar faces sat side-by-side on the same-time train each day. When one went missing, the rest inwardly wondered where. When a new face turned up, they took note. It was a diversion she'd engaged in during inclement weather, or whenever running too late to walk the distance; before Eloise.

Now, for the first time, she understood that faces mask the amatory lives defining people and that their caliber of intimacy is exposed by the choices made in words spoken (by vocabulary, volume and tone), food eaten (by quality or quantity via utensil or hand), cleanliness kept (whether covered or bare), expressions adopted (in intensity of look or manner), and beverages drunk (by bottle or glass). Private lives are recklessly exposed in precisely such telltale ways.

Imogene closed her eyes and took a deep breath. She felt Eloise.

• • •

When Charles answered his door, Eloise introduced herself as a friend of Imogene's and asked to borrow equipment to clean up a mess they'd made.

"You don't look like the messy type," Charles said, leading her to the locker beneath the staircase and offering her a choice of supplies. "Pansy, on the other hand..."

"Right on both counts. But Pansy had accomplices this time."

Charles studied her. It wasn't the same as when he first met Imogene, who had charmed Mr. Singer and made Charles jealous. Eloise was quieter. She had a casualness he appreciated. He knew he'd never feel the same fondness for her as he did for Imogene, but he liked her, right off.

"I wanted to yell down from the roof when I saw you drive up. Tell you that's a mighty fine Electra 225 you have there."

"Thanks. It is, except when rising at daybreak to switch sides of the street. I dread that."

Charles' face brightened. "I can help you with the parking if you want."

"How so?"

"I park cars for people in the morning." He didn't, but knew he could. He'd love getting in that Buick daily, warming the engine, drinking a cup of joe and listening to Imus In The Morning on the radio until a space freed up.

"How much?"

"How much what?"

"How much does it cost for the service?"

Charles hadn't thought of it as a service, much less getting paid for it. He simply wanted to drive that car down the street, or maybe around the block, and he wasn't about to miss out on an opportunity by charging for it. "It's included in the lease. It extends to visitors."

Eloise didn't delay. She removed the extra car key she kept on the set in her pocket and handed it to him. "In that case, her name is ZonaBee and she's all yours."

• • •

Once their whiskers and paws were washed and coats combed, Eloise placed all four pets on pillows in the bathtub for safekeeping before closing the door and going to work on the apartment. By noon she'd mopped, dusted, polished and plumped. The ashes from the fireplace had been emptied. The sinks, cupboards, and appliances were scoured and scrubbed; the dishes were washed and put away. Everything that hadn't been chipped, cracked, or broken was back in place, along with the lone gift she'd held back: the figurine of the redheaded girl at her typewriter. She'd intended to give the porcelain image to Imogene as a 'someday' promise, but that was now a misbegotten goal. Eloise knew she'd sooner forsake her soul than to ever leave Imogene.

She rearranged the furniture by placing the wing chair within reach of the phone and the hassock directly in front of it so the kids could lounge there while she, or Imogene talked. She'd always treated pets as her children and now knew Imogene did the same.

Finally, after surveying the room one last time, she reheated the leftover coffee from earlier, lit up, sat down, and dialed her mother.

"Eloise Ann, where have you been? I've rung and rung. James said you went to Boston and never returned. He said he didn't know if you'd been killed, or frozen in snow, or what. Land alive girl, I've been beside myself."

It hadn't occurred to Eloise that James might be looking for her and she didn't care.

"I met someone, Mom. We'll be driving down there for Aunt Edna's birthday party in May if that's okay." Eloise didn't know what possessed her to promise this. She and Imogene hadn't discussed it yet.

"Well, I be John Brown. I'll get the rooms made up. What do you want to eat?"

"You've got six weeks to decide, Mom. One room. Nothing fancy."

"Your daddy will be beside himself. Oh! I wish he were here. He's up to the lake with your cousin Clyde."

"Tell him I'm sorry I missed him. Here's my new address and number. Got a pen?"

"Let me fetch it. One minute now." Mrs. Fitz always kept a pad of paper and pencil next to the phone but she pretended she didn't so she could hold her daughter on the line a bit longer. Even hearing her breathe long distance would suffice. She loved her daughter. She wasn't always good at showing or saying it, but she was very good at feeling it, deeply.

"Are you still there, Ma?"

"I'm here. Go on."

"Twelve West Eighty-fifth Street. I'm living in New York City now."

"Near the Park?"

"Yes. I bet if I leaned out the window I could see it from here."

"You be careful 'bout leaning out windows in New York City Eloise Ann!"

The two went on chatting about nothing much, as was their tendency. Her mother didn't delve into whom she'd be bringing home — but if she had, Eloise had already decided to follow Imogene's lead and tell the truth. Not a flaunting truth, or a challenging truth, or a hesitant truth, or a truth clouded with fear, or colored with shame.

Instead, she would have simply said, "Her name is Imogene LaPin."

Somewhere between cleaning and coffee, Eloise flipped through the Sunday edition of the *New York Times* that Imogene said no true New Yorker could live well without. When she got to the classifieds, she circled an advertisement placed by the New York Bell Telephone Company:

~ NOW HIRING ~
Applications are now being taken for operators
to fill our 3 wire centers in the garment district, at the
Murray Hill Office on West 37th Street, and in our regional
office on 34th Street in the Empire State Building.
Full-time, part-time, competitive salaries and benefits.
Apply weekdays from 9 to 5. Drop by today!

Eloise thought that could be her calling. After all, as a bartender she'd made a minor career out of listening to people. More important, she felt indebted to an unknown operator at Ma Bell.

It didn't take long for Eloise to find a skirt among Imogene's many outfits, even with their waist sizes being off by an inch. She fixed it by looping a rubber band through the buttonhole and then back onto the button, covering the extra space with a long sweater. The length of the skirt was more of a challenge. At five inches taller that Imogene, Eloise had to accept that it looked like a miniskirt on her. *Good thing I inherited my mother's legs*, she thought.

By half past three she was on a train heading downtown to the Herald Square Station, and by a quarter past five she was back uptown, standing at the West 86th Street subway entrance, eagerly awaiting Imogene's emergence from the underground. She held a bouquet of daises bought off a street vendor in one hand and an employee benefits package in the other.

Eloise felt like a New Yorker, as if she and Imogene had lived there together all of their lives.

FIFTY-NINE
Tuesday, March 31, 1970
Open Sesame

A tall, pasty-faced, paunchy, steely-eyed, silver haired man of sixty-six with tea stained teeth, sliver thin lips and a plastic giveaway pen guard in the left breast pocket of his short sleeve drip-dry shirt approached Imogene in the corridor outside the office she shared with Patsy Wolf.

"I'm Adam Snow, Vice President of Finance." He extended his hand. "We haven't met."

"Imogene LaPin." The man's grip was so anemic and clammy, Imogene's first instinct was to wipe it off on him.

"Do you like it here?"

"Very much."

"Okay. That's all. Carry on."

Once Patsy returned from replacing sizes and colors of salesmen samples 'borrowed' by employees needing a quick gift, Imogene brought up Snow.

"Oh, Puke. The numbers cruncher creep. Keep your distance whenever he's here."

"I've never seen him here."

"They keep him caged at our Cheat Mountain plant. He's from there. Third generation coal miner's son, but a true guru with numbers."

"Not a friend then."

"Archenemy! Anytime corporate calls for cuts he targets me."

"Because...?"

"The bastard thinks I'm overpaid. He knows I make twenty per cent less than every man holding my same position in the different divisions. You do, too."

"Why twenty per cent less?"

"For being female. Watch what you say around him and on the phone. All Puke's information comes from 'Miss Wiretap' there in reception."

Imogene's jaw dropped.

"What? What did I say?"

"Shouldn't you have told me that a year ago?"

"Probably." Patsy grimaced. "Yes. Sorry. You rarely got any calls the first year and he only comes here when corporate is on the warpath. Damn. I didn't think of it before. Why?"

Imogene groaned. "Nothing. Too late now."

"Spit it out."

"I keep being told not to tell if I want to keep my job. Not that it registers."

"So, it's true then?"

"What?"

"What Ronald told me about you and your blonde bombshell."

"She's not a bombshell," Imogene reddened. "Okay, she is."

"Ronald said Wink said she's hot."

"You've met Wink?"

"No. Ronald's a score whore who doesn't mix tricks with true blues. He did tell me about the two of them. And your cab crossing."

"That was a shock."

"I didn't believe him after you flunked my test."

"I was tested?"

"Ronald goaded me on and on."

"The night I stayed over in Brooklyn?"

"Yes."

"Then I really must find a way to pay him back."

"So, now that the cat's out, tell me," Patsy ventured, "if you *had*..."

"No."

"Why the hell not? What's wrong with me?"

"I lost my heart, Pats. Not my mind."

Patsy had taken Imogene by the elbow to hurry her down to the conference room and through the door before locking it behind them.

"What I'm about to tell you now is strictly between us because it could get me fired. Not that they'd have grounds. But Snow would raise a shitstorm."

"My lips are glued and stapled."

"Me, too!"

Imogene was stumped. "You, too...what?"

"I'm in love, too, same as you. I'm in love! I'm in love!"

"How same?"

"The normal same. I met him over the weekend. Believe me Imogene, he's the one. I'm definitely going to marry this guy."

"Normal, is it?"

"You get the drift."

"You're saying he's already dropped down on bended knee?"

"Did he ever! We fucked for forty-eight hours. This morning he asked me to move in with him. And, get this — his apartment is on 67th Street near Central Park West. I'd be living in the city, same as you."

There was that 'same' word again. Imogene didn't know how to react. Her mind searched for similarities between her fortnight courtship and Patsy's forty-eight hour fornication. It was as if they both spoke English, but with different definitions of identical words: communicating perfectly, without fully understanding each other at all.

"Earth to Imogene. Aren't you going to congratulate me?"

"Yes, Pasty, yes that's great. I was thinking we had dinner at O'Neal's near there last night. A friend of ours once lived in an old high-rise on 67th."

"That's where I'll be! He has the one bedroom garden apartment in the back. Isn't it exciting? I mean it's cramped — but choice. And perfect for the two of us."

"What does your guy do?"

"Something for his dad. He hates it, but is set to inherit it all."

"So, not a doctor, or a lawyer, but money?"

"Gobs."

"Jewish?"

"Swedish."

"Lutheran, then?"

"Christ, I hope not."

"Good looking?"

"Good enough."

"Tall?"

"Tall enough."

"Smart?"

"Smart enough."

"Talented?"

"Eh."

"Well, he sounds like he's met all your criteria. Except, of course, for the tall, dark, handsome, doctor, lawyer, artist, genius, Jewish parts."

"I'll be out window-shopping for a ring at break time."

"Tiffany's?"

"Winston's!"

"Oh-h," Imogene whistled. "*That* rich!"

There was a knock on the door from the sales manager needing the room.

"I'm happy for you, Patsy. For us both. Wow. Talk about riding high on the same merry-go-round."

"And catching the brass ring!"

"Better than brass." Imogene showed her the antique opal ring Eloise had placed on her left hand.

"How quaint, Imogene. See ya!"

SIXTY
Monday, May 11, 1970
Home Style

Mrs. LaPin stood on the sidewalk in front of her home with a dainty white handkerchief clasped in her hand, alternately dabbing at her eyes and waving it as her daughter backed the big blue Buick down the driveway. When it slid into the street, Imogene lowered the window to call out one last "I love you, Mom" before leaving her behind with nothing to do but reheat the leftover coffee and talk to her cats.

Other than the time she gadded about during an occasional visit by one of her children and the hours she kept vigil on the graveyard shift at a hospice house, Mrs. LaPin had devoted most of the two hundred and eighteen days since her husband of thirty years died to being alone. There were no additional demands made on her. Her friends at the senior center where she went on Tuesdays and Thursdays said that most wives die within seven years after being widowed. If true, it gave her 2,337 more days to go on twelve more biannual bus trips to Mackinaw Island before being zipped into her burial dress.

She looked around at the other houses on the block, searching for a neighborly invitation, knowing there'd be none. Mrs. LaPin was now the oldest in a neighborhood of working parents with kids in daycare. She longed to be young again with babies to nurse, and toddlers to chase, and stories to read to children gathered around, begging for one more chapter before bedtime.

Nevertheless, it was a heavenly spring morning with the forsythia in full bloom, so she took her cup and sat in the cane seat rocking chair kept in her back yard by the bright cadmium bush, happy to inhale the beauty of it all.

They'd had a good visit, although she'd have preferred for Imogene to come home alone. Yes, she wanted her children to marry and lead happy lives, but she resented sharing the time she had with anyone *but* them. If that meant leaving an in-law or friend behind while her sons and daughters visited solo, so be it.

This marked the first time Imogene ever brought anyone home. Even as a child, she never had friends in to listen to records or play games. Her husband's drunken stupors had eliminated all possibility of it. The other children would risk his contemptuous manner of showing up and embarrassing them, but not Imogene.

"Dolly's careful like that," Mrs. LaPin told the birds and the breeze that served as her audience over the years. "Too much so if you ask me." She took a sip of her coffee. "Which no one ever does."

Mrs. LaPin was proud of the fact that she'd raised talented, intelligent, polite, respectful, and well-versed children.

"But of them all," she informed Eloise over a breakfast of Stokey's orange juice, brown eggs fried in bacon grease, Maxwell House coffee, and Roman Meal buttered toast, "it's my dear Dolly who has never given me even an ounce of trouble. She's always been my little lion, so brave. After my husband died last October, she began calling me daily." She batted her eyelashes, intended as gauntlets going down. "Except for those two after meeting you."

Imogene reached across a corner of the table to take her mother's hand. "In other words, Eloise, Mom's lost count of the calls."

Mrs. LaPin had decided not to pump Imogene about her relationship with Eloise, the same as she'd decided against grilling Imogene years earlier when her second daughter gave up Christianity for Lent, or years before that when Imogene refused to be baptized with her siblings at church camp and was returned home after less than a day away. In each instance, Mrs. LaPin marked it off to a phase her daughter was going through and would eventually outgrow before returning to the fold.

Not that there was a fold per se to return to. Her own mother had been born in Sweden, where Lutheranism ruled. She assumed her mother was Lutheran, but couldn't verify it since all 'old country' talk had been off limits.

Her father was of Scotch-Irish Presbyterian descent with an American lineage going back before the Revolution. His parents were much older when they accidentally had him; passed on by the time he turned fifteen. Or, he was raised by his grandparents. Or, adopted. Definitely orphaned at fifteen though.

Regardless, Mrs. LaPin was raised a Baptist until becoming a teen, when she strayed from its formalities and didn't return until her first child was of school age. Even then (and with the five children who followed) there were no prayers before meals, no bedtime rituals, no discussions, and no deep devotion shown by any of the six before Imogene took flight. The fact that Mr. LaPin was a devout atheist who deposited the family at the Church of Christ on Sundays because it was close by and, if he disappeared to nobody's business, or tied one on, they could all walk home, was of no consequence.

So, when Imogene (whose constant challenge to accepting 'faith' as the answer to anything logical) divorced the church altogether, Mrs. LaPin ignored it. The same as she ignored Imogene's ten years of Jewish studies, lessons in Hebrew, conversion classes and invitation to her bat mitzvah, and Imogene's lack of interest in boys, dating, marriage and babies, and Imogene's decision to return to New York rather than remain home with Mrs. LaPin after her husband died.

Now, here she was, faced with a daughter who had fallen in love with another mother's daughter.

"Mark my words, Amos and Andy. It's a phase."

• • •

Imogene eased the Buick into the flow of traffic heading south on Route 127.

"So, what did you think?"

"I gotta say, your mom is the funniest character I've ever met."

"Truth?"

"I swear. The woman should have been in show biz. She's a natural."

"I always thought she could have made it big, given the opportunity. It's what she wanted for my brother and me."

"Why didn't she go for it?"

"No money, I'd guess. Or, maybe she felt an obligation to take care of her own mother, even though it was my grandma who helped feed and care for us most the time. Who's to say?"

"You didn't want to know?"

"I did and I do. But she's a shusher and an evader. Is yours?"

"No. Mine harps. Mine's a harper."

SIXTY-ONE
Monday, May 11, 1970
True Grits

In the weeks before Eloise left Florida for New Hampshire, her parents began the process of packing up the contents of their Crystal Beach bungalow and moving back to Alabama, where both had been born into a large families and raised on neighboring farms.

As a young man, Padraig Fitz was nicknamed Pappy, partly due to the Americanization of his Irish name, but mostly because he was the oldest in a family of five boys whose dad died of a coronary when Padraig was sixteen and his youngest brother was nine. To keep the family intact, the boys all went to work at whatever each did best.

Pappy was tall and sinewy with earnest eyes set deep into a high forehead above an oblong face. His berry-brown skin, from overseeing the family fields during the long growing seasons under an unrelenting Alabama sun, was a salubrious complement to his rakish looks and quiet style. As a child he demonstrated a natural knack for bringing scorched earth back to life. As he aged, his soft drawl and gentle touch esteemed him as a peacekeeper.

But Pappy's expertise was in engineering, self-taught from borrowed books. So, when his heart was shattered after the death of his fiancé in a car crash he caused, and suicide-by-combat was thwarted when he was exempted from duty, Pappy took a civil service appointment to build, fix, and test airplane engines for the WHA war effort, setting him on the course that resulted in the emergence of Eloise.

"At least, that's how I heard it. I was an 'emergence' from my mom."

"Gotta say," Imogene giggled, "you rival Cliff Notes for giving a bare essentials bio."

"Cliff Notes?"

"Those yellow and black striped study guides students read instead of books."

"How'd I miss out?"

"When did you graduate?"

"Class of '57."

"That explains it. A guy from Lincoln, Nebraska published the first booklets in 1958, starting with Shakespeare. By the time I graduated in '64 he was doing most of the classics on our required reading lists."

"I lived in Lincoln once."

"Tell me."

"My folks owned the restaurant on the Wayne State College campus."

"No joke, there's a Wayne State in Nebraska? I went to Wayne State in Michigan."

They rode in silence for a bit; wowed at that.

"I was six when we first moved Wayne. My folks worked all the time, but they took a day off once to go to the horse track in Lincoln. I was too short to get into the bleachers, so we had to stand near the rails. Dad let me pick the quinella and it turned out the big winner that day. We went home with a wad."

"Gambling at six? Nice!"

And so it went on for hours as an inexhaustible exchange of events, leaping like frogs on parallel lily pads whenever an account by one overlapped with a similar account by the other in an uncanny way.

"Come to think of it, Eloise, my Mom has a jar of red dirt my brother brought back from Alabama."

"He's been there?"

"Went to college there. Met Harper Lee when she was invited to speak at his graduation."

"Which school?"

"Troy."

"No way! My third cousin, Tray, went to Troy."

"My brother's roommate at Troy was named Tray."

They left it at that.

Upon crossing the line into Ohio and picking up State Road 20

West, Eloise took over driving until they got to Indiana and the interstate heading south outside of Angola. Imogene had never traveled much, so wanted to make their trip to the land of cotton as memorable and leisurely as possible.

"Let's see," she enumerated. "I was accepted by Northwestern, so I visited Chicago once. And, I think there was a family trip to Pennsylvania when I was four. Then there's my stint as a camp counselor one summer in the Berkshires. But otherwise, my itinerary was limited to my home state and New York City, with weekends on Long Island."

"Portsmouth and a whiteout through Rhode Island and Connecticut," Eloise added.

Imogene slid over to rest her hand on Eloise's leg. "But of course."

All along the way they stopped to take photographs and gather souvenirs for their Happybox in the forms of chestnuts (still in green pods) from Ohio, a miniature metal race car from Indiana, plastic ponies from Kentucky, corn cob pipes from Tennessee, and matchbooks from every pit stop.

Each took the wheel for 49 miles as a good luck gesture before trading off. They stayed two nights in motels, renting room number 13 and paying an extra buck when pretending to lose the key they kept at checkout. It was an idyllic trip, an unpretentious honeymoon that couldn't have been happier if legal or planned.

• • •

Pappy Fitz bought a three bedroom, three bathroom, single story ranch house situated on a half acre of property in an upper middle class neighborhood of old Montgomery.

Built in the 1950s, the house had beige wall-to-wall carpeting throughout with a bland contrast of tawny walls, natural woodwork and off-white ceilings. It featured a sizable living room with an oversized picture window looking out onto a long lawn sloping to the street, a dining room large enough to fit a maple china cabinet and sideboard with a matching set of table and chairs for seating twelve, and an eat-in kitchen with three double-hung windows that provided a view of the backyard's spectacular flower and vegetable garden, privatized by a seven-foot redwood fence wrapping around the back lot and connecting to the house.

A ten by fifteen-foot sunroom with private bath sat off the kitchen with access doors to the front yard, garage, backyard, and laundry. The room was wallpapered in a pink peonies floral pattern and lit by fairy lamps arranged on two cloth-draped tables. Next to each table was a chintz slipper chair (covered in plastic, like every other piece of upholstered furniture and lampshade in the house). A music console occupied one corner, a bookcase filled with *Southern Living* magazines sat in another, and a single bed made up with white sheets and one pillow was positioned under jalousie windows.

Mrs. Fitz had mailed Eloise the key to this room well in advance, giving them the freedom to show up at any hour and come and go as they pleased, which they did by arriving at one in the morning, long after the rest of the household was sleeping soundly.

Imogene looked at the narrow, blanket-less bed.

"Did you tell your mom you were bringing a guest?"

"She knew."

"And *this* was the biggest bed available? Not that I'm complaining."

Eloise had already stripped bare and jumped under the sheet.

"The other bedrooms went to relatives here for Aunt Edna's eightieth. I told her a single bed would be fine."

"Oh! So, it was envisaged. Well, then...by all means...move over."

SIXTY-TWO
Thursday, May 14, 1970
Check Mate

The smell of coffee awakened Imogene to a sight at the edge of the bed that startled her.

"How you?" simpered Mrs. Fitz, scantily clad in a sheer pink negligee draping breasts the size of basketballs. She had somehow managed to ease her backside up against the bent waist of Imogene's body in order to pose with a silver-plated tray of steaming Folger's in mismatched mugs resting on her knees.

Imogene's lips peeled apart as her face flushed.

It's not that Imogene had never seen breasts before, because she'd now seen Eloise's. But she'd never seen breasts of such magnitude, nearly nude, at an ominous angle and of short-range.

Yes, she'd viewed magazine photos of Jane Russell and Jayne Mansfield in formfitting sweaters, staged with goggle-eyed men in tow. But she thought their bras were at least partially padded with the amount of tissue used by braggart schoolgirls. Having grown up in a dress code household, and having been excused from taking biology after refusing to stab a dead butterfly, and having never attended gym classes where health and fitness films were shown, for all Imogene knew, the brassieres of mothers and movie stars were endowed with rolls of Charmin.

"Mom," came Eloise's muffled voice from under the sheet. "What are you doing?"

"Why Eloise Ann, I've brought you and your little friend some coffee s'all."

"Leave it, Ma-a."

While Imogene remained stupefied, Mrs. Fitz stood up and flitted across the room in her downy tufted satin slippers on the most beautiful pair of legs Imogene had ever seen on street or screen. Once there, she slowly bent down and carefully placed the tray on an end table. Then she twirled around and glided back to the kitchen in all her semitransparent glory.

"Ya'll shake a leg now, hear? I've bacon and eggs and grits and biscuits hot for the takin'. The rest will be gatherin' in the dining room soon, but you girls are welcome to sit a spell with me and your Aunt Edna in the kitchen if you've a mind to."

Glancing over her shoulder at Imogene on her way out the door, she paused long enough to wink.

Imogene quick-flipped over towards Eloise to talk, their noses nearly touching, their lips stretched wide enough to break their faces.

"*What* was that?"

"That was Mother."

"Why didn't you warn me?"

"I swear I have never seen her pull a stunt like that. I didn't even know she had it in her."

They stared in silence for a second, each one trying to figure out what was up.

"You're sure she knew I was coming?"

"Yes. I told her I was bringing someone. I told dad about you. He had to have told her."

Imogene rolled over and reached down for their clothes, dropped with the dogs on the floor before they collapsed on the bed hours earlier hoping to sleep fast.

"Why didn't the dogs bark?"

"She slides beef jerky under the door as a bribe. I bet they've been there begging for it."

Imogene got dressed under the sheet, afraid that someone else might mosey in on them. Eloise did the same.

"What did you tell your dad about me?"

"Not much."

"I'll need more than that."

"Can't we eat first?" Eloise begged. "Shower, maybe? I need a smoke before being forced to think this early."

"At least give me an inkling as to what else I'm walking into here."

They hopped up to grab a cup of coffee off the tray, then sat back down on the bed to slip into their tennis shoes.

"I told him we're living in New York, I was bringing you home, and to get used to you being around for awhile."

"Get used to me being around for a while? That's how you put it?"

"You said to be casual. That's me being casual."

"Okay, okay," Imogene waved it off. "So, pretend you are your mom, and your dad told you that your daughter was bringing home a woman who was going to be around for awhile. How would you, *as her,* respond to that?"

"Come to think of it, I didn't say for awhile." Eloise searched her pockets for her cigarette case, removed a smoke, and lit up. "I said, from now on."

"Nice save, but still. How would you take it?"

"I might not take it seriously."

"No?"

Eloise shrugged.

"What was your dad's reaction?"

"None. He said I'm his baby, same as always, and to come see him."

"So. This is all good?"

"Half good, anyhow."

"And, the other half?"

"Hard to say. They never agree on anything." Eloise took a deep drag as they both sat thinking and sipping. "Hey! Maybe that's it."

"What? What did I miss?"

"My folks are straight."

"Again, what did I *miss?*"

"Maybe my mom thinks my dad got it wrong. That if you're truly a lesbian you'd hit on her. You didn't, so you can't be. It was a Patsy test."

"Patsy test."

"Yes."

"You're sure?"

"Pretty sure."

Eloise snuffed out her cigarette as they headed for the bathroom. Her mom had left a new toothbrush in the medicine cabinet for each of them, paper cups in a plastic dispenser and clean towels on a rack behind the pink flamingo shower curtain. Eloise splashed her face and ran her fingers through her hair. Imogene brushed her teeth. Then they switched places and tasks, using their reflections in the mirror over the basin for eye contact.

"So you're saying your mom was toying with me."

"Kinda."

"And, now she assumes we aren't involved because I flunked?"

"Yep."

"Sleeping nude together in a single bed is...?"

"Ignored."

"So are we back to square one?"

Eloise spit and rinsed and spit again. Then she pushed the bristles of the two wet brushes together (as if they were kissing) before sticking them in a 'for show only' glass next to the 'for show only' hand towels near the basin. "I wouldn't say that."

"What then?"

"They'll end up rationalizing it the same way as segregation is rationalized down here."

"Which is?"

"The thinking is, Southerners like coloreds as individuals, but not as a group. Northerners like coloreds as a group, but not as individuals."

"Ah-so. Then to paraphrase, straights like gays as individuals, but not as a group?"

"Yup. It's the best any of us can hope for right now."

Imogene wove her arm around Eloise's waist and hugged her. "You know, that almost makes sense to me."

"It does?"

"Not the racism, but the parallel. As a group, I don't like men. But as individuals, I have a few men friends whom I think of as women."

They opened the backyard door and followed the dogs out to wander with them.

"My mom will always love me," Eloise assured. "She'll be like your mom in that way. Denying the details. But I'm not sure if mine might feel forced to take a stand against us if she's backed into a corner. She's more controlled by what others think than your mom seems to be. She's a great mom all the same. Don't ever tell her I said that."

• • •

Mrs. Fitz bought everything new only once in her life, determined it would last until the day she died. The fact that the size and shape of the Fitz households changed over the years was immaterial; interiors remained locked in a late 1940s time warp. No couch, chair, or bench (except those matching the stainless steel, padded Naugahyde kitchen set) had ever been sat on without a plastic zippered cover intact. No tables were without the felt padding and cloth in place. No side chairs were without washable slipcovers secured.

Accordingly, the same turquoise and grey Frankoma pottery that filled her china cabinet in 1940 remained displayed in 1970. The same Phillips television console from 1949 sat facing the same French provincial living room settee. The same rotary phones adorned the same side tables with the same cellophane covering the same paper lampshades on the same lamps set next to the same photographs in the same frames. Even the curtains and kitsch were carryovers.

Eloise was seeing the house for the first time while giving Imogene the tour.

"I hate it," she said. "It's tacky."

"Don't. This is the seat of luxury compared to the home we had."

"Your mom has a nice enough home."

"Now, maybe. At least it's gotten a little nicer than it was when we were kids. My father was notorious for not spending money on anything but booze, philandering and the one thing none of us wanted."

"Which was?"

"A newer house."

"I don't follow."

"We were born in an 1850s farmhouse. It was updated with electricity and plumbing but it still had the coal fed furnace in the basement and a block-icebox in the kitchen. The attic and walls were insulated with layers of newspapers dating from the Civil War. My folks had their bedroom, the boys shared one, and the girls shared one. My dad wasn't home much, so we kids were close and happy and we loved that dilapidated old place."

"Why the move?"

"A colored family bought a house a mile away."

"White fright."

"That's it. He moved us into a two-bedroom house in a Catholic neighborhood where we were shown contempt. A kind of racist meets bigot scenario."

"Karma?"

"Not for him. My folks and the boys took the upstairs bedrooms, while my sisters and I shared a double bed in an unheated, unfinished cement block basement beside a gas boiler, two standing washtubs with a wringer apparatus, and an ash trap. That stench memory of wet cinders in bloated corrugated boxes can still sneak up my nostrils."

"Gosh, Imogene, I'm sorry."

"Oh no-no, darling, don't be. I am who I am in spite of burdens and because of blessings. My mom always wanted a home filled with French provincial furniture, that's all. I swear she'd be bowled over by this place."

Imogene and Eloise took time to call Patsy, who was cat-sitting Pansy and Petunia while they were away. When they finally entered the kitchen, Mrs. Fitz and her sister, Edna Boyle, were seated for breakfast. Mrs. Fitz had changed into an ordinary housecoat and scuffs by then, with an apron tied tight around her waist and a linen dishcloth stuck in the strings.

By contrast, Edna was in evening clothes (her atire of choice regardless of the hour). Like Mrs. Fitz, she was a tall woman with striking good looks that aging hadn't hampered. Her burnt brown hair had streaks of white; her high cheekbones had a tad too much rouge; her pool-blue eyes glistened and she flashed a set of teeth that were her pride and joy.

"Land alive, child," Edna squawked when jumping up to bear hug her niece, "I thought ya'll would never walk through that door!" She shook Eloise by the shoulders some and hugged her again. "I be bitten by a snake if you don't look more beautiful than ever. Child, there's elation in them baby blues. Someone fancyin' your pants?" She chortled at her own mischievousness before turning to Imogene. "And who's this pretty little miss?"

Imogene stepped forward, taking both of Edna's hands in hers. "I'm Imogene LaPin. You must be the birthday girl, Aunt Edna. I've so looked forward to meeting you. Eloise says you've always been her favorite aunt."

"Oh my-my-my, I do like a lady who panders," said Edna. She jerked her head in Mrs. Fitz's direction. "Have you met that one?"

"Hurricane? Why yes. Yes I have."

"Hurricane?" said Edna. Her eyes grew wide. "Well ain't that the berries and perfect name for the old coot. How'd you come up with it, shug?"

"Instantly." Imogene peered over at Mrs. Fitz who hadn't a clue as to what the girl was up to. "She snuck into our room like an unpredicted storm. Caused a sensation, too! Even made landfall for a bit." Imogene nodded at Mrs. Fitz. "Then she sashayed out as fast, with a big old 'gotcha' left behind."

"Like a cyclone," Eloise added.

"Almost. But a cyclone often rotates counterclockwise and inwards. Whereas your mom? She took immediate aim, hit her mark and stayed the course. Classic hurricane."

"That's her, all right, to a tee," Edna cackled. "By gum, Hurricane it is!"

Mrs. Fitz pursed her lips, trying to contain a twinkle creeping in. "Well I be John Brown. No one's ever given me a nickname before."

"Hell, Hurricane," Edna roared. "That's because no one's had the audacity to find you endearing 'til now. Eloise, honey, I like this youngun' you got yourself. I like her lots!"

"Whose dogs are digging in my garden?" Pappy growled before spotting Eloise sitting at the kitchen table scarfing down a side buttery biscuits soaked in syrup. She jumped up and ran to him. "Baby!" he beamed. "If you aren't a sweet treat for these old eyes."

"She looks like she slept in her clothes," Mrs. Fitz stabbed, "but she didn't!" She quickly covered her lips, glancing over to see if Imogene had caught the slip. Imogene had.

"The pups slept on them," Eloise covered. "But we threw them on anyhow the minute we smelled Hurricane's coffee."

"Who's Hurricane?"

"Isn't that the darnedest thing?" Mrs. Fitz feigned fussing, proud that she had a pet name and Pappy didn't. "This one here," she pointed towards Imogene, "dubbed me Hurricane and now my sister and your daughter are tail-wagging along."

Pappy turned to Imogene. His face lit up. "Then I've got myself another daughter. How 'bout that?"

The tension between Eloise's parents appeared evident to Imogene, as if the two were engaged in an ongoing battle over their daughter's attention, each making certain the one didn't infringe on the other's time. But the truth be told, Pappy was a scalawag and his wife was a scamp. They adored each other. They weren't open about it, but their underlying mutual admiration was solid. Each had loved and lost and assented to second best. At first, it got them by. But they'd developed a kind of reverence for each other over time, with a bond built on trust and loyalty. They came to realize their union was meant to be and were both the better for it. Sure, acting cantankerous was the script they followed when the spotlights were on. But once out of the earshot others, he was her man and she was his woman and Lord help anyone who dared to say otherwise.

Pappy was the mollycoddler and Hurricane the disciplinarian when it came to Eloise, who was deft at playing them against each other. Now he had two girls to spoil and she had two to make toe the line.

"Another daughter, huh?" she mumbled when the three excused themselves to spiffy up some before going out on a walkabout. They'd left her behind in the kitchen with her sister to decorate a birthday cake. "Fat chance of Eloise allowing that!"

"What's that you're jawin' about, Hurricane?" poked Edna.

"Not jawin'. Just sayin' is all."

SIXTY-THREE
March 1970 - June 1972
Bedtime Stories

Imogene and Eloise sat together in the pastel pink back bedroom where they'd placed the double brass bed that Micky Bee helped them take apart to cart down from a fifth floor East Village tenement and lug up to the top floor of their Brooklyn Heights duplex. They'd seen the bed advertised in a Village Voice classifieds for fifty dollars and chose to take a wary look-see in a risky area on the lower east side.

The bed belonged to a biracial couple whose apartment door was spray-painted in red with slurs from nasty neighbors. It didn't help that she was his minion, as light as he was dark, as soft-spoken as he was harsh, and as pregnant as he was not. Her meek, disheveled image clashed with his angry, unrelenting attitude. Dressed immaculately in an exotic West African tribal robe and hat, he blamed the 'hoodoo bed' for creating the beggar in her belly.

"We will sleep on the floor as penance for our foolishness!" he proclaimed. "I will hear no more of it."

The girls compassion for the woman prompted her overlord to callously assure that the bed would go, regardless of her pleadings, even if he had to take a machete to it. That wouldn't happen. Imogene's and Eloise's hearts skipped a synchronized beat upon seeing the bed.

The head and footboards stood six feet and four feet high respectively, with monk style caps atop matching cylindrical posts and bulbous bottoms linking horizontal bars framing five columns. Except for the cast iron side rails, the entire bed was formed from thin, seam-sealed sheets of solid brass, stamped in block letters at the bottom of the four posts: May 10, 1876 CIE, proving its provenance from the first Centennial International Exhibition.

"We'll take it," bargained Eloise, "if you'll accept a ten dollar deposit now, and the rest at five when we pick the bed up."

"I accept. But if you do not return by five I will keep the ten and the bed. I am a very busy man. Very busy! I have no time for nonsense."

Hotfooting it down the grimy stairs and out into the fried food fetor of the prideless street, they were halfway to the subway station before stopping to do the Snoopy dance of joy.

"But let's make a pact to never again profit by the misfortune of another," Imogene said, feeling guilt slither over her. "I'd hate to be haunted by this."

"Okay, but in fairness, the bed was doomed. All we did was pay to rescue it."

"We did do that, didn't we? And, we paid top dollar!"

"In today's market, yes."

"And, we'd be complicit in a cultural crime if we let the bed be destroyed."

"Absolutely!" Eloise didn't know what a cultural crime was, but as long as the end game remained the same she was all in.

· · ·

From that day, the bed had been their go-to place, regardless of the activity or hour. Often they'd sit and chat among piles of pillows propped up against the headboard with a TV-tray of hot coffee and croissants, cold butter and Dickinson's Black Raspberry Preserves set adjacent to an unadorned south side window, inviting the warmth of the morning sun to engulf them.

"It seems inconceivable," Imogene reflected, "that we've lived in Brooklyn Heights for two years since Patsy got engaged and moved to Manhattan." Before then, Patsy had encouraged Imogene and Eloise to take over her existing lease by explaining, in doing so, she'd save the loss of her security deposit and they'd get a much larger living space. A dual income easily offset the rise in rent so they jumped at the offer.

"It's even more inconceivable that I've held down a job that long," Eloise added, laying the groundwork and searching for the nerve to ask Imogene if she could quit it.

• • •

Eloise had proven popular with her coworkers at the West 36th Street wire center across from a no-name bar where she and several of her cohorts dined daily on hot meat sandwiches ordered in for them by the bartender, Micky Bee.

Micky Bee was often pigeonholed as a goombah (which he was) and Eloise as a dumb blonde (which she was not), but neither took the other for being gay, nor did they engage in the kind of conversational fishing used to ferret out details about the lives of others.

Initially, Micky Bee took a liking to Eloise because she spoke to him with an unguarded ease about her friend, Imogene, and Eloise took to the politeness and geniality of Micky Bee. But it wasn't until she said, "I think there should be a liquor named Kindred Spirits," that he knew she knew and vice-versa. In response, he served her a vodka martini with an olive still attached to its branch, kept special for that purpose.

Their friendship proved unusual in another way. From the moment Eloise first entered the no-name bar, something felt old soul between them.

For her, it was more in his mannerisms than his looks. He was bald and skinny but tall and sturdy with a scraggly face and meticulously manicured mustache emblazoning the length of his ultra-wide, thin-lipped mouth.

Eloise wasn't like Imogene, who had the kind of charm that could embolden strangers to confess secrets within minutes after meeting her. To wit, in almost every conversation Eloise began about Micky Bee, Imogene interrupted with commonalities that hadn't occurred to her to ask, like the whereabouts of his hometown, his parents heritage, if he had siblings, his pet status, birthday and year, whether he preferred glazed, or jelly donuts, and the model car he drove.

"Eloise isn't inquisitive," Mrs. Fitz once told Imogene.

"Imogene is curious about everything," Mrs. LaPin once told Eloise.

A day after the sound of Micky Bee's voice finally getting the better of her, Eloise begged

Imogene to meet her at the dive. She knew Imogene wouldn't be caught dead in such a dump, but depended on her ability to tailor a conversation in such a way as to explain why she felt such an affinity to Micky Bee.

"Why don't you come out and ask him, Eloise?"

"You can't pry people about their lives. They'll clam up if you do."

• • •

Micky Bee always kept one an eye on the barroom door and one hand within reach of a sawed off shotgun, but whenever he saw Eloise coming in he dropped his guard to greet her.

"This is Imogene," Eloise boasted.

Micky Bee's face crinkled up as he took a fresh white dish towel used for wiping down the bar top and dried his hands before extending his right one.

"Happy to finally meet you, Imogene."

"My pleasure, Mr. Bee. Is that your true last name as Eloise says?"

"Everyone assumes it is, so I say so. But no. It's more of a Sicilian work name. The initial 'B' stands for Bolla."

"As in the Soave?"

"The same."

"Hold on," Eloise interrupted. "Big Mike Bolla? The trucker who stopped at Fortyville weekly back in the 40s?"

Micky Bee stepped back. "Nobody's called me Big Mike Bolla in twenty years. Not since I stopped hauling hooch after losing two toes and a hundred-thirty pounds to diabetes. Easy? Really? Easy!"

Over the months that followed, the three became close friends. Eloise learned, Micky Bee sidelined as the backup limousine driver for Italian businessmen. He learned Eloise and Imogene sidelined as pickers for the row of Atlantic Avenue antiques dealers. Micky Bee offered to pick up and deliver any oversized items they found to their mutual liking. They responded in kind by having him to dinner at least once a week and always on holidays. As a bonus to both, Eloise appeared as Micky Bee's toy date for the rare family function he was expected to attend.

"You can't imagine the pressure it takes off when you're with me," he'd tell Eloise upon entering Junior's in Brooklyn, or Sparks on East 46th Street.

"Show me the steak," was her standard reply.

"You two got anything goin' on for the weekend?" Micky Bee asked Eloise around noon every Thursday.

They always did. It could entail pitchers of beer with rowdies at Shine's on Long Beach, back room conviviality with the boys of Julius' on 10th Street, a weekend of card games with Marie and Lisa, brunch at Mr. William Shakespeare's in the West Village, a double feature at the Midwood theater on Avenue J, a foreign film at the Paris across from the Plaza, dinner at Uncle Charlie's South on Third Avenue, or two nest days alone. Whatever the choice, Imogene proved the more innovative and Eloise the more adventurous — but both had a flair for the romantic.

One rainy weekend they went camping on Bear Mountain with an Army surplus tent big enough to fit themselves, the pups, two cots, a picnic table, their gear, and the VW Bug inside.

Imogene had purchased the VW from James for its payoff balance after he blamed Eloise for his loan being in default. His accusations so incensed Eloise, she threatened to expose him for fraud. But Imogene didn't want any venom spat by James to tarnish the memories she and Eloise were making together. What's more, she thought the Bug was the sweetest of rides.

The buyout allowed Eloise to sell her Buick to Charles (raising the old man's spirits on the day they moved away), and fostered the idea of a weekend camping getaway to celebrate having bought their first car together. The weekend they went, it rained the entire 48 hours starting within minutes of getting the tent set up and their gear situated. Imogene recorded the adventure in her journal as "simply divine."

Micky Bee depended on Izzy's retelling of hers and Imogene's escapades as his major means of entertainment. Whenever they stayed in town, he liked knowing where they'd be for safety's sake. Not that he ever discussed business with those outside the family, but he was vigilant about steering them away from designated places on parley-days.

To dissuade inquiries into why he sought her whereabouts, he'd hand Eloise a bag twice a month with two size 8 and two size 4 outfits that had 'fallen off the delivery truck' from various New York fashion houses. The garments were often samples, created with the finest materials and expertise, intended for the catwalk rather than mass production.

Not that the women knew the source of Micky Bee's bimonthly gifts. Not that they ever asked.

SIXTY-FOUR
Saturday Morning, June 3, 1972
After 825 Days

Imogene and Eloise were up early laying out the garments Micky Bee had procured for them to wear to Patsy's wedding. Imogene's was a sleek, full length, lemon-yellow knit sleeveless gown with a knee-high slit up the center. It arrived with a pair of I. Miller open-toe pumps and opera gloves reaching past the elbow. Eloise's was a white-on-white coordinate of a quilted skirt and blouse in French silk with a pink cummerbund sash and pink leather sling-backs.

"Who's yours by, Imogene?"

"Beene, I think. The label's been cut, but that's what Micky said. Yours is a Blass."

It was nearly eight and they were late, having dawdled in bed pondering Pasty's imminent nuptials.

"Did you ever wish we could get married?"

"Instead of our RAVE Day, Iz? Or, for real?"

"For real."

"Truth?"

"Of course."

"No."

"Eh. Me neither."

Imogene saw Eloise was troubled. "What's all this about, Hon?"

"Nothing. I was making a comparison, that's all."

"Of?"

"Of how our ceremony was all about romance planned between the two of us, but straight marriages require lots of flash and exhibitionism as a means of validation."

"True. But they marry for different reasons. Not us. We aren't joined by arrangement, or for prestige, or out of necessity."

"Or for a dowry."

"No promises of benefits."

"No dictates by religion."

"No merger between families."

"Or for the sake of unborn children."

"Think of that, Eloise. We're only connected by love."

"It's what makes us special." Eloise pulled Imogene into a never-let-me-go hold.

"You know what, Izzy? Sometimes I think, whenever people seek societal recognition and acceptance for what's been divined, it acts as the pride that goeth before the fall. As if love, being the supreme blessing, isn't reward enough for them."

"It could account for all the unhappy couples out there."

"Maybe. All I know for certain is, if Goddess nicknamed God nicknamed Powers That Be nicknamed Betty truly *is* love — then what we have is sacred." She cuddled closer. "Because only those genuinely in love want it and wish it for everyone."

Eloise buried her nose in the freshly unwrapped curls atop Imogene's head, closed her eyes, and pressed a kiss into them.

"Thank you for that."

SIXTY-FIVE
Saturday Morning, June 3, 1970
Of Anglers & Wanglers

Patsy's wedding was set to start at 12:15 sharp atop the south side balcony of Byron Steele's penthouse on East 48th Street in Manhattan.

Byron had taken over the top floor of the entire east wing of the rent controlled building (with its ground level courtyard and two 24 hour doormen posted in gatehouses at parallel street entrances) after landing several high profile accounts for his market research firm: a company that consisted of himself, his lover, Sheldon Piro, a clerk, and anyone they could snag off the street for videotaped product testing.

His penthouse had a private elevator that opened into a large, checkerboard floor foyer of multiple doors leading to eleven rooms, each of them larger and more lavishly decorated than the next with Tiffany lighting, Dresden porcelains, 19th century art, and European antiques.

Beneath the charade of opulence and pretense of devotion for the sake of a shared income, the envied bon vivants no longer liked nor loved each other, sleeping separately and living licentious lives. To preserve the need to profit through testimonials by satisfied clients, the men hosted dinners and holiday parties that often required fake dates. On these occasions, Byron called on his old friend, Eloise, who now included Imogene as compulsory if the pact was to continue.

"Byron has a bad habit of buying boys," Sheldon remarked condescendingly upon being introduced to Imogene. His petulance was emitted by way of a chronically congested nose cartooning a tiny head with Eddie Cantor eyes set above a scrawny frame to match his vapid personality.

"I buy them for Sheldon," Byron disparaged through clenched teeth and mustached lips, looking like a stylish version of Captain Kangaroo and sounding like a ventriloquist without a dummy. "He once caught them fresh, but they kept throwing themselves back." He wagged his fingers at Imogene. "Do you get that, or must I translate?"

Imogene smiled, coyly. "I *dare* you to."

"Tell me where you found her, Eloise. I want one!"

Whenever they stayed over at Byron's penthouse, Eloise and Imogene were given their own bedroom and bath with a door that opened onto a private balcony facing north where one could sit and gaze upwards at the skyline and the stars, or peer over the four foot high brick wall onto the traffic and people below, or let their pups piddle on the raised beds of grass installed for that purpose. At the far end was a locked portal leading to the wraparound lanai that ran the east side width of the building before intersecting with a much larger rooftop patio stretching half the length of south side of the building and ending at two sets of sliding glass doors: one entering the prodigious living room and the other the kitchen. It was on this patio, landscaped with potted trees, blossoming gardenia and rose bushes, a side wall waterfall, a canopy, a grand piano, and ten tables seating forty guests coveting fresh flower centerpieces spritzed with Joy *parfum* that Patsy was to be married.

Byron had never met Patsy before her wedding day, since the single purpose for lending out his penthouse was conditioned on Imogene and Eloise agreeing to be his and Sid's dates to two trade shows, and act as participants in a hidden-camera commercial he had rigged to guarantee a positive reaction for his instant coffee account.

But when Byron's private investigator learned Patsy's fiancé hobnobbed with influential people in high places and was the heir to a sizable fortune, he acted magnanimously by saying he'd host the nuptials, no strings attached.

Rightly suspicious, Imogene avoided feeling indebted by agreeing to attend the trade show functions, but nixed the commercial.

"To be honest Byron, I don't think I could inveigle anyone into believing I couldn't tell the difference between fresh brewed coffee and icky instant, on or off camera."

"Of course you could. You have theatrical training."

"True. But Eloise doesn't and she wouldn't like us being used as collateral."

However, Eloise wasn't thrilled for an entirely different reason. She felt Patsy had taken advantage of Imogene's friendship by putting her in a precarious position when saying she hadn't been able find a suitable place in Manhattan to stage her wedding.

By then, Patsy knew of their connection to Byron, primarily because Imogene shared the details of their nights out on the town that invariably included dinner at the finest restaurants and third row orchestra seats on the center aisle to numerous opening nights on Broadway.

"I had no choice but to beg Byron," Imogene rationalized. "She's my boss."

"Which proves my point. She made her wedding *your* problem, like you made it his."

"You're right. I'm sorry. But Byron went from wangling quid pro quo out of me..."

"Us."

"...to falling all over himself for the gig. It worked out."

Eloise was resolute. "I still don't like the way you were played."

"That's the last time."

"It better be!"

"It will."

Eloise appeared to be appeased, but in order to make certain Imogene proffered, "Shall we squeal the deal?"

SIXTY-SIX
Saturday Morning, June 3, 1972
Unpredicted Snow

Patsy Wolfe knew Adam Snow was in town and purposely didn't invite him to her wedding. Even if she had, it wouldn't reverse the downsizing approval he'd secured calling for her firing when she returned from her honeymoon. He drafted and typed the termination letter himself to keep the details private before getting it signed by both Jerome brothers whom he'd duped, yet again.

The brothers co-owned the company: Frederick, by obligation of being the eldest son and Jerard, by having the directorial reins handed him when the elder became too old to manage the enormity of everyday operations. By then, they had factories in five states employing six thousand garment workers.

Because Frederick Jerome was a short, aloof, effete man who abhorred commerce and cared only about funding the company provided for his philanthropic work, Snow knew it was easier to persuade him to do his bidding. Jerard Jerome was much taller, much kinder, and a much harder sell.

"She's been with us for nine years, Adam. Right out of high school."

"I'm aware of that, sir. But she makes twice the salary of Miss LaPin whom, I've been assured by the plant manager, is doing as good a job, if not better. Some say Miss Wolfe isn't doing anything at all — that Miss LaPin often handles the entire workload."

Jerard Jerome was wary. He didn't like Adam Snow. No one did. But he couldn't ignore the man's prowess when it came to profits and how to obtain them.

"May I go on, sir?"

Jerard motioned Adam to continue.

"If we bump Miss LaPin up to manager of both divisions and rid ourselves of the records clerk — whose job is better handled by the factory accountant — and let go the salesmen who cost us the Stillman stores, we're looking at a savings of fifty-five thousand, plus six more in benefits and bonuses.

"Ricardo Alvarez? You're saying he goes, too?"

"Yes."

"And Sam Levine in sales? Sheldon Melchick is okay with firing him? "

"He is. We're also letting go two seamstresses, a presser, a packaging clerk, a piece goods clerk, and one of the trimmings buyers. All their duties can be absorbed by our current staff."

"That adds up to how much?"

"Over a quarter mil onto the profit side of the books if we act now."

"It won't help for long if we don't increase sales."

"That's not my department, sir. But I can look into it if you want."

Instead of facing Adam, Jerard sat swiveled towards the windows of his corner office with an eagle's view of Central Park. He'd never believed the rumors of an affair between Patsy Wolfe and Myron Stein circulating years before, but now Adam Snow was telling him Patsy was pregnant with Myron's child. It was a clear violation of their morality clause, even if Myron was single, which he wasn't. Adam said the man she was marrying didn't know he wasn't the father. It was the kind of behavior that company protocol didn't dare condone.

"Should I consult with Myron about it, Adam?"

"Absolutely not. We couldn't afford for him to quit over this. And, what if she hasn't told him?" Adam knew she hadn't because according to medical records he had access to for annual insurance evaluations, Patsy wasn't pregnant. Furthermore, the steel brace strapped to Myron's back precluded him from acting as a Lothario, and the side effects of his medications to reduce spinal pain caused impotency. "I'm saying it's bad for company morale to ignore an affair that could also cost us additional funds in maternity leave and raise our insurance rates."

Jerard sought an easy way out and Adam was offering it. "I got an

invitation you know. I took your advice and bowed out. Sent the gift."
Jerard checked his watch. "She's getting married about now, isn't she?"
"It's why we needed to meet today. Except for us, no one's here. This keeps the lid on."
"Who does the firings?"
"I'll take care of everyone but Ricardo. Miss LaPin will need to do that herself. It's her department now."
"She's consented to this?"
"She will. I guarantee it."

Jerard closed his eyes to ease a headache coming on. With his father at the helm, he hadn't been involved in the lives of the staff, preferring to be the liaison between the corporate office and plant managers. Given a choice, he would have fired Adam and let Patsy and Myron figure it out. But he had no choice if what Adam said was so and there wasn't pretext for believing otherwise.

"Lock up behind you, Adam. I'm going to camp out here a while longer."
"Will do."

Adam Snow raced away like a roach on the wall when a light's flipped on. He was stoked over what he'd done, eliminating a decade-old adversary and replacing her with someone he knew he could control through coercion. Rita provided him with all the ammunition he needed for that.

• • •

Sheldon Melchick was the Executive Vice President of Sales with his neck in a noose. He'd been told by Jerard Jerome to either boost sales by fifty dozen units each week, or start looking for a new job.

"I don't care how you do it," Jerard said. "All I want to see on my desk from you at the first of each week are total sales. Do I make myself clear?"

"Yes, sir," was the most Sheldon dared reply. If it had been anyone else giving him an ultimatum he'd have wined him, dined him, and gotten him laid. But not the executioner, as Jerard Jerome was referred to when he was pushed too far. Sheldon had reached the pushing point.

The pressure to perform had taken its toll on Sheldon's ulcer until

Adam Snow showed up with a ruse. He'd agreed on it without understanding the details of how the embezzlement of goods was going to increase sales. So far, Sheldon had done as he was told. But now he felt like a lamb being lead to slaughter, having waited an hour for Adam in a booth at Schraft's, milking his milk. When Snow finally sailed through the door it felt like a reprieve to him.

"How'd it go?"

"Like clockwork." Adam ordered a club sandwich, black coffee and a slice of custard pie before showing Sheldon the termination papers.

"I swear I'll never understand how you got them to do this. When are you telling her?"

Adam checked his watch and saw it was 11:30. "Well, I was going to wait to send it by courier, but I can cut costs and let it go regular mail now. The last pickup from the lobby box is at noon. I'll drop her termination papers in it now so it's in her Monday morning delivery, waiting for her when she returns in two weeks." He rubbed his hands together expectantly.

"That's cold."

"All of a sudden you have a soft spot for Patsy Wolfe?"

"Never." But Sheldon wasn't thinking of Patsy. He was thinking of himself in case Adam was out to target him next.

"Where's my proof of transfer and bill of lading?"

Sheldon pulled out two pages torn from the weekly production tally. One indicated five dozen of the terry lined polished cotton robes retailing at seventy-five dollars a pop appeared to have been sold out. The other showed a transfer of five dozen garments into a catch-all sale lot priced at twelve dollars a dozen with five dozen sold. "That's forty-five grand worth of retail merchandise for seven hundred and twenty dollars shipped to your storage locker. Now what?"

"Simple. This proves it works, so we'll get an extra printout of the sales and production figures each week. Once LaPin has reviewed the two and filled each unit with its production quota, we siphon off the best style finished goods, transfer them into sale lots, and sell them to select jobbers. The sales totals will rise, and since that one number is all Jerard cares about, he won't question it. You keep your job, and I'll get all the discounted goods I need to restock my flea market boys."

"What if LaPin catches on?"

"Let me worry about that." He gestured to the waitress to put his order in a doggie bag. "Trust me, I have her between a rock and the harder place of never finding another job in this town again. Maybe even her arrest."

"Arrest?"

"I've got it covered, Sheldon. That's all the information you need."

"What if the plant manager catches on?"

"He won't. But if he does, we'll blame it on LaPin. After all, she's the one responsible for production and finished goods transfers. They're her divisions now."

"But we'll stop once the spring line comes out, right? That's all the time I need to turn sales around legitimately."

Adam took his take-out and patted Sheldon on the back. "We'll see." He gave Sheldon the bill. "You wanna get this?"

Once outside the restaurant, Adam Snow stood in the nearly-noonday sun thinking he'd finally come into all that was due to him. After years of being derided by her behind his back, he was getting even as the henchman who replaced Patsy Wolfe with a lesbian he could out and have arrested if she didn't do as told.

Adam wasn't sure what riled him most about Patsy Wolfe: that she avoided being fired during the first scandal he circulated about her and Myron Stein, or the smarmy way she and her faggot friend, Ronald, acted when mocking him with sexual innuendo whenever he was nearby.

He didn't absolutely know Ronald was a fag, just as they couldn't absolutely know he was anything other than a happily married man. After all, he carried pictures of his wife and kids in his wallet wherever he went, and even put framed photos of them on his temporary desk whenever he had business in the New York office.

Besides, he'd never been unfaithful to his wife, not once in twenty-two years, unless you counted buying young men for a quick release as being so, which he did not. Neither did it make him queer like he bet Ronald was, nor deserving of the suspicion leveled at him by Patsy — canards that could have cost him his career and marriage.

Anyway, except for once when he was shaken down by a young Aryan looking bastard who needed money to take a potato truck trip out of town, he never again made the mistake of finding a trick closer to home than Philly. He'd helped that kid, too, by telling the boy he was a Jew when he saw the kid was circumcised.

"The irony," he commended himself to himself while crossing the street to the Tishman Building, "is that I got to replace a straight butch with a lady dyke. If that doesn't beat all."

Once inside, Adam stopped near the stainless steel letter boxes built into the lobby walls, opened a chute, and dropped in the postmarked envelope containing a check for six weeks' severance pay along with the letter terminating Patsy Wolfe from Jerome Brothers.

When the door snapped shut and he watched it slide down the glass enclosure, he imagined Patsy's face when breaking the seal to extract her fate. It made his walk to the Waldorf Astoria for checkout before returning home to Cheat Mountain worthy of a quick trip to the Continental Baths.

SIXTY-SEVEN
Saturday Morning, June 3, 1972
Dogged Determination

Gracie stood on her hind legs and woofed, scratching furiously on the rim of the tub while Imogene bathed. She sat on Imogene's feet and yapped as Imogene combed out the curls of her shoulder-length auburn hair. She whimpered as Imogene applied her makeup. She nudged her as Imogene padded the cups of her training bra with two soft cotton handkerchiefs embroidered with dainty red hearts in the corners. And she nipped at Imogene's heels for attention, twirling and begging to be picked up once Imogene descended the stairs and entered the living room, ready to depart for Patsy Wolfe's wedding.

Eloise was swept away.

"Is something wrong?" Imogene stuck out her leg to check her nylons for snags.

"No."

"Then what?"

"My daddy always said there's one moment in every woman's life when she looks as beautiful as she's ever looked before, or will ever look again. That's you right now. Stunning."

Imogene wanted to thank her, *really* thank her, and might have if Gracie hadn't begun to bark nonstop. It wasn't a 'take me for a walk' yap, or a 'feed me' plea, or a 'pick me up' appeal. It was an unprecedented baying mingled with sharp explosive yelps.

"Gracie, that's enough!" scolded Eloise to no avail.

"It's okay. She doesn't want me to go. You run ahead and I'll be down in a sec."

Eloise wheeled the car out of its space a half block away and double-parked it in front of the duplex while Imogene swaddled Gracie in a towel (so she could hold the dog close without getting hair on her

369

clothing) and carried her to the front door landing. There she sat to soothe her beloved and devoted friend.

"Listen to me. I won't be long, an hour or so, two at most. And I promise to come back to you. I love you and Lucy and Pansy and Petunia like no tomorrow. You're my earth angels." The two nuzzled and touched noses. "So, be my brave, loyal little girl and wait for me, okay? No tears. Momma will be home soon, Gracie. I'll *always* come back to you."

Imogene was distraught when she finally set a quieted Gracie down and slipped out the door. But the minute the lock clicked in place the dog began to howl. She continued howling as Imogene slipped into the VW driver's seat. Once the doors were locked with Eloise safely by her side, Imogene released the clutch, put it in first and drove slowly down the block towards the turnoff to the Brooklyn Bridge. All the way, Gracie cried out for her.

"She's never acted like this before, Izzy."

Eloise reached over to gently wipe the tear-smeared mascara from Imogene's cheek with a moistened tissue. "She didn't want you to leave, that's for sure."

"Can we not stay for the reception?"

"Aw-w, come on Imogene. It's free food. And Byron serves the best of everything."

"I'm sorry, sweetie. I am. But something is telling me not to go."

"We must."

"Maybe we should come right home after the ceremony. I know I'll be worrying about Gracie the entire time."

"The cats will take care of the dogs. They'll be fine. The same as I take care of you."

Imogene derived no comfort in Eloise's words. Absolutely none.

SIXTY-EIGHT
Saturday Morning, June 3, 1972
Runaway

Harold Hennessey was a slender, sandy haired, sallow skinned slacker. If he could have devised an easier way to pay his bar tab than driving a cab on the streets of New York City, he would have done it in less time than it took pork-barrel politicians to piss away a dime.

But he couldn't. Handling a hack was all he ever knew to do. It allowed him a regimen of stopping along his dispatch route to take a swig from his flask, or double-park for a fast bar shot, or tie one on at the end of the day before starting anew, driving through one hangover to the next.

Harold knew he was committing socially accepted suicide, one that people were quick to pity, but not condemn. To him, that was swell. Pity was what he depended upon when dragging dollars he never intended to repay. He was willing to wallow in woebegone for the price of a full flagon and didn't give a damn what anyone thought of him as long he could guzzle free booze.

The sole exception to his dismissal of others' estimation was in his rank among the hack runners, a banded bunch of cabbies vying for championship in a secret competition of who could make the fastest nonstop trips while covering the greatest distance in the least amount of time on Manhattan streets.

The attempts at record making and breaking was primarily confined to novices during the wee early hours when cars were sparse and the preset timers dictated the top speed one could travel in order to score the longest run of green. But as the day wore on and traffic became heavy, skill and expertise in spotting car clusters, guestimating split seconds before a red turns green, avoiding pockets of pedestrians, and maneuvering jams to jump red lights proved the difference between the winner bellying up to the bar for his free drinks and the bumper-butts buying them.

Among hack-runners, Harold Hennessey was legendary.

If asked, he might tell you he'd not always been a drunk, that he was born the second son in a middle class family with three boys who went to public schools, attended mass, ate breakfast together every morning, and dined as a family four nights a week. His father was a copywriter and his mother worked the graveyard shift at Mount Sinai Hospital as head nurse.

In high school, Hennessey was a varsity all-star with enviable good looks capable of bagging any babe he wanted. But he had no passion for his dad's dream of playing pro ball, or for his mother's fixation on granddaughters. All Harold Hennessey loved was opera: studying its history, listening to it sung, watching it performed, mingling among those with careers in opera and aspiring to produce opéra bouffe.

It was due to this indubitable dream that he interned as a stagehand for the Metropolitan Opera Guild, filling in on nights his parents thought he off pursuing sports.

"So here I was," said Hennessey, slurring his words to a bartender who'd heard the same soppy story time and again over the course of twenty years. "Was. I was on my way home from the opera when I was *supposed* to be at staying late at school for football practice, see?"

"Can I top that off for you, man?"

Hennessey stared at his glass before nodding for his fifth refill. "Where was I?"

"On your way home after playing hooky."

"Right! And, then what?"

The bartender bit his lip, pretending he couldn't imagine.

"Outta nowhere this Jew steps in front of the cab I'm in." Hennessey acts amazed. "I mean from nowhere he, boom!, appeared with this woman in his arms — covered in blood!"

"You don't say."

"Bizarre, huh? So what can I do, man? Ignore them?"

"Can't do that."

"Right you are. So I jumped out of the cab — in the middle of traffic, this is — and I helped them. They coulda been killers for all I knew, with her blood all over me me. But the guy was so upset..."

Hennessey threw his arms up in the air. "What could I do but act? On instinct."

"That was good of you, man."

"But wait! Wait. You haven't heard the worst part yet."

Even though the bartender *had* heard it a hundred times, he asked, "What's that?"

"We go to the hospital. Mount Sinai, see? You got where that is, right?"

"Yes."

"Well, that's where we went. And they saved her life. The bleeder-er-er one."

"That's good."

"But the baby?" Hennessey shook his head. "Nope. Not the little baby. That's why all the blood. See?"

"I see."

"And then!" Hennessey reached out and poked the bartenders arm. "And this is the part I still, after all this time, I still can't believe. My *mom* comes out. She catches me there!" He held his flattened hands against his chest. "After I helped save a life, that's the thanks I get."

"From your mom."

"No, no, no-o-o. You ain't listening, man. Don't you see? Don't you get it? That was the end of it. No more opera."

"No opera."

"*Because*," he almost said. "Because," he reconsidered. "That's the night my nose and kneecap broke." He winked. "Bada bing bada boom, I'm driving a cab." He burped. "The end."

Hennessey dropped his head in a huff, raised it slowly and stared into the mirror behind the bar. The bleary eyed guy staring back helped him chug what was left of his drink, push him up, pay his bill with wadded ones, knock twice on the bar as his way of saying thanks, and stagger out into the bright sun of a glorious June Manhattan morning.

• • •

Hennessey got the idea to make a run for it while stopped at the red light at 45th Street, in the center lane of the front row of cars stretching the width of Third Avenue going north.

It appeared miraculous to him that there were no cars in front of him for a full two blocks — none that were part of the actual traffic flow, anyhow. He counted three double-parked on the west side of the avenue and another two on the east side of the next block, but nothing in front of him blocking his way. He bet, if he peeled out the moment the light turned green and outpaced the light changes by split seconds, he could catch the cars two blocks ahead, dodge the front runners and set an unbreakable record for a ten block run in midtown during midday.

He knew from experience that four Manhattan blocks equaled a quarter mile. That meant, if he went from zero to seventy in five seconds, it was possible he could do the ten blocks in fifty-six seconds, or less.

But if he ramped it up even higher, he might clear the quarter mile mark at 49th Street in thirteen seconds. That would be a record all by itself, even if he got no further.

Granted, it hadn't been done, at least not in a Marathon cab, the biggest and heaviest hack of its kind and only one left in his boss's fleet. He knew the old tank was due to be retired soon and wagered it should go out in a blaze of glory.

At the first inkling of the light turning green, Hennessey clicked the stopwatch taped to the top of his visor, flipped on the taximeter and floored it.

The time was 11:57:21.

• • •

The cab never reached Hennessey's projected speed until too late to break any record and too late to brake at all. It took him 39 seconds to cover the four block quarter mile, but when he was about to take the 49th Street intersection on the sidewalk where he'd jumped the corner curb — the car crashed at 11:58 on the dot.

SIXTY-NINE
Saturday Morning, June 3, 1972
Pomp & Circumstance

It infuriated Ronald Newman that Patsy Wolfe expected him to go downstairs and be on the lookout for Imogene and Eloise.

"They're driving a white Volkswagen Bug with red leather seats," she instructed.

"Like I can see inside?"

"It's a 1969."

"Like they don't all look the same?"

"It has a sunroof."

"What's with the details? How many white Bugs do you think will be circling the block with two dykes in wedding duds?"

"Do this for me, will you? Think of it as a wedding present."

"I thought my flying here from London was your wedding present."

"Then think of it as the wrapping."

Ronald stood silently by the elevator doors, pretending he'd take the next compartment heading down the fifteen flights. Instead, the minute he saw Patsy return to the room Byron Steele had cordoned off as the bride's area, Ronald darted down a corridor and slipped through a door posted as off limits.

Once inside, he lingered long enough to admire the first room he'd seen in the stately penthouse decorated in a purely feminine fashion: ribbon papered pastel walls, period paintings of female subjects, Art Nouveau bronzes, Parisian furniture, two Tiffany dragonfly lamps, and fresh cut tulips in Steuben vases with a faint fusion of vanilla and lavender added to the air.

He strode across the antique Persian rug to where burgundy silk drapes were drawn and tied back with dark gold acorn-end cords,

375

exposing voile panels and a sliding glass door leading to a private balcony. Stepping out, he took in the sight stretching uptown towards the East River and Queensboro Bridge, the scattering of iconic rooftop water towers, the multilevel bustle of lives and the synchronized streaming of traffic. It calmed him.

Ronald Newman was happy to be hiding from all the hullabaloo happening before a bride walks down the aisle and makes promises she can't keep to a man she doesn't know. The way he saw it, this latest frenzy centering on the whereabouts of Imogene served as yet another reminder of how Patsy had come to prefer her to him, all because Imogene's contacts scored Patsy a lavish venue for her wedding. A venue he now coveted.

He assumed he'd eventually come to accept that Patsy chose to marry a man he'd never met, elevating him to being foremost in her life. What he couldn't bear was that it seemed Imogene was displacing him, too. Imogene, who should have been there to assist Patsy before now.

It hurt because he'd always been there for Patsy, making her his priority, on call day and night, professional and personal, the two of them inviolable until now. He'd traveled three thousand miles to be her hero, only to be treated like her houseboy. It made him feel used and abused, undervalued, unappreciated and sorry for himself, especially when he looked at the Rolex watch given to him by his lover, whom he'd left behind in London and now sorely missed.

It was 11:57. Ronald knew time had run out for them all: for his and Patsy's exclusivity, for Patsy's freedom, for any excuse to ever return to New York City, and for Imogene's career if she was a no-show. Not that Patsy would fire her, but she'd take umbrage and make her pay.

Peering down over the terrace wall onto Third Avenue, he spotted the top of a taxicab barreling towards the five lanes of traffic stopped at the intersection of 49th Street.

"He's going too fast," Ronald said aloud, fearing one of the red light targets was about to be rear-ended. "Slow down!" he shouted, as he caught a noontime reflection off the aluminum framed sunroof of a white Volkswagen clearing the intersection and easing into a parking space on the northwest corner of 49th.

It seemed slow and surreal, how Ronald heard the crackle of his muscles, and felt the friction in his nerves as his head jerked and his jaw snapped open to inhale a cool breath of terror, spellbound, watching the mammoth cab lunge to the left and sail over the sidewalk to skirt the light and broadside the Bug.

The explosion could be heard even from that height, as the airtight compact burst when struck by thirty-five hundred pounds of steel traveling at lethal speed.

He knew it was Imogene.

He sensed she was dead.

But he ran to her all the same, down the fifteen flights of steps, past the last of the guests arriving for Patsy's wedding, out into the street, slapping the hoods of cars while sliding over them, dashing by strangers stopping to stare and sprinting up the one short block to meet chaos and reach heartbreak.

SEVENTY
11:58:00, Saturday Morning, June 3, 1972
Prolonging

Imogene had easily made it through the East 49th Street intersection and was aiming her VW Beetle towards a choice corner parking space on the far side of Third Avenue when she caught a glimpse of the Marathon cab in her peripheral vision. Its driver had careened the curb and employed the sidewalk to bypass the traffic stopped at the red light blocking his path.

The impact from the taxi broadsiding her was so ferocious, it ripped her car in half lengthwise, fusing the driver's side door and partial body to the reinforced steel bumper of the cab while hurling the VW's sheared remains through the air for ten feet before it crashed to the pavement, skidded, and smashed into the lobby window of a branch bank.

It happened without warning. No slamming of brakes. No scattering of pedestrians. No perception of impending doom.

There was just her mild look of astonishment upon meeting her fate with a whispering of five final words.

"Oh my God. I'm dead."

SEVENTY-ONE
Saturday, June 3, 1972
Imogene's Elegy

You can hear me.

You can always hear me.

I am your inner voice saying when to stay, what to acknowledge, whom to embrace, where to go, when to act, why to remember and how to flee.

I happened to here in similarity with the swirl a camera lens takes when the shutter quickly closes and reopens: primary, practical, prosaic and precise.

In less than a click of a blink of a flash of a snap of a second of a moment of a fraction of a fraction of an instant to the nth degree, I became assimilated with everything.

There is no bright white light.

There are no halos, no wings, no gates, no streets of gold, no sentiment, no cauldrons of fire, no pain, no punishment, no prophets, no antecedents, no greeting, no goodbye.

There is no sound, no smell, no touch, no taste.

Sight, alone, remains.

I am the essence of infinite eyes, floating; expanding and contracting; being drawn in one direction, then another; zooming upward, downward, over, in and out, backwards and forwards.

I am evolved atmospheric magnetic energy, conducive to your emotions and made constant by your conscience.

I am primarily of the universe as life everlasting.

I am infrequently of the body as death undertaking.

As primarily of the universe I flow within a clonal time span.

I was present during all the prior periods when celestial bodies in untold galaxies aligned to duplicate the exact degree of magnetic field first embodied to form

379

my core.

I can convey the emotions of each language spoken in all my previous infrequent vessels, perfectly and accurately, in accordance with thoughts, dreams, premonitions and imagination.

I can recognize everyone, everything, and everywhere when summoned within our two aligned-time domains.

I am all I ever was to you, for now and within, unto eternity.

I am your forte and intuition.

I am your unequivocal answer to everything.

You need but listen.

I am connected to you by the absorbing and shedding of energy containing parallel elements within your encircling median: the magnetism encompassing your entirety.

I am drawn in opposite directions without a breaking point.

I swirl as pure volition, governed by the inherent law of the universe.

I am your initiative, eternally primed for returning to here.

But, lo! Those subliminal thoughts that now occur to you?

Those thoughts are indefinable to me.

You are a face I can recognize but can't identify; a sound I can recognize but can't grasp; a word I can recognize but can't translate; a taste I can recognize but can't place; a touch I can recognize but can't distinguish.

As primarily of the universe, I possess recollection and portent of all things channeled to guide you, without knowledge or understanding of anything from having been there.

As infrequently of the body, you possess knowledge and choice, without recollection or understanding of anything from having been here.

SEVENTY-TWO
Saturday Afternoon, June 3, 1972
SOS

The officers struggling to free Eloise from the wreckage restrained her from reaching back for Imogene, ordering her to concentrate on helping them get her out. They'd already determined the listless driver (her eyes fixed and dilated and no pulse noted) was dead upon impact.

As the passenger door was being lopped from its hinges, and the air-conditioning unit was being jacked up off her lap, and her legs were being dislodged from under the leveled gearshift at her feet, a corner of Eloise's left eye caught the image of something flopped over a buckled metal claw like a red rag mop on a hanger.

She shrieked.

Shh, Eloise, easy does it. Stay with me now.

You are about to realize, all vested energies are linked. I'm here because I didn't listen to the very voice I've come to be inside of you. If only I'd chosen to obey the presage to stay. It's all the end of being there comes down to: choosing wrong.

Had I not, mine wouldn't be the voice you hear. Yours wouldn't be a face I can't quite place, now that I'm void of the knowledge of who you are, and the meaning of each thought I insert to ensure your fortitude and longevity.

Your forte and intuition are now merged with mine, evolved for all eternity.

I am no longer there with you, but here — for you.

I flow free of the fears hobbling rationale and silencing decision.

By choosing me you choose you.

Listen.

An officer crawled into what remained of the VW's back seat and reached around Eloise's headrest, positioning his hands to force her face away from the corpse beside her.

"Don't look!" he commanded.

His partner grabbed Eloise by her wrists through what remained of the burst windshield.

"Don't move. You could be hurt. Don't...move."

Eloise felt snared. She stared, deaf and dumb ahead at a third officer, questioning her.

"Are you in pain? How do you feel? Can you move your legs? What's your name?" He asked all those within earshot. "Does anyone know if she can hear me?"

Let's go back, Eloise, to when you were thirteen and unexpectedly made your first connection to here. Do it now. Relax your fingers. Flatten your hands. Hold them as close as possible without them touching until you find the warmth of the path. Feel the field?

The scowl on Eloise's face eased. The tightness in her jaw lessened and the rigidity of her body in its rage of resistance, calmed. She opened her hands and held them as close together as possible without touching in front of her face. The officers weren't certain if she was in shock, or praying. When they relaxed their guard, Eloise automatically turned towards Imogene. Once again her face was physically forced away. A chorus of men scolded her.

That's right, Eloise. You remember. It was February, 1952. Miss Bacchus. First period. You won a red ribbon for your science project. What did you say?

"When you enclose a magnetic field inside a circuit and close its path, you alter the field to produce an electric current," Eloise mumbled. "Flip a switch. The light goes on."

"Step it up," an officer yelled. "She's babbling. Could be the sign of a concussion."

As evolved magnetism, you are keyed to that simplicity-of-expansion. When enclosed in an organic receptacle, the field is altered to ignite life. Alter the field. Close the path.

Eloise saw what remained of their car had been crushed like an accordion. She felt the coils of Imogene's seat angled hard against her left thigh. It dawned on her that Imogene's body had taken the full brunt of the blow, acting as a human cushion to insulate her upon impact before being flung half back out a mangled frame to hover lifeless, inches above the pavement.

In the reflection of the dangling mirror now mixed with the smashed dashboard and debris hindering her escape, Eloise spied an immaculate blonde haired man arguing with officers behind her, swearing that he knew Imogene and pleading that he be allowed to help.

I am rising higher now, spreading wider. I see congestion, lights flashing, dual places, revolving reds, static, distance and delay. Say it, Eloise. Close the path.

The officer holding Eloise's head dropped his hands to her shoulders and pushed while the one gripping her wrists began pulling her upright and out until she could stand alone. Responders swarmed around her.

"Two ambulances," she told them, "are caught in traffic. I need to help her."

They said she was in shock. They swore medics would arrive soon. They offered her water. They uttered canned condolences. One took her by the elbow and forced her to walk with him to a police car, away from Imogene.

I'm surging. Growing lighter. Eloise!

It might have happened because the officers were compelled to subdue the young blonde man who'd become rowdy by insisting he be allowed past the barriers cordoning off the crash. Or, maybe it was because Harold Hennessey saw his chance to escape and bolted. Or, traffic in two lanes of Third Avenue opened to a slow flow of gawkers going uptown. Or, the rookie assigned to Eloise became distracted while monitoring radio calls.

Or, it was all those disruptions coinciding that allowed Eloise to slip away from her escort and return to Imogene's side, where she knelt in shards of glass splattered with blood.

Gently, ever so gently, Eloise used her palms to push Imogene's shoulders up until her head lopped back against the crumpled seat, and her vacant eyes were turned skyward toward the missing sunroof through which the two, as one, had traced the course of rising moons and falling stars.

I am the breeze blowing beneath my soul. Close the path.

Imogene's lips were parted, frozen in awe on the final inflection of her last five words. Eloise rose to wedge herself onto the edge of what remained of the car's chassis, tilted Imogene's chin up and, tenderly, sealed her lips, wiping the blood from the corner of her mouth with a gentle press of her thumb. She tried to brush away the slivers of glass that glittered in the wedding day rays on Imogene's cheek, but the sparkle of tiny crystals embedded like tears near her eyes caused Eloise to gasp.

Stopping. Turning. What?

"You promised, Imogene," Eloise choked. "You said you'd never leave me."

Taking one long last look at the woman she'd forever love most, balanced before her like a broken doll, Eloise leaned in to press her chest hard against Imogene's, holding it there for as long as she dared before drawing back to kiss Imogene's lips as delicately, and as hopefully, and as truly as she had kissed them that very first time.

I am the quondam north wind blowing west as a cyclone on nigh.

Warm tears flowed from her blue, blue eyes into Imogene's barren browns as she rested her cheek against Imogene's forehead, the same as she had each night of their lives together, sealing all space between them so neither could detect where the face of one ended and the other began.

"Please, Imogene, please," she whimpered. "Don't go."

I am whirling. Falling as a downdraft. Barreling backward. Integrating the periphery. Processing. Grasping. Wait! Are those...eyes?

I am zooming inward outward, oh, no-o.

I am primarily of the universe. I can recognize, but cannot know those eyes are mi...

Blink!

Imogene awoke wondering if she was awake, disquieted by eyes stuck open before complete consciousness settled in. She instinctively knew where she'd been and instantly understood the recollection as unintended; that the sanctity of such knowledge was inalienable, poised now to either break, or embrace her.

She could not feel her limbs. She could not feel her torso. She could not feel her neck. All Imogene felt was radiant as a harbinger of the hereafter. She sensed the inability to feel the pain of her broken body would not last. But the radiance? The radiance would be hers forevermore.

"Hey babe."

Eloise stiffened, startled by the words she thought she'd heard whispered near her ear; so very desperate to hear them again. Cautiously, deliberately she pulled back and stared, clinging to that faint possibility.

She leapt up.

"Help!" she screamed. "Help! All of you! Help!" Once she started she didn't stop, raising her fists, daring them to defy her. "Now dammit! Now! Help me! Help me no-o-ow!"

It was Ronald who got to Imogene first and kept her body from tumbling back over. "I'm here, Imogene. I've got you."

He held her up until two ambulances arrived.

Finally.

ABOUT THE AUTHOR

Marguerite Quantaine lives in Florida where she is at work on *Eloise's Imogene*, the second book in this planned trilogy.

Follow her at www.margueritequantaine.wordpress.com/

Made in the USA
San Bernardino, CA
17 December 2014